Valor's Calling

by Kal Spriggs

GW00776879

Books by Kal Spriggs

The Shadow Space Chronicles

The Fallen Race
The Shattered Empire
The Prodigal Emperor
The Sacred Stars
The Temple of Light
Ghost Star
*The Star Engine**

The Renegades

Renegades: Origins
Renegades: Out of the Cold
Renegades: Out of Time
*Renegades: Royal Pains**

The Star Portal Universe

Valor's Child
Valor's Calling
*Valor's Duty**

Fenris Unchained
Odin's Eye
*Jormungandr's Venom**

The Eoriel Saga

Echo of the High Kings
Wrath of the Usurper
Fate of the Tyrant
*Heir to the Fallen Duke**

*Forthcoming

Chapter One: I Should Have Known Better

While my parents had hardly been excited about me attending the Academy, I had expected a bit more enthusiasm from my best friend. After all, it would mean we'd be there together.

"You're what?" Ashiri Takenata stared at me through my datapad.

"I'm coming to the Academy," I repeated, feeling stupid. I'd meant to tell her and Alexander Karmazin the news as soon as the Admiral had accepted my application. But Mom had sort of freaked out about it and with all the chaos after my misadventures at Champion Enterprises, I hadn't got around to it until now.

"But..." Ashiri shook her head. "I mean, the acceptance lists have already been posted, you weren't on them, so we assumed..."

"I had a letter of explanation that I put in with my application packet, I'm accepted," I answered. The Admiral hadn't pulled any punches, either. Someone *might* assume that, being my grandmother and all, she would show me some favoritism. Of course, I'd say they were crazy. The Admiral had barely spoken a dozen words to me outside of what could be strictly viewed as professional terms. I hadn't even met her almost until my fourteenth birthday... and as far as I knew, my Mom only spoke to her around the holidays, and then only in a formally stilted video call.

What can I say, my family is a mess.

"Did you tell Alex?" Ashiri asked.

"Karmazin?" I replied. I didn't really think of him as an Alex. I mean, he was far too... imposing for that. Alexander Karmazin was almost two meters tall. With his olive complexion, curly dark hair, and handsome looks, he could have passed for an actor on one of those daytime shows. When I'd first met him, I'd instantly hated him, he'd seemed to be everything I wasn't: tall, confident, and his father was the richest man on the planet. Now I considered him a friend, maybe something more. He'd certainly hinted that he was interested in something more, the last time we'd talked in person, almost five months ago.

I flushed as I considered that, "No, I just had time to call you. I've been digging into all the course work. Did you see we have an entire research paper due on the first day of classes for Military

Ethics?"

"What, yeah, I knocked that out a month ago. We... that is, Alex and I, we've had the past five months to do all that stuff," Ashiri said, looking distracted. "You really should tell Alex."

"Yeah, I'll do that," I said. "The welcome packet mentioned we can select our roommates, do you have one, yet?"

Ashiri looked nervous, "Uh, yeah, we can talk about that later, after we get in. You might change your mind, you know. Oh, I'm hitting the limit on my bandwidth for the month, got to go, see you later!"

She cut the call and I stared at my home screen for a long, puzzled moment. I'd met Ashiri at the Century Military Academy. We'd been in the same squad of Sand Dragon. We'd slept on the ground together, been shot at together, and struggled through some really rough times together. I wasn't sure why she seemed nervous at being my roommate. It wasn't like I was anything like her old roommate, Rakewood. I wasn't going to dump on her or anything, I could pull my own weight.

For that matter, I had no idea why she was out of bandwidth. I sort of remembered that her family didn't have the best financial situation. They'd come here as refugees or something, back when the Guard had annexed their homeworld in the Ten Sisters system. But bandwidth for video calls was plentiful. She'd have to have been spending eight or ten hours a day to put a serious chink in even a basic bandwidth plan with the planetary network.

It was different out here at Basalt Mesa Outpost. It was an archeological and research station, with a permanent population of only thirty. The video call had used up a lot of my family's non-research bandwidth. In fact, I'd probably talked longer than I should have, but I'd wanted to see Ashiri. The past five months had been rough. I hadn't really had any friends... well, none besides Ted. *He's dead now,* I reminded myself. The accounting intern who'd been friendly to me had been kidnapped and probably killed by the smugglers who'd been buying stolen military equipment from rogue elements of Champion Enterprises.

Officially he was missing, but I'd talked with Ted's parents. They planned on holding a quiet funeral after all this blew over. I felt horrible for them. If I were them, I would have blamed me. But they hadn't. They'd actually *thanked* me for uncovering the corruption at Champion Enterprises... and for bringing their son's killers to justice.

That left me feeling adrift. I shouldn't have got Ted involved. I should have handled it all differently, should have gone straight to the Admiral when it all started, but I'd screwed it all up. I'd been kidnapped, nearly killed. Ted was vanished, as if he'd never been. I'd been able to fall back on my military training from the Academy Prep Course, which had saved my life... but I'd killed six men in the process.

I wasn't fifteen Century years old yet and I was a killer. That was one more reason I'd chosen to attend the Academy. Someone should have been there to protect me, to protect Ted. Maybe I could prevent someone else's family from having to hold a quiet funeral for their child.

For just a moment I felt the urge to call Alexander Karmazin. Of anyone, I felt he'd understand. He'd had to fight for his life, too. But some measure of Ashiri's nervousness made me hesitate. Why had she been so insistent that I call him?

It can wait, I told myself. In a couple more days, I'd fly to Duncan City, and I could meet him and Ashiri there. I could talk to them in person and figure out any problems. Besides, I'd already used too much bandwidth and I had a full ethics research paper to knock out.

I flipped my datapad back over to the course material and got started.

* * *

"Jiden, how's the coursework going?" Dad asked as I came into the dining room.

"Good," I replied. Of my parents, Dad took my decision to go back to the Academy the best. My mom adopted a pinch-faced expression that I knew only too well. It was her you're-making-a-terrible-decison-but-one-day-you'll-realize-it-and-wish-you'd-listened-to-me expression. "Lots to do, still, but I've got a few more days."

The prep work was supposed to take around three months. Since I'd been accepted less than a week ago and classes started in a week, which meant I had around two weeks to do it all. Thankfully there was a lot of crossover to coursework I'd done for my

Champion Enterprises internship. I just hoped this worked out better.

"I saw some navigational data in your last download, are you going to be taking pilot classes?" Will asked. My little brother sounded annoyingly eager.

I gave him a glare, "You've been checking my downloads?" Still my glare faded as I saw his enthusiasm. I suppose it wasn't his fault. We both had to share data from the family network access. Mom and Dad used the university research access for the most part, so they hadn't bothered to install any kinds of privacy filters or anything

"Yeah," I admitted after he looked a little sheepish. "It's one of the first courses. We'll do a first year of navigation and simulation, and then next year I'll start actual piloting."

"Assuming you don't decide to take up a more reasonable career," Mom sniffed.

I rolled my eyes at that. Mom was the one whose mother was the war-hero and all that. Of anyone, you'd think she'd actually support my decision. Strangely enough, it was Dad, whose family had been in archeology for generations, who seemed to accept my choice.

"That's so cool," Will said, ignoring what my mom had said. "Do you think you could teach me some things?" Will had always sort of followed me around, but this level of interest in something I was doing surprised me.

Then again, I remembered when our cousins, Mel and Rawn had last showed up. Will had been very interested in their ship and what it took to be a pilot. I wondered if he'd already made his mind up about flying and my attending the Academy simply looked like the best route. "We'll see," I hedged, "I don't know how much time I'll have to hang out or how complicated it all is." Judging from my initial course work, piloting in atmosphere was pretty difficult... and that was child's play compared to piloting a ship with a warp drive.

For that matter, my one attempt at piloting a skimmer had ended up with me crashing. Of course, I'd been shot down, technically speaking, but that didn't change the fact that I wasn't exactly a stellar pilot.

"That would be great!" Will said.

Dad gave me a smile, the one he hadn't given me in a long

time. It was the one of thanks, for making his job as a parent easier. It was the one he used to give me when I helped watch Will when we were both younger, the one I hadn't really seen since I'd started hanging out with Tony Champion.

Of course, now Tony was in jail. So was Tony's father. Both of them were there because of me.

"Well," Mom said, "I went to the effort of making Christmas Dinner, the least everyone could do is eat it." I rolled my eyes at that too. Mom had made this dinner about as much as I'd landed the skimmer I'd crashed. It was pre-cooked; lab grown meat with hydroponics-grown vegetables, all cooked, packaged, and shipped to our desolate little outpost. It used to be that I'd enjoyed the meal, it was far better than the simple protein cubes that we'd mostly made do with.

But I'd had real food at the Admiral's house and then again at the Academy. I picked at the food, too polite to complain, even as Will and my parents dug in. It was weird how some things had gone back to the way they'd been... and how others would never be the way they once were.

For a second I flashed back to the pain and terror as the thugs sent by Tony's father had come to kill me. My heart raced and my breath came quickly. The moment passed and I was back at home. Everything was alright. Nothing ever changed here at Black Mesa Outpost.

Just yesterday I'd spent most of the morning down in the catacombs, I'd practically grown up in that warren of tunnels. The excavations were the life's work of my parents. The million-year-old ruins below the huge basalt outcropping jutted out of the desert sands, a looming, familiar presence, as full of wonder to my parents as the day they'd first moved here, before I was even born. Black Mesa Outpost was the closest settlement to the equator, hotter and less hospitable than any other place on my dusty, barren homeworld... but it was home. It was a constant in my life that hadn't changed and I was grateful for that.

As my dad told a goofy story about one of Mom and his fellow archeologists, my gaze went to the rifle over the mantle. It was a hunting rifle, from when my dad's grandfather had first come to Century, but it had also seen use when the Culmor had invaded. It was a battered and old testament to rougher times.

My parents had chosen a life of research, of quiet, uneventful days and little personal risk. They enjoyed ferreting out secrets of a long-dead alien civilization. I had been called to a different path.

***

Dad was the one who flew me back to civilization. He'd raised an eyebrow when I'd asked him to drop me at the Enclave, but he hadn't questioned it. He talked as he flew. Dad wasn't as good a pilot as mom, so the skimmer bobbed a lot, but Dad's stories were interesting enough to keep me distracted. It sounded like they'd found a lot of interesting stuff in this next level down of the old alien ruins under Black Mesa.

I was glad for the distraction, because I'd started to feel nervous. I'd messaged Alexander Karmazin to let him know I'd be coming by on my way to the Admiral's house. He hadn't responded other than to say he'd meet me at the Enclave's landing terminal. Most towns on Century just had landing pads in residential areas. With almost all of Century's surface being land mass, it wasn't like we didn't have enough room to spread things out a bit.

The Enclave, though, was supposed to be different. Karmazin had told me that they were refugees of some type, military refugees if you could believe that. His grandfather was the Enclave's leader, his mom was some kind of important official there too, so Alexander should know.

The terminal we set down in looked like a military base. Most of it was underground, with a few buildings with sensor masts and what looked like weapon emplacements above-ground. Off to the side, past a few big cargo and personnel transports, I actually saw a row of military skimmers and beyond *them* I saw the big, sleek forms of Mark V Firebolt warp-drive fighters.

Okay, I thought, *maybe there's a reserve unit doing drill here or something.*

Dad talked with traffic control and then settled us down near one of the personnel transports. As he dropped the ramp, I looked over to see Alexander Karmazin and Ashiri Takenata come out of the nearby terminal building.

I unstrapped quickly and hurried to the ramp. I felt a smile growing on my face, it felt good to see them in person. Alexander Karmazin stood tall, almost two meters, with dark brown hair and olive skin. Ashiri stood next to him, her short black hair tossed in the hot dry wind. I opened my mouth to shout a welcome... and then I saw them standing close to each other, holding hands.

Oh.

I forced myself to smile, "Hey, guys, good to see you." My voice sounded robotic and I felt like an idiot.

"Yeah," Ashiri smiled back, her expression was wooden, "good to see you too." She sounded nervous.

"So, these are your friends?" Dad asked from behind me.

All I wanted to do was turn around and run back up the ramp. I felt so embarrassed. Of *course* they were together. It wasn't like Alexander Karmazin had showed any real interest in me. We'd been friends... and the one time he'd even hinted at wanting to be anything more, I'd thrown it back in his face by telling him I was leaving the Academy.

Instead I forced my face into something between a smile and a grimace and turned to my dad, "Yeah, these are my friends, Karmazin and Takenata." I deliberately used their last names. It let me distance myself from it. If I thought about them as classmates, it didn't feel like a betrayal.

"Great, well, I commed the Admiral, she's covered your ticket from here back to Duncan City, so I guess I should get back home," my dad said cheerfully. On impulse, I stepped forward and gave him a hug, burying my face in his shoulder. I wanted to cry, but I told myself that was silly.

He patted me on the back and gave me a last squeeze, then turned away and walked up the ramp.

I turned back to face my friends, they still held hands. It hurt, like my whole chest constricted around my heart... but at this point, I should be used to pain. "Let's get out of his way, right?" I said as casually as I could manage. I shouldered my duffel bags and moved out of the way of the skimmer.

I was thankful for the sound of the turbines. It meant I had some time where I didn't have to talk. Carrying the weight of my bags meant I had an excuse not to look at my friends. As the hot air blasted over us, I could pretend that the tears in my eyes were from the turbine wash.

***

"So..." Ashiri said a few minutes later as she and I stood by the curb, waiting while Alexander Karmazin brought up a ground vehicle. "We didn't know you were going to be coming back. Alex and I started spending a lot of time together and..."

I realized with horror that she was going to explain how she and Karmazin had hooked up. The last thing I wanted was to hear any details. "Ashiri, it's fine. Really, you don't need to explain." I swallowed, "It wasn't like Karmazin or I were dating. We're just friends, like you and me." I said the words with as much sincerity as I could manage.

Ashiri shot me a look. I forced myself to meet her brown eyes. "You mean that... I mean, I thought you two..."

"There was nothing between us," I interrupted before she could finish. "And clearly, you two are together. It's fine. I'm happy for you both."

"You're okay, then?" Ashiri asked, her voice intent.

"Yeah," I replied. "I'm okay." It wasn't like I had some sort of claim to Karmazin. Besides, I liked Ashiri, she was my friend. I couldn't be angry with her. We'd been through too much together.

I'd be okay. Everything would work out.

If I just kept telling myself that, maybe I'd even believe it.

***

The Enclave was weird. As we drove through it, I couldn't quite put my finger on it. The buildings were all squat and low to the ground, vehicle garages were all underground. It wasn't a big city, or at least it didn't seem to be.

That was, right up until Karmazin drove down into what looked like an oversized garage... and the road kept going. I craned my head around in surprise as I saw that the road descended into the ground, winding deeper and deeper.

Karmazin gave his smirk, "My people come from Dalite Three, what we call Acrotan, where the cities are all underground. The planet's environment isn't as friendly as here."

I shot him a disbelieving look. Century was a dry, dusty world. We didn't get anything near a winter and it only ever rained near the two polar seas. I hadn't ever heard anyone call our world "friendly." *It's a dry, barren dust-ball, and most of us think our ancestors were crazy for leaving behind the cool green hills of*

Earth...

"We're used to living underground," Karmazin went on. "Most of the Enclave is below ground. It's easier to maintain temperatures and it provides better defenses that way, too."

"Who are you defending against?" I asked.

"Anyone who might attack," Karmazin hedged. It was a vague enough statement to make me feel uneasy. I'd heard that Enclave citizens were prohibited from service in the Century Planetary Militia by a recent Charter Council decree. Was that because they felt the Enclave was some kind of security risk? *For that matter, if there is some kind of fight, which side would Karmazin pick?*

I knew they were refugees, from the Three Day War with the Dalite Confederacy. I hadn't expected them to have defenses or for their aerospace port to look so militarized.

Karmazin pulled into a side street and then into a vehicle garage. He climbed out, "I'll help you out with your bags," he offered, moving to open the cargo compartment.

"I'm good," I said quickly. "I can't stay long, this is just a quick visit on my way to the Admiral's house." The words came out before I could help them. I'd planned

He cocked his head at me, "You're sure?" There was something in his voice, almost an edge of disappointment. I wasn't going to think about that, though.

"Yeah," I forced myself to smile. "I've got a lot of the pre-class assignments to knock out." That wasn't a lie. I still had several papers to write and three more books to read. I hadn't even started the military ethics research paper itself yet, in part because I felt like it was sort of pointless.

I'd planned on working with Ashiri and Karmazin. *I can do it on my own.* The very thought of spending hours with them left me feeling sick. "There's an evening flight I'll need to catch, I just have a few hours."

I *had* seen there was an evening flight. I had no idea if they had any seats left, but I was going to the aerospace terminal regardless. I'd spend the night there if necessary.

"Well," Karmazin said, "I'll give you the quick tour, then." He gave me a solemn nod, almost as if I'd hurt his feelings. *Well, he probably should have thought of that before he started dating my best friend.*

I banished the thought before I could go on. I wasn't going to resent my friends. This wasn't their fault. I was the one who'd changed her mind. I was the one who had been wrong and I couldn't expect things to be the way I'd secretly dreamed they'd be.

"This way," Ashiri said, leading the way. I followed them through the door.

Alexander Karmazin's home was far more spartan than I'd expected. There was a small dining room, a smaller living room, both with a few simple prefabricated tables and chairs. There were a couple of decorative holoprojectors, which painted two of the walls with vistas of a rainy, lush planet. I thought I recognized the pattern as one of the default settings, one that most people typically replaced with some kind of custom display.

A tall, dark-haired woman greeted us as we stepped inside. She have Ashiri and I both nods, "Ashiri, welcome back." Her gray eyes locked on me. There was something watchful there, evaluative and somehow threatening, as if she didn't know what to make of me. "You must be Jiden Armstrong. I've heard quite a bit from Alexander about you." She had the same olive skin, the same quiet watchfulness as Alexander, I saw.

"Jiden," Alexander Karmazin said, "this is my mother, Diane Karmazin."

"It's a pleasure to meet you, ma'am," I said.

"Yes," Alexander's mother said. I wasn't sure if that was agreement with what I'd said or simply an acknowledgment. "Alexander tells me that you'll be staying for a few days?" Her voice almost sounded resigned.

"I'm afraid not," I replied. "I'd meant to clarify, I only had time to swing through and say hello, I'm quite a bit behind on my studies."

"That's too bad," Alexander's mother replied. She somehow managed to make that sound both sincere and insincere at the same time. I didn't know if that was because she really didn't want me here or if she somehow realized *why* I didn't want to stay. Either way, I was eager enough to take that as a way to make my exit.

"Well," I said, studiously glancing at my datapad, "I probably should get back to the terminal if I'm going to catch my flight." I looked up, "Thank you for inviting me to your home."

"Of course," Alexander said. He was looking at his mother though, almost as if he sensed something was wrong. I had no idea what was going on, but I felt like leaving was going to be the best thing I could do.

All I wanted to do was get out of there and I think Alexander was really regretting the invitation to visit. I felt like an idiot, but I managed to say polite things as I backed out and Alexander gave me a ride back to the terminal. I passed the trip in silence. Thankfully, he didn't seem very talkative, either.

***

A few hours later I'd boarded a commercial skimmer and had my datapad out while I worked on some of my projects. I'd been lucky to get a ticket on the flight, the only one leaving the Enclave that day... but I'd scrapped my plans of staying with Karmazin and his family. Not with his relationship with Ashiri.

I'd managed to message the Admiral to let her know I was coming a few days early, just before I boarded. Now I was buried in work. Some people hated to work on a flight, but I welcomed the chance to tune everything out, to not think about how my expectations had been completely overturned.

The skimmer was surprisingly empty for a holiday season flight. It made me wonder if Karmazin's people celebrated Christmas... or for that matter, if they celebrated off-season from everyone else. After all they were from another world. I knew there were some Christian and Jewish sects that followed the standard Earth twelve month calendar, in spite of the fact that it didn't remotely match up to Century's fifteen month years and three seasons.

My mind went off on a bit of a tangent, sort of wandering as I stared out the window. I watched the hydrogen-powered gas turbine, just sort of staring at the heat distortion from the jet wash. It was mesmerizing and I just sort of watched as the superheated gasses blurred the setting sun and desert.

I had a perfect view of the missile that came streaking in at us.

My eyes went wide as I realized what I was seeing. But by the time I could open my mouth to shout a warning, there was a flash of light and the entire skimmer shuddered. The detonation was muted, but the skimmer went into a spin. I heard shouts and screams from the other passengers and the whine of the turbines altered pitch. The smooth flight became a rough spin and I was smashed against the side window. Staring out, I had a great view of the burning engine as the skimmer cork-screwed towards the ground.

I'm going to die. The thought wasn't as jarring as it should have been. I'd nearly died several times. It just seemed unfair that I'd survived being shot down and attacked by criminals, only to be shot down in a commercial aircraft.

There wasn't time to panic. There wasn't time to do much of anything. I found my hands going to my seat restraints, tightening them, even as I heard the skimmer pilot come on over the intercom, "Brace for landing, brace for landing," his voice sounded abnormally calm and some absent part of my brain wondered if he was a graduate of the Century Military Academy.

The remaining engine roared as the pilot fed it power. The skimmer stabilized and the nose swung up. I watched the spinning sky and sand transition to mostly sand and some sky. This side of the aircraft was lower, the damaged engine providing little or no lift. The sandy, rocky ground whipped past, far too fast for me to pick out details and far too close for me to focus on it.

We hit, a bone-jarring, grating, sliding, and world-ending chaos. Passengers and their possessions flew through the compartment. Something heavy struck me a glancing blow to the head and I saw stars. I saw the skimmer engine ripped away and then a moment later we smashed, hard, into something and the entire craft jerked to a halt.

I unbuckled my restraints and stood. Passengers looked around dazedly. An attendant fumbled with one of the doors up front, but I didn't see the attendant here near the rear. I pushed past my seat-mate and moved to the door, moving on impulse. The skimmer was damaged, the hydrogen tanks were probably leaking. We had to get off the craft before the hydrogen caught fire or exploded.

I wrenched the door open and the smart-plastic ramp extended. I started to jump down it, but then I saw that no one was following me. I stared at the passengers, most of whom were either in shock or possibly denial. "Move it!" I shouted, "Get out of here!"

I reached over, popped the restraints off a nearby woman and jerked her to her feet. Without thinking I pushed her down the ramp, then grabbed the man next to her. "Go!"

Passengers started to move. Some fumbled with their restraints and I hurried to help them, pushing them towards the door. I didn't want to think about how little time we had. Hydrogen gas would be spreading through the aircraft. All it would take would be a spark and the entire skimmer would go up like a bomb.

"Go!" I shouted, shoving a business-man ahead of me. I looked around, not seeing anyone else near the rear of the aircraft. I started towards the door when I heard a whimper of pain. I looked over and saw movement under a pile of bags. I reached down, throwing stuff out of the way and found an arm. I pulled, dragging the attendant out from under the pile. She was battered and bloodied, her eyes unfocused. "Let's go!" I shouted, pushing her towards the door. We ran out, sliding down the ramp and then plowing into a group of passengers milling around the bottom of the ramp. "Get clear!" I shouted at them. "It's going to catch fire!"

I pushed and shoved at people, even as I heard a whoosh. The sound turned into a roar and I felt a wash of heat, even as I stumbled away. The dusk turned bright as daylight and I looked back to see the entire aircraft engulfed in flames. "Go!" I shouted angrily at people as they stopped to gawk.

We weren't anywhere near a safe distance away. I helped an attendant to herd people away from the crash site and the roaring flames. We'd managed to get two hundred meters away when the hydrogen tank exploded like a bomb. As the blast knocked me to the ground, I finally gave up and just stayed down. A moment later another hydrogen tank detonated, then the third.

I lay on the ground, listening to the roaring flames and the panicked shouts of the people around me. *Someone shot at me... again.* There was no reason that I thought of myself as the target, but somehow I knew that I must be. Someone had fired a missile at me. They'd nearly killed dozens of people... trying to kill me.

As I lay on the hard, hot ground, I had a dread certainty that they wouldn't stop until they succeeded.

***

The Admiral was one of the first people to greet me as I came down the ramp from the rescue craft. She and James pulled me to the side, even as the media swarmed the other non-injured passengers.

The first transport had carried the wounded passengers and crew. They'd settled down near the crash site within minutes. I'd come off it all with nothing more than a few bumps and scrapes.

"The car is waiting, miss Jiden," James said.

The Admiral didn't say anything, she just waited until I followed James towards the vehicle. "Isn't there some kind of interview or something?" I asked, gesturing at the Enforcers. The law enforcement personnel seemed to be managing the flow of personnel.

"This became a military matter as soon as we found the expended ML-7 launcher near the crash site," the Admiral said. Her voice was calm, pitched just high enough for me to hear over the sound of the crowd.

I swallowed convulsively. "So I didn't imagine the missile?" I had half-convinced myself that I must have imagined it, that surely I was wrong. I felt light-headed as I climbed into the Admiral's ground car.

"No," the Admiral said as she followed me inside. James shut the door behind her and then moved to the driver's seat. As the vehicle pulled away, the Admiral went on. "Military inspectors did a full analysis of the crash site, passenger manifests, and the Enclave's passenger terminal. In addition to the expended ML-7, they discovered a bomb in cargo storage at the terminal, scheduled to go on the flight in three days."

It took me only a few seconds to realize that flight must have been the one I'd originally booked. I swallowed again. "Someone is trying to kill me?"

The Admiral nodded. "Someone had you under close observation, they noticed when you changed plans and they had someone in place to take a shot. More, we've identified the lot number for the ML-7. It's from a lot of weapons that were listed as destroyed... the main contractor was Champion Enterprises and Isaac Champion signed for their destruction."

I closed my eyes. Isaac Champion had been behind the theft of military equipment from various storage and maintenance sites run by Champion Enterprises. Apparently that included actual weapons. He'd been selling the stolen equipment to smugglers, but as far as I knew, they had identified and arrested most of them. *Apparently not all of them.*

"So some smuggler wants to kill me because I ruined his good deal?" I asked. I didn't bother to hide my bitterness. I was fourteen years old, I shouldn't have to worry about someone trying to kill me.

The Admiral shifted uncomfortably, her lips pressing together in a hard line. "Unfortunately it's not that simple. A smuggler would probably have cut his losses, found some other job... if he didn't, we could rely on a criminal to be sloppy. The average criminal doesn't have military training. They'd probably slip up and we'd catch them." She shook her head, "No, this is a little more serious. The bomb maker used C9-X, it's military-grade explosives whose lot number we *also* tracked to the same lot of 'destroyed' weapons and equipment. Same with the detonator and initiator. The ML-7 requires military training to pick out and lock onto a specific target, especially at the altitude you were traveling."

I felt my stomach sink. "You're saying?"

"Officially I can't say anything," the Admiral said. "This is a military investigation. I'm not at liberty to discuss the specifics of the investigation, not beyond basic facts."

I wondered if she was really that detached. After all, I was her granddaughter. *She's telling me this for a reason. This is a warning, that someone with military training and access to military grade weapons wants me dead...*

My eyes widened. It might well be someone still *in* the military. An officer, maybe someone senior enough with access to the Academy. I'd thought that I would be able to go to the Academy, to become an officer and protect the people I cared about. I thought that I could leave this whole business with the smugglers and Champion Enterprises behind.

I should have known better.

***

Chapter Two: Back To School

The first time I went to the Century Military Academy, I boarded a late-night bus, which took almost eight hours to arrive. This time, as an actual Cadet, they gave me an itinerary that let me take the train.

James had dropped me off at the Duncan City Train Station. I'd already coordinated with Ashiri Takenata and Alexander Karmazin, so I knew where they'd be as I boarded. "Hey guys," I said as I found them.

"Hey Jiden," Ashiri smiled from where she sat with Alexander. I did my best to ignore how close the two of them sat. After two weeks, I'd managed to mostly come to terms with their relationship. It helped a bit that I had the more immediate priority of someone trying to kill me. It sort of put things in perspective.

"I heard about the attack," Alexander said. "Glad you're okay."

I hadn't told either of them what the Admiral had told me. "Thanks," I said. I stowed my one bag in the overhead. All my uniforms had been destroyed in the skimmer crash. The Admiral had told me what forms to fill out to request replacement uniforms, which I'd be issued when we arrived. So all I'd brought was my datapad, a few changes of clothes, and undergarments.

"Alexander and I were talking," Ashiri said as I took a seat. "The news is saying it was some kind of terrorist attack, but then it all just disappeared. I mean, this was an attack on a civilian aircraft and there hasn't been a mention of it on any of the major media channels since three days after! As far as Alex and I can tell, they haven't caught anyone, they don't even have suspects!"

"Yeah," I said. I felt uneasy at the turn this conversation was going. I knew that someone wanted to kill me. I didn't exactly want my friends dragged into this.

"What if they didn't get all the conspirators in that smuggling ring you helped to take down?" Alexander asked. His face was intent and I could feel his gray eyes boring into me.

I didn't meet their gazes, "Well, what makes you feel this is related to me?"

"Come on, Jiden!" Ashiri threw her hands in the air, "Three

months ago you uncovered Isaac Champion selling military equipment to smugglers and they nearly killed you... then two weeks ago someone took a shot at the skimmer you were in? You think the two things couldn't possibly be connected?"

I looked down at the floor. "Maybe you guys shouldn't be looking into this."

"You don't want to drag us into it?" Alexander asked.

I shrugged. I didn't really know how to answer. The Admiral had only given me hints. I didn't know if I'd be breaking some military regulation by passing on what I knew. I didn't know if I'd be endangering them or putting them in the line of fire. Someone had tried to kill me, and they'd nearly killed an entire skimmer of people in the process.

"We're probably already in the line of fire," Ashiri said, her voice soft. "As your friends, whoever attacked you will probably assume you've told us everything. Besides, shooting down a skimmer isn't exactly a precision attack."

I snorted at that. "Yeah... neither was the bomb."

"Bomb?" Alexander asked.

I bit my lip as I realized what I'd said. After a moment, I sighed, "Yeah. There was a bomb on my original flight." I hoped they didn't ask *why* I'd changed flights, so I went on quickly, "When I changed flights, they sent someone to shoot me down, instead." I'd been thinking about all this for the past two weeks with no one to talk with about it all. Now it all came out in a rush, "The military is conducting a full investigation... but they suspect that there's a military officer involved, someone who had ties to the smugglers but who didn't get picked up when they took them down."

"Why go after *you* though?" Ashiri asked. "I mean, revenge is one thing, but killing a whole skimmer full of people just to get you?"

Alexander frowned, "He might--"

"She," Ashiri interrupted, "remember, they never identified the woman that Jiden heard talking with Isaac Champion."

"Fine, *she* might think you know enough to identify him," Alexander finished.

I nodded, "But I don't know *anything*. I've already told the original investigators everything I knew. They had a couple military investigators interview me last week, but I couldn't tell them anything new. They seemed pretty frustrated by it all."

"I bet," Ashiri nodded. She cocked her head, "Do you think the train is safe?"

I blanched at that. I hadn't even thought of an attack on the train. Still, I shook my head, "The Admiral and the investigators both told me that whoever this was, they're going to be laying low. If they attack me again, so soon after the last one, they risk being caught."

"Huh," Ashiri said. "I suppose that's true."

"The train is a harder target, anyway," Alexander said. "It is military infrastructure, designed for transporting military personnel and equipment across the planet, especially in times of war. Most it is buried thirty meters below bedrock, it's hardened to withstand near-misses by nuclear weapons."

We were in a mostly-empty passenger compartment. The handful of windows just showed darkness outside. I didn't know much about the train network. I supposed Alexander was right. It would be hard for whoever wanted to get me to get me here. "Okay," I said, "Well, once we get to the Academy, I should be safe enough."

Ashiri and Alexander shot one another solemn looks. "Maybe," Alexander said, his voice heavy with discomfort. "But if this is someone in the military, then he--"

"She," Ashiri corrected automatically.

"Whatever... *she* could have pulled strings to get transferred to the Academy. There's always a high turnover of instructors. Reservists rotating through, active duty militia taking a term as instructors while they wait for their next position..." Alexander sighed. "It would be *easy* for an officer to get a transfer there."

My stomach sank. I had hoped that I'd be safe. Well, perhaps not safe, but at least I'd be able to focus on classes, maybe even be able to be a normal person. I'd nearly been killed, twice now. Three times if you counted the bomb. I just wanted a chance to live my life without looking over my shoulder.

"Okay," I said, "I'll have to keep an eye out."

"We'll help," Ashiri stated. "We've got your back." She grabbed Alexander by the shoulder and while I felt an ache in my chest at the familiarity they had, I also felt almost pathetically grateful for the fact that they were going to be there for me.

"Alright," I said, "the bad guys won't know what hit them."

***

I'd never been to the Academy's train stop before. After graduation from the Academy Prep Course, I'd flown back to the Admiral's house with my parents, then gone straight from there to my internship at Champion Enterprises.

The train pulled into a broad, wide-open cavern, carved out of solid rock. It didn't feel like the lower levels that I remembered. This felt deeper and somehow reminded me of my parent's excavations of the alien complex at Black Mesa.

We pulled up to a platform and the others in the passenger car began to shoulder their bags and move for the doors. I took my one, small bag and followed.

Within a few minutes, I found myself lined up with my section in one of the subterranean parade squares. I had an odd, goofy grin on my face. These were my friends and it felt good to be with them again. By habit, I was formed up as second squad leader. It felt odd, though, to see the shoulders of Mikuluk ahead of me instead of Sashi Drien.

Then again, since Sashi had shot me in the face at the final exercise last summer, she wasn't exactly popular in Sand Dragon Section. From what I'd heard, the other candidates in my section had refused to have anything to do with her.

"Welcome back to the Academy," a familiar voice spoke. I kept my eyes forward and forced myself to look properly stern as I recognized Senior Cadet Instructor Mackenzie.

"At ease," he snapped. As we went into a more relaxed position, he gave us his friendly smile. My eyes widened a bit as I recognized the rank on his collar. "I'm Cadet Commander Mackenzie, and I'm in charge of Sand Dragon Company. I hope you all had a good holiday break with your families. Last time we saw each other, you all had just graduated as candidates during the summer Academy Prep Course. Well, I'm happy to say that now you are here as Plebes."

I swallowed nervously as I realized that while I'd remembered reading the term, I hadn't paid much attention. I'd been focused on the class work that I'd had to rush to complete, I'd just sort of skimmed all the military stuff. *That was probably something of a mistake...*

"For those of you who didn't pay much attention," Mackenzie said, "Plebes are our most junior cadets. The term comes from an old earth language, it means 'citizen' or 'civilian.' While all of you have learned basic military procedures, what you haven't done yet is master the skills that will make you valuable cadets in the Cadet Reserve Regiment."

Cadet Reserve Regiment? I'd read that, but I'd assumed it was just another way to refer to the Cadet body as a whole. The way Mackenzie said it, it was like we were an actual military force.

"All of you know that the Century Planetary Militia has a large force of reservists, men and women who work civilian jobs and who, in time of war or emergency, are called up to serve our planet." He gestured around at them, "As you might imagine, it takes a while for those reservists to form up, they've got to be ordered up, travel to their drilling centers, and get their equipment out of storage and mobilized. Uniquely, all of us are already *at* our drilling site and because we train with our equipment on a daily basis, we're ready to go within a few hours if we get called up. What that means is that our cadet regiment acts as one of the emergency reserves for our planet."

I felt a weight settle on my shoulders as he said that. I knew that the Star Guard limited the forces we could have in our Planetary Militia, like they did with everyone. While they limited what we could have on active duty, their restrictions were far less tight on our reserve forces, which meant we could have a lot more people and ships in the reserve. It was supposed to prevent star nations from attacking one another, but way out on the edge of human space, it made me feel like we weren't very well protected.

Officially the Star Guard would come to the protection of any nation attacked. Our active forces were supposed to be just enough to prevent someone from taking the planet over without resistance. But not only were we way out on the frontier of human space, but we also weren't included in the Star Guard charter, which meant we weren't going to be a priority for them to save us.

"The Academy has a squadron of corvettes and several squadrons of warp fighters," Mackenzie went on. "Each company in the Regiment falls in on our assigned positions. Sand Dragon Company has two squadrons of warp-drive fighters, Firebolt Mark

V's. Maintenance and care of those fighters is our duty, just as completing our assignments and coursework is our duty."

"But while you know how to study, you don't know your assignments within Sand Dragon Company, or our overall duties within the Cadet Reserve Regiment. That's why you're not full Cadets... you're Plebes." He smiled, "I'm sure you'll learn your duties quickly. Once your class, as a whole, has proven their skills, then you'll all be accepted into the Regiment of Cadets, as Cadets Fourth Class. In the meantime, you'll fall under our Company Training Officer, Cadet Lieutenant Webster." He gestured at the cadet standing nearby. "Now, I've got the utmost trust in you. So do me proud." He nodded at us and then snapped, "Section, attention!"

"Cadet Lieutenant Webster, take charge!"

Webster came up, saluted Mackenzie, and then waited while our Company Commander moved off. As he turned around, I couldn't help but feel there was something ominous about the silence he held us in. After a moment, he barked out orders and marched us off the parade ground and then down into the familiar corridors. He broke us down into a single file line and had us line up against the wall. Just down the hallway I recognized my old room. It was odd to see it, like the whole place had shrunk a little bit.

"Alright, *Plebes,*" Webster snarled at us, "you may think that because you've graduated the Academy Prep Course, that you're good to go. You can't be further from the truth." He walked down the line, counting us off, "One, two, three, one, two, three..."

"Ones," he said, "step across the hallway and turn to face your former section-mates." He gloated as he said that and I felt puzzled as I watched Ashiri Takenata and others step across the hallway and face us. "One third of Plebes won't finish the year," Webster snapped. "They'll fail out, or they'll be released for honor code violations or misconduct. One in three... think about that!"

I shivered as I considered it. I'd walked away from several offers at other colleges. I chose to come here, instead. I didn't think I'd fit in at a normal school, not after what I'd been through. More than that, I felt I *had* to be here. I'd seen how dangerous the universe could be. I'd nearly been killed. My friend and fellow intern, Ted Meeks, had disappeared, probably been killed.

"Two's... step across the hallway," Cadet Lieutenant Webster snapped.

I stepped across and turned to face my section. "One third of cadets don't graduate with their sections. They either fail to get their coursework completed on time or they are delayed for misconduct or other violations."

I swallowed as I stared across the hallway. Dawson stood opposite me, and he looked rather lonely. In fact, as I realized that the entire line of my section looked pretty lonely. There were big gaps between each of them. Of the twenty of us, only six remained. *That can't be right,* I told myself. We'd started with forty candidates. If only six out of forty graduated...

I couldn't understand the amount of effort they went to for such poor returns.

"Ones and twos, step back across the hallway," Webster barked. As we complied, he walked up and down the line. He had an odd, rushed movement, it was nothing like the confidence of the Cadet Cadet Instructors, it was almost like nervous energy and it left me feeling uneasy.

"Now, since I have you here, I'm going to outline your duties as Plebes. First off, we drill every Saturday. For those of you who don't realize it, that's tomorrow morning. Drill days are intensive. Not only do we have the squadron of Firebolts, we also have a ready platoon who are assigned to defend the Academy Grounds and several Cadets assigned to the Academy's air defenses."

He stopped opposite me and gave a scowl, glaring at me as if he found my very presence offensive. "Most Plebes are utterly useless for those duties, so we'll start you out doing simple tasks: grounds defense and helping to ready the squadron."

"The rest of today you'll be going through in-processing," he looked up and down the line, still standing in front of me. "Medical screening, equipment issue, and weapons draw." His gaze returned to me, "And since some of you apparently managed to lose your uniforms and gear, we'll do an equipment issue as well." His glare at me was all the more imposing for the fact that it seemed very personal. It was like he didn't like *me.*

I didn't understand that. Even the Cadet Instructors had been impersonal about their treatment of us. In fact, as the Academy Prep Course had gone on, they'd become almost friendly... in a distant and authoritative sort of way. For some reason, Cadet Lieutenant Webster really didn't like me.

"Some basic ground rules before we go over to in-processing. We have the cadet military structure which falls under the Planetary Militia. Cadets First Class often are given positions of authority and rank within the Academy. I'm a Cadet Lieutenant. Cadet Commander Mackenzie is in overall command of Sand Dragon Company. We have several other officers and you'll be expected to memorize their ranks and positions. You will render salutes and greetings to them."

He began to pace up and down the line again, "Cadets First Class have been here five years, sometimes more. We have all been through what you've been through. We are about to be commissioned as officers in the Planetary Militia. You will treat us with the respect of our experience and rank, regardless of whether or not one of us is a Cadet Officer."

"Cadets Second Class have completed four years. They act as our squad leaders and non-commissioned officers, or NCO's. They'll carry out Cadet Officer instructions and orders. They typically tell the Cadets Third Class what to do."

I recognized both of them, they'd been two of our Cadet Instructors. It seemed that they'd continue on in a similar role. That gave me an odd sense of relief. On the one hand, they utterly terrified me, but on the other, both had been fair and even-handed before.

"Cadets Third Class typically are totally focused on their duties and assignments. Most of them are training on their second tier of combat skills, gaining proficiencies in weapons systems, vehicles, and spacecraft. If one of them gives you a direction, you will acknowledge it and obey."

"When your class, your year group, has learned their assignments and becomes a valuable contribution to the Cadet Reserve Regiment, you will be *recognized* and you will become Cadets Fourth Class. You'll be given opportunities to display your skills... and unfortunately a great many of you will fail. Military service is not for everyone. Failure is something that you can learn from, but the level of stress, the very real danger that you face in military service, is such that we have to push every one of you to the breaking point."

Webster looked around at us. "Some of you will break. Some of you do not belong here." He stopped opposite me, again and this time I couldn't help but flinch back from the vitriol on his face, "It is my job to make sure that we find the weak ones and weed them out."

My heart sank. I'd hoped that after the Prep Course, things would be easier. Apparently I'd been wrong. I wondered if I'd made a terrible mistake in coming back and as I stared at Cadet Lieutenant Webster, I wondered what I'd done that he hated me so much.

***

In-processing went much the same as it had before, only without all the yelling and shouting. Actually, it was... boring. That left me feeling surprised. It had all seemed so alien before, the brusque treatment, the poking and prodding. Now it was almost soothing in the boredom. No one was trying to kill me. No one was shouting at me. A couple of times, standing in line, I had to fight the urge to nod off.

I fought that urge as well as I could, downloading the various rules and regulations for the Academy and reading up on it all, looking for things I'd missed. It turned out that there were a lot of rules. At first I tried to take them all in, then I just skimmed. After a few minutes, I closed it out. Otherwise it was going to put me to sleep, worse than standing in lines. I just sort of turned my brain off at that point, everything settling into a vague haze.

That was, until I got to supply.

It was the same female Petty Officer I'd seen here last summer. At least, I thought it was her. She had the same pinched expression. The same glower. She looked at her datapad, then up at me. "You lost *all* of your uniforms and gear? *All* of it?"

"Uh," I looked around, "Yeah. There was a skimmer crash, it caught fire..."

"You cadets..." the petty officer growled. "Worse than officers. That stuff is expensive! I can't believe someone signed off on your loss requisition, not with a cockamamie excuse like that. Skimmer crash... yeah right." She tapped her datapad and the machinery next to her spat out the required uniforms. "It'll be tonight for the rest of your gear, the machine's got a queue that will keep it running all night. *Half* of you cadets lost some or all your gear. I'll message you when you can pick it up."

It seemed that not everyone was so happy to work here at the

Academy.

Leaving supply, I checked my datapad for my next stop. I frowned, though, as it updated to show an appointment back in the medical section. I thought I'd cleared all the physical and mental examinations at this point. Still, maybe I'd missed one.

I headed back that way, following the directions on my datapad until it led me into a hallway that seemed rather empty. It was strange, everywhere else there had been a line of cadets waiting... but this corridor had no one. In fact, I looked back the way I'd come... and it was just empty corridor as well.

I swallowed nervously, remembering what my friends had said. Someone wanted to kill me and that someone might be here at the Academy. As I came up to the door that my datapad indicated, I hesitated. What if this was a trap? What if someone just wanted to lure me away from everyone else?

I swallowed and started to take a step back.

A hand fell on my shoulder, "You lost, Plebe Armstrong?"

I flinched back from the contact, and then realized that I recognized the voice. "Uh, Cadet Commander Mackenzie, good morning, sir." I was pretty sure I was supposed to salute him, but he'd caught me entirely by surprise.

"Hello, yourself," Mackenzie smiled. "You lost, Armstrong?"

I shook my head, "No, sir, I've got an assignment here, I think." I held up my datapad.

He frowned down at the screen, "I guess you do. This is the implantation section, normally plebes don't ever come down here. You don't get your implants until your second year."

I stared at him, not understanding. Then something clicked. *Implants... he means the neural implants.* It was something that I'd forgotten about. All cadets received a neural computer implant, with a communications device, memory augmentation, and a variety of other resources. It was an expensive procedure, though, and since we weren't obligated to stay at the Academy until after we completed our first, full, year here, they didn't do that procedure, or the life extension procedure, until they knew we'd be sticking around.

"Well, maybe they want to do some kind of calibration or something. You were injured in that crash, a few weeks back, right?" Mackenzie smiled. "Maybe they just want to make sure it didn't knock anything out of place."

I couldn't help but smile back, "Yes sir, that makes sense, I suppose."

Like most places, cybernetic augmentation wasn't exactly popular here on Century. I felt repulsed by the idea and it wasn't something I looked forward to at all. Still, I couldn't fault them for wanting to check me out for any kind of brain damage or something.

"Well," Mackenzie said, "Since I've got you here, I thought I'd ask you something."

At his words, my heart raced a bit. He was a cadet first class, what did he want from me? I felt a flush climb my cheeks, "Sure, go ahead." I felt so flustered that I forgot to add a "sir" in there, but he just smirked at my response.

"Well, all cadets are encouraged to join a sports team here at the Academy. We do intramural events, but we also do some competitions with other colleges. Now, I don't know if you've signed up for anything yet... but I'd like to ask you to join the grav-shell team."

"You want me to join your team, sir?" I stared at him in surprise. As far as I knew, most plebes weren't able to get on any of the truly competitive teams, not until they proved themselves. Then again, I didn't really know much about grav-shell racing. It had always seemed like sort of a silly event. *That was before I got invited to join Cadet Commander Mackenzie's team.*

"Yeah," Mackenzie said. "You're small and light, I think you'd make a great coxswain. If you want to give it a shot, I'll transfer all the details to your datapad." He looked up as I heard footsteps coming down the corridor behind me. "Now, thank you for your time, Plebe Armstrong." Mackenzie finished, his tone becoming formal.

Before I could respond, he walked off. I turned around to find Alexander Karmazin and Ashiri walking up. Karmazin's expression was suspicious. "What was that about?" He asked.

"Nothing," I replied. "Cadet Commander Mackenzie checked in on me to make sure I wasn't lost. Then he invited me to join his grav-shell team." I couldn't help but put extra emphasis on the '*his*' part. Mackenzie had been our senior cadet instructor during the Academy Prep School. The offer felt like a bit of vindication with my decision to attend the Academy... and it also made me feel more than a little excited.

"Grav-shell racing?" Ashiri asked with surprise. "Isn't that a little dangerous?"

I blinked at her, "Why should that matter?" There was elements of danger in everything we did, after all. "It's a sport, right? I'm sure it can't be too dangerous."

Ashiri shook her head, "People have been killed..."

"You shouldn't do it," Alexander Karmazin growled. I didn't miss how he glowered in the direction that Cadet Commander Mackenzie had departed. *He's jealous,* I thought to myself, *which is immature and stupid, plus it isn't fair to Ashiri.*

"I can do what I want!" I snapped back, angry on behalf of myself and my friend. What right did Karmazin have to think he could tell me what I could and couldn't do? And he was seeing Ashiri, he shouldn't be jealous about me!

"Cadets!" A voice snapped. All three of us spun to find a short, red-headed woman stood in the now-open doorway. "Not only are all three of you delaying the others by your absence, but you are causing a disturbance. I would advise you to step inside immediately." She said the words in a cold fashion that made me think there would be painful consequences for not doing as she'd said.

I recognized Doctor Aisling with shock. I hadn't seen her since last summer. But as I stared at her narrow, fox-like face, I couldn't help but shrink on myself. She'd done something to me, strapped in her chair. For a moment, strapped into it, I'd felt my mind shift, as if I'd become something... else. The experience had been maddening and terrifying... and yet part of me had felt smaller since she pulled me out of her machine.

I'd overheard a confrontation between her and the Admiral. She was here for some kind of purpose, but I didn't understand her interest in me, or in my friends.

"Let's get the three of you ready, shall we?" Doctor Aisling said, adopting a friendly smile. It made me uncomfortable to be the target of that smile. It was such a real smile, so obviously sincere, that I felt fear over how she could project that reassuring smile. After all, I'd heard how coldly clinical her voice could be.

None of us could come up with any kind of argument. In moments, she had us each cocooned in her machines again, I didn't even have time to see anything more of her lab. Before I could think to ask how long it would take, I stood on the green field of grass, under a brilliant blue sky. *Back in her simulation.*

The others stood around me. I knew and recognized them, now. Alexander Karmazin, Ashiri Takenata, Tyler and Ryan Zahler, the twin brothers from Sand Dragon who liked to try to game the system.

"Oh," a voice spoke from a short distance away, "Look who we have here..."

All of us spun. I recognized Bolander from Ogre. Bolander was my polar opposite. She was big and muscular, with dark hair and a tan complexion. Behind her was Thorpe, also from Ogre, and Thorpe was tall, blond-haired, and his arms were bigger around than my legs. Next to Thorpe stood Sashi Drien.

I hadn't seen Sashi since graduation from the Prep School... and the last time I'd seen her for any real length had been when she shot me in the face during our final exercise.

Two more candidates from Ogre stood behind them. *Equal numbers,* I realized. If this turned into a fight, the odds looked unfortunately even.

It shouldn't come to that. This was a simulation, it should all be under control... right?

"Cadets," Doctor Aisling's voice spoke from overhead, "Welcome to Phase Two of the Sensory and Cerebral Interface and Mapping program. Now that we have confirmed neural interface, we will begin the integration process. Please relax and do not resist the procedure."

The world vanished. In its place, there was nothing but a void.

***

Chapter Three: A Warm Welcome

You left. The voice spoke in my head, but it came from outside, from the void.

"Excuse me?" I asked. Or at least, I thought I did. I couldn't hear my own voice, I couldn't hear or see anything. I should have panicked. There wasn't up or down, there was no ground, no air. I didn't know if I was breathing. I couldn't feel anything.

Why did you leave? The voice asked. It was a familiar voice, I realized. It was my voice. Yet it was more than my voice. This didn't sound like how I really sounded, this voice was how I wanted to sound, how I thought I should sound.

"I don't have any control over this," I said. "This is some kind of testing. When the doctor puts me in here, this is what happens." I couldn't imagine being trapped here, in the dark, empty, nothing. I'd go mad, I was sure. Maybe I had gone mad, maybe I was just talking to myself. "Who are you?"

The voice didn't answer. For what felt like a long time, I was simply alone. Then I felt it, the other mind: the consciousness that sounded so much like me. It joined with my mind and it felt like coming home. The world filled with light, color, and sound. For a moment, it overwhelmed me, I couldn't make sense of it all... and then the other mind was there.

It was an entire world. It was Century. From the almost temperate polar areas to the deep desert near the equator. I could see everything, every building, every road, every vehicle. I didn't need to zoom in to see those details, I simply sensed them, while still seeing the greater whole.

I could track them, too. In fact, I could sense the movement of every skimmer, every near-planet space-craft. I was guiding them. With a single thought, I messaged a dozen skimmers to avoid an oncoming sandstorm, transmitting corrected flight paths even as I adjusted their arrival and landing times.

What are we? I wondered. Yet I knew the answer to that. We were an integration, two parts joined together to become a greater whole. We were both human and... something else. Separately, we had functioned, but combined we had our abilities multiplied.

To what purpose? The question came from me, but as a whole, we didn't care. We were stronger together, we could solve so many problems. We were like a god, all-knowing, all-seeing...

Doctor Aisling's cold voice interrupted the moment, "Integration and calibration complete. Simulation terminating."

No! Before I could fight it, before I could even comprehend the moment, it all ended. I blinked up at the ceiling lights and listened to the machinery come to a stop around me. I felt dull and empty, as if she'd cut open my head and removed half my brain.

I wanted her to strap me back in. I wanted to feel that smart, that powerful. All I could do, was mumble to myself. It was hard to make my eyes focus. Before I could protest, she had me up out of the machine and at the door. "Thank you for your time, Cadet."

The door closed in my face. I trembled a bit as I tried to even form words. It was too late. I felt like I wanted to cry, but I couldn't. Dully, I took out my datapad. I had no more appointments.

I didn't remember going back to my room. I didn't remember flopping on my bed or going to sleep. But the next thing I knew, I heard Ashiri's voice.

"...and then it was gone. I mean, for just a second, I felt like so much more."

I sat up, wiping at my face. "You too?" I asked.

Ashiri and Alexander stood in the doorway, talking in low voices. They both looked over at me. "Yeah. What was that?" Ashiri asked.

"Some kind of computer interface," I replied. "But it felt like it was an artificial intelligence."

"Those are illegal, for good reason," Alexander scowled. "AI is dangerous."

I shook my head, "I don't know. It was... weird. It didn't feel dangerous. It felt like it was..."

"Like it was me," Ashiri nodded. "Like it was part of me."

"This is strange," Alexander shook his head. "We should ask someone--"

"Plebes," a sharp voice spoke from behind him. We all started a bit. Cadet Lieutenant Webster stood in the corridor behind Alexander, "Why are you not headed to the Arena?"

"Sir?" I started to my feet and we all went to attention.

"All Cadets and Plebes attend the welcoming brief at the

arena in..." he glanced at his datapad, "five minutes." He glared at us. "If you are not there, then you will face punishment. Unless you have a reason why you three would not be in attendance?"

"Sorry, sir," I spoke up, "we just got out of--"

"The proper response is 'No excuse, sir.' Do you understand Plebe Armstrong?"

"Sir, no excuse, *sir*," I bit off in response.

"Then you three had best get moving," Cadet Lieutenant Webster gave a nasty smile. I hated him already, but I controlled my expression and followed Alexander and Ashiri as they took off at a run.

***

We made it in time, and I was seated in the right place at the right time. The huge indoor chamber was dim, with just enough light for us to find our seats and take them.

I still felt dull and stupid from whatever it was that Doctor Aisling had done to me. In the dimness I had to fight to stay awake.

That was, until the lights came on. "Attention on Deck!" A crisp voice snapped out.

As one, we all snapped to our feet. Central to the chamber, on a platform that overlooked us, the Admiral stepped forward. She wore her normal desert-tan khaki uniform. From where I stood, I couldn't read her expression, but her posture and voice carried professionalism. "Cadets," she said, her voice crisp, "welcome back to the Academy. Today, we start the one hundred and seventieth year of this institution. I welcome our new Plebe Class, the Class of Two-Ninety. I also welcome our First Class, Class of Two-Eighty-Seven, who will graduate at the end of this year and go to their follow-on assignments."

Her voice went stern, "Now that the pleasantries are out of the way, I will tell you this. You are here to train to become officers within the Century Planetary Militia. Everything you do here, every choice you are given, is aimed at that. Every one of you is under constant supervision. Those of you put in positions of authority are there for further evaluation. Your cadet officers will make mistakes. All of you will make mistakes. You are here to learn from those mistakes, to further yourselves as potential leaders, and to perform to the best of your abilities."

"That said, there are some things which we will not accept. Violations of the honor code will be reviewed and adjudicated by a committee of your peers. Lying, cheating, and stealing are unacceptable. You all are expected to report such violations as you witness them."

I felt more than a little uneasy at her words. I thought about why my parents had sent me to the Admiral in the first place: I'd forged my mother's signature on my application to Champion Enterprises. That was technically lying. Did that count? The Admiral knew about it already.

I wasn't in the Academy at the time, I told myself.

"We have reasons for the Honor Code, just as we have reasons for the many other rules we have here. Violations of our administrative rules will receive administrative punishments. Violations of military law, especially fraternization, corruption, and undermining the good order of a unit, will face military justice, possibly even a military tribunal, which I will sit as your final court of appeal."

I could have heard a pin drop in the silence that followed her pronouncement. I wasn't even really certain what those violations meant, but I certainly didn't want to have to throw myself at her mercy. I might be her granddaughter, but if anything, I thought she'd be harder on me than any other cadet here if I was stupid enough to do something illegal.

"Now then," The Admiral went on. "In a more positive but not entirely unrelated note: leave policies have been reinstated now that the construction is complete in the Bahta Town Station." Much of the audience cheered at that, but I wasn't sure why. "All Cadets may take weekend leave passes so long as they are not restricted to campus. Plebes will have to earn passes by showing progress at learning their military duties."

"Additionally, I'd like to introduce some of your new teaching staff," she finished. "Commander Bonnadonna has just come back from an assignment as an observer with the Guard Marine Corps. He will teach Military Law, Military Ethics, Military History, and their introductory courses." The Commander stepped forward into the light. Bonnadonna was a short, stocky man with a grizzled face. There was something about him that intimidated me.

"Commander Pannja has just arrived from a tour at Militia

Headquarters at Duncan City. He'll be taking the role of primary instructor for our Pilot and Navigation tracks of instruction." The piloting instructor stepped forward. He was tall and handsome, with hair just inside tolerable regulation. He wore a friendly smile, his white teeth bright against his tan face, and I felt a little relieved knowing I'd have an instructor for flying that seemed to be at least a little easy-going. After all, my first flight had ended in a crash.

"Additionally," the Admiral said, "Commander Scarpitti has recently come to us from a stint on Admiral Drien's staff. She's an active Militia officer with a great deal of engineering experience. She'll be teaching several of our engineering and technical classes and since she has a great deal of experience in logistics, so she'll be managing our Academy Logistics." Commander Scarpitti was a tall, blonde woman, she had a friendly smile, too. That made me hope that I'd enjoy her engineering classes. I thought I remembered seeing her name on some of my class schedules, anyway.

"Lastly," the Admiral finished, "Doctor Aisling has decided to assist with Academy Instruction." I didn't miss the edge to the Admiral's voice. It was something so subtle that even I would have missed it... except it was the same tone that my mother would adopt when she was annoyed but didn't want to show it. "Doctor Aisling will take over instruction of the cybernetics and medical tracks of instruction."

Part of me felt fear at that. The Doctor terrified me. Yet another part of me felt eager. I'd never felt so alive as when she'd had me connected to the device, I'd felt so strong, so smart...

The Admiral's next words brought me back to reality. "As always, all Companies, Sections, and Individual Cadets are judged based upon a point system. Your grades, your performance in exercises, and your punishments and successes will all count in this process. Last year's winners, by a slim margin, were Sand Dragon Company. The honor graduates, Anderson, Silva, and Chung, were all within hundredths of a point of one another. Honor Graduates often are recruited to some of the better units and choice assignments."

I wondered about those who *didn't* score well. Was there some kind of outcast unit where they ended up?

"Please keep that in mind as all of you train and educate yourselves. Failure in one area can rob you of those possibilities.

Do not neglect one aspect of your profession. Strive to be the best that you can." She looked around the chamber and as her eyes went over me, I felt an almost electric jolt. "Dismissed."

***

"Listen up, *plebes*," Cadet Lieutenant Webster snarled. "In the future, at the end of a ceremony, you will be expected to join in as the Cadets sing our Alma Mater." He stalked up and down in front of us, his movements jerky. Thinking back, I remembered how the other Cadets had sung a song after dismissal. I'd just stood there awkwardly. "The Alma Mater is the heart and soul of our Regiment. You will memorize the Alma Mater. You will sing the Alma Mater with pride and you will pay proper respect to our school. Do you understand?"

"Sir, yes, sir!" We all snapped back.

He didn't seem particularly impressed. "That said, you have to *earn* the right to sing it. Tomorrow we will have a drill day. I have your assignments, based off of your performance through the Prep School as well as your competency examinations. Eventually we'll rotate you all through every position so that you are cross-trained in the necessary duties."

"Now, we should finish our drills by evening, assuming none of you *plebes* screw anything up. If that's the case, we'll have our first regimental dinner at the dining hall. Plebes are not allowed to talk during the meal unless directly asked a question. Additionally, several personnel will be chosen from each section to serve the Regimental Officers and Staff. You will receive food trays and deliver those to the head tables. You should expect to provide service, answer questions, and do as instructed by your cadet officers."

He stopped and looked around. "Sunday morning there will be chaplain services for those of you who want to attend. Those who don't, I will conduct additional drill instruction for those who require it... which will be all of you."

Let's see, I thought, *go to the chapel or get additional training with Cadet Lieutenant Webster, tough choice.* I'd be certain to go to the chapel and I would be very surprised if anyone stuck around for the extra training.

"Sunday afternoon you will have time to set up your rooms

and prepare any classwork for turn-in on Monday morning. I will conduct room inspections Monday morning at zero-five, prior to classes. If you fail your room inspection, you will be inspected again at zero-seven." The way he said that, I got the feeling that he planned to fail all of us.

"We will have a training meeting every night after your classes. There is no excuse for missing or being late. Those of you attending some form of sports activity are required to attend the training meeting first and receive updates from me, after which time I will dismiss you."

It almost felt like Webster had rehearsed all this or like he was going down a list. I felt exhausted listening to him, especially after such a long day. It was frustrating, too, since I'd hoped that I'd be treated just a little bit better after graduation from the Prep School.

"Additionally, cleaning the barracks is the duty of the Plebes. Even after your recognition, as Cadets Fourth Class, you'll still be expected to clean the barracks. I will conduct inspections of the heads, the recreation areas, and all public and commons areas just after I complete your room inspections. These areas will be assigned on a rotating basis, and that list will be sent to all of you before I am finished speaking."

"Now, let me introduce Cadet Petty Officer Salter." We all perked up at that. Salter had been one of our Cadet Instructors. To hear her voice was something of a relief after Webster.

"Plebes," Salter's rough voice snapped. "Welcome back."

Her gruff welcome was like a breath of fresh air. I felt myself stand straighter at it. Compared to Cadet Lieutenant Webster's dismissive hostility, her gruff tone was positively heartwarming. Salter didn't hate us, she didn't care enough about us as people to do that. She'd treat us fairly based on the result of our performance.

"The chow hall will not come online until tomorrow evening. Meals in the meantime are E-Rats. You can pick up yours at the end of the corridor. Cadet Lieutenant Morgan will sign each of you three of them, one for tonight, two for tomorrow," Webster looked around at us. "That's all I have, any questions?"

No one said anything.

"Good. Dismissed."

We broke formation and headed for our quarters. It had been a tremendously long day. I wanted nothing more than to climb onto my rack and put a pillow over my head. But if we were drilling tomorrow, then I had a lot of work to do.

It was going to be a very late night.

***

The next day was about twice as brutal as I expected. We drew our weapons sometime well before dawn. I received Private First Class Santiago Ballanco's rifle, a hero's weapon, in a ceremony similar to what had happened during Prep School. At the same time, every member of Sand Dragon Company went through the process. It was a sobering event, especially with how tired we all were.

They issued us ten magazines of ammunition. Five held training rounds, designed to hurt and incapacitate. Five held live rounds. We received several lectures on the various penalties for confusing the two. Salter and Webster both made it clear to all of us that if we ever suspected live rounds were being fired mistakenly, then we were to immediately put a halt to training.

After that, we performed what Cadet Lieutenant Webster called a "Familiarization Drill" which consisted of us rushing to our assigned positions at full speed. I'd hoped to be assigned to the fighter support. Instead I was assigned to a firing position. Our fire team leader was Cadet Third Class Trask, also of Sand Dragon. The first obstacle I ran into was that I didn't have any of my gear, not yet. So as soon as they learned that, I had to rush over to supply and draw my gear. Thankfully it was ready... but that meant I had to adjust the fit, put it all on, and rush back out to my position.

By the time I arrived, the all-clear went out. I showed up just as we were told to stand down and return to our starting location. So I jogged with the others back to the barracks area in the hot morning sun. If I'd needed any reminders that the Academy lay close to the deep desert, I didn't anymore.

No sooner had we arrived at the barracks and removed all our gear than the drill siren went off again. Doing that in the sun, with a weapon, and all my gear was more than tiring, it was exhausting. Once back at our assigned firing position, a cadet officer came along and inspected our position. He repositioned several of us and departed.

The all clear sounded. We went back to the barracks. Then the drill alarm sounded again.

By late afternoon, I was covered in dried sweat. My uniform was stained with sweat and dirt. I'd managed to eat both of my rations and I'd drained and refilled my water bladder at least four times over. We staggered back to the barracks and I was so tired that I didn't want to sit down, mostly because I didn't want to have to stand up again.

"That's it, *plebes*," Webster snapped from the corridor. "Change out and clean up for dinner. Uniform and gear inspections for everyone. Dinner is in one hour. Armstrong, Takenata, Dawson, and Phillips, you're on server duty for the week."

Oh no, I thought. The last thing I wanted to do was stand for a few more minutes, much less have to answer questions and serve food. I wanted to curl up into a ball and cry. Instead I said, "Aye, aye, sir."

Cleaning our gear took most of that hour. I had just enough time to wash myself, get on a new uniform, and get in line to get a tray of food with the other Regimental Servers. The civilian cooks in the chow hall gave us smirks and smiles as we came through, along with loading our trays down with food to the point that my tired arms trembled.

The smell was torture. First off, there was real meat, not the vat-grown stuff that I'd had all my childhood. I hadn't realized there was a difference, really, not until I'd had the real stuff during the Academy Prep Course... and had to try to swallow the fake stuff when I went back home. Real meat smelled better, it had texture and flavor.

The butter-covered vegetables and thick, creamy mashed potatoes brought growls from my stomach. I'd choked down rations throughout the day, but compared to this, rations didn't really count as food. Nevertheless, I followed the line of servers as we stepped out of the kitchen and started up to the platform where the Regimental Officers sat. These were all Cadets First Class, Cadet Officers. Most of them ignored us. I copied the actions of my fellows and placed trays where they'd fit. To my surprise, the Cadet Officer nearest me gave me a nod of thanks and a slight smile, "Been there, Plebe Armstrong. Don't worry, you'll get food soon enough."

"Yes, sir," I replied and stepped back to stand at ease, like the other servers.

We stood there for a while, while the Regimental officers ate and talked. I listened with half an ear while they discussed this or that event. Most of them seemed focused on their assignments, either comparing their duties or discussing what they hoped to achieve. I didn't understand a lot of it. They used a lot of acronyms and slang.

"Plebe Armstrong," one of the Cadets asked. She wore a rank of Cadet Commander and her name-tape read: Givens.

"Ma'am," I straightened to attention.

"What is the maximum effective range of a ML-7 anti-air missile?" Her voice was relaxed, but the question made me break out in a sweat. That was the same type of missile that someone had tried to kill me with only fifteen days earlier.

I could feel her dark eyes locked on me as I considered the question. "Ma'am," I said after a moment, "I don't know, but I will find out for you, ma'am."

One of the regimental officers laughed, though whether it was at my expense or at the question, I didn't know.

"It's fourteen thousand meters," she answered. "What types of seeker heads does an ML-7 use?"

I swallowed. Was Cadet Commander Givens messing with me... or was she involved in the attack, somehow? "Ma'am, I don't know, but I will find out for you, ma'am."

"Infrared and active radar," she snapped. "You can't win anything if you don't play the game, Plebe Armstrong."

"Being a little tough on her, eh, Amy?" the cadet officer who'd given me a smile said. "This is day one, you can't expect much from Plebes today, right?"

"She's not just any plebe, Teddy," Givens snapped. "She's the Admiral's granddaughter. And from what I understand, she's been in a firefight before... plus she was on that skimmer that got shot down around two weeks ago. By an ML-7. So if she takes this military stuff seriously, she better know some of this stuff."

She looked back at me. "Here's an assignment for you, Plebe Armstrong. Look me up. Figure out what kinds of questions I'm going to ask you. Because I *am* going to ask you. And if I don't like your answers, I'll request you to be our server next week, too. And the week after that. And I'll keep grilling you until you can give me the right answers. Understand?"

"Ma'am, yes, ma'am," I snapped.

"Good." Cadet Commander Givens gave me a nod. Then she pushed her plate to the side and stood up. "See you tomorrow, Plebe Armstrong."

***

Chapter Four: Setting the Example

After room inspections, I made it to my first class of the day with just enough time to find a seat. I'd been dismayed to learn that I wouldn't spend the first year with my section-mates. Instead, it seemed that they split us up for the first semester, while we took the introductory classes and selected our military track. Out of the forty others in the class, I only recognized Dawson, who at least gave me a nod as I came in. Since this one was Introduction to Military Ethics, I had hoped to be at the back, possibly where I could work on some of my other classwork. Instead, I was pretty much right in the front and center.

"Class, Attention!" One of my classmates barked as Commander Bonnadonna stepped into the classroom.

"Take your seats," Commander Bonnadonna barked. He had an abnormally deep voice, especially at how short he was. He walked briskly to his podium. I realized pretty quickly that he had an implanted computer, because he'd dimmed the lights and brought up the display along the way, without use of a datapad or other device.

He stood near the podium, looking over the class, his hard-planed face unreadable. I took the time to study him. He was short, shorter than my father, but with broad shoulders and thick muscle. He looked like he was carved out of rock, his face grizzled and scarred. I found his dark eyes unsettling as they went across me, as if he were cataloging me like an item.

"Welcome, Plebes," he spoke, his deep voice resonating in the classroom. "That's an interesting term, isn't it? Plebe, from *pleb*. The Roman term for commoners... it has become a derogatory term throughout the military culture in general. In ancient times, the Roman Legions would sometimes be called in to restore order when their *plebs* got out of line... an interesting fact, don't you think?"

I sort of knew who the Romans were. They'd built roads back on Earth, long before we'd gone to space. I thought I remembered them having some kind of Empire, though I couldn't remember if that had been in North America or Asia. He was talking ancient history so I didn't really see the relevance.

"Here on Century, citizenship is granted by birth, and some

few of our immigrants, gaining it through renouncing their old homeworlds and swearing an oath to the Charter Council and Century," he nodded to one of the students. "Plebe Martinez, you and your family immigrated from New Madrid in the Evistar Sector. Did you or your family find it arduous to gain citizenship here?"

We all looked over as Martinez stood, "Sir, no, sir."

"Thank you, Miss Martinez. For the purposes of timeliness, consider these classes an open discussion, rather than a traditional lecture. Feel free to answer my questions and elaborate," Commander Bonnadonna said. "We are going to use something of a Socratic method for instruction. I will introduce concepts, we will discuss them, and I hope that all of you will come to the correct understanding in the end."

That left me with a headache. In my mind, a teacher should teach. We should learn the right answers so that we could solve a problem in the right way. Engineering problems didn't involve discussion, they were settled with calculations and hard numbers. There was a right answer and a wrong one.

"So," he said, "having reviewed all of your papers and seeing where you all stand, I think we'll start with a group discussion and practical exercise."

My eyes widened at that. We'd turned in our research papers on Friday when we reported. The ethics paper had been ten pages at a minimum. There were forty of us in the class, I didn't see how he could have reviewed all of our papers, much less all of the papers from his other classes.

"All of the examples we'll use are real world examples, though I adapt them a bit to simplify them," Commander Bonnadonna said. "We'll start with a relatively recent one." He brought up the scenario on the screen. "Plebe Duchan, please read it aloud."

"Uh, yes sir," Duchan stood. "You are a cadet detached to work with a civilian company for a broadening experience. During your time there, you uncover inconsistencies with the company's records, particularly with their military contracts. You suspect they are stealing military equipment for sale on the black market. What do you do?"

I wanted to sink into my chair. I could feel stares from around me. I was the example. I wanted to throw up. I already doubted myself enough, why did I have to be dragged back through all this? I kept my eyes forward and my mouth shut, though I felt anger at the officer for doing this to me.

"Well, anyone?" Commander Bonnadonna asked. "No one? Surely someone has a suggestion?"

Someone raised their hand, "Yes, Mister Naghi?"

"Uh, sir, possibly contact the authorities?" Naghi answered. "I guess the Enforcers, since it is a civilian company, right?"

"Technically, the civilian authorities would have jurisdiction over criminal wrong-doings, yes," Commander Bonnadonna nodded, "But the military would have jurisdiction over military equipment." He nodded at another student, "Miss Do, yes?"

I looked over to see a short plebe, clearly from the second wave of colonists, her sharply slanted eyes and straight black hair distinctive, "Shouldn't we gather more information or evidence? I mean, it just says we suspect, it doesn't say we have any proof."

"Indeed," Commander Bonnadonna nodded. "Without some measure of proof, it is unlikely that a cadet would be believed, especially if the company is in good standing." He looked around, "Ah, yes, Miss Drien there in the back."

I went cold as he said that and I couldn't help but look over my shoulder. I hadn't seen her at the back of the room. Sashi stood up, "Sir, I don't think further investigation is warranted. I think the cadet should contact the military authorities, possibly call back to the Academy. With someone in authority involved, the cadet can then have guidance on how to proceed so as to not alienate either the civilians or endanger any personnel."

My stomach fell as she said that. I had second-guessed myself about that since I woke up in the hospital. I should have done exactly what she'd said. I should have messaged the Admiral, let her take charge. I shouldn't have looked into it myself or endangered Ted Meeks.

I agreed with her, that's what I should have done.

Yet I found my hand going up.

"Ah, yes, Miss Armstrong?" Commander Bonnadonna smiled. There was something about that smile that suggested he'd known this would happen. He had planned for it. He *wanted* me angry.

"Sir," I bit out, "I think it's unfair to look back at a situation like this and judge what the person *should* have done without being in the moment."

"Exactly right!" Commander Bonnadonna nodded. "And spoken exactly as I would have expected. As most of you no doubt realize, this situation was drawn from an experience that Miss Armstrong went through. She brought up a very good point." He put emphasis on that with his resonant voice, "We can simplify the situation, we can make it abstract, and we can look at a situation knowing far more information than the person on the ground. We can discuss what she should and should not have done all day long... it's the person at the time who makes the call. Just as Miss Armstrong made this decision, all of you, as future officers, will be put in situations where others will second-guess your judgment, where they will question your decisions, your reasons."

"There will come a day where you will have to justify your choices, not just to others, but to yourself. That, ladies and gentlemen, is why we are here today. Not to talk about the decisions that will cost the lives of men and women under your command, but to talk about *why* we make those decisions."

His dark eyes settled on me and I felt cold at his next words, "Because we are the ones who will have to live... or die... by those decisions."

***

"Take seats," Commander Pannja said. The Intro to Piloting and Navigation instructor was as friendly-looking in person as he'd appeared to be before. He was tall, handsome, and his light brown skin stood out against his khaki uniform. He was definitely a Second, that was, a descendant of the second wave of Century's original colonist, but he had a swagger that suggested he had more than enough confidence.

"We're going to be deep diving into piloting theory, today. I'm impressed with the scores from your coursework during the prep course and I want you all to know that I'll be pushing you hard throughout this course."

He pointed at one of the students, "Plebe Beacham, what's our course objective here?"

"Uh," Beacham stood up. He read off his datapad, "To prepare and certify plebes for warp drive and atmospheric craft?"

"Exactly, so what does that really mean?" Commander Pannja asked with a friendly smile. When no one volunteered an answer, his smile grew, "Not a lot, actually. What we'll be doing in this class is basic familiarity. Enough to get you in trouble if you try to use any of it in real life."

He brought up the classroom display. "This is the Mark Five Firebolt Attack Fighter, it's a light fighter, initially designed and built for Guard Fleet over three hundred years ago. We use it, with judicial upgrades, as our standard warp fighter. We also use a stripped-down version as our training craft."

He looked around at us. "Anyone know how many hours of simulator time you're required to have before we can legally put you in the seat of one of these?"

"Sir," I recognized Duchan's voice, "I think the manual suggested a thousand hours."

"Correct, that's what the manual suggests," Commander Pannja smiled. "But the Charter Councils has laid some additional safeguards on us. Every one of you, before we put you in the seat of one of these, has to undergo fifteen hundred hours of simulator time and be signed off on by no less than three qualified officers." He nodded at Sashi, "Plebe Drien, at the maximum recommended simulator time of four hours per day, how many days of training would you require to be trained?"

"Sir, that's three hundred and seventy five days, sir," Sashi Drien replied. *She probably expected that question,* I thought to myself. Granted, I could do the math myself, but it would take me a bit longer than that.

"Correct. Very good. Now, to the rest of you, why do you think we have such heavy restrictions?"

I hesitantly raised my hand, "I assume it is due to the effects of warp drives on atmospheres, sir?" If I remembered right, warp drives generated massive currents in atmosphere, causing tremendous storms.

"That's close enough that I'll give you credit, Armstrong," Pannja nodded. "Atmospheric effects from warp-drives are bad, but there's another issue. Warp drives warp normal space-time around themselves to achieve relativistic velocity. There's not normally much kinetic force, in fact, there shouldn't be *any*, really, from the ship itself striking a planet."

"The problems are twofold: you have the warping effect from the warp field. Generally that causes massive gravitational shearing forces. In a little fighter like a Firebolt, you'd just blast apart a kilometer or so of dirt before your drive burned out. On a bigger ship, like say a Nelson-class battleship... well, you could obliterate a planet and keep moving."

"The second problem is that our warp-drive fields require antimatter power plants. If you plow yourself into a moon, you'll blow out your warp drive. In the process, you've got a good chance of creating a feedback loop into the antimatter core, or maybe just shattering it yourself from the collision. If that goes..." his screen shifted to show a massive explosion. "This is the result, people. This happened just last year, when a Drakkus Imperial Space Korps fighter, a Havoc Heavy Assault Fighter, collided with a small planetoid during a training exercise. Over three thousand workers on the planetoid were killed. So was the pilot, but I think that goes without saying."

I felt a chill as I stared at that fireball. At the relative velocities that warp-drive craft traveled at, the pilot might not have even had time to realize what had happened before he died.

"So, we have three hundred and seventy five days of training before you're certified to go up. That's a massive investment of time and resources...and don't think for even a second that we're going to start you on that in this class or even this year. We lose five months of time during the summer semesters, but between drill days where you'll receive more simulator time, and some very intensive training events in your second class year, all of you will be certified by the time you are First Classmen."

I was more than a bit daunted by that. Two complete years of training? I wasn't even certain I wanted that level of responsibility.

As if he read my thoughts, Commander Pannja went on, "Warp craft training isn't for everyone. We'll see where your interests and abilities lie. By the time you complete this class, you'll have a good grasp for the basics of both. After summer semester, I'll have you all back in here and ready to start the flight course, where we'll go hands-on with the air-breathers and reaction-powered thrusters. By the end of that, we will get you your unlimited aircraft and non-warp capable aerospace craft licenses. All of you will achieve basic proficiency in both areas in order to stay here at the Academy."

"Now, some of you may be thinking you already have civilian licenses for these things," His grin grew broad, "that's great. It's wonderful. And I'll tell you right now, thinking that you already know this material will get you killed. That's if you're lucky. Because if you're really unlucky, thinking you already know everything will result in you being a picture like this," he waved a hand at the fireball image. "And in that case, you probably killed a lot of people in the process."

"So," he said. "Let's start off with some basic aircraft theory..."

***

"Welcome class, to your medical and implantation class," Doctor Aisling said. She either didn't notice that we'd all come to our feet or she didn't care. In ones and twos, we all settled back into our desks as she continued to talk, "Normally this class would be an abridged familiarization, but some elements of the Century Planetary Militia feel that more of a preparation for the process will limit the number of implant rejections."

"Implant rejections?" another plebe asked.

"Yes, they are unfortunate, but they're also rare. I see that I got ahead of myself, though." Doctor Aisling gave us all a sunny, friendly smile, her red hair bright against her white lab coat. "We'll follow the course curriculum that I've just uploaded to your datapads. Our initial focus over the next few weeks will be over the current level of technology. What you can expect, what the medical process entails, and how to best integrate your biological systems with the cybernetic augmentations that you all will receive."

"Ma'am," Plebe Beacham raised his hand, "Plebe Beacham, Dust Company, I thought that cybernetic implants were purely on a voluntary basis."

"That was correct, until recently. The Charter Councils has just signed into law a requirement that all officers receive cybernetic implantation as a requirement for commissioning. All cadets, including this year's seniors... that is, first classmen, will be required to receive implants."

Mutters filled the room. Cybernetics weren't popular. Being

required to get them was even less popular. I'd sort of resigned myself to the idea of it, but knowing there was a choice about it had sort of given me a bit of relief, just in case I couldn't go through with it.

"Now," Doctor Aisling went on, her light, friendly voice somehow cutting through the discussions, "I can imagine that's not an entirely popular decision. So we'll put off some of the technical discussions and go into a bit of history. Most of the predisposed distrust of cybernetics comes from the Chun-La Massacre, I assume?"

No one really said anything. Most people had heard stories of cybernetic augmentees going nuts and killing people. The Chun-La Massacre was simply the most famous incident.

"You, there," Doctor Aisling pointed at Dawson, "Give the class a bit of a history lesson. Tell us about the Chun-La Massacre."

Dawson stood, "Ma'am, Plebe Dawson, Sand Dragon Company. The Chun-La Massacre happened before the Star Portal. I'm not a hundred percent certain on all the details, but as I understand it, a unit of cybernetic-augmented mercenaries attacked a Chinese colony, Chun-La, in the Alpha Centauri system. They massacred the entire population."

"A succinct explanation," Doctor Aisling nodded. "It misses some crucial details. The mercenary company was made up Russian survivors from a Russian colony that the Chinese military had wiped out. They were hired by the Russians to make an example of the Chinese colonists. While they were paid to do it, it wasn't an attack motivated by money, it was done based on revenge."

Her voice stayed light, but there was anger in it, as if Dawson's explanation had irritated her. "Now, the vast majority of the so-called berserk incidents that have been reported since then have also come back to similar motivations. Rare incidents of lone cybernetic augmentees going insane have often been tracked back to a variety of causes ranging from mental instability to poor installation of equipment or malfunctioning implants. Believe me when I say that a properly installed implant that receives proper maintenance is of no risk to anyone."

No one had a reply to that. Her words, however she delivered them, still didn't make me any more comfortable about the idea of her cutting open my head and putting hardware inside. It didn't matter how safe she assured me that it would be.

"Now, then," Doctor Aisling said, "the vast majority of hesitation that you all feel about the idea comes back to fear of the unknown. This is to be expected. It is basic human psychology to fear change. That's part of what this class will be about, allowing you to learn that you have nothing to fear from the process. You will not be harmed, this will not disable you in any way. You will in fact, be *enabled*. I'll go over the many abilities that you'll gain throughout the course, but the sum up the highlights: instant access to all manner of communications, data management, the ability to record events as they unfold, and the ability to download information and examine it at your leisure."

What she'd pitched made it sound like having a datapad. *Except the datapad is in your head and may or may not drive you insane,* I reminded myself.

"Additionally, many of our ship and weapon upgrades require a direct neural link to operate with full functionality," Doctor Aisling said off-handedly. I couldn't help but perk up at that and wonder how it related to the testing she'd put me through. "A neural computer implant will allow you to control such equipment with far greater speed than a non-augmented human."

Despite myself, my hand went in the air. "Ma'am, Plebe Armstrong, Sand Dragon Company. What about interfaces with artificial intelligences?"

Doctor Aisling's expression went hard. "Yes, well, anything like that would not only be purely theoretical, it would be highly illegal. Production of artificial intelligences violates the Non-Human Intelligence section of the Alien and Telepathic Act of the UN Star Guard Security Council." She stared at me, as if daring me to mention the testing she'd put me through. "Any potential results would be immaterial. Any nation that conducted such experiments would be declared rogue. The Star Guard would dispatch a task force to seize and destroy any such research."

I nodded in reply to her warning. This wasn't something she was going to discuss in class and doing so clearly had the potential for drastic repercussions. Yet some part of me wondered why the Admiral allowed such experimentation to take place, given the consequences. There had to be some threat equally dire to risk the intervention of the Guard.

The thought was not a comforting one.

***

Chapter Five: Walking on Eggshells

"Ma'am, Plebe Armstrong, reporting as ordered, ma'am," I snapped as soon as I'd set my tray down. I braced at attention and just hoped that I'd managed to pick the right things to read in preparation.

Cadet Commander Givens glared at me, "Well?"

"Ma'am, you are the Regimental Tactical Officer. You are responsible for evaluating and coordinating defensive plans in case of attack," I reported. She waited, as if expecting more, so I went on. "Six years ago, you were aboard Long Station, where a pirate gang boarded the station and killed several civilians." I'd managed to find that much from comparing her public profile to news files.

"Good enough. For details, I was one of the hostages they took, and I was forced to kill one of them to save my own life." I simply nodded in response to that. "So, Plebe Armstrong, you carry an Alpha Eleven assault rifle, what's its maximum effective range?"

That was easy, "Eight hundred meters without optics, ma'am."

"What's the maximum effective range of a Trascom eleven millimeter hunting rifle, with scope?" Cadet Commander Givens asked.

I froze as I flashed back to the wreckage of the crashed skimmer, the hunting rifle held in one arm and braced with my other hand, three of the fingers broken. It was the weapon I'd used to kill two goons who'd tried to kill me. I had no idea how she knew that. "Ma'am," I said after a long moment, "depending on the circumstances, up to two thousand meters with optics."

"Tammy, what's up with that question?" One of the cadet officers asked.

"Plebe Armstrong's seen combat, of a sort," Cadet Commander Givens said. "She killed two men with a bolt action hunting rifle and a broken hand."

"Holy..." the Cadet First Class looked back at me and I could see a weird mix of respect and worry on his face. "I guess the apple didn't fall far from the tree."

Cadet Commander Givens just gave me a little nod. It seemed I'd passed her test. She went back to talking to the other cadet officers. Yet in the moment she'd met my eyes when she told me she'd killed a pirate, I wondered if she ever had times when she closed her eyes, and like me, she was back in that moment when she took the life of another human.

***

The grav-shell team seemed to meet in an isolated steel shed just inside the Academy grounds. Past the open bay doors on the shed, I could see miles of open desert. We'd run out there during some of Indoctrination, but seeing it in the late afternoon sun left me feeling tiny and insignificant.

"Armstrong!" Cadet Commander Mackenzie greeted me. "Glad you could make it!"

I could only nod at him. I felt more than a little awkward. He and most of the other team wore sleek, almost skin-tight, bodysuits. They didn't leave much to the imagination. I felt oddly self-conscious in my academy shorts and t-shirt, yet I couldn't imagine wearing anything like what they wore.

"You know anything at all about grav-shells?" Mackenzie asked, waving at one that hung from a rack on the ceiling.

"Not really," I replied.

"No problem," he grinned. "I'll show you the basics and then we can launch."

"Wait, you want me to drive one of these things, already?" I asked in shock.

Mackenzie chuckled, "Don't worry, you'll pick it up quick. Besides, we won't go very fast."

It wasn't the speed that I worried about. The sleek-looking craft looked decidedly fragile. The outriggers, with their sliding chairs, were mounted on thin struts. The main body, where the pilot –coxswain, I reminded myself-- sat was slender and tapered. The entire contraption wouldn't have looked out of place floating on the water, yet it was designed to fly.

"So," Mackenzie ran a crank and the entire rack lowered down, "every grav-shell runs off gravity-inductor coils. Most of them are custom designed, some are salvage jobs from wrecks."

"Wait, gravity inductor coils?" I asked. "Aren't those part of a warp drive?"

"Yes, same tech, but re-purposed," Mackenzie waved a hand.

"With a large enough power source, you could generate a warp field. Of course, if they're not arranged properly, it would be a really messed up field that would probably kill you." He grinned, "I wouldn't recommend it. Luckily, those exotic particles we generate at much lower power levels have a sort of ground effect. If their frame is light enough, you can float them with human-powered muscle." He pointed at the big torsion machine at the center of the craft. It lay square in-between the outriggers, with pull cords run down each outrigger, and a broad grip at the end of each cord. "The rowers crank the generator. The coxswain adjusts the angle of the inductor coils, and the whole thing floats."

"How does it move?" I asked as I ducked underneath it to look at the underside.

"The ground effect from the coils can be adjusted to allow it to slide 'down' in one direction or another. You trade height for speed... then readjust with a bit more power to compensate."

"All powered by muscle?" I couldn't help but wince as I thought about that. It sounded incredibly exhausting.

"Yep, and lots of combined effort," Mackenzie smirked. "If the rowers get off beat, the generator loses power and the shell loses balance. If the coxswain exhausts the rowers, the whole thing could crash."

"What happens then?" I asked. I couldn't help but tap the hull of the grav-shell. It wasn't particularly thick, and it made a dull noise from my knuckle. Clearly it was some kind of fiber, rather than sturdy metal.

"Well, you can really get going in one of these. In the professional races, they're going as fast as two hundred kilometers per hour. You hit the ground at those speeds and, well, it's not good."

I turned to look at him in shock. "Don't worry," Mackenzie's easy smile reassured me, "Daisy here is only rated for around sixty kilometers per hour. We're strictly in the amateur leagues. I've had her at seventy KPH before, but that was with my previous cox, and he graduated last year."

I shook my head, "I can't imagine going that fast in something like this."

"Oh, trust me, even going at thirty KPH feels like you're in serious trouble," he replied. "We'll start you off slow. Competition racing doesn't start for another month, so we've got time to break you in. But practices are two hours every evening and two hours every morning from here on out. You'll be getting up before your inspections in the morning, so you'll get a pass on those, but you'd better keep your room inspection-ready. This isn't a free pass."

I straightened at that, "Yes, sir."

He waved a hand, "None of that, no rank in the grav-shell bay." He snorted, "I'm the team captain, though, so if I tell you you're out, you're out. So don't abuse the little perks you get from being on the team, understand?"

"I do," I said. Honestly, I didn't see many perks to the sport. I'd be up even earlier than the other plebes, I'd spend four hours a day at this, and there looked to be a solid possibility of death or injury. Still, I didn't see a good way to get out of it. Maybe I'd get lucky and he'd think I wasn't cut out for this.

"Go ahead and mount up," he said with a nod. He flipped down a thin cord ladder and I fumbled up it and climbed into the cockpit. "Snug, right?"

I felt like I could barely breathe. The seat was formed of the same thin spun fiber material as the hull. I had a tiny harness that probably wouldn't do much to keep me from flying out in the event of a crash.

"Mind the back-bar. You're short enough that you can rest your head on it, at least." I did so and I could barely see over the front. "Perfect," he said. "Here's the controls."

I had expected some kind of digital display. Instead there were some thin rods, which were connected in with wires. Mackenzie reached in and shifted one, pointing to the side. I looked over and saw the left outrigger shift slightly. "It's a mechanical control system. You've got pitch and yaw, here, with altitude there. The trick is to trade speed for height. When we hit a slope, you milk it for everything it's got, when we're going across flats, you call a power ten or twenty and the rowers pile in the effort to build height, which you trade for more speed."

"Um," I frowned, "how do we stop?"

"Why would we want to do that?" Mackenzie laughed at my expression. "There's an emergency safety. That's here," he flipped up a clear plastic cover and pointed at a big red button. "It's a capacitor with enough juice to bounce the whole thing. It goes on and the coils will bring us to a stop, then lower us to the ground. It disconnects our generator in the process." He shrugged. "Never had to use it, not even with a temporary cox."

"Okay," I said, "what about non-emergency?"

He laughed and reached down to grab the central strut. To my surprise, he lifted the craft, me included, right out of the rack. "Generally you just need to slow us down and we can hop out and stop it. It's not too heavy, even with you in it."

"Got it," I said.

"Great," Mackenzie smiled. He waved to one of the others, "Stroud, we're going to take Daisy for a quick spin."

"Sure thing!" Stroud jogged over. He was just as tall and lanky as Mackenzie, though with blonde hair and blue eyes as opposed to Mackenzie's brown hair and blue eyes. Stroud had a similar, easy-going smile and attitude. I wondered if they were related or something.

The two of them pushed Daisy out of the bay and into the desert. "For now, focus on keeping her straight and on the flat," Mackenzie said. The entire craft shifted as he and Stroud mounted up. They were seated above and behind me on the rower chairs that projected off the two outriggers and they'd scampered up faster than I thought was possible. "Now," Mackenzie said, "normally, the coxswain calls out commands, but I'll walk us through, since we need to get moving before we sink."

"Power ten, three, two, one, power ten!" He barked. He and Stroud began to row. I couldn't help but watch the pair of them move, in perfect synch so that the craft didn't as much as shift. "Alright, ease us forward a bit, but be gentle, she's very responsive," Mackenzie said.

I tweaked the controls ever so slightly. The entire craft surged forward. I was so startled that my first instinct was to jerk at the controls, but I stopped myself before I could do that. Instead I eased back a bit and our pace slowed. "You're drifting starboard," Mackenzie puffed.

I tweaked the controls and we swung to port, then further in that direction. I over-corrected and brought it back into more or less a straight line.

"Good, now we've lost some altitude," Mackenzie puffed, "so to gain it, we're going to do a power five." He paused for a moment, then bellowed, "Power five on two! One, Two..." Both Mackenzie and Stroud began to take deeper strokes, the entire craft surged as more power flooded into the coils, "one, two, three, four five!"

We'd risen almost a meter in the air. I tweaked the controls and turned some of that into speed. To my shock, the Daisy responded a lot more than I expected. It felt like we were racing across the desert and I started to panic.

"We're good," Mackenzie puffed. "Ease up a little and turn us around, that's a good introduction, for now."

I followed his instructions and turned us in a broad, slow circle. As I did so, I searched for the grav-shell bay, thinking I must have missed it somehow. Then I realized that it was the distant spot, near the horizon. "Wow," I gasped.

"Yeah, we go a lot faster and further than you realize. Most of these races we go fifteen or twenty kilometers, but some of them are forty or fifty kilometers," He puffed. "Take us back nice and slow. Stroud and I need to practice different rowing speeds. I think you're about ten pounds lighter than our last coxswain, which is good, but neither of us have been practicing at all for the last couple of months, so we need the workout."

I nodded, but I didn't know if he saw. As we headed back, I tweaked the controls steering us in as straight a line as I could manage, slowly feeling more and more confident as the shed drew closer. Surprisingly, I even found myself enjoying it. There was something incredible about harnessing the power of the two rowers. The entire craft floated in the air from the brute force of two men. The Daisy sped across the desert, hovering just above the sand. We arrived back at the shed just as the sun began to dip towards the horizon. Stroud and Mackenzie hopped out at the same time and Mackenzie gestured at me to dismount.

I did so, feeling oddly stiff as I did so. I watched as they racked the light craft. I felt oddly forlorn as they did so. I missed it. I didn't have a clue what I was doing, I doubted I'd be much more than additional weight to the two rowers without lots and lots of practice and effort. But I already enjoyed it.

"Well," Mackenzie patted Daisy. "Thanks for coming Armstrong. See you in the morning?" He gave me a smirk, as if he knew exactly how I felt.

"Yeah," I said, "Sure thing."

***

"Look what we have here," A deep voice growled from behind me in the corridor. I'd just got back to the barracks areas from grav-shell practice. I hadn't expected to encounter anyone, not for how busy everyone seemed to be, especially not for this time of day.

I turned and saw Bollander. The big woman gave me a smirk. Beside her I saw Thorpe. The two of them were so big that I didn't even notice Sashi Drien standing in front of them until she spoke, "Armstrong, you lost?" Sashi's hostile tone shouldn't have hurt, but it did.

"Just on my way back from practice," I replied. I took a reflexive step towards the stairwell as I did so. I didn't like being outnumbered and alone, especially not by Ogre.

"You're in our barracks area," Bollander growled.

"I'm *under* your barracks areas," I replied, taking another step towards the stairs. Yet as I did so, Thorpe sidestepped to block my escape in that direction. *I might slip past him, but his arms are long enough that he might grab me.*

"You shouldn't be down here, anyway," Bolander growled. "Right Drien?"

"Yeah, you shouldn't," Sashi snapped, glaring at me.

This didn't look good. I didn't really know much about fighting. "I don't want any trouble."

"You think you're tough, just because you killed some thugs?" Bolander growled. "You think we should be afraid of you?" There was an edge of anger and something else in her voice. I didn't understand it. I didn't understand any of this. I had beaten out Bolander and Thorpe in the final exercise during the Academy Prep School, but it hadn't been personal, they'd been trying to do the same thing. For that matter, Sashi had shot me during the same exercise... after I'd saved her from Bolander.

"Well, you're about to get a lesson, one you should have learned already. Don't mess with Ogre!" On her cue, Sashi lunged forward to grab me, but I dodged to the side. Thorpe leaned in, his arms going to grab me, but I ducked under his grasp and then ran for the stairs. I saw Sashi and Thorpe collide and both of them went down in a tangle.

Bolander was quicker than I'd expected, though. She caught me just as I reached the stairs and spun me into the wall. I tried to punch at her, but she caught both of my wrists and cranked them up over my head. "Time to teach you a lesson..."

"Stop right there!" A deep female voice snapped. "What do you think you're doing, *plebes*?"

Bolander released me and Thorpe and Sashi Drien untangled themselves. "Plebe Armstrong was in our barracks area uninvited, ma'am." Bolander started.

"Assault upon another cadet is against Academy policy," Commander Scarpitti snapped. Her harsh accent added extra force to her words and I saw all three of my attackers go pale as she glared at them. "Worse than that, you're beating up on another cadet with unfair odds and a significant size advantage. Bolander, Thorpe, and Drien, I'm putting the three of you on report for this. Do you understand?"

"Yes, ma'am," All three of them snapped.

"Now get out of here," Commander Scarpitti barked. As the three of them departed, she waited and then gave me a friendly smile, "Seems I arrived at the right time, eh, Plebe Armstrong?"

"Yes, ma'am," I nodded in response. I was still shocked that they'd been so willing to resort to physical violence.

"You should use a bit more caution," Commander Scarpitti said. "A certain level of rough-housing is to be expected. They probably wouldn't have done more than rough you up a bit, but they might have gone a bit far. Many companies have rivalries going back several decades. Ogre and Sand Dragon have been feuding since as far as anyone can remember."

"I see, ma'am, thank you, ma'am," I spoke on autopilot. I still couldn't believe that they'd been willing to pound on me just *because*.

"The three of them will be in trouble with the rest of Ogre for getting caught. They'll also face some administrative punishment, but that's not going to make them like you any better. So in the future, I'd recommend that you travel with friends late at night, or at least avoid empty corridors. Understand?"

Commander Scarpitti didn't wait for a response. She strode off, leaving me in the empty corridor. I was more than grateful for her intervention. But I was also surprised by how little she seemed to care about what they'd intended to do. In my mind, violence like that wasn't warranted and it should have received serious punishment. Instead, I felt like whatever punishment they'd receive would only make them come after me even harder... or in a more devious fashion.

Alright, I told myself, *I have enemies, I already knew that.* I'd just have to keep my eyes open. First, though, I needed to get back to my barracks room, hopefully without any other incidents.

***

Chapter Six: Knowing Where I Stand

The alarm klaxon went off well before dawn on Saturday morning. It was followed a moment later by a voice, "This is a drill, this is a drill, this is a drill. Load practice ammunition and proceed to grounds defense positions."

My clock said it was just after two in the morning. Sashi and I fumbled around, drawing on our uniforms and gear and then rushing into the corridor. I loaded my rifle with a magazine of practice rounds as we ran. The first set of drills had been dry; that was, without any ammunition of any kind loaded. If we were loaded, that meant there was at least a chance that we'd face some kind of opposition.

I arrived at my assigned position. Cadet Petty Officer Trask waited as the rest of us funneled into our positions. Our bunker overlooked a desolate stretch of desert. "Third Squad, Sand Dragon Company, we have reports of enemy infiltrators in our area of operations. Expect contact with enemy forces in team size or smaller. They'll have small arms, expect harassing fire. If you take fire, call it up. If anyone is hit, we'll go through evacuation procedures."

Team size, I thought, *that is four or five personnel.* We'd gone over the evacuation procedures the last drill, but only as a basic exercise. I had a cheater card so I could read off it, but I felt nervous at the thought of reading it out on the net.

Despite that, I hurried to my firing position. It wasn't much more than a notch in the trench, with a little bit of overhead cover for when the sun came up. I turned on the night vision setting on my helmet visor and scanned the desert. I didn't see how anyone could hope to sneak up. The desert looked flat and empty. I figured someone would have to be stupid to try to sneak up on the position. There wasn't anywhere to hide.

I heard what sounded like a shot. A moment later, I felt an impact on my shoulder, just between my shoulder armor and my chest armor. "Shot fired," I reported, "I'm..."

The world went dark.

***

I woke up, flat on my back. There was a bit of camouflage netting above me. I looked around and saw that I was on a stretcher. "Took a round already, eh?" A soft voice spoke. I saw another plebe seated next to me. "Yeah," I said. I sat up, "I guess I should get back to my unit."

"Nope, you get to sit this one out," a cadet said from the other side of me. "All casualties remain here until reset." She grinned at me, "I'm Cadet Third Class Connie Elliot, by the way. Welcome to the aid station. You're our first guest this morning."

"Cadets run the aid station, ma'am?" I asked. She was surprisingly cheerful for someone who's job it was to patch people up.

"That's correct," She gestured at the plebe on my other side. "Ivy Company are medical officers in training. We operate as medics and nurses during the drills. Your company dropped you off here as a casualty, we treat you, and get you back to the fight after the drill ends."

"How long will it go?" I asked.

Before she could answer, I heard a shout from the front of the room, "Casualties inbound!"

"Got to go," Elliot said. She and the plebe rushed to the front of the room. I watched as they went through a full inspection of the two cadets they'd brought in. "Gunshot wound to the leg, hear-rate irregular..."

I tuned it out as I got off the stretcher and winced at the bruise on my shoulder. The training rounds were heavy enough to leave bruises and they delivered a mild tranquilizer. I'd been hit by them before, but it wasn't something I'd been eager to repeat.

A moment later, they put the comatose cadet's stretcher down next to me. "She's terminal," Cadet Third Class Elliot said. "Call it."

"Time of Death, zero-seven-three-nine," her assistant reported.

"Got it, dose her," Elliot nodded.

I looked over and I paled a bit as I recognized Sashi Drien. Apparently she'd been a casualty, too. The hit had caught her on the side of her neck and she already had a massive bruise. I watched as they hit her with a stimulant to counteract the tranquilizer.

She sat up a moment later. When she saw me, she glowered,

"You shot me!"

"I did not," I snapped.

"Play nice," Elliot chuckled. "Both of you were hit by the raid teams. Neither of you came in from even the same sector. So shut up and play dead."

"Dead?" Sashi and I both asked at the same time.

"Dead," Elliot grinned. "Both of you took fatal wounds. You're combat casualties until the drill resets. After that, you get to go back out there... until you die again. So play nice and shut up, I'll have more casualties to triage."

We stayed quiet as she walked towards the front of the room. Sashi and stayed quiet for a long moment. "Sniper?" I asked after a long moment.

"Yeah," she said.

After a long, awkward, silence I said, "Me too."

Neither of us said anything for a long while. I sat on the edge of my stretcher, facing away from her. I thought about how she and Bolander and Thorpe had ambushed me earlier in the week. "You get punished?"

"That's what you want to know?" Sashi's voice was harsh. "Do you have any idea... you know what? I've got nothing to say to you." I could hear the hate in her voice and that hurt more than anything she'd actually said.

Part of me wanted to turn around and shout at her. It felt like she wanted *me* to apologize. *Like that would ever happen,* I thought to myself. She was the one who'd betrayed me. It was her family's stupid feud that had ruined our friendship.

I wanted to scream all that at her, but instead I sat fuming. How dare she think she deserved anything from me? Less than a week earlier she and her Ogre section-mates had tried to attack me. If not for Commander Scarpetti, they would probably have succeeded. She'd literally shot me in the face. I had thought she was my friend and she'd betrayed me.

Sitting there, only a few meters away from her was almost intolerable. I couldn't wait to get back out to my squad, as far away from her as I could be.

***

"Welcome back, Armstrong," Cadet Third Class Trask said

as I rushed to my position. "Have a nice nap?"

"Negative, sir," I replied. "It won't happen again, sir."

"Don't make promises you can't keep," Trask replied. "The opposition force takes all of us out, at one time or another. That's their job. Our job is to make it harder on them."

"Aye, aye, sir," I said, even as I took up my position.

They'd sounded the reset and the medics had sent me back out. Things remained quiet as I sat there, waiting. "Is this usual?" I heard Ryan Zahler ask.

"Oh, yeah," Cadet Petty Officer Trask said. "Some days we'll be out here for hours and nothing will happen. Other days they'll hit us with one thing after another. Long periods of boredom interspersed with brief moments of terror. But don't worry, it's all part of the training."

Great, I thought to myself. I kept my eyes open and kept scanning my area. I wanted to learn. I wanted to be more capable, but it was hard to think of this as being educational. Still, there was a part of me that enjoyed it. It was frustrating and at times boring, but at the same time, here I was, armed, wearing armor, and training to fight those who would harm my world.

I couldn't help a glance at the sky. The Admiral had fought the Dalite Hegemony, fellow humans who'd sought to conquer our world. Before that, the Century Planetary Militia had fought the Culmor on two occasions. Century had been invaded three times, twice we had faced extinction. There'd been smaller encounters with pirates, single or multiple small actions in our star system and against some of our merchant or missionary ships.

Over the course of almost three hundred years, Century had only ever faced three major attacks. Odds were that I'd face another one in my lifetime. Granted, things had been peaceful since my mother was a child, but things could change. This drill had shown that I might not even see the person who killed me... yet I didn't feel fear. I almost felt serene about it. My presence might be enough to save the life of Ashiri Takenata or Alexander Karmazin. Me serving in uniform might be enough to tip the scales, to protect my family and friends.

For that, I'd gladly put myself in a bit of danger.

The recall sounded, followed a moment later by the announcement, "All hands, reset from drill. Assemble at your company areas for after action review."

***

The after action review was more than a little interesting. I'd expected a critique of our individual actions, but the one from our squad wasn't oriented at that at all. Cadet Lieutenant Artho led it, and he instead showed images from around the perimeter, including some from the opposition force as they'd moved up on us unseen in the dark. "As you can see," Artho said, "there's some dead-zones near the bunker. In the future, it would behoove you to reposition some personnel to keep these areas under observation as well as to place anti-personnel mines."

Trask took the critique well, "Yes, sir."

"Let's move on to your casualties," Artho went on, "Plebe Armstrong was hit in the shoulder, but you waited almost fifteen minutes before you requested ground evacuation."

"Yes, sir," Trask nodded, "my concern was that our position is rather exposed. There's sections where anyone coming to evacuate our wounded could come under aimed fire from outside the perimeter. I didn't want to put first responders at risk for what wasn't an immediately life-threatening wound."

"Okay," Cadet Lieutenant Artho nodded, "but during that time, observers adjudicated that Plebe Armstrong would have lost enough blood to be in life-threatening condition. When evacuation did arrive, they didn't have the equipment they might have needed to save her."

"Sir," Trask nodded, "that's on me, I didn't take into consideration that our Plebes don't have full emergency responder training yet, so she didn't receive any on-site treatment."

"That's well and good to say. But if this were a real event, Plebe Armstrong would be dead. You would have to live with that for the rest of your life." Artho's voice was somber. "Don't forget, you had some other options. After initial contact, you could have requested aerial support. One of our combat skimmers could provide air cover for ground evacuation. Any sniper would be stupid to stay in position and come under fire from a combat skimmer."

"Yes, sir, I hadn't considered that," Trask nodded.

"Something to keep in mind, particularly when we're on the defensive and we have plenty of resources at hand. Overall, as a squad, you did well. You didn't defeat the enemy snipers, but you only lost the one casualty and you held the perimeter. Well done by Sand Dragon, that's five points for your company. Of course, you also *lose* five points for losing one of your personnel who might have survived."

I saw Trask wince a bit at that. I wasn't sure how the points system worked for him as a squad leader, but for me during the Academy Prep School, I'd had an additional percentage based off what we earned as a squad. We hadn't lost any points this exercise, but we also hadn't gained any.

At least I'm not really dead, I thought.

***

"You know," Ashiri said as we cleaned our gear in our room, "if someone really wanted to kill you, doing it at one of the drills would be the time."

"What?" I looked up from my wiping down my rifle. I hadn't had a chance to fire it yet, but it had dirt on it from when I'd been hit and fallen.

"We have combat loads with real rounds," Ashiri said. "If you'd been hit by a real round, none of us might have realized it wasn't part of the exercise."

I felt a chill at her words. "But they'd know who fired it, right? It doesn't seem like a good way to avoid getting caught." *That only works if the person trying to kill me really wants to avoid notice.*

"Maybe," Ashiri nodded, "But maybe they could get around that somehow..."

"Well, if I needed more incentive to avoid being shot, then I've got some." I hadn't told her yet about my encounters with Sashi. I probably should, I knew. She was the one who'd shot Sashi after she'd shot me during the final exercise. If Sashi hated me, she probably hated Ashiri, too.

At the same time, I didn't want to worry her. We already had the very real threat of someone trying to kill me. Ashiri was already involved in that. I didn't see the need to pull her into things if Sashi hadn't already.

"So, how are things between you and Alexander?" I asked. I regretted the question as soon as I'd opened my mouth.

"Oh, really great," Ashiri gushed. I managed to keep control over my features, but I couldn't come up with much of anything to say in response.

"That's good," I said. *I sound like a robot.* Luckily, Ashiri didn't seem to notice.

"Yeah, he really understands me and we spend a ton of time talking. We're taking things slow, though, you know, we don't want to rush it," Ashiri's voice had changed. She sounded almost... *bubbly.* I had to fight a pang of jealousy. I wished that I was that happy about *anything.*

"Well," I said, "it's good you guys spend time together."

"Not as much as I'd like, but at least we don't have to worry about the fraternization policy," Ashiri said. I wasn't sure about that. Really I hadn't finished reading the whole list of all the rules we had to obey. *I have to make time for that.*

Ashiri must have noticed my silence and she clearly misinterpreted it as disapproval, "We're not doing anything wrong." Her voice was nervous. "Fraternization only applies if there's some kind of favoritism or opportunity. We're the same rank, we're both plebes, and he's in a different squad in our section. I mean, it'd be a whole different thing if he were a different class or something, you know, like with Cadet Instructor Hilton and Rakewood."

"Oh, yeah," I replied. That made a lot of sense, actually. I remembered how I'd felt when I'd overheard the two of them discussion how they planned to falsely testify about another cadet candidate being injured. *I guess fraternization is to prevent other unfair situations,* I thought.

"I mean, plebes aren't even allowed to associate with upperclassmen at all," Ashiri said. "The only exception is sports teams, like with you joining the grav-shell team, and even then, only inside the accepted parameters of a team."

"Oh," I said. "Yeah, Cadet Commander Mackenzie and I... that is, there's nothing going on there." I found myself stumbling over words and Ashiri gave me an odd look. *Oh, no,* I thought to myself, *I do* not *have a crush on our company commander.*

I didn't want to think about that just now. Even leaving aside the whole fact that it would violate one of the academy's main military regulations, there was no way he saw *me* that way. *I mean, yeah, he did invite me to his team, to be his coxswain, but that's just because of my size... right?*

"Anyway," I said quickly, "what do you think of classes so far?"

Ashiri pursed her lips as she stared at me, almost as if she really wanted to ask me a question. She seemed to think better of it and then nodded, "Classes are good. I'm a little frustrated that we aren't going straight into our tracks. I mean, the medical people are already digging into their training, heavy on biology and anatomy classes... and everyone else is stuck in the general studies. I mean, most of us already know what our focus will be, I'd like to get started!"

"Yeah," I nodded. "And we've got these stupid filler classes like the military ethics one..."

"Oh, yeah, I heard about Commander Bonnadonna using you as an example, that must have been brutal," Ashiri shook her head. "He used another plebe as an example for my class with him. I wouldn't say that's a waste, really, I mean I find it interesting..."

"We're just *talking*, though," I grumbled. "That and ten page papers about people who've been dead for over a thousand years." I spent as little time as possible thinking about those subjects. I'd long since developed the ability to churn out a paper without much thought. Really I didn't even remember the subject of the last ethics paper, I'd simply thrown in a lot of quotes and some hand-waved interpretations and called it good. I still hadn't seen a paper back from him and I really doubted that he'd read all of the papers like he said he had.

"Yeah, but it's a discussion meant to bring out what we really think... and to make us think." Ashiri shook her head, "It's actually sort of refreshing, having a teacher who wants to hear what we think, you know?"

I didn't respond directly, "Commander Scarpitti seems to care about her students," I said. I'd enjoyed the engineering class I'd had with her. She'd kept us all engaged and I'd come away from the first week feeling as if I were actually learning something.

"Yeah, that's true," Ashiri nodded. "She's pretty personable. I like some of her teaching style, too. I just really want to get on with the space tactical track, which means flying, not just going over the theory."

"You're planning on tactical track?" I asked in surprise. I'd known she was space oriented, like me, but I'd thought...

"What, you don't think I'm capable?" Ashiri demanded.

"No, it's not that at all!" I protested. We'd filled out our initial preferences just before arrival. I had no way of knowing what she and Alexander had chosen, but I'd still made an assumption. "I just thought, well, I assumed that you'd go technical. I mean, that's what I did..."

"Jiden!" Ashiri stared at me as if I'd grown a third limb, right out of my forehead. Or maybe as if I'd passed gas in front of a large crowd. "Please tell me you aren't serious. You did *not* select one of the technical tracks!?"

"What?" I asked. "I've always been more interested in engineering..."

"Jiden," Ashiri shook her head. She grabbed her datapad and typed something in. "Don't... I can't even..."

I opened my mouth to respond and she held up one hand, "No. Don't talk. Wait a second, okay?" I nodded, feeling both a bit humiliated and amused at the same time. I didn't see what the big deal was, anyway.

A moment later, Alexander Karmazin stuck his head in, "What's up, Ash?"

I flushed a bit as I heard what he called Ashiri. *Oh, god,* I thought, *they're using pet names...*

"Jiden selected technical track as her preference," Ashiri said.

"Oh, she..." Alexander stared at her for a long moment. Then he looked at me and started laughing. "Oh, that's hilarious.... you totally got me. Her expression is so serious and..." he trailed off as neither of us laughed. "No." Karmazin looked at me and his jaw dropped. "No, you can't be serious. *Why?!*"

I flushed, "I'm more interested in engineering and research than..."

"Are you stupid?" Alexander demanded.

"Don't call me stupid!" I snapped back.

"Okay, calm down, *both* of you," Ashiri sighed. "Look, Alex, she just doesn't understand."

"Ash..." He put his hands over his face. "Nine Fates. This is more than a mess. I don't even know how to explain..." He shook his head. "Look, Jiden, you know that the technical track guys, they take them out of the normal chain of command, right? They're like the medical track. Inside their field, they'll have some authority, but outside that, anyone, even a lower enlisted-man can give them orders."

"Okay, yeah, I think I remember that," I nodded. It hadn't seemed all that important of a detail to me. I just figured I'd be left alone to do what I enjoyed.

"Okay, so in effect, it's like taking yourself out of the race before they blow a whistle," Ashiri said. "Everyone else in a graduating class is fighting for points, trying to get a plum assignment... trying to get commands, since those are hard to get short of a war."

"What do you mean?" I asked.

"Command time is the only time that counts towards promotion when it comes time to select a tactical officer," Ashiri said. "Staff time is there and if you get a bad evaluation, it can take you out of the running, but that's a pass or fail situation. When it comes time for a promotion board, the only evaluations they look at, the only thing in your packet beyond any certifications you have, will be evaluations from when you commanded a unit."

I frowned, "Okay, so why does that..."

"Every cadet realizes that. They know that only the best officers are selected for commands. Promotions aren't required, the Planetary Militia will let you serve for fifty years as an ensign if you want. So the ones who want to move upwards, to get the good assignments, compete early on to get those chances to prove themselves."

"I still don't understand," I said. "What's the big deal? I don't *want* to command."

"Yes, Jiden, you *do*," Alexander snapped. "Because tell me honestly, if you go technical track as an engineer... would you really be happy? Turning a wrench, overseeing the drive on a ship, maybe eventually progressing up to the point where you're working in a military research lab? You'd be happy doing nothing more than that?"

"Well," I said, "it's an important job..."

"Jiden," Alexander said softly, "you've killed six people."

I swallowed. The words had caught me off guard. "Yes."

"Do you regret it?"

I looked away. I owed him an honest response, but I hesitated because I didn't want to see a look of disappointment from him and Ashiri. I forced myself to meet his eyes and answer, "I regret that it was necessary. I don't regret doing it. They were trying to kill me."

"Good," Alexander nodded. "That means you're a warrior. In your heart... and that's *good* Jiden. Our world *needs* warriors. People who will stand against evil. I've taken a life. I know the burden it involves." I remembered then, that he'd been attacked and that he'd killed one of his attackers, prior to his attendance at the Academy Prep School.

"Now, what the people who run this school will think, knowing that you've fought for your life before, and knowing that you graduated *number one* during the Academy Prep School, is that you're on track to graduate at the top. You could have anything you wanted, right out of the gate. You could command a squadron of fighters or a platoon of infantry, you just have to keep working hard..."

"But I don't want..."

"Hold on, let me finish," Alexander said. "In their eyes, seeing you take yourself out will make them think that you doubt yourself. It'll be on the record, a red flag that says they must have missed something. I bet they'll have a psychologist pouring over your file. They'll wonder if you'll crack under the pressure. If you stick with technical track, they'll curve your points downwards. They'll assume you're self-selecting out of any position of risk. They'll put you on a starting assignment of little or no importance. You'll never move on from there, or if you do, it'll be to something of less consequence. How would you like to manage inventory of engineering equipment for the next fifty years?"

I stared at him, "That's not... that doesn't make any sense. I want to make a difference, I'm just more interested in engineering and science..."

"That doesn't matter," Ashiri shook her head. "They don't have a way to read our thoughts and subconscious minds. They have to guess based off your decisions and actions. If you go from having the choice of anything to selecting from a track that most people write off... then you don't have confidence in yourself."

"I don't think that's the way it'll work out," I said stubbornly.

Both Ashiri and Alexander winced. "Look, they may not have explained it to you that way, but that's the way it really works. Trust me," Alexander said, "I did a lot of looking into this. Between us three, we're top graduates from the Prep School. We'll have targets painted on our backs with all the other plebes. We scored a major coup for Sand Dragon Company last year, even though we didn't know it, because our good performance helped last year's First Classmen graduate at the heads of their classes. I guarantee you that if any of them had gone technical track, they probably are kicking themselves right now."

"I don't understand," I said. "Look, I want to do engineering, I like math, I like technology..."

"You can do that as tactical track," Ashiri said. "*I* plan on doing that. Between commands, you work engineering staff jobs. If things work out, you could end up running an engineer lab or engineering section on a ship... but you'll be in *charge*, not just a technical expert."

"I've got to think about this," I said. "You guys are making my head hurt."

"Don't take too long to think about it," Ashiri said. "And whatever you do, don't switch to tactical and *then* back to technical, or they'll be certain you gave up. You might not even graduate then."

"What?" I asked. "If I pass all my classes and stay out of trouble, why would I not graduate?"

"Well, you'd graduate," Alexander said, "but they wouldn't commission you. They'd think you lost your nerve. They'd say thanks for your time, here's your diploma, but we don't have need of your service. It happens," he glanced at Ashiri, "There's one or two cadets every year that it happens to."

That sounded incredibly unfair to me, but what did I know, I was just a plebe. "Alright," I said. I'll think about it." This had all gone a long way off topic. "Hey, it's almost lights-out, you should probably leave the room before..."

"Plebe Karmazin!" Cadet Lieutenant Webster shouted from down the corridor. "You had better have a good reason for why you aren't in your room at lights out!"

Alexander winced, "Moving, Cadet Lieutenant!" He shouted. He gave us a wave as he ran out.

I listened with only half an ear as our Cadet Training Officer laid into him. I figured Cadet Lieutenant Webster would head here as soon as he finished up with Alexander. *So much for getting to bed early,* I thought to myself.

***

Chapter Seven: I Find A Peaceful Place

Sunday morning I went to the chapel service.

Outside, I found myself drawn to the outside wall. I remembered, vaguely, one of the Cadet Instructors calling it The Wall. As I moved closer, I saw it held hundreds of brass plaques. Each one held a name, a birth year, and a death year. They were in clusters of years, I saw, mostly centered around conflicts. Each one was a cadet. At first I didn't realize the meaning... but then I did. These were cadets who had died while attending the Academy.

I found myself choking up a bit as I realized just how many had died. Each plaque had a signal and I pulled one up on my datapad. "Cadet Second Class Ann King, born one-sixty-nine, died in one eighty-eight at the Battle of Rowan III. Cadet King was killed in action serving against the Culmor at the Battle of Rowan III when her vessel was struck by..."

I ended the playback. This was a memorial. It hadn't registered until now. This was to cadets who had lost their lives in service.

I made my way into the chapel, feeling overwhelmed. Yet as I took a seat, the plaques outside took on a deeper meaning. They had felt the same calling as I had. They were brothers and sisters of a sort... and the school remembered them. If something every happened to me, I would be remembered here too. As I came to that realization, my head cleared a bit and I started paying more attention to my surroundings.

I felt odd, sitting there, in the quiet, peaceful room. It almost felt as if time had slowed. The simple beauty of the place left me feeling relaxed, refreshed. In the constant movement of the Academy, it felt like the chapel was the only place I could really clear my head.

"Plebe Armstrong, welcome," the chaplain greeted me at the inner doors again.

"Sir," I nodded in reply. The chaplain was an odd position for me to understand. He was a commissioned officer, so I had to salute him and speak respectfully, but for services he was dressed in traditional priestly garb.

The last weekend I'd been so tired that I had barely listened to the sermon. This week, I listened with half an ear, mostly just glad to have a quiet moment to think. I still wasn't certain about my religious convictions, but I was just happy for a quiet place to sit and not be bothered.

After the service, as I stood to leave, the Chaplain gave me a smile, "Feel free to come by any time you need to talk."

I was more than a little tempted to take him up on the offer. I felt like I had plenty on my mind, some things I could talk with Ashiri or Alexander about... but other stuff I couldn't... like their relationship.

"Thanks, sir," I smiled, "I'll keep that in mind."

***

"Military ethics is very different in principle from civilian ethics and morality," Commander Bonnadonna said. We'd only just taken seats and he was already diving into the lecture. Personally, I was exhausted from being up early for grav-shell practice, then room inspection, and here, Monday morning, I had ethics class. I hid a yawn as he continued talking and just hoped he wouldn't call on me.

"Now, I just finished reading your papers on the subject and I was impressed by the... creativity that some of you showed. So we'll dive into some that. Hopefully by the end of today's lecture, you'll all have a better grasp for the differences," Commander Bonnadonna said.

I felt my stomach sink at his words. I still didn't believe that he had time to read all of our papers. I'd barely had time to finish writing all ten pages in just a week, especially with all the other coursework, the grav-shell practices, and all the additional military stuff I had going on throughout the week. Still, I knew that my paper had been extremely vague about those differences.

"So," Commander Bonnadonna began, "Miss Armstrong, let's start with a rather simple example. A man and woman fall in love and things take their course. In a normal world, how would morality come into effect?"

The answer was simple enough that I didn't trust it. He'd ensnared too many of our section before with "simple" questions that didn't have right answers. "As long as they're both willing, I don't see a problem with the morality," I answered, choosing my words with care.

"Good, they're both willing, that implies that no coercion is involved," Commander Bonnadonna nodded. "Excellent Miss Armstrong... but what if one of them were already married to someone else?"

I flushed, "Uh..."

"You can see that in such a condition, the morality could be called into question. In the civilian world, how might this affect things... Mister Dawson?"

"Ideally, they'd get a divorce," he said.

"Yes," Commander Bonnadonna nodded, "And should the person in question have children, they might not see those children again, except under judicially mandated circumstances, in fact, his spouse might take everything, including his most loyal dog. Not a good position to be left in and I don't recommend it." He said it with a smirk on his face, as if he were telling a story, but I didn't know if he were joking or not. I wasn't sure if he'd made up the details to be humorous or if he were using someone in the class as an example.

"Now, in the military, there could be rather more extreme effects, could there not, Miss Drien?"

"Yes, Commander," Sashi replied. Of everyone in the class, she seemed to enjoy these discussions the most. It was one more reason that I'd come to hate the class. "If one or both of them were in the Militia, then there would be effects on morale, on their work performance, and potential for problems over time."

"Yes, very good, Miss Drien," Commander Bonnadonna nodded. "So what if *both* were in the military? What if they were from the same unit? If the woman were the commander and the man were one of her junior officers? Can you see grounds for an unfair situation to arise? Would there not be suspicion of favoritism... justifiably so?"

Despite myself, I nodded. It came back to the ban on fraternization. I was actually surprised at how much it mirrored my own thoughts on the subject. *I've been tricked,* I thought, *he's got me thinking about this stuff outside of class.*

"Or worse, what if the man were married to one of the unit's junior officers?" Commander Bonnadonna asked. "How would that junior officer then interact with her commander, knowing that her former husband had chosen someone else, possibly abandoning a family? How would other members of the commander's unit trust her after that?"

No one answered. I couldn't imagine someone doing something like that. How could you work for someone who would do such a thing?

"This is the difference between the military and civilian world. Things we think of as unfortunate or inappropriate as civilians can destroy the capabilities of a fighting unit. If that commander were charged to defend our world and such actions had just taken place, she would not be able to lead her unit. She would endanger countless lives over her own desires."

That was quite a bit more profound than the gibberish I'd written in my paper.

"So," Commander Bonnadonna said, "the same applies to a variety of other ethical considerations. This is the root of our Honor Code: I will not lie, cheat, or steal. The implication, of course, being that you won't do this to your fellow classmates or your instructors. Doing so is a failure of character, it undermines our community and trust."

That made a lot of sense, I supposed. The problems came back to definitions, I supposed. All of the implications sort of made my head hurt, but almost in a good way. This was both frustrating and oddly interesting. *I guess I see why Ashiri likes this class...*

"Now that I've given you all something to chew on, I'd like you to take another look at your papers. Go ahead and do any revisions you feel necessary to give me a good product," Commander Bonnadonna smiled. "And get those to me by tomorrow."

I restrained a groan, but much of the class didn't. Revising my paper, orienting it on some of the things we'd talked about would take hours. *Never mind,* I thought, *I hate this class.*

***

"Plebe Armstrong," Commander Scarpitti said as her class ended, "hold on a moment." Her harsh, strange accent was gentled a bit as she smiled at me, as if to say that I wasn't in trouble.

She'd gone a bit past her time, discussing engineering principles and I had my next class in only five minutes, so I wasn't exactly eager to wait, but I let the rest of the class funnel out and then moved up to her podium, "Yes, ma'am?"

I couldn't help a reflexive look up at the clock. My calculus and differential equations class started in just three minutes. I felt a lot more confident about that class than some of my others, but I still didn't want to be late.

"I just wanted to check with you to ensure that you haven't had any further trouble from those other plebes," Commander Scarpitti said. "I also wanted to tell you that all three of them received demerits. So they'll all have extra duties." She put extra weight on that, as if she were personally overseeing those duties.

"Okay, ma'am," I replied. I was glad that they had received some kind of punishment, but I wasn't happy that they'd blame me for it. I didn't know how they'd react, but they'd probably just be sneakier about trying to get me. I was still hazy on the whole concept of demerits. If I remembered right, they counted as negative points until they were worked off, typically with extra work like cleaning the kitchens or classroom areas.

Since all of us plebes already had non-existent free time, I had no idea how they'd find the time to do anything like that.

"I know what it's like, feeling a bit like a fish out of water," she smiled at me. "When I immigrated to Century, I was just a young woman, little more than a refugee. I felt *very* out of place. If you ever feel like you need someone to talk to, a mentor, please, feel free to ask me."

"Thank you, ma'am," I replied. I sort of remembered that one of the other plebes had heard that she'd immigrated from Drakkus, which had explained the accent, but I hadn't really thought about that. Still, I didn't want to seem like I was currying favor or anything like that. I didn't know what else to say, so I just stayed quiet, glancing up at the clock. I was going to have to run to make my next class on time.

"Well," Major Scarpitti smiled, "let me know if you need anything else."

"Of course, ma'am, thank you," I replied. I glanced at the clock on my way out. I had just under a minute to get upstairs and into a seat. Normally I would have walked fast, but this time I ran. I made it to the stairwell and took the stairs two at a time, dodging around other cadets and plebes. Just as I reached the next floor, my boots skidded out on the slick, wet surface of the landing. I let out a yelp as I flailed for something to hold onto. Just ahead of me I saw water trickling down from above.

"Careful!" A voice shouted from behind me.

I tried to grab the railing but I missed. I felt a sick feeling as the world started to slow, as I knew I was about to fall.

A set of hands caught me and shoved me against the railing. "Be careful, Armstrong," Sashi Drien bit out, even as I realized that she'd caught me. Before I could so much as say thanks, she let go of my shoulder and walked past me.

It took me a few seconds to catch my breath. The steep metal staircase would have been more than painful to fall down, it might have killed me. I looked at the floor where I'd slipped and then up at where water trickled down from a pipe in the ceiling. The entire stair landing was slick with water. *Done in by stairs, how embarrassing would that have been?*

As I looked up, I saw Commander Bonnadonna staring at me from the landing. "Had a bit of a slip, Miss Armstrong?" His dark eyes were unreadable and I wondered how long he'd been watching me. He had a datapad in his hands, and I saw that he was off to the side of the landing, out of the stream of water. I almost wondered if he'd been there when I slipped, if he might have caught me... but he hadn't.

"I'm fine, sir," I stuttered, even as I straightened. I was going to be late for class. "Excuse me, sir." I stepped past him, careful on the slick floor.

I kept my head down as I took my seat in the classroom. Commander Anson had already begun the lecture, but I saw him note my late arrival. I'd try to explain it to him after class. Hopefully it wouldn't make me late for my next class. Part of me was still in shock at the near miss. Part of me was wondering just how much of it had really been an accident. I'd been rushing, yes, but it had looked like the pipe had just burst. What if someone had seen me running up the stairs... or known I was coming? *Commander Bonnadonna was right there,* I thought, *he could have shouted a warning, could have said something, but he didn't.*

Sashi Drien had caught me, though. She'd literally saved me, from a painful fall, if nothing else, and possibly from serious injury or even death. I glanced over at where she sat, her attention focused on the teacher as he spoke. Why had she saved me? I would have expected her to let me fall, possibly to laugh, certainly not to grab me and make sure I had a good grip on the railing before she let go of me.

It gave me a lot to think about as I sat there in class. *Like I didn't have enough on my plate already...*

***

"Hello, class," Doctor Aisling said cheerfully as she stepped into the room. "I hope all of you are having a wonderful day." She flashed us all a sunny smile. With how cheerful and friendly she'd been so far, I had half convinced myself that I must have imagined her earlier words and actions.

Or maybe she's just evil and messing with me...

"We've actually gotten quite a bit ahead of our planned curriculum, so I thought we'd go off the outline a bit and talk some about future cybernetics that are just over the horizon," she said. She toggled the class display with her implant and dimmed the lights at the same time. "Now, we're seeing substantial increases in device miniaturization as well as adaptive hardware. What do you think some of the implications of that might be?"

No one raised their hand at first. Finally, though, I saw Sashi Drien's hand go up. "Ma'am, Plebe Drien, Ogre Company," she said, "I would guess substantially increased capabilities as far as data integration and usage, possibly a true data-link?"

"Interesting," Doctor Aisling nodded, her eyes narrowing. "Clearly you've been doing some research, like others in the room, I'm certain. Yes, for those of you in the class who haven't read into it, what she's discussing is an implant that fully integrates computer systems with a person's mind as opposed to what we have now, which is more like a data access process." My eyes crossed a bit as I tried to understand that.

The doctor seemed to realize that she'd gotten a bit technical, so she explained further. "Right now, our current generation of neural computers are like very sophisticated datapads. You can browse data, conduct calls, compose papers, record notes, all of it in a sort of request-access process. It's a conscious process which we will train you in after we implant your neural computers. It quickly becomes as second nature as using a datapad, so that you can access information quickly and act on it. Combat implants allow you to interact with a ship or weapon system and use it to control these things." On the displays, we could see signals from several regions in the brain connecting with the implanted neural computer. "You will basically be able to fly a ship, fire a weapon, or operate systems all through your implant."

I nodded at that. It would cut down on reaction times and, in theory, it would make it easier to control whatever we were hooked in with. It still made me feel uneasy. I didn't like the thought of being wired into equipment like I was just another machine.

"What Plebe Drien is suggesting, and what some of our cutting edge technology suggests *may* soon be possible, is a full integration. Where a human mind directly interfaces with computer systems and control systems, so that an implanted human could control a weapons platform or control system as fast as they could think. Their data access would be subconscious, and their implant would adapt on the fly, delivering greater computational power as needed or converting to deliver more synapse links for greater integration with the user's mind." The displays shifted to show an implant that wormed through the brain, with signal activity triggering throughout. It looked something like a cross between a crawling snake and a spider web. "Essentially, the human mind could process data far faster, control systems without conscious thought..."

The classroom door opened and Commander Pannja stuck his head in the door, "Doctor Aisling, it seems there's an issue with the classroom sensors and recording devices, Admiral Armstrong asked me to check in and see if there's any problem." The piloting instructor's voice was polite, but his normally cheerful smile was absent. Instead, his face was serious, his dark eyes intent. He was angry, I realized.

"Ah," Doctor Aisling smiled, "I might have shut those off on accident when I dropped power to the lights." The lights in the room came up, even as the displays cleared, "There, is that better?"

"One moment," Commander Pannja said. A moment later, he nodded, "Yes, tech support says their systems are back online."

"Ah, sorry about that, we'd gone a bit off topic, anyway," Doctor Aisling smiled. The displays came live again, this time showing the biology topics we'd had on our course curriculum.

I felt a chill go down my spine as I realized that it hadn't been an accident. Doctor Aisling had turned off the Academy's security monitoring in order to tell us something that she didn't want the Admiral knowing. That probably meant that her "theoretical" technology wasn't theory, it was probably related to whatever testing she'd done on us.

In fact, it sounded an awful lot like what I'd experienced.

"Now, class," Doctor Aisling said, "please go to page three in your notes..."

As we dove into the lecture, I didn't have any more time to think about it, but it was something that I needed to figure out.

***

"Hey, Jiden?" I looked up as Dawson stood at the door.

"Yeah, what's up?" I asked. Adam Dawson had been a huge help when I'd been stuck as the squad leader during Prep School. We were in a lot of the same classes, but I hadn't had time to talk with him other than in passing.

"I hear you're on the grav-shell team, and I was just wondering if you could put in a word for me," Dawson said.

I stared at him, not understanding for a moment. "What do you mean?" I couldn't imagine why he hadn't applied himself.

"Well, normally plebes aren't allowed on the varsity teams, but me and Farmer from Tiger Company both did grav-shell racing back in high-school.... anyway, we were hoping to get on the team, but our applications were rejected since we're plebes. Anyway, you got accepted, so I figured you had enough experience in it that they'd probably take your word that we're qualified."

"Oh," I said. I hadn't realized that there *were* applications... and it suddenly made me feel really uncomfortable. I hadn't applied. In fact, I barely knew the basic concepts. The practices had been brutal for me, not just in trying to figure everything out but also the long hours. Four hours a day, every weekday had left me basically without free time.

"Farmer and I are pretty skilled. We qualified for our regional competition. In fact, we planned to come here as a team, with our coxswain, but she didn't make it through the Prep School, she broke her foot. She may come in next year, but..." He shrugged.

"I'll definitely talk with the team captain," I said. I had no idea what weight that would carry, but I'd do it.

"Thanks, I appreciate it," He gave me a relieved smile, "We

were really worried that we wouldn't have a chance to get out there, and it's a sport we really love."

"Yeah, I bet," I replied. I didn't know what else to say. I barely knew the terms for the basic events. I wasn't anywhere near the level that Dawson obviously was as far as the sport.

"Well," Dawson said, "have you heard that we're getting approved for a two hour pass next weekend?"

"Yeah, I hadn't planned on taking it," I said. After the past couple of months at the Academy, I hadn't really had much time to think about taking a pass. Not that Plebes were allowed, normally, but I guess they thought we'd all been doing well. I was so busy that using two hours of my Sunday afternoon for anything besides studying or homework seemed ridiculous. From what I'd heard, the pass was only good to go to Bahta Town, which had a dubious reputation. It was where cadets and trainees from the nearby training facility got to go on pass. I didn't have much money to buy from the stores there and I wasn't interested in anything else the place had to offer.

"Probably smart of you. I heard they're going to stage it to trap plebes who violate regulations. Simple stuff, like drinking age or pass times. Anyone who leaves will only have one train that will get them back in time, so if they miss it..."

I nodded, "Yeah, that would be bad." Rumor had it that breaking the terms of a pass led to restriction to post and a lot of demerits. That would be bad not just for the plebe in question, but for their company. Which meant any plebe that got in trouble would have even more attention from their upperclassmen as a result.

"Thanks for the heads up," I said. "How're classes going?" Dawson had always seemed to study with a different group than me, but since we shared a lot of the same classes, studying with him made sense.

"Good, I'm in a study group with Josephic. We just finished the engineering assignment for Commander Scarpitti. That was brutal." He shook his head.

"Oh, yeah, I haven't started that yet," I groaned a bit. I'd been working on editing my paper for Commander Bonnadonna. I'd almost convinced myself to scrap the whole paper and start over. Going back through my own paper after his class had actually made me feel a bit ashamed for the quality of what I'd turned in.

"Well, it's a beast." Dawson nodded. He didn't offer to let me look at his assignment. I didn't ask, either. One of the things our instructors had told us was that they wanted to see our original work... and copying or even just using someone else's assignment as a starting point was considered cheating. They allowed study groups for most assignments, but they'd specified that meant the group worked together on problems, with each member doing their fair share of the work.

Since Dawson had already finished the assignment, I'd be violating the honor code if I even looked at his assignment. Since I'd already seen plenty of evidence that they monitored us, the last thing I wanted to do was get kicked out for cheating. *Besides,* I thought to myself, *I need to figure out how to do it for myself so I can pass the exam and so that I learn the material.*

I still hadn't decided whether to switch my track back to tactical or to stay technical. Engineering was what I was passionate about. I really didn't want to get away from it... but Alexander's warning stuck with me. "What track are you doing?" I asked.

Dawson grinned, "Oh, tactical, of course. Us winning top section didn't hurt our prospects for good assignments on graduation."

"No thoughts about technical?" I asked.

"Are you kidding?" Dawson laughed. "Any of us from Sand Dragon would have to be using recreational drugs to select anything besides tactical. At best, I'd get pigeon-holed into some engineering lab. At worst, they'd think I lost my nerve and they wouldn't commission me. Of course, that goes double for people like you and Ashiri," he nodded at my roommate's empty desk. "Between you two, Karmazin, myself and the wonder twins, I think we have a solid chance at locking out most of the top ten slots for our class at graduation."

"You're looking that far ahead?" I asked in surprise.

"Got to be," he nodded. "The only one who comes close to us in competition is Thorpe and Bolander from Ogre, and Drien, too, but she's out of the running with..." he trailed off. "Well, she's probably not competition now."

"Why do you say that?" I asked.

Dawson looked down, "Well, she transferred companies. She probably won't get much help, if any, over at Ogre. That means she'll be on her own as far as studying and all that. Plus there's the whole fact that she selected technical track. That's going to be a big negative mark on her record if she stays with it."

"She went technical?" I asked in surprise. "I thought she wanted to command a ship?"

"Yeah, that's what I thought too, but Farmer is dating Manning from Ogre, who's her roommate. She said that she saw Drien's initial pick on her datapad, she requested technical track. Our instructors will think she's lost her nerve, they'll probably throw some heavy stuff at her to get her to quit. She's basically done for."

"Oh," I said. I had more than a few mixed feelings over that.

"Granted, it's not like she finished in the top three, so it's not as bad as it might have been if someone like you or Karmazin had listed technical track, but they're still going to hit her pretty hard. Odds are, if she did lose her nerve, she'll crack and either fail out or resign." Dawson shrugged, "but I guess it's better that someone fail out here rather than failing when they're in a leadership position and lives are on the line."

"Yeah, I guess so," I replied. I felt sick to my stomach. "Hey, I've got a lot of work to catch up on..."

"Yeah, no problem, and thanks for agreeing to put in a word for me about the grav-shell team," Dawson stepped out into the hallway and left me to my thoughts. One thing at a time, I told myself, as I went back to my paper. I had to think about what I'd learned about Sashi, about the confirmation that the technical track wasn't the best idea, and all the rest... but I had to get my assignments done first.

Hopefully I'd have time to do all that.

***

Chapter Eight: I Ruin A Perfectly Good Dinner

As I collapsed face first onto my bed, I heard Ashiri stumble into our room. "I want to curl up and die," she said from behind me.

I mumbled something into the mattress, half-asleep. The week had been killer. Between sports practice, homework, and classes, I felt like I had about three good hours of sleep. Then we'd hit Saturday...

"I think they shot me a few times that last drill," Ashiri groaned.

I didn't respond. The day's drill had started with a warning about a full ground assault. We'd just gotten in position when a hundred or more attackers had swarmed over our squad's position. Most of us hadn't had time to do much more than fire off a couple shots and then we'd gone unconscious.

Then we'd reset and gone back to our barracks... then we'd heard the drill siren again. And we'd been hit again. Then we'd reset and repeated the process. I'd sprinted across the academy grounds six times. "The last time they didn't even wait for us to get in position," I mumbled.

"We need to clean our gear," Ashiri mumbled. Her voice would have held more conviction if she hadn't collapsed on the floor. I had thought I was tired at the Grinder. This wasn't just physical exhaustion, though, it was mental exhaustion. The classes we were taking were hard. Harder than I had expected my internship at Champion Enterprises to be, back when I'd thought that would be the most challenging program that Century had to offer.

Still, I rolled off my bed and more or less onto my feet and started pulling my gear off. My body armor protected me from hits by training rounds, but it didn't cover my arms or legs... and I was covered in welts from hits.

"Poor Alex caught one to the neck," Ashiri shook her head, "he can barely talk."

"Ouch," I winced. Having been shot in the face, I had a deep understanding for that kind of hit. "Is he going to be okay?"

"Yeah, they gave him something to reduce the swelling and pain," Ashiri nodded. We'd both sort of flopped on the floor, a pile of soiled gear on the ground around us. "He thinks he'll be good to take pass tomorrow."

"Oh, you guys are going out?" I asked.

"Yeah, getting dinner," Ashiri sat up. "You should come. It'll be nice to get out."

"Uh..." I didn't know what to say to that. It sounded awkward to tag along on their outing. "I've got a ton of homework..."

"It'll be fun," Ashiri said.

Sure it will, I thought. But I didn't know how to get out of it. Maybe I'd get lucky and they'd cancel our passes. "Okay, I'll go."

"Great," Ashiri started getting out cleaning supplies.

It was close to midnight. It would take us a couple of hours to get our gear cleaned and inspection ready. We'd have to be up around five hours after that. *Then I can go to chapel services or spend three hours with Cadet Lieutenant Webster doing whatever tortures he thinks up...* It wasn't too hard of a decision, especially since I actually liked the chapel.

It would have been great to have more than a few hours of sleep. But maybe if I caught up on all my studying and classwork and...

I woke up, face down on the floor, drooling a bit. The lights were still on and I looked over to see Ashiri passed out, snoring slightly. I put my gear up, shook Ashiri awake and then crawled into bed. I'd just have to find time to work on things in the morning.

***

I scanned my pass at the terminal and purchased my ticket to Bahta Town. That done, I wandered around the platform for a short time. It looked like I was one of the first to show up, and I took the time to check the train arrivals and departures. Just as Dawson had told me, there was only one train coming back in time. It *looked* like there was a second one, but while it departed at seventeen-fifty, it didn't arrive here at the terminal until eighteen-oh-five, which was five minutes after all plebes were supposed to be back.

"Jiden!" Ashiri shouted, "over here!" I looked over and saw her and Alexander Karmazin standing at the end of the platform. I walked down towards them, "Hey," I said.

"Glad you decided to come," Alexander said, though he looked more resigned than eager to see me. *This is awkward*, I thought to myself. "The last car will be the least packed. I figure we'd want some breathing room."

"Great," I said. We stood there. Ashiri and Alexander were hand in hand. I started to put my hands in my pockets and stopped. I was in uniform. So were they, but holding hands was sort of on the boundary of what was allowed in uniform.

"So, where are we going?" I asked.

"Oh, there's this neat little restaurant that my parents took me to in Bahta Town," Ashiri said eagerly. "They do authentic *chennai*, I thought Alex would really like it."

"Yep, sounds good," Alexander said.

"Yeah," I said. I had no idea if this 'chennai' stuff was a food or a place or a type of people.

The silence grew long. Thankfully, dozens of other plebes and even upperclassmen arrived before I had to think of something else to talk about. All of us plebes stood quietly, but most of the upperclassmen laughed and talked. Down the way, I recognized Sashi Drien, who stood with Bolander and Thorpe. *Great,* I thought to myself, *well, maybe she'll go do something fun and hate me a little less for it.* I'd thought that having demerits would have prevented her from taking pass, but maybe she'd worked those off already.

The train arrived and we all rushed aboard. Like Alexander had said, the car at the end was less crowded, I even had room to take a seat next to Ashiri and Alexander. Yet as I saw how close together they sat, I reflexively stood and grabbed onto a bar. *Stop being stupid,* I told myself, *they're your friends. So what if you liked Karmazin, you missed your chance.*

Our train arrived and cadets and plebes swarmed off. I followed my friends as they worked their way through the crowd. We had to work our way up the stairs, the crowd pressing against us. The stairs opened out and just sort of dumped us out onto the street. I looked around, not really sure what I expected, but Bahta Town certainly wasn't it.

About a dozen ships lay in the desert. Most of them were obviously old, little more than rusting hulls. Cords strung with lights ran from one to the next, glittering in the late afternoon sunlight. Walkways, roads and alleyways wound between the ships, while cloth curtains screened off some areas of the street and around the ships. A host of people in military and civilian clothing moved through the chaos. A man with glass jars of some amber liquid stepped in front of me, his accent thick, "Drakkus Aromatics, very nice for a pretty young lady..."

I pushed past him, trying not to get separated from Alexander and Ashiri. A young girl rushed up to me, trying to sell me some kind of jewelry. Before I could decline, Alexander reached back a hand and pulled me along. "Just ignore them," he shouted over the din.

It seemed rude, but I didn't argue. I felt like I couldn't breathe. I could barely move. I saw a couple of plebes stumble past, their feet unsteady as if they'd already been drinking. *They'll get in trouble if they have.* We weren't supposed to drink, even if any of us were old enough. Since the drinking age was eighteen, that wasn't likely.

"Isn't this great?" Ashiri shouted. She'd picked up a bouquet of flowers from a stand.

"Yeah," I shouted back, "great..." I felt overwhelmed and uncomfortable, not great.

We finally wound out way off the main street and the noise level dropped a lot. We had room to walk side by side. Ashiri and Alex walked close, hand in hand. I kept a meter or so to the side. I saw all kinds of shops, some little more than a blanket on the ground, others were stalls or tables, while some were whole stores, with rooms cut out of the ship hulls.

"Bahta Town is where the Culmor landed during their invasion," Ashiri said. "After they were defeated, the hulls were just sort of left in place, some stuff was salvaged, but the hulls stayed in place. I read that after Century established their military schools in the area, lots of people just sort of moved in."

We passed by a stand where someone served barbecued lizards of some type. I wrinkled my nose at that. "Where did all these people come from?" I couldn't help a tone of distaste. I didn't like the crowds and I'd thought that most of Century's population was from Firsts, Seconds, or Thirds.

"Refugees, mostly," Ashiri said. "Those applying for citizenship can speed the process up if one of their family members signs up for the Planetary Militia. Since there's recruiters here and it's close to the military bases, lots of families come down here. My dad worked in a shop down here for a few months."

"Oh," I said. I stepped around a group of running children. In the late afternoon sun, the place was hot, dusty, and the smells of cooking food and unwashed people mingled in a way that turned my stomach.

"Here we are," Ashiri said. She led the way down a narrow alleyway between two rusting hulks, then up a rickety metal ladder and through a hatch. I wasn't really sure what to expect, at this point, but it certainly wasn't what I found on the other side.

Carpets and rugs covered the floor. Soft music and the sound of falling water filled my ears, cutting off the noise of the town beyond. A short, dark haired woman greeted us, her face painted in an elaborate fashion, "Welcome!" she said, "table for..." she looked between Ashiri, Alexander, and I. "Three?"

Ashiri nodded, and then replied in a different language. My eyes widened as the two chattered back and forth for a moment. The hostess looked at us and then gestured towards a curtained doorway, "This way."

Ashiri led the way. Past the curtains, we walked down a long corridor and then into a small, private room. "They normally keep this for distinguished guests, but since I speak the language..."

"Nice," Alexander said, taking a seat at the table. The entire wall of the room was taken up by a large window, which caught the light of the sinking sun. We were high enough up that I could see out, over the town, and into the desert. It looked remarkably beautiful, in a stark fashion.

I took a seat. A moment later, a young woman entered and passed each of us menus and filled our water glasses. The way she poured water, a single smooth motion, struck me. It was like she practiced it. *What a strange place.*

"These are traditional dishes," Ashiri said as she opened her menu. "So most of them are spicy. If there's a mild version, I recommend that."

The menus were actual printed ones, rather than what I was used to at restaurants, where they would just populate on my datapad. I looked at it for a long while, not really understanding what I was reading. I sort of listened while Alexander and Ashiri talked about classes and their families. I felt left out, but I couldn't blame them. I was the one crashing their date, after all.

My gaze kept going to the window. The view really was amazing. The sun had begun to draw close to the horizon and the sand took on a golden hue. From our height, Bahta Town looked peaceful, almost beautiful. I could sit there for hours and just enjoy the view.

"Are you ready to order?" Our server asked. I blinked at her, not realizing how much time had passed. I wondered if I'd dozed off, staring out the window.

Ashiri began to order, still in the same language. A moment later, Alexander ordered, haltingly pronouncing something off the menu. Then everyone stared at me. I felt a flush climb my cheeks. I pointed at something, more or less at random. "Ah, the *phall*, a good choice," the server gave me a friendly smile.

"Oh, good," I replied.

She took our menus and I really wanted to ask Ashiri about this place, about how she spoke this other language. I knew she'd come from the Ten Sister's system, but I didn't know that they spoke a different language.

But I didn't want to seem ignorant. So I kept my mouth shut.

Food came far more quickly than I'd expected. Ashiri had some kind of rice topped with cubes of meat and all of it smothered with a bright orange sauce. Alexander had slices of some kind of meat that had been grilled, with several odd-looking vegetables.

Then they set the plate down in front of me. The smell hit me first. It was some kind of soup or thick gravy with large chunks of fish, with a strong spicy scent that made my eyes water. There was rice to go with it. I looked up, wondering if this were some kind of joke, but Ashiri and Alexander were diligently eating. I fumbled with the silverware and then tried to pick at it. My stomach rumbled to remind me that I'd missed lunch, having to try to scramble to get homework done before I left on pass.

I brought a mouthful of rice and fish up to my mouth and took a bite. It actually tasted better than it had smelled, right up until the spice hit. Then it felt like fiery doom. I reached for my water and started gulping it down, even as I felt my eyes well up and my nose began to run. I had to look like a crazy person as I gulped down my glass of water, then poured the glass full again.

"Uh, Jiden," Ashiri asked, "are you okay?"

"Yeah," I croaked, feeling as if the spiciness had seared my vocal cords, "I'm great, this is really good." I felt like what I'd eaten was trying to eat its way through my stomach.

"If it's too hot..."

"No, no it's *fine*," I insisted, "just fine."

"You look a little red," Alexander said, his voice neutral.

I felt like my face was on fire. I could barely breathe and I just hoped my nose wouldn't drip onto my plate. "No, this is great." I brought another mouthful up and took a bite. *Kill me now, please...*

I kept eating, my mouth, throat, and stomach protesting at every bite, my eyes welling up. It was sheer agony. I felt like every bite burned its way through my throat, into my stomach, and then headed deeper in my intestines to cause me further pain. The other two finished their meals and we sat there in awkward silence until they pinged our datapads with the bills. I had never felt so embarrassed in my life and I just hoped we'd be able to get out of here and I could go back to my room. I didn't want to see Alexander Karmazin ever again. I wasn't even sure I wanted to see Ashiri again.

I paid my bill and stood quickly, stumbling a bit and feeling off-balance. "We'd better go," I croaked. "Don't want to miss the train."

We still had plenty of time, but I stepped out of the room before they could argue. I didn't see them coming behind me, as I hurried out of the restaurant and down the stairs. I had my head down and my eyes were still burning, so I didn't see the group of three people ahead of me until I ran into one of them.

I bounced back and landed on my backside. I stared up at the plebe I'd run into, barely able to see through my watering eyes.

"Crying, Armstrong?" Bolander said, her voice mocking, "I didn't even hit you that hard... yet."

I heard laughter and looked over to see Thorpe laughing at my expense. Next to him, I saw Sashi Drien, her expression hard. Three of them, one of me, and I felt like I could barely walk. They were going to pummel me. I looked around the alleyway and I didn't see anyone. I didn't know how they had gotten here, if they had followed me or if I'd just had that kind of luck that I ran into them.

I almost felt like I deserved it. I was stupid. I shouldn't have come here. *Maybe I can run*, I thought, but I didn't want them to jump me from behind. It was hopeless, yet I somehow found the strength to stand to my feet. If they were going to beat on me, I was going to at least meet them on my feet.

***

Chapter Nine: It Was In Self Defense, I Swear

I had stumbled upright and took a step backwards, only to bump into someone behind me. I looked over my shoulder, expecting another enemy, only to see Alexander Karmazin had come up behind me. He gently pushed me out of the way and stepped forward, "Bolander, you have a problem with us?"

"Sand Dragons," Bolander spat, "more like sand *lizards*." She took a menacing step forward, but Alexander stood his ground. Ashiri came up next to me and I saw her tensing up, as if she were getting ready to run or fight. I wanted to run, but looking back, I didn't see anywhere to run. I'd probably fall and break my neck if I tried to run up the rickety metal stairs.

As I looked forward, I saw Thorpe had circled to the side and I saw him lunge forward in a punch. "Look out!" I shouted.

I needn't have bothered. Alexander dodged the punch and kicked Thorpe in the stomach. Bolander went after him, then, but before he could do a thing, *Ashiri* leapt forward, kicking and punching like a madwoman. I just sort of stood there staring as the two of them brawled with Bolander and Thorpe... and that's why I didn't see Sashi coming.

My former roommate didn't do any grandstanding. She just stepped up in front of me and punched me right in the face. As I stumbled back, I caught a boot in the stomach and I fell back against the wall. As I gasped for air, I looked up in time to see Ashiri grab her by the hair and drag her away from me, but then Bolander swung a punch at me and I did the only thing I knew how to do: I stood there with a dumb expression on my face as she punched me.

I fell to the ground and for a moment, I saw stars. Bolander picked me up by the front of my uniform, slamming me against the metal hull of the old ship behind me. As she drew back her fist to punch me again, my stomach had finally had enough.

I vomited, blasting her in the face and hair with the contents of the spicy, fishy, food. She opened her mouth to shout in disgust and I kept puking, throwing up still more as she reflexively dropped me. I emptied the entire contents of my stomach in the alleyway, the burning, acidic bite leaving my throat and nose in pain... but my stomach at least finally felt better.

I heard the sound of running feet and then Ashiri gave me a hand up. "Jiden, are you okay?"

"Yeah," I gasped. She passed me a handkerchief and I wiped at my face and lips. Looking down, I'd somehow managed to avoid throwing up on myself, but I had dirt and dust from the street on my uniform.

Ashiri looked a little scuffed up, with a small bruise on her cheek and dirt on her hands. Behind her Alexander looked a bit more roughed up, but their bruises could have passed for what had happened at the training the previous day.

My left eye was already swelling shut from where Sashi had hit me and it still hurt to breathe from being hit in the stomach twice.

"We should get you some ice, get you cleaned up," Ashiri said.

I dabbed at my face. I didn't think I'd broken my nose, but I honestly didn't know. I pulled out my datapad to use it as a mirror and then noticed the time. *The train...*

"We don't have time," I said. "The train leaves in five minutes."

The others checked their datapads and I heard Alexander curse. "We have to run, let's go!"

We ran back, dodging through the twisting streets and crowds, then running down the stairs and into the train station. As we ran down the last set of stairs, we could see people filing aboard, but the train cars were filling up quick. Each of the cars were full as we came to them. Alexander and Ashiri held me up as we ran down the length of the platform, finally squeezing into the last train car just as the doors closed

"We made it," Ashiri puffed. I could barely breath, my throat was on fire. *From now on, I'm asking just what it is we'll be eating and I'm looking it up ahead of time.*

I started to say something to her and then froze as I saw who we shared the car with.

Bolander, Thorpe, and Sashi stared at us from only a couple of meters away. Bolander's face and uniform were still covered in vomit. Thorpe's face was a mass of bruises and his uniform was torn. Sashi Drien sported a black eye and her hair was still wild from where Ashiri had grabbed her. The three of them stood from their seats in a menacing fashion.

Even as they did so, the doors on the end car opened and Commander Bonnadonna and Commander Scarpitti stepped through. "See," Commander Bonnadonna said, "as I said, the last cars are a bit less crowded." He looked at us, his eyes narrowing at the bruises and contusions. His gaze seemed to linger on our clenched hands. "Plebes," he simply nodded and stepped past us to take a seat.

Commander Scarpitti looked between us. Her gaze seemed to linger on me, almost as if she wanted to ask what had happened. She probably wanted to help, but I didn't think her getting involved would make things any better. *It would just make Bolander angrier.*

She didn't say anything though, she just followed Commander Bonnadonna to the back of the car and took a seat there. The eight of us waited in silence as the train headed towards the Academy.

As the train slowed to a halt, I turned and the three of us got off as soon as the door opened. "We have time to get cleaned up a little," I panted as we ran through the corridors of the lower levels. There was supposed to be some kind of uniform inspection at the upcoming formation.

We ran back to the barracks and Ashiri gave me a hand patting the dust and dirt out of my uniform. She'd avoided anything noteworthy. I took a moment to wash my face off in the sink and then we ran back toward the parade ground.

We were just in time and I stepped into the formation just as they called us to attention. "All present," Dawson muttered to me. "And what happened to you not taking pass?"

"I'm never taking pass again," I croaked, my throat still burning. Off to the sides, stretching off in all directions in the massive, underground chamber, I saw other plebes in formation. I wasn't sure, but it looked like there were a lot of missing people. *We're probably all going to get in trouble for that.*

Cadet Lieutenant Webster squinted at us, his eyes angry. I wondered why *he* hadn't taken pass, but I didn't ask. We went through a quick accountability and then he snapped, "Open ranks!" First squad immediately took four steps forward, my squad took two steps forward, and Alexander Karmazin's Third Squad didn't move. Cadet Lieutenant Webster stalked down the ranks, his expression angry. Here or there he paused and criticized scuffed boots or stains on uniforms. I grew more and more nervous until he finally got to me. He stopped, only a few millimeters from my face, and looked me up and down. He sniffed loudly, "You smell like you've been eating curry. Really, really spicy fish curry." He frowned, "*Phall*?"

"Sir, yes, sir," I snapped, hoping that I didn't reek of vomit.

"I hate *Phall*," Cadet Lieutenant Webster snapped.

"I'm not much of a fan, either, sir," I replied, before I could stop myself.

Behind me, I heard Alexander Karmazin snort, barely controlling his laughter. *Don't make this worse for me, please,* I thought to myself.

Webster squinted at me and opened his mouth as if to chew me out.

Down the way, I heard a training officer begin to shout, "Bolander, you smell like you fell in a fish-market dumpster! You have vomit on your uniform, in your hair, there's even some in your eyebrows. I could smell you from the front of the formation! Do you want to try to tell me it's not your fault again!?"

"Sir, no excuse, sir!" Bolander shouted in response.

Cadet Lieutenant Webster looked in that direction, then back at me. He seemed to consider the situation for a long moment, and then gave me a slight nod, "Uniform is acceptable, Plebe Armstrong." Then he moved on.

I let out a slight sigh of relief. Though from the continued shouting over by Ogre, Bolander wasn't getting off lightly. *She and Sashi and Thorpe are going to hate me even more now.* Yet I didn't feel any pity for them. They were the ones who had cornered me. They'd picked the fight. I hadn't even managed to defend myself, not really.

The inspection ended and Cadet Lieutenant Webster called us all to attention. As he did so, I saw a largish group of plebes forming up on the other end of the parade ground.

"Class of Two-Ninety," the Regimental Training Officer shouted. I could see him, now, out of the corner of my eye, standing on a large pedestal. "You have failed as a class!"

Well, that's not good, I thought to myself.

"We give you all the opportunity to enjoy a few hours of freedom, and you spit in my face! Over a hundred and thirty plebes were out of ranks, a *hundred and thirty*! I am disgusted, I am disappointed! Not only that a hundred and thirty of you were unable to read a simple train schedule, but that so many of you made it back in time! From this point on, Class of Two-Ninety, you either pass as a class, or you *fail* as a class. That is in every regard of the regiment. Every drill exercise, every training event! If one of your classmates is late to a formation, from this point on, *all* of you will receive the demerits! If one of your classmates fails to pass one of their drill exercises, then *all* of you will continue to drill until that individual passes, am I understood?"

"Sir, yes, sir!" I shouted with the rest of the plebes. My stomach sank at the thought, though.

"Now, as a show of unity, I want you all to do one push-up for each of your absent or late classmates! Class of Two-Ninety, half-right face!" We shifted over, and I stifled a groan as he put us on the ground. "Count with me, in cadence!" he shouted. Out of the corner of my eye, I could see him assume a push-up position. "One, two three..."

"One!" we all shouted.

"One, two, three..."

"Two!" we shouted. It was going to be a long night.

***

The next day, waiting for ethics class to start, my arms aching, I looked up in surprise as someone stopped in front of my desk, "Armstrong, right?"

"Huh?" I asked, "Yeah." I recognized Regan, the tall, red-headed plebe was from Dust Company, if I remembered right. I was just surprised he spoke to me.

"Nice job with Bolander," he said. "You know, biological weapons are against the Guard Charter, right?" He grinned at me. He had a nice smile, I noted.

I found myself smiling back, "Well, I used what I had." I had no idea how he'd heard about the incident already. I certainly hadn't told anyone.

"Still, throwing up in her face... You're something of a biohazard, eh?" He snorted.

"Yeah," I laughed. It felt good to laugh about it, to put it behind me a bit.

"Very good, Miss Armstrong," Commander Bonnadonna said, his deep voice alarmingly close. I jerked to attention along with the rest of the class. None of us had seen him come in the room. "That's actually part of our discussion today: the morality and ethics of warfare and the myth of the 'fair fight' that has permeated society."

He had a slight smile as he saw us guiltily waiting. "At ease, ladies and gentlemen. This is a class, not a dressing down. Take your seats." I sat down hurriedly, noting that Regan took the empty seat next to me. Maybe, just maybe, I'd made another friend.

"Now, then," Commander Bonnadonna said. "What does it mean to fight fair, Mister Regan?"

He straightened, "Sir, I suppose it means to face your opponent head on, to follow the rules of war."

"Ah, a rules lawyer, are you?" Commander Bonnadonna nodded. "What are the rules of war?"

"Uh, the Guard Charter, I suppose, sir," Regan replied. "No use of biological weapons, no destruction of inhabitable planets, that sort of thing, sir."

"Tell me, Mister Regan, are the Erandi or the Culmor signatories of the Guard Charter?"

"Of course, not, sir," Regan answered. "They're aliens..."

"Exactly, and any contact with aliens is strictly prohibited under the Alien and Telepath Act of 451 SP, which, while we *also* aren't signatories of the Guard Charter, we're still kept to," Commander Bonnadonna's voice took on a hard note. "And why would that be, Miss Senacal?"

"Uh, because they make the rules?" Senecal replied her voice hesitant.

"Yes, but why do they make the rules?" Commander Bonnadonna asked. "Are they the bastions of morality? Do they possess some divine insight into the nature of right and wrong?"

No one answered. "It's not a difficult question to answer. Perhaps, Miss Armstrong, you could shed some light on the truth?"

I felt sweat bead my brow. Yet I'd begun to learn that when he asked a question like that, Commander Bonnadonna knew that the person would provide an answer. I thought about my fight in the alleyway with Bolander. She would have preferred I fight her fair, I knew. That might be it. "Because they're stronger than everyone else."

Commander Bonnadonna cocked his head, his dark eyes

contemplative. "Which means?"

"If people fight according to their rules," I said, thinking of my last two encounters with Bolander, "then they'll win."

"Exactly," Commander Bonnadonna nodded. "Exactly as a medieval peasant stood little chance fighting a mounted knight in hand to hand combat, the rules are designed to favor those in power. The moment those rules change, such as to say the introduction of longbows and later gunpowder, the paradigm shifts."

He looked around the classroom. "Now, in some regards, the rules are designed to make warfare more merciful, less destructive, and to prevent atrocities. What we know of as war-crimes: willful murder of innocents, use of indiscriminate weapons such as biological weapons and chemical weapons, and use of weapons of mass destruction against inhabitable planets, among others, are checks and balances to prevent warfare from becoming too heinous... yet these rules have been violated on occasions, even by those charged to implement such safeguards."

"Plebe Drien, your paper addressed one such incident, please tell the class about it," Commander Bonnadonna said.

"Sir," Sashi stood up. She still had a black eye from our fight in the alleyway. I didn't feel any better about it for the fact that I hadn't given it to her. After all, I sported one, too. "In the Sepaso Sector, during the War of Persecution with the Culmor. The planets Kutai, Bengalon, Wreath, and Idalia surrendered to the Culmor on terms. Their human populations reportedly provided material aid to the enemy and they did not pursue any significant insurgency against their alien occupiers. When the Guard recaptured those systems, they utilized chemical and biological attacks to kill off the surviving human and alien populations of those worlds."

I'd read about that, of course, in history books, but it took on a deeper meaning after having gone through all the training that I had. The Guard had killed billions of humans at Kutai alone. The men and women who dropped the bioweapons wore uniforms. They'd signed up to defend humanity... yet they had murdered billions of their own people.

"So," Commander Bonnadonna said to the quiet class, "does might make right? Were they justified to take such action through the fact that they have the power to state that it was the right thing to do?" It was a trick question, I knew, but I wasn't sure how.

"No, sir," Duchan said from the back of the room. "Might doesn't make right, but they did the right action in order to win the war. Human worlds that surrendered gave the Culmor an edge. They could occupy those planets with minimal forces, which allowed them to conquer other planets with more forces. By not resisting, they gave the Culmor the ability to shift more forces forward. The Guard had to make an example of those worlds or else it might have cost us the war as other worlds surrendered."

To my surprise, Regan spoke up next to me, his face flushed, "No, that's not right. The Guard had already defeated the main Culmor attack at that point. The Culmor had begun to withdraw, the war was already won when the Guard reached the Sepaso system. At that point, it didn't matter what happened on Kutai and Bengalon."

"Interesting," Commander Bonnadonna nodded, "please, go on."

Regan flushed, but he continued to talk, "The Guard *abandoned* Kutai and a dozen other worlds. They evacuated their personnel and ships and even stripped police stations and their planetary militias of weapons, in a panic because the border systems were overrun within days. When the Culmor arrived, the planets that surrendered had nothing to defend themselves with. Those planets did the only thing they *could* do. And as a matter of fact," it was clear that Regan had warmed to the subject, "this was the first time that the Culmor ever accepted surrenders from human worlds." He swallowed, "I think the Guard forces that murdered those billions of people did so to cover up their own incompetence."

"Interesting, very interesting," Commander Bonnadonna nodded. "Duchan would you care to counter?"

"Humans have a duty to oppose the Culmor or the Erandi," Duchan snapped. "The Culmor have killed us in the billions and the Erandi have enslaved millions of humans. The Guard is all that stands between humanity and extinction and any action they take is justified."

"Ah, Mister Duchan," Commander Bonnadonna said, "you said 'justified' and I think that's a very particular word to use. When someone kills another person in self-defense, this is often termed a 'justifiable' homicide. It is not accepted that this killing is 'right' but that it is the better of two evils."

"Of course killing a billion people isn't *right*, sir," Duchan replied. "But this is the fate of humanity. The Guard had to show that anyone who joins the enemy, human or alien, will not receive mercy."

"But they didn't join the enemy!" Regan protested, "They surrendered when faced with no other option to but be massacred... and then the Guard did it to them, instead!"

"Yes," Commander Bonnadonna nodded, "I think this conversation has been very fruitful, but let's avoid bickering. Both of you have some important points, and I'd like to move back to the original topic: what is the grounds for an ethical form of warfare?" He nodded at Martinez, "Miss Martinez, in your paper you mentioned treatment of prisoners of war. Please elaborate."

I wasn't sure whether Commander Bonnadonna wanted us to come to a decision about the War of Persecution. I really hadn't thought about it, much. I couldn't imagine commanding a ship with orders to do such a thing. Yet as I thought about it, I wondered if his goal had been just that: to make us think. Perhaps there wasn't a right answer... and maybe that was another lesson entirely.

***

Chapter Ten: I Have A Name

"Morning, Biohazard, you ready to take her out?" Mackenzie asked.

"Sir?" I blinked at him, not understanding for a moment. Then I flushed as I realized what he meant. *He knows, somehow, he knows about my fight with Bolander.* "Sir, I can explain..."

"Relax, Armstrong," Mackenzie grinned. "We're a bit more informal here at practice, it's nothing to worry about. I haven't officially heard of it as Cadet Commander Mackenzie. I doubt that anyone will go that route. It's purely informal, word of mouth." He gave a shrug, "It's a funny story. People are going to talk."

"I thought fighting was against the regulations," I asked.

"It is," Mackenzie nodded, "and if you were caught on campus, you'd face some charges. If you *do* get caught on campus in a fight, don't try to deny it either, or else you'll face charges *and* an honor board investigation. Then you'll probably get thrown out." He shrugged, "But stuff happens off campus. As long as the authorities don't get involved and no one is seriously injured, the regiment doesn't care and the staff is generally willing to look the other way. Besides, some companies have rivalries that go way back. Ogre and Sand Dragon is one of them. Dust and Tiger is another. These things happen, especially when there's pressure on plebes to 'prove' themselves."

"So if I got roughed up by the three of them..."

"Three of them?" Mackenzie asked.

"Yeah," I said, choosing my words with care. "There were three of them and three of us."

He cocked his head, "I can imagine who was involved from Sand Dragon. I don't know Ogre well enough. Sorry to interrupt, continue."

"If three of them had roughed me up, but they didn't seriously injure me, then I wouldn't have had any recourse?" I asked.

"That depends what you mean," he said. "If they'd done something really vile, trust me, they'd face charges, possibly expulsion, and maybe even jail time if they really crossed a line. But a few bruises, about what we get during an intensive drill day? Most of us would just take it as a lesson learned: don't go anywhere alone, don't pick fights that you can't win, and learn how to fight for yourself."

I flushed, "Sir, are you saying that I can't defend myself?"

He gave me a level look, "Armstrong, while half the Academy has heard the story and some of them might think you ate something vile to intentionally throw it up in the face of someone beating on you, I think we can both be honest here: you got lucky."

I looked down. I couldn't meet his eyes when I found my voice, "Yes, sir."

"That's fine. Luck is a part of combat," Mackenzie gestured at the grav-shells in their racks. "It's a part of racing, it's a part of life. But you don't plan for luck. You're a target for Bolander and the rest of Ogre, now. You made them not just look bad, you *embarrassed* them. And they're not dumb, they know you don't know how to fight, so they're going to keep coming at you that way until they think it won't work."

I winced at that. "I don't really see much of an option, then..." I'd just try to avoid them as much as I could. *I'll try to go places with classmates, too, when I can.*

"You're probably thinking dodge and hide, which will get you through some of it for a little while," Mackenzie seemed to read my mind, "but that's not going to work forever. They're acting like bullies, Armstrong. You know the best way to take on a bully?"

I shook my head. It wasn't really something I'd thought about. Back at Black Mesa Outpost, there were only a half-dozen kids. Bullying wasn't really a problem.

"You punch them in the nose. Hard. And when they try again, you punch them again," Mackenzie shrugged. "Bullies go after people that they see as weaker than themselves. It's human nature, we like to have a social pecking order. We're in a physically demanding profession, so physical roughness is what the human mind defaults towards. You want them to leave you alone, you show them that you're not weak."

"I did fine in the final exercise," I grumbled.

"That was with a weapon," Mackenzie nodded, "which is a different sort of game. Guns are the great equalizer. Your small size actually gives you an advantage there, you're a smaller target than someone like me. And you've got a good natural movement with a weapon and killer instincts... as I'm sure you know after your experience at Champion Enterprises."

I felt a chill at his words. I'd almost pushed all that out of my mind, especially with how busy I'd been over the past few weeks.

"Honestly, that whole bit has probably made you *more* of a target to them," Mackenzie rubbed his chin in thought. "You've seen combat, of a sort. They haven't, so they want to see what you're made of in order to decide if *they* are capable." He shrugged, "Either way, your best bet is to learn to fight and go after them. Bolander for sure, but I'd suggest you take down one of her cronies first, she's a big girl and I'd wager she knows how to fight."

"Any recommendations?" I asked.

"Don't fight fair," Mackenzie shrugged. "She'll clobber you if you let her. Jump her, hit her when she doesn't expect it. Don't get caught. Don't do it on campus, or you *will* get caught. Don't hurt her too bad, or else you'll still get in trouble. And if you get in trouble, I'll have to train up a new coxswain for my grav-shell. I wouldn't like that."

"Sir," I nodded. It felt odd to be getting advice on how to beat someone up, especially from someone who was nominally in charge of enforcing rules against such things.

"Now, I think we've wasted enough time, Armstrong," he nodded at the rack, "Let's do some racing, eh?"

I nodded and helped to get our grav-shell down. In the past few weeks, I'd learned a lot about the sport. I still didn't feel skilled, but I felt able to at least steer and control the craft. "Sir, did you have a chance to talk with Dawson about joining the team?"

"Yeah, Dawson's good, but Farmer's not going to make the cut," Mackenzie said. He shot me a look, "this stays between you and me, as my coxswain, understand?" I nodded. "Dawson's doing well with his grades and on the military side of things, but Farmer's barely keeping his head above water. I don't think he'd make it with twenty hours of sports practice a week to endure."

I considered that, "But Dawson seemed pretty intent on getting in as a pair..."

"We can match him up with some of our other rowers. Besides, I'd already viewed his performance, I endorsed his application because I watched him race. I just wanted to see how he handled getting on the team." He rolled his eyes, "I *wanted* him to come to me. That would have been the best way. Going to you, as my coxswain, was smart, but the more professional way would have been for him to talk with me directly, as the Team Captain."

The analysis in his voice shocked me a bit. I hadn't thought organizing a sports team involved so much thought. I wondered if that was a product of the training here at the Academy or if that was simply how Mackenzie's brain worked. "We'll match him up with Rufus. He's a plebe from Ogre."

"I thought you said Ogre and Sand Dragon don't get along," I replied.

"Glad you were listening. Normally that's true, but you need to remember we won't always be at school. Someday we'll all be officers in the Planetary Militia and we'll need to work together." He finished adjusting the strap on the grav-shell and we pushed it out of the bay. "Besides, Rufus is alright for an Ogre and Dawson is pretty easy-going. The two of them might be a good way to bridge some of our differences."

"Okay, sir." I didn't know enough to really say one way or another.

Stroud showed up and he and Mackenzie started to get ready while I got into the coxswain seat. "One other thing, Armstrong," Mackenzie said. "Signups for Cadet Instructor slots start this week. I think you should put your name on the list."

"Me, sir?" I asked in shock.

"You learn a lot, it's a great leadership challenge, and it's a good way to get ahead in points. You need all three." I winced at his words. Clearly I wasn't doing that good of a job if he felt the need to say such a thing.

"Don't get me wrong," he said, "you've got lots of potential, but you signed the technical track on your application. It's going to take a lot to come back from that. Best way for you to do that is to switch back over to tactical and then do a stint as a Cadet Instructor."

"How did you know..."

Before I could finish asking, he and Stroud mounted and we started going, "Focus on the task at hand," he puffed. "Get us in position. We'll wait until the others get on-line, then we're going to do a mock race, forty kilometers down the main course." There was a set of markers leading out into the desert. Forty kilometers meant going the full distance out and back. It would be a brutal challenge.

I still wanted an answer about how he knew my selected track, but I didn't have time. I had to focus on the simple controls for the grav-shell, not only getting it into position, but then keeping us steady while the other craft formed up around us.

Once all five of the crewed shells were in position, Mackenzie blew a whistle.

I brought our speed up slowly, but several of the other craft dashed ahead. Two of them swooped down low, almost scraping the ground to gain speed. I could hear their coxswains shouting encouragement and they weren't alone. There was something exhilarating about the speed, the feeling of being just out of control.

One of them came sideways at me and I tweaked the controls over, diving down and then accelerating. The light aircraft swooped down and the outrigger of the other grav-shell seemed to pass only a few centimeters in front of me. I found myself shouting at the top of my lungs, calling out cadence to my rowers, and tweaking the controls at the same time.

I felt more alive than any other time I could remember. Stroud and Mackenzie were panting behind me, cranking in synch on the rowing machine, feeding power to the grav-coils and keeping us aloft even as we slid through the air, just above the ground.

As we flashed past markers, I lost all sense of time, all sense of movement, everything was a measure of tweaking the controls and shouting commands to the rowers. As we reached the end of the course, it barely registered, except to realize that Mackenzie and Stroud had stopped rowing.

I brought us to a slow halt and looked around, realizing that my face was covered in dust and sweat. I blinked at our surroundings, only then realizing that we'd covered the entire forty kilometers.

"What a rush, right?" Mackenzie panted.

I couldn't even form words.

The other shells came to a stop around us. We hadn't finished first, but a solid third place. I was stunned that I'd done so well. "Was that okay?" I asked, "I mean, the commands and piloting and everything?"

"Yeah," Mackenzie grinned, "you'll make a good Cadet Instructor."

***

Ashiri Takenata stared at me later that week, when I finally had time to talk with her about it, "Well, yeah, of course you need to sign up for the Cadet Instructor position. Alex and I already have. You've switched over to tactical track, right?"

"Not yet," I admitted. "I've just been so busy..."

"Jiden!" Ashiri shook her head. "Just do it now, okay? Not later, not tomorrow, not when you get time, do it now!"

I stared at her. She put her hands on her hips and I sighed and pulled out my datapad, "You're acting like my mother."

"Maybe that's the only way to get you to budge," Ashiri snorted.

I ignored her as I pulled up the administrative site on my datapad. I hesitated as I stared at the track change form. I'd actually filled everything out already. I just hadn't submitted it yet. I closed my eyes, took a deep breath, and hit the send button. I hated making irrevocable decisions.

"Good, now sign up for the Cadet Instructor course," Ashiri waved her hand. "Get it done with, let's go."

I opened my eyes and gave her a glare, "You sure are bossy lately."

"I'm practicing to be a Cadet Instructor," Ashiri grinned. "Though I hear you can be bossy too... Biohazard." I groaned. It seemed like everyone had taken to calling me that. I had my first race coming up soon, I'd lose a weekend for that, then come back into midterms for the semester.

I was staying on top of my coursework and I'd gone around my squad and checked on everyone. We'd all sort of scattered a bit as we started our separate classes. Originally I'd expected us to stick together, but it seemed like the academy had deliberately split all the companies up. I supposed there was some intent that we become a cohesive class... but I found it really hard to relate to some of my fellow plebes. *Especially the ones from Ogre.*

That wasn't entirely fair. Rufus from Ogre wasn't bad. He and Dawson were now on the grav-shell team and every other day I operated as their coxswain. He didn't really talk with me much, but he wasn't rude or mean, not like Bolander.

Sashi pretty much ignored me. But twice more Bolander had tried to corner me. I didn't know how to fight hand to hand. I'd never done any martial arts. I'd never even thought about it, and I really didn't know where to start.

Although... "You handled yourself pretty well in the fight in the alleyway," I said to Ashiri.

"I have two older brothers," Ashiri grinned. "I learned how to fight just to survive. But I've also taken *koryu* and *dato-ryu*. I'm actually on the *koryu* team here." I remembered that now. I'd thought it was sort of silly at the time, but now I sort of wished I'd done that instead of the grav-shell team. She hesitated, "You haven't done any martial arts, have you?"

"No," I answered, "I haven't."

"I sort of guessed that when Bolander bounced you off the wall," Ashiri snorted.

"Spare me my blushes," I grumbled.

"It's not *really* your fault. I guess you just grew up sort of sheltered," Ashiri smiled. "My childhood was a little rougher. Like I said, I had to learn how to fight to survive." She sighed, "I really think you should join one of the self-defense classes. But you're doing four hours every day on the grav-shell team, right?" I nodded in reply. "Then you just don't have time."

"I guess I could ask for some days off in the evenings," I thought out loud. Most of the practices in the evenings were rowing practice on stationary machines. Taking a grav-shell out was too dangerous with the afternoon winds common to the desert. I rehearsed controls and such, but that was only so useful at this point.

"Then I'd recommend Commander Pannja's *kerala* class," Ashiri nodded.

"*Kerala*?" I asked.

"It's a modern take on one of the older classes of martial arts, and it's suited for someone our size, rather than some of the other ones that favor bigger people," Ashiri shrugged. "You'll get more out of it and from what I'd heard, Commander Pannja doesn't mess around. He gets you sparring right away and you'll learn quickly."

"Okay..." I said. I wasn't really sure what sparring meant. "I'll ask tomorrow morning, I guess. I've got my first race this weekend, after that we'll see if they even want me on the team."

"I'm sure..."

Alexander knocked on the door frame. We gestured at him to come in and Ashiri went on, "I'm sure you'll do fine. From what

Dawson's said, you're picking it up pretty quick. Not that I know much about the sport to judge."

"Grav-shell racing?" Alexander scowled. When I nodded in response, he glanced at me, "I hear that Rufus from Ogre is on one of your crews?"

"Yeah," I replied, irritated at his protective attitude, "I'm the coxswain for the amateur heat, and then for Cadet Commander Mackenzie's shell in the collegiate varsity heat. Dawson and Rufus are the rowers for the amateur shell." I was allowed to coxswain for both, since I could go up a level in the competition... just not downwards. Next year, if I stuck with this, I'd only be eligible to coxswain in the varsity level.

"I don't like that," Alexander muttered.

"From what Dawson says, Rufus is alright," Ashiri said. "For an Ogre, of course," she amended.

"I haven't had a problem with him," I scowled at Alexander. "And it's not like he's going to try to beat on me in front of the whole team." I'd taken the precaution of walking out to practice with Dawson or Cadet Commander Mackenzie, so I pretty much wasn't ever alone.

"Yeah, but he might sabotage you some other way," Alexander growled. "He could tweak the controls on one of those grav-shells or loosen a bolt or something."

I rolled my eyes, "Please, if he did that, he'd risk hurting himself when we go out!"

"Not if he does it to your other shell," Ashiri said thoughtfully.

"You don't think he'd risk getting kicked off the team just to injure me or make me look bad?" I looked between them. "Look, getting accepted on a varsity team is a big thing. We all earn bonus points for our companies and ourselves based off performance. And with how fast those shells could go, anyone fiddling with one is as likely to *kill* someone as hurt them."

"That's why I don't like you doing it," Alexander growled. "Someone's already tried to kill you once."

"Twice," I muttered.

"Wait, what?" Ashiri and Alexander both asked at the same time.

"I'm not sure about the second time," I didn't meet their eyes.

As they stared at me, I explained quickly about the burst pipe and how Sashi, of all people, had saved me. I put emphasis on how Commander Bonnadonna had been standing there, watching me.

"You think he was involved?" Ashiri asked, shaking her head. "That's a big stretch. Anyone could have tapped into the monitors and saw you running up those stairs. And that's even assuming that it *wasn't* an accident."

"A burst pipe *could* be staged," Alexander hedged. "You can buy a pipe-bursting kit on the planetary network, they sell them for pranks and such, and you can activate one with a wireless signal. But unless he knew you'd be running up that staircase, I don't know how he could have prepared."

"But he was right *there*," I said. I felt somehow certain that he'd been involved. "He didn't even try to grab me."

"Maybe he saw Sashi right behind you," Alexander said.

"Yeah, and if he knows anything about our family history, he certainly wouldn't have expected her to catch me," I scoffed. Granted, I hadn't known a thing about that rivalry until last year, but everyone else seemed to know. *I really wish my mom had told me some of this stuff...* But then again, my mom had pretty much closed the book on this part of her life. She'd never gone to the Academy, she barely talked to her mother, the Admiral. For all I knew, she didn't even know about it.

"Maybe, maybe not," Alexander pursed his lips. "But it still seems a stretch... I mean, he's the *ethics* teacher, you really think he's the one gunning for you?"

"Why not?" I asked. "He was off-world on assignment with the Guard Marine Corps. That might be where he linked up with off-world smugglers."

"That seems pretty far-fetched," Ashiri frowned. "Besides, do you think Admiral Armstrong would let him teach ethics here if she didn't trust him?"

I didn't have an answer to that, but for all I knew, she was using me as bait to bring out my attacker. "Well, he's new to the school," I ticked off fingers, "he doesn't seem to like me, and he would know how to use a ML-7, plus he was at the site of that accident, so that's four indicators."

Alexander frowned, "It doesn't make a lot of sense to me."

"Well, we have two other new instructors," Ashiri said.

"Commander Pannja and Commander Scarpitti. Other than that, there's a dozen or more staff, it could even be one of the cadets..."

"Doesn't make sense for it to be someone on staff," Alexander shook his head. "Staff wouldn't have access to cadets. Cadets are under constant observation. Do you really think that any of us would have the time and opportunity to try to kill Jiden? Whoever wants to kill her would want to be able to get close to her, maybe even find out what she knows."

"Commander Bonnadonna used me as an example in class," I said, "maybe he was fishing for information."

"I think you're just bitter over that," Ashiri scowled. "I don't see it, sorry."

"Well, I'll keep an eye on him, anyway," I grumbled in reply. I didn't understand why the other two didn't see it. It wasn't enough for me to take to the Admiral, sure, but I thought my friends would believe me.

"Well, whether or not he was behind that incident, I still think you should drop grav-shell racing," Alexander said. "It's too dangerous..."

"You aren't in charge of me," I snapped. "I *like* the races, okay? I'm not going to live in a safe bubble." It felt like when I was with the grav-shell team was the only time someone treated me like I was human. Even my friends had taken to bossing me around. "Anyway, if you guys are done, I need to get to sleep, I've got to get up early for practice."

I saw them roll their eyes, but I didn't care, I was tired, I was stressed. Someone was trying to kill me, Bolander wanted to pound me into a mass of bruises, and I felt like my friends were pushing me into something I didn't want.

I didn't say anything as Alexander left and Ashiri closed the door. She left the light on, she still had several assignments to work on, I knew. I wanted to apologize, I knew they were trying to help. But all the same, I felt like they wanted to do things *their* way.

And right now, I didn't want to do things their way. I was tired of doing things everyone else's way. I'd made the decision to come here... and some part of me was wondering if that had been the *wrong* decision. I'd thought that I could make a difference, that maybe I could protect people, people like my family and friends.

Instead, I felt exhausted, confused, and tired. I'd thought this was my calling... but what if I'd been wrong? What if I simply wasn't good enough, smart enough, or strong enough? What if I failed... or worse, what if I caused other people to fail?

I lay there in my bunk, trying to sleep, but just staring at the ceiling above me. Long after Ashiri shut off the light, I lay there, wondering, worrying.

***

Chapter Eleven: Barely Scraping By

As the day of my first official grav-shell race arrived, I really worried that I was going to throw up. Somehow, I knew that wouldn't help with my new nickname. I walked down in the dark, it wasn't even two in the morning. We had to load up and we'd have a three hour flight, from what I understood.

"Biohazard!" Mackenzie greeted me as I arrived at the shed. "We already got the shells loaded in the cargo bay, go ahead and get loaded up!"

I glanced at my datapad, "Sorry, sir, am I late?" I'd checked the schedule three times the previous night, just to be sure I'd be there on time.

"No, you're good. Normally we don't have the coxswains help with loading the shells. You're not all that tall, so it's just awkward trying to get things in position with most of us rowers being two meters tall," Mackenzie grinned. "But if it makes you feel better, you can go check out our work and see that we loaded everything right."

"Thanks, sir," I replied. It wouldn't hurt, I figured, to make sure that they'd been loaded right and I could verify that Rufus from Ogre hadn't sabotaged the Daisy. Not that I thought he would, but it didn't hurt to check.

I walked over to the cargo skimmer and then up the ramp. The Daisy was the varsity grav-shell I'd been using and I started towards it first.

"Miss Armstrong," Commander Bonnadonna's deep voice startled me. "Good morning to you."

I spun around, not having seen him in the shadows near the ramp. His short, broad stature made him look menacing, and the way the cargo bay's lights made his eyes and teeth glitter gave me a chill.

"Sir," I felt my heart race. If he *was* the one trying to kill me, then this might well be the perfect opportunity. I half expected him to draw a pistol and confront me, like some kind of holovid villain.

"Just checking the manifest," he nodded. "Sometimes plebes try to sneak off campus. We wouldn't want anyone having any fun, now would we?" He gave me a slight smile, as if he'd said something particularly amusing.

I smiled weakly, "No, sir."

"Good luck, Miss Armstrong," he nodded at me and stepped out of the shadows and down the ramp. As soon as he'd departed I started looking over the Daisy, examining it for any sign of tampering.

"Biohazard!" Mackenzie shouted a few minutes later, "Get out here, we need to roll!"

"Yes, sir!" I shouted. I still hadn't had an opportunity to search the Arrow, the amateur shell, but I'd be certain to do it when we landed. *If he's the one who was working with the smugglers, then I'm not going to let him do me in that easily...*

***

The skimmer flight left me feeling remarkably nervous. I tried to sleep. Most of the rest of the team slept, passed out in their seats, some of them snoring softly. Except for Rufus from Ogre, he managed to snore loudly over the drone of the skimmer's engines, his head thrown back and his mouth wide open.

I had to fight the urge to throw something at him. It wasn't his fault. I just couldn't sleep. I was by the window and part of me was watching for a missile to come streaking in at us. Nothing happened, though, we just continued on over the desert.

That sense of dread stayed with me though. I pulled out my datapad and started working on some of my homework. I had a hard time focusing though. I felt like my mind just ran in circles. I had classes to study, I had my duties as a plebe, I had to deal with Bolander before she cornered me and beat me to a pulp, and someone was trying to kill me.

"How's it going?" A soft voice spoke from over my shoulder.

I started, I'd thought I was the only one in the skimmer awake besides the pilot. I looked over to see Mackenzie kneeling next to my seat. "I'm good, sir," I responded automatically.

"Sure you are," he shook his head. "I know you're stressed out, plebe year is hard. But don't be afraid to reach out for help. And when someone asks you how you're doing, you can tell the truth."

"I'm afraid of failing, sir," I blurted out, not even really sure where the words came from.

"That's a reasonable fear, Armstrong," he nodded. "And to tell you the truth, I'm afraid of that myself. Fear of failure means you understand the nature of the risks we all take." He pursed his lips and in the dim light, he looked particularly thoughtful. "Look, the only advice I can give you is the advice I've been given. None of us are perfect and no one should rightly expect a perfect solution from you. What people will expect is your best. And from what I've seen of you so far, Jiden, you don't have it in you to give anything less than your best. So just keep up the good work and carry on."

"Yes, sir," I nodded, "thanks."

"No problem, now get some sleep," he said, "I don't want you passing out while we're speeding along the ground at fifty K-P-H."

"That would be bad, sir," I replied. He stood and moved back to his seat and I tucked my datapad away and sat back. It took me a moment to realize that he'd used my first name. I hadn't even known that he *knew* my first name.

I closed my eyes, thinking about that and how much I liked his smile. I wasn't sure when I fell asleep, but I didn't have any nightmares.

***

We landed at the outskirts of Duncan City and unloaded near the racing track. It wasn't much to look at, especially not in the twilight just before sunrise. It was just a flat stretch of desert, roped off, with stretches of seating being assembled as we watched.

I helped to unload our food and drink supplies, even as the rowers got our grav-shells out and racked on the portable stands. From what I understood, they'd be inspected by race officials and then we'd race. I was a bit nervous because the varsity race was one of the first of the day.

I walked over to the racks to look over the Arrow, the grav-shell I'd use for the amateur race, and I ran into Commander Scarpitti. The tall woman was speaking with one of the female rowers, and as I came forward, I recognized Cadet Salter. I hadn't seen much of my former Cadet Instructor at the practices, she had her own coxswain and she mostly kept to herself. "Yes, I'm very glad to be invited to attend. I was a grav-shell rower all four years on a women's shell," Commander Scarpitti was saying.

"Thanks for agreeing to come, ma'am," Cadet Salter replied. "I know you've got a busy schedule..." She looked over and saw me, then waved me over, "Here's another of our female team-members, ma'am."

"Ah, yes, Armstrong!" Commander Scarpitti smiled. "You're the only female plebe on the team, did you know that?"

"Uh, no, ma'am, I guess I hadn't noticed," I admitted. I'd been aware there was a separate female-only set of heats, but I didn't know if there were even any female plebes who'd be interested in the sport. Much like the difference between varsity and amateur, women could race on the men's teams but not the other way around.

"Well, we need to make sure that we get other representatives involved," Scarpitti shook her head. "The year after I left, there wasn't another female on the team, can you believe it?"

Given the peculiarities of the sport, I supposed that I could, but I didn't say that. "That's too bad, ma'am." I noticed that Cadet Salter had made a hasty retreat. *What a rat,* I thought to myself. Not that I blamed her, Commander Scarpitti just seemed to like to talk, and always at the least convenient times.

"It's great to see you doing so well," Commander Scarpitti went on. "A plebe, and already on the *men*'s varsity team. Very accomplished!"

"I'm just a coxswain, ma'am," I said.

"Still, a good cox makes all the difference!" she said earnestly. "Do you mind showing me the grav-shells? I'm sure the ones I used have been retired by this point, but I'd love to see what your team uses to race."

I forced myself to smile. "Of course, ma'am."

We walked through, and I pointed out what details I remembered about each of them. Commander Scarpitti would pause here and there to pat one or stroke the smooth lines of another. "I miss this sport," she said, practically gushing, her harsh voice softening to the point that she almost sounded girlish. "I'd forgotten how much. The rush, the joy of competition... isn't it great?"

"This is my first race," I admitted.

"Really?" She looked down at me, "well, I'm certain you will represent the Academy well. I dare say that you'll impress us all!"

"Thanks, ma'am," I said. I still wanted to check out the Arrow, but I hadn't had a chance to do more than a cursory look at it as I showed the Commander around. As I tried to make my escape to do that, I heard Mackenzie shout, "Biohazard, it's screening time!"

I sighed and ran in his direction. As soon as I arrived, two judges escorted me to the side, had me strip down in a booth, and then ran the scanner equipment, checking me out for illegal cybernetics or drugs, from what I understood. I didn't know why anyone would want to cheat at a college event, but I wasn't going to ask that question of these two women. One of them gave a nod, "You're clean. You can get changed into your race suit."

I flushed a bit as I started pulling that on. It was the school colors, gray and blue, but it was a skin-tight, sheer material that clung to my body in a fashion that made me feel rather uncertain. The older of the two judges gave me a smile, "Don't worry, dear, you look fine, and the only curves people will be watching are the ones of your grav-shell."

I flushed in response, but I felt a little better as I stepped out and walked over to our shells. Mackenzie gave me a nod, "Ready, Biohazard?"

"Yes, sir," I replied.

Stroud gave a chuckle, "We're not on campus, out here, you get to call him by *his* nickname: Captain Crunch."

"What?" I asked.

To my surprise, *Mackenzie* flushed. "I, uh, wrecked a grav-shell on my first day on the team."

"You *wrecked* a grav-shell?" I asked in surprise.

"He got off-synch with the other rower and the coxswain tried to correct," Stroud grinned. "Then Captain Crunch here tried to save it by throwing his weight to the side... he wound up running the whole thing into a sand dune. Total loss. We all thought that the team captain was going to kill him... but here he stands."

I looked between them, not sure if they'd made the entire story up. Mackenzie shrugged, "It's true, Armstrong. So don't worry so much about *your* nickname. I had commissioned officers calling me Captain Crunch in class."

"Sir," I snorted, unable to really find a response for that.

"Racers," a voice blasted over the desert, "all Varsity Men's racers assemble your shells at the starting line. Race will begin in five minutes."

"Here we go," Mackenzie grinned. "Mount up, Biohazard."

I climbed into the seat and they pulled it down from the rack, and carried it over to the starting line. I wasn't sure what to really expect, possibly four or five grav-shells.

Instead, there were twenty or more. I couldn't count them all, not from my low-down position. "Is there room for all of them?" I asked.

"It'll be crowded," Mackenzie nodded, "First heat always is. But if we do well enough to get to the second heat, the numbers thin out. We should only have to race three heats today, including finals. I've been to some races where we have to do five... let me tell you, that's exhausting."

I couldn't imagine. I already felt like a nervous wreck. What if I messed things up? What if I disappointed Mackenzie? I couldn't imagine being thrown off the team, but maybe there was a first for everything.

Before my nervousness could really tear me up, it was race time. "Racers, ready!" a voice shouted. Around us, grav-shells jockeyed for position on the starting line. A red one, just to the side, edged so close that I was worried they'd hit us, but their coxswain, his head barely visible in his cockpit, held it steady just short of collision.

"Racers, five, four three, two, one, go!" There was a gunshot and then Mackenzie and Stroud were running forward, driving the Daisy forward until they mounted. For just a second, I stared at my controls, forgetting what they all did.

Then something in the back of my head took over and I started shouting commands.

The red shell to my right edged ahead and I dropped us down, picking up speed. We edged ahead of the red shell but we'd lost height so I shouted, "Power Ten on five!"

I counted it down and then the explosive power of the two rowers behind me hit, practically vaulting us in the air as they fed power to the grav-coils. We'd trained hard, before, but this was a race and it felt like they held nothing back. We surged forward, racing across the flats, wind and dust stinging my face, just as the sun came up behind us, lighting up the entire desert.

We covered forty kilometers in what seemed like mere seconds, dashing across the finish line so fast that I wasn't certain we *had* crossed, not until the two rowers went limp behind me and the shouts of the other coxswains cut off.

I coughed, my throat raw from shouting, my vision blurry and my body feeling at once exhilarated and exhausted. We curved around in a slow turn and I brought us to a halt near the scoreboard. They already had the results posted by that time.

"Third place, not bad, not bad at all, Biohazard," Mackenzie gave me a broad smile. "That gets us to the second heat."

Stroud finished draining his bottle of water, "Good race, Armstrong."

"Thank you," I croaked. I wished I'd brought water for myself. We made our way back along the course with the other racers, moving far slower and on the return side. As we did, I saw the female racers blast past, before we even really started on the way back. "They must have started right after we finished," I said.

"Nope," Mackenzie shook his head, "They start a few minutes after we started. They don't go quite as fast, but with how many races they have to do, they try to get everyone through as quickly as they can. That's why I didn't let you coxswain for our female rowers, no way you'd make it back in time, which would disqualify you immediately."

I didn't respond. I wanted to save my voice, especially since it looked like I'd be mounting up on the Arrow as soon as I got back. I wasn't wrong, either, as we pulled in, I saw Dawson and Rufus ready to go.

I hopped out of the seat and ran over, even as I heard, "Racers, amateur men's racing heat racers report to the start area."

I had just enough time to suck down a cup of water that someone passed me and then climb in. As we got to the start area, Dawson looked down at me, "You ready?"

"Absolutely!" I shouted back. The crazy energy of the race was contagious. It was addictive. I wanted to race again and I could barely wait. The speed, the excitement... in the light grav-shell, it was the next-best thing to flying, just above ground.

They did the count down and I braced myself, feeling my heart race, feeling the thrill of anticipation. The shot rang out and Dawson and Rufus ran us forward. I gave a shout of exhilaration as we started to move.

Then it was back into the fury. I shouted out commands as we moved forward and it seemed like we were at the head of the pack. As we went faster and faster, the wind and dust pelting my face, skimming across the ground, I felt *happy* for the first time in as long as I could remember.

That's when the strut supporting the starboard grav stabilizer let go.

The whole starboard outrigger separated and we started to roll that way, the ground screaming past less than a meter from my face. I mashed on the emergency stop button by reflex, but nothing happened.

I didn't have time to scream before we slammed into the ground.

***

Chapter Twelve: Picking Up The Pieces

I came to as someone dragged me out of the grav-shell. Everything was chaos and confusion. Someone helped me to stand and I limped off to the side, trying to make sense of the world. I blinked and for a second, all I saw behind my eyes was spinning earth and sky.

"Look at me, are you okay?" the emergency technician asked. "How many fingers am I holding up?"

"Three," I said, even as I tried to calm my breathing. This was the third time I'd survived an aircraft crash. I would have liked to think I'd handle it better. I looked up, "Is everyone okay?"

"Don't worry about anyone else, okay?" she smiled at me, "Now, sweetheart, I'm going to go through some questions with you..."

She worked me over, checking to make sure I didn't have any breaks or numb spots. By the time she'd finished, I saw an emergency vehicle pull up. A moment later, she helped me in the back and we drove off. "I need to contact my team captain," I said to her.

"We've already contacted your school, they've sent an air ambulance since you don't have any live-threatening injuries," she said. "We'll meet them at the landing site."

"Okay," I said. I lay back on the gurney, too shaken to talk. As my eyes closed, I saw spinning sky and ground again, but this time I saw what I'd seen in the crash. Pieces flying off the grav-shell. Bodies flying free, being flung into the air... and into the ground.

I opened my eyes, "How are Dawson and Rufus?"

The technician didn't answer at first. She looked towards the front of the vehicle, then back at me. "The two boys were both flung free. As I understand, one of them was thrown pretty far, but he landed alright. The other one..."

"I need to know," I said, staring at her. The woman flinched back from the intensity in my voice. "Rufus," the technician said, "he was thrown into the ground and the grav-shell landed on him and then dragged him. He's not in good shape. We evacuated him, I don't know any more than that."

My fault, I thought to myself. I must have messed up somewhere. Maybe I'd pushed the grav-shell too hard, maybe I'd messed up steering and put too much stress on the frame. I'd seen the side strut give way, it had come loose from the outrigger. Without the stabilizer, the ground effect forces had rolled us over.

"The emergency power never kicked on," I said. That might not have stopped us in time, but it should have done something.

"What?" the woman asked.

But I didn't say anything. She didn't need to know. The Admiral needed to know. The emergency power should have kicked in and at least slowed us down. It hadn't. The strut separating was one thing. I could believe that I'd caused that, that I'd messed up. But the emergency failsafe should have kicked in. That was one thing that had been hammered into me, that pushing that would slow us to a halt. It might not have prevented the roll-over, but it should have at least brought us to a stop rather than the long, skidding nightmare crash I saw every time I closed my eyes.

Someone must have sabotaged the grav-shell and I thought I knew who.

***

"Someone did sabotage the crew shell," the Admiral nodded. "The race investigators have determined that the power cable for the emergency failsafe had been disconnected. They also determined that two of the three bolts attaching the strut to the outrigger had been loosened."

"What are you going to do about this?" I demanded.

She gave me a look and I sat straighter, "Sorry, ma'am."

"I understand you are concerned for the well-being of your team-mates. Believe me, girl, I already *have* taken precautions, many of which you've not seen. I've also taken actions as a result of this event," the Admiral's cold voice held an edge of anger that terrified me. She had a level of raw intensity that almost made me quiver in response. She was, quite simply, terrifying.

"Ma'am," I started to speak, "I saw Commander Bonnadonna in the cargo hold for the skimmer..."

"His presence wasn't related to the sabotage," the Admiral dismissed my statement.

"Ma'am," I began, "I--"

"He was not involved, I assure you of that," the Admiral snapped. "Now, if you'll excuse me, I have to speak with young Plebe Rufus's parents, who need to know how this happened. You are dismissed, Plebe Armstrong."

I stood stiffly and gave her a sharp salute, so angry at the dismissal that I could barely breathe. I turned sharply and stepped out of the Admiral's office. I'd managed to talk my way out of the Academy hospital and into her office, but as I walked out, I could feel the aches and pains of my entire body. I paused in the outer office and saw a man and woman in civilian clothes. Rufus's parents. I wanted to go up to them and tell them I'd been in the grav-shell, that it was probably my fault that their son was in the hospital.

But I couldn't make my feet work that way. Instead, I walked past them and out of the office. I went down the corridors in a daze, my body hurting, my mind running in circles again.

I got back to my room and found Alexander outside in the corridor, his face hard. "I told you." He shook his head, "I told you that it was too dangerous." He walked away before I could respond.

I went into my room and closed the door. Ashiri wasn't there. I just sort of crouched down, my back to the door. After everything else, Alexander's words hurt the most. It *was* my fault. Dawson was injured, Rufus was in the hospital. All three of us could have died.

I just sort of crawled over and got into bed, tears streaming down my face. I had nearly died. Why did they want to kill me? I didn't know anything. I was just a kid.

"Jiden?" I hadn't heard Ashiri open the door.

"Yeah," I said, "what is it?"

She came over and put her hand on my shoulder. "It's okay."

"It's *not* okay," I snapped. I didn't look at her, I didn't want her to see how weak I was. "I was stupid. I'm going to resign from the grav-shell team. I'll find something else, something that won't make other people a target. Maybe I'll resign from the Academy..."

"Shut up," Ashiri snapped. She pulled me around by the shoulder and I hissed in pain. I might have come through without broken bones or other serious injuries, but bruises covered my body. "It isn't your fault. You didn't put a gun to Isaac Champion's head and force him to work with those smugglers. You didn't do the same thing to whoever is trying to kill you now. None of this is your fault."

I couldn't meet her eyes, "But I knew someone wanted to hurt me. I made Rufus and Dawson targets..."

"That's a load of *hidoi*," Ashiri snorted. "You didn't make them a target, whoever is after you is a callous enough person that they're willing to kill innocent people to get you. Yeah, taking up a dangerous sport like grav-shell racing probably gave him a route to hurt you, but it probably didn't matter *what* you do, he's still going to be after you."

"Commander Bonnadonna," I muttered, "it has got to be him."

"What?" Ashiri asked.

I told her how I'd seen him in the cargo compartment of the skimmer. She frowned, "You told someone, right?"

"I told the *Admiral*," I snapped, "and all she did was tell me that it wasn't him. She didn't even let me *finish*." I felt so angry about that. It was like I was just a child, someone who didn't need to know everything and who could be ignored. This was my life, I wanted some input on it.

"Maybe it isn't him," Ashiri said. "There were plenty of other people with access. For all we know, Rufus did it for Bolander from Ogre..."

"And hurt himself?" I shook my head. "That makes no sense at all. No. I saw Commander Bonnadonna in the cargo bay. I checked over the Daisy but I didn't get a chance to look over the Arrow before the race."

"I still think you shouldn't jump to conclusions," Ashiri cautioned me. "Alex said..."

"Alexander blames me for what happened to Dawson and Rufus," I snapped. "And he thinks I'm an idiot for putting other people at risk."

"That's not it at all!" Ashiri shook her head, "he's angry at you for putting *yourself* at risk and for not having one of us to watch your back. Dawson's on the grav-shell team with you, but he doesn't know that someone tried to kill you. Maybe if he had, then *he* would have checked the grav-shell for sabotage."

"I can't tell *everyone*," I sputtered. The last thing I wanted was more attention and that was exactly what word getting out would give me. Things were hard enough already. I felt like every action I took was under a microscope.

"You don't *have* to tell anyone else, but it would be nice if me or Alex could watch your back," Ashiri rolled her eyes. "Geez, Jiden, just accept some help, now and again!"

"Okay!" I threw my hands in the air, "Help me!"

"Well, me or Alex could join the grav-shell team, if you could get one of us in," she mused.

"I'm not going back," I growled.

"Don't be stupid," Ashiri shook her head, "whoever tried this is going to lay low. You like the racing, right?"

I thought about that for a long moment. Right now, the last thing I wanted to do was get back in the seat. Yet as I thought about the feel of the wind on my face and the raw joy I'd felt, I really wanted to experience that again. "Yeah, I guess I do."

"Well, we'll see how this all shakes down," Ashiri said. "They brought us down from a drill event for it, ended the exercise and everything. Word got out pretty fast that Dawson was injured and Rufus was in the hospital, though we haven't had any more details since then. Really, it's a minor miracle that you walked away from it..."

"I was dragged away," I thought back. I couldn't help a flashback to the spinning sky and ground and the jarring, tearing impact. I shivered. "But yeah, I'm walking now." My body had really begun to ache, though. I had the feeling that come tomorrow I'd be using the painkillers that the doctor had shoved in my hand as I left the Academy hospital.

"Still," Ashiri shook her head, "you're really lucky."

Lucky, I thought to myself, *that's hardly what I consider myself.* If I were really lucky, then I wouldn't have stumbled into this situation. If I were really lucky, I could have lived a normal life.

"Let's see how tomorrow looks," Ashiri said.

"Yeah, tomorrow," I didn't want to sleep, didn't want to close my eyes, but after talking with Ashiri, it seemed like it was all I could do to stay awake. *Biology, Doctor Aisling talked about it, I've come down off the adrenaline rush, I've gone through the other coping mechanisms, and now I'm crashing.* It was a distant part of my mind thinking that, observing it all. The rest of me was simply exhausted.

I lay back in bed and the last thing I remembered was Ashiri turning out the lights.

***

At Sunday morning formation, Cadet Lieutenant Webster officially broke the news to us. "As some of you have no doubt already heard, it seems that there was some kind of accident at the grav-shell race that several of our cadets and plebes competed in yesterday. Two of our plebes as well as Plebe Rufus were involved. While Armstrong walked away with no more than bruises and scrapes," he shot me a hard look, almost as if he blamed me for that, "Plebe Dawson will spend the rest of the weekend in the Academy hospital for observation, and Plebe Rufus was seriously injured."

He waited and let us take that in. I was glad to hear that Dawson would be out, hopefully by Monday. I was also glad that Rufus was still alive, I'd secretly worried that he had died and no one dared to tell me.

"While it looks to be purely an accident," he went on, "as I understand it, the race investigation is still incomplete and the Enforcers have been called in." I didn't miss how he put extra emphasis on that. Then, to my surprise, Cadet Lieutenant Webster stopped in front of me and looked straight at me as he continued, "If *anyone* knows what might have caused this accident, either negligence, incompetence, or something of the sort, I suggest they come forward."

I just stared right back at him, not really understanding what he meant for a moment. Then, as I realized his intent, I felt first shock and then rage. *How dare he...* it was all I could do not to shout at him that it wasn't my fault, that it was sabotage. Instead I clenched my jaw and stared straight ahead.

"Well," he said after no one spoke up, "I'm sure they'll get to the bottom of things on their own." He walked back down to the end of the corridor. "Now, normally I would hold inspections this morning, but the Superintendent has instructed that all cadets be allowed the morning to take a mental health break. So all of you are free to take the time to do what you need to do. I understand that Plebe Dawson is allowed visitors this morning. I suggest that *some* of you see him." The emphasis he put on that made me clench my jaw again.

"Plebes, you are dismissed."

As we fell out of formation, I nodded at Ashiri and then in the direction of the Academy hospital. She nodded in reply and we jogged off in that direction.

The hospital section was mostly empty. A couple of plebes and a female cadet were on duty. I hadn't realized that the Academy made so much use of us, but I saw their company patches and realized that they were Ivy, the medical company. After a moment, I recognized Cadet Third Class Elliot from my first drill. I wasn't sure how they saw enough real trauma to get certified as doctors here at the Academy. Then again, I'd been here twice now, so maybe I was wrong.

They let Ashiri and I back to see Dawson. The broad shouldered young man was seated upright in bed, wearing one of those hospital gowns that makes everyone look absurd. "Jiden!" He perked up when he saw me, "I heard they let you out, I hope you're not here because you're actually hurt!"

"Me?" I waved at that, "No, just some scrapes and bruises." I felt self-conscious, seeing him in bed here at the hospital when I'd made it out without any real injuries.

"Thank God," he shook his head, "that was a bad one."

"Yeah," I nodded in agreement. "Look, Dawson, I wanted to apologize..."

"Apologize?" He shook his head, "Are you kidding? I saw Rufus's strut separate, I was looking right at him when it happened." Dawson looked down at his hands, "It was all I could do to remember my training and unstrap. I looked down to give you warning and you'd already done the emergency fail safe, more than that, you steered us off to the side, out of the way of the other racers, otherwise we'd have been run over, that's when you finally lost it and we flipped."

"Wait, what?" I asked. I didn't remember any of that.

"Yeah, you were mashing on the emergency fail safe and steering us for the side at the same time," Dawson nodded. "If you hadn't done that, things would have been way more serious." He cocked his head, "Hey, have you even seen the video?"

"No... no I hadn't," I replied.

"Cadet Commander Mackenzie sent it to me earlier, told me that I was lucky I had a coxswain with a cool head..." he brought up his datapad and I recognized the Arrow. It was weird to watch myself on video, I didn't look the way I thought I would. We were at least ten meters ahead of the next grav-shell, we must have really been booking it. The footage was shaky, like what someone would get on their personal datapad, not a professional camera. It was good enough, though, that I could pick out right when the strut let go. The starboard outrigger separated almost instantly. Then, to my shock, I watched as I steered hard over, getting out of the main track even as the entire craft dropped, starting to roll. I'd turned hard to starboard, which had provided a momentary stability, just enough for the Arrow to get clear of the next craft behind before we smashed into the ground and started rolling. It was a small thing, but I felt relief that I'd managed even that much. Dawson was right. If I *hadn't* done that, consciously or not, the next grav-shell would have smashed right into our wreckage, probably killing all of us.

As the Arrow hit and rolled, though, my stomach dropped. I winced as I saw Dawson flung free... but what left me feeling nauseous was when Rufus disappeared *under* the rolling grav-shell. It wasn't particularly heavy, but we hit at high speed and the strut he was on crumpled like tissue under the impact.

"Any word on Rufus?" I asked, passing the datapad back.

"Not yet," Dawson shook his head. "They didn't even want to tell me that you were okay. I think everyone's tight lipped about this because they still don't know the cause. I *saw* you press the emergency fail safe. That strut came off without warning... I'm still trying to make sense of it myself, you know?"

"Yeah," I answered. I couldn't meet his eyes, "I really hope they find out what really happened." I didn't know how he'd feel about my steering when it was me that had been the target of the sabotage. I didn't know how much of the investigation would be public or what they'd want me to keep secret, so I didn't want to say anything about it at all.

"Well, I'll just be glad to get out of here," Dawson shook his head, "should be tomorrow."

"You need anything?" Ashiri asked.

"Nah, I've got my classwork and stuff," Dawson said. "And the food's pretty good. As long as I can get back to the company tomorrow, I'll be fine." He met my gaze, "And thanks, again, Jiden. You really saved our backsides with that steering."

I flushed. I didn't feel worthy of praise. It was my fault that someone had tried to kill all three of us. But I didn't say that. Instead I mumbled something about hoping he felt better and I left. Outside, Ashiri said she was going to head back to the barracks. I looked at the time and decided to head down to the chapel.

I arrived well before the scheduled services and I just sort of wondered inside. Without thinking about it I found myself sitting in my usual spot. I sat there, just enjoying the quiet and peace. I didn't even notice the chaplain sit down next to me. "Had a rough spot, eh, Jiden?"

It seemed that everyone knew my first name today. "Yes, sir," I replied.

"It's funny," he said, staring forward at the altar. "In the military, we do things that are hard and dangerous. In battle, it seems like we handle injuries and deaths a bit better. These things are terrible, but expected. It's incidents like this that can catch us off-guard."

I didn't know about that. Loss was something I hated. I hadn't been close to Ted Meeks but I'd been responsible for his death. I hadn't been close to Rufus, either, but it was my fault that he was in the hospital. "It's my fault."

"Bull," the chaplain snorted. "I'd be willing to believe a lot, Jiden, but not that."

I should have kept my mouth shut, but I spoke anyway. Maybe I was just tired of people telling me it wasn't my fault. "It was sabotage. The person who did it was trying to get me."

"Sounds like it's that person's fault," the chaplain replied after a moment. He didn't seem surprised by the revelation. I wondered if he'd already known or suspected... or if he was simply that even-keeled.

"I knew someone was trying to hurt me," I said. "I *made* Rufus a target when I decided to join the grav-shell team." I couldn't help it, tears welled up. "Just like I made Ted Meeks a target when I asked him to look into the crooked accounting at Champion Enterprises. He's dead. They never even found his body, his parents had to have a funeral without a body... and it's my fault too."

"Sounds like you're taking on a lot of responsibility," he said after a moment. "I never met this Ted, but it seems to me that he made a decision, too, didn't he? Clearly he thought it was important to look into things or he wouldn't have done it, no matter what you said. And as for the people who killed him... well, I think we can both see that *they* would be the ones who made that decision. Not you."

I closed my eyes. As much as I wanted to believe that, I found it hard.

"Well," he said, "if my words don't help, just think about this: here at the Academy we teach our students to take a great deal upon themselves. At the same time, we have to strike a balance. We can take ownership of the things we can control. Jiden, none of us can control everything. Some things are in God's hands."

I closed my eyes. For a moment I saw spinning earth and sky. I didn't know how I had managed to steer the Arrow out of the way of the race. Maybe the chaplain was right in that at least. Maybe some things were in God's hands.

"Thanks, sir," I said.

"It's what I'm here for, Jiden," he said gently. He patted my hands and stood. "I'll just be down by my office if you want to talk some more."

I closed my eyes as he walked away. This time, though, I didn't see spinning earth and sky, I saw the Arrow swerving out of the way of the following grav-shells. Maybe I should focus on the things that I could control.

***

Chapter Thirteen: One Day At A Time

"Ladies and gentlemen," Cadet Commander Mackenzie stood in the doorway of the grav-shell shed, "Plebe Rufus."

He gave a wave to the doorway as Rufus hobbled in, on crutches. He gave everyone a sheepish wave and everyone rose to their feet clapping, me included. It was such a relief to see him that I felt tears welling up in my eyes.

"Hey, everyone," Rufus said. "Thanks for the warm welcome."

"When did you get back?" Salter asked in surprise.

"I got released last night," he cleared his throat, "I've already missed three weeks of class and I'll have five months or so of physical therapy. With all the classes I've missed, I've already started the paperwork for being setback a year."

"Oh, no," I said. I wasn't the only one, either.

"It's fine," Rufus waved one hand. "I'm just happy that I'll be able to come back. It was..." his gaze went distant, "well, let's just say it wasn't looking good, there at first. But I'm coming back. They're assigning me to a different company, Dust, so I won't have to be behind my former section mates. It's good. I'll have a head-start when I come back, now that I know what to expect."

He was so positive, so upbeat about it that I couldn't help it. I walked over and gave him a hug. He patted me awkwardly and I stepped back, feeling suddenly self-conscious. "Sorry," I said. "I'm sorry that--"

"Not your fault, Biohazard," Rufus gave me a nod. "And trust me, when I get back, I'll want *you* as my coxswain. I saw the videos of the crash, if you hadn't steered us clear, I'd be nothing more than a red smear."

I didn't respond.

"Anyway," Rufus said, looking around at everyone, "I just wanted to drop by and say hello. I'm headed back home today, but I'll be back."

We all clapped for him as he went out, but I felt sad as he left.

"Alright, guys," Mackenzie stepped forward. "Now, I know everyone's been hang-dog over all this. The best way to tackle an event like this is to take it head on, learn from it, and grow. Rufus has the right spirit about it. Now, we have our next race in a week. Dawson's back into it and our newbie, Karmazin, is fitting in well. We're hosting the next race."

I'd talked to Mackenzie and he'd brought Alexander onto the team as a replacement for Rufus. He hadn't seemed all that eager to let him in, but I'd convinced him that having someone that Dawson knew would work towards getting a new partner integrated. And Alexander had caught up quickly. We still had some issues with him not knowing the commands and getting out of synch, but he'd picked everything up pretty quickly.

In the meantime, I'd also obtained permission to take nights to do a self-defense class with Commander Pannja.

Mackenzie looked around at all of us, "That race we host is also parents' day weekend. So not only do we host it, but we're going to have families all over this place. You all know what that means."

"Other cadet's cute sisters!" Someone in the back of the room shouted.

"Cute brothers," Salter grinned. I flushed at that. I really didn't want to think about her dating my little brother. *Thankfully, he's a little young for that.*

"Well, that too," Mackenzie smirked. "But it mostly means being on your best behavior and making us all look good. Because parents like to see sports and if they like to see sports, they'll try to get us more funding, and we're down a grav-shell in case no one else noticed."

I winced at that, but no one shot me any glares. I'd had no idea how expensive a grav-shell was, not until I'd taken a look at the paperwork that Mackenzie had put together to request donations for a new one.

"Now, then," Mackenzie said, "there are a few more admin details related to parent's day. But we can handle that at the First Class level."

I perked up at that. There'd been rumors that our plebe class might get accepted before Parent's Day. That would mean we'd have a few more liberties and I knew I'd certainly be happier talking about the place to my parents and little brother if I was no longer a Plebe. I'd have far more freedom to walk around, I wouldn't have to snap to attention every time a cadet officer walked past… I'd almost be able to act like a normal human again.

Mackenzie didn't drop any more hints though. "We'll need to set up a demonstration for families at the track. Salter, I want you to run that, you're pretty good at handling people. Gallagher, you and Tyson get rowing duty for that, since you're down a coxswain." I saw both of them nod. Their coxswain, a cadet third class, had just failed a series of projects. From what I understood, he'd been told to drop all extracurricular activities until he brought his grades back up.

"Everyone else, plan on doing ferry duties and helping out in general. We'll all be pretty busy with a parade and formation. You know, standard dog and pony show. Remember to smile a lot and all that, right?" We all chuckled at that. One thing that being on this team had taught me was that the upperclassmen were under just as many pressures as us plebes.

Of course, they don't have someone actively trying to kill them...

I had been careful to keep an eye out for Commander Bonnadonna, but I'd only ever seen him in class. Other than some awkward encounters with the overly chatty Commander Scarpitti, I'd not spoken or dealt much with any of my instructors. Even in class, most of them seemed distant and unwilling to discuss anything outside of class.

I wasn't sure what to make of that. I wondered at what kind of discussions happened at their level, at what they saw that we didn't.

Commander Bonnadonna's classes hadn't changed, that I could tell. He still engaged us with discussions that seemed aimed at making us examine our own conclusions. Half the time I came away from class frustrated and annoyed, half the time I came away reconsidering some of my assumptions. It was all the more frustrating for the fact that he seemed to be the only suspect I had as far as who might be after me. Yet he'd not given any indication that he wished me harm, I just found myself uneasy around him.

As we got ready for practice, I just hoped things stayed that way.

***

"Strike hard," Commander "Panda" Pannja snapped at me.

The normally easy-going piloting instructor turned over a new leaf during his self-defense classes.

I stepped forward and attacked my practice partner with as hard a punch as I could muster. Hargrave reacted with the drill we were supposed to be learning and I found myself tasting the practice mat.

"Technique and speed are essential," Pannja said as Hargrave helped me to my feet. "But delivering blows with real force is just as essential. Do not forget, we are here to learn to defend ourselves and to hurt those who would hurt us."

Hargrave drove a fist at my stomach and I caught her wrist, clamped her elbow and rolled her forward. It was still an awkward motion that I had to think my way through, but I was getting better.

We went through a couple more iterations before he called a pause. "Alright, everyone, Commander Scarpitti has agreed to help me teach this next session."

I restrained a groan as the chatty officer stepped into the gym. She'd come by the grav-shell practices a couple times since the crash and she'd told all of us how glad she was that none of us had been seriously injured. The way she went on, though, just left me irritable. Everyone was sorry that it had happened. Everyone was glad that none of us had been killed. I got very sick of hearing that, and she'd repeated the sentiment a lot.

"Commander Scarpitti and I have practiced a lot, so this demonstration is one where we'll be free to use some techniques that I don't want any of you to practice. Some of these, against an untrained opponent, will be lethal. Using them improperly will lead to your own injury. So don't try any of this until I give the go-ahead and walk you through it."

He finished talking and stepped into the sparring ring. So far, I'd done a few rounds of sparring. Most of the time I either felt like I flailed blindly or I acted as someone's mobile punching bag.

"Begin," Commander Pannja said.

Commander Scarpitti moved faster than I'd expected. The tall, blonde woman lashed out with a kick and followed that up with a series of punches, all of them at full force and speed. Commander Pannja sidestepped and brought his knee up into her midriff. As she bent forward, he started to bring his elbow down in a strike towards the back of her head, but she turned to the side and he missed.

Faster than I could follow, she somehow kicked his feet out from under him and then stomped at his face with her heel. He managed to roll to the side and sweep for her feet, but she jumped back. I couldn't believe how fast she moved on her feet for her size.

The two of them went back and forth, now and then a fist or elbow struck flesh with a meaty thunk and one of them would stumble back, but the sparring session didn't slow or stop. It went on for what seemed like forever and I actually began to feel worried as I saw Commander Scarpitti catch Commander Pannja a glancing blow across his jaw. As he stumbled back, he looked dazed, barely able to keep his feet.

She followed that hit up with an elbow that stopped just a few centimeters from his temple. "Match," he groaned as he stepped back and then out of the ring. We all stared at the pair of them, both sporting bruises and a bit of blood running down out of the corner of Commander Pannja's mouth. I glanced at the clock and felt shock as I realized that less than two minutes had passed.

Commander Pannja seemed to need a moment to catch his breath and get his bearings. When he finally spoke, his voice remained unsteady, "That, ladies and gentlemen, is full speed, full contact. As you saw, neither of us had time to consider our moves. And let me assure you, neither of us was going for the quick victory. This was a demonstration, only. Were this real, it would have been two or three such strikes, only."

"Two, in my case," Commander Scarpitti grinned. Her friendly smile seemed off, after what I'd just witnessed. It was like she viewed dealing potentially lethal blows as being equally humorous as teaching us in class.

Commander Pannja gave her a nod of acknowledgement, his expression somber, "She's right. At any time during this demonstration, she could have bested me, and several of her counters would have been lethal had she not pulled the strikes."

"How come she's not teaching the class?" One of the cadets muttered.

"I'm not as good at teaching," Commander Scarpitti smiled. "And I can be a little less patient with new students than Commander Pannja. So unless you'd like to nurse some broken bones, I'd recommend you take his instruction." She said it in such a friendly fashion that the words almost didn't sound like a threat. Yet, for me it was as if she'd pulled off a mask. She had no compunctions about violence. Her friendly, cheerful nature was only one facet of her attitude. I'd missed that, and I wondered what else I'd missed about her.

She was at the grav-shell race, I remembered. It was possible that *she* had been the saboteur. I dismissed the fears, though. I'd accompanied her, I would have noticed if she'd been the one to loosen the bolts... wouldn't I have?

"Now, then," Commander Pannja said, "we'll return to your standard drills. You need to practice them until they become muscle memory. Commander Scarpitti and I will make corrections as necessary."

Hargrave and I went back to our spots and began to practice our take-downs again. I felt slow and useless as I did it. What use was such a thing if everyone here was better at it than me? It seemed as if I were getting worse as I practiced. As Hargrave threw another punch at my midriff, I botched the block and caught the blow right in the sternum. I bent over, coughing and trying to breathe for a moment.

As I straightened, Commander Scarpitti stood over me. "You're off balance, Jiden," she said, her voice gentle. She repositioned my rear foot and then grabbed my shoulders and shifted me backwards slightly. "There, always keep your center. You're low to the ground, which means you have a lower center of gravity. Use that." She stepped back, "Now, try again."

Hargrave punched at me again and this time I blocked and went straight into the take-down. And this time, it worked, it felt like everything flowed together and this time it was Hargrave whose face bounced off the mat. I helped her up and gave Commander Scarpitti a nod, "Thanks, ma'am."

"Of course, Armstrong, keep it up, you'll get better," She nodded at me and turned to the next set of trainees.

We went back to practicing. The shift to my feet and change in my posture helped tremendously, but it didn't stop me from feeling every bruise and ache. I was tired. I was tired of hurting, tired of crawling into my bunk for two to four hours of sleep every night. I was tired of classes, tired of drills.

As Hargrave threw me face forward onto the mat again, some part of me wondered if this was really what I wanted for the rest of my life.

***

"Move, move, move!" a voice bellowed in my ear.

I didn't know who was shouting. I didn't care. I scurried down the trench and into my position, just as explosions began to go off all around us. They were deafeningly loud. Trask had called them "arty-sims" and they gave off ear-rupturing shrieks just before they went off, to simulate inbound fire of some kind.

All of us were in position, though, so none of us were flagged as casualties from the simulated bombardment. A moment later, a group of opposition force emerged from cover and charged our line. I opened up as they passed the engagement marker. My target went down, followed by a second and third, and then, before I knew it, the assault broke off.

"Counter attack!" I heard called out over our fire team net. I was up and over the barricade before I'd really processed the words, running forward, pausing every third step to bring my rifle up and fire at one of the retreating enemy. As we reached the spot they'd retreated to, I heard calls of "LOA," which signaled we'd reached the limit of advance. I stopped running forward, dropping to one knee and then taking cover behind a convenient body.

The "casualty" snored loudly, tranquilized from the training rounds. I almost envied him, but for now I rested my rifle across the unconscious opposition and scanned my sector. A moment later, I heard, "Armstrong, Takenata, search."

I rose up to a crouch and fell in next to Ashiri. We moved from one enemy casualty to the next, checking them for booby-traps and then rolling them over to check for anything of importance. Weapons and equipment we threw to the side, papers and datapads we piled up for retrieval.

"Withdraw," Cadet Third Class Trask ordered over our team net and we all moved back to our positions in the trench. Ashiri and I brought back our cache of items, while Trask threw a smoke grenade on top of the pile of captured weapons to mark them as destroyed.

I took a moment to suck down water and try to replace some of what I'd sweated out in the near-summer heat. *This is the third time today.* This drill, like the last two, had gone smoothly and efficiently. I felt almost like a robot as I carried out my activity. Then again we hadn't messed anything up, so I felt a lot better about myself.

"End exercise!" A voice shouted over the net. "Exercise complete, all cadets report to their ready rooms."

I looked around in surprise. We hadn't had an exercise end before mid-afternoon in weeks, maybe months. Normally, even if *we* did our role well, then we'd remain in place while other teams across the campus went through their drills until they got them right. It wasn't really resting, not in the intense heat, but it was better than going through the drills over and over again until we collapsed.

I stood up from my position, looking out I saw some of the training cadre dragging away the unconscious bodies of our opposition forces. I half expected an order to go assist them, like we'd had to do during other drills, but Trask just waved at us to head back to the ready room.

Sand Dragon's ready room was crowded. This was the first time we'd all been in the room. I saw all the plebes, all the third classmen, second classmen, and even the cadet officers. I was honestly surprised to see *everyone*. *Something is up, normally there'd only be the people under review.*

A moment later, Cadet Commander Givens stepped into the ready room. "Sand Dragon Company, congratulations on completing your drill to standard." She said it in a clipped, professional tone, but then she smiled, "As usual, Sand Dragon never disappoints."

"Hooah!" Cadet Commander Mackenzie grinned, "Thanks, Givens, always good to hear it."

I hadn't realized that Cadet Commander Givens was from Sand Dragon. She adopted a more serious expression. "Now, there's still room for improvement, but I can say with confidence that all of you, plebes included, have reached an acceptable level of training." She nodded at Cadet Commander Mackenzie, "And just so you know, Sand Dragon scored second-highest, overall in this series of drills."

I saw Mackenzie's smile waver a bit at "second." I didn't get that. Second place was still pretty good, in my book. But then again, I wasn't up on all the points ratings. *Is the difference between first and second on one drill that big a deal?*

"Well, thank you Cadet Commander Givens," Mackenzie said formally. "I appreciate the good news. We'll conduct a review and we'll see if we can get better for the next set of drills."

I let out a groan at that and I wasn't the only one. Next weekend was supposed to be Parent's Weekend. *Everyone*'s parents would show up. We'd hoped to have that Saturday to show our families around the grounds and maybe to get off campus with them. I wasn't looking forward to being exhausted, sweaty, and covered in sand instead of hanging out with mom, dad, and Will.

"Now, then," Cadet Commander Mackenzie swept his gaze around the room. "Let's break this exercise down by the numbers..."

***

"I don't see the big deal," I said to Ashiri a few hours later after we finished cleaning our weapons and gear and we both pulled out our datapads to start on homework. It was ridiculously early in the day. In fact, I actually thought I might get to bed not long after sunset. I wasn't even certain I'd be *able* to sleep that early, not anymore, but I wasn't going to complain. "What's wrong with second place?"

"Are you kidding?" Ashiri asked, looking up from her paper.

I gave her a level look. *I'm not stupid, I just apparently don't get the secret undertones for how to get through this place.*

She read my look and rolled her eyes. "Look, Jiden, it goes back to the point system. If we got second place as a company, then as our company commander, *Mackenzie* gets a percentage based off second place. But that means someone *else* got first place."

"Yeah, Tiger Company," I nodded.

"Right, so Cadet Commander Argunpet, gets the bonus points. The company commanders for the other companies may be further behind, outside of direct competition. And remember, not all the companies are in the standard path, Ivy Company is medical track, for instance, so it's not really second place out of twenty, it's more like second place out of ten... which percentage wise would put him in the top twenty percent, not the top ten percent. Mackenzie is on space tactical track, he's *just* under the top ten in his class right now, and seven of *them* are in regimental command slots, so there's no way he's going to even catch them unless he gets a regimental officer slot next semester..."

I shook my head, "Why would he leave Sand Dragon? I mean, he loves it here!" The very idea of Mackenzie leaving our company left me uneasy.

Ashiri gave me a level look. I glared back at her, daring her to say something. I wasn't doing anything inappropriate. It wasn't like he treated me any better or anything. There wasn't a relationship. I just really liked him. I felt a flush climb my cheeks as I realized just how much I'd come to like him. *Stop that*, I told myself, *you do not have a crush on him.*

Fraternization was against the rules. I could be kicked out over it. Worse than that, I didn't want anyone to think that *he* had given me any kind of favoritism. I'd worked hard for everything I'd done. *And yeah, I do kind of melt when he flashes that smile at me.*

"Anyway," Ashiri rolled her eyes, "Regimental Officer positions, especially Regimental *Command* positions give major points, with an overall rating based off performance. Normally the first semester is the easy bet, it's based off improved performance. Second semester is the complex training scenarios, from what Alex heard, some of those exercises are really brutal. So that's a risky proposition. If you get unlucky or if you're not at the top of your game, you can actually lose out pretty bad."

I shook my head, "All of this sounds like gambling. I don't see how it benefits the Militia to have so much determined by luck."

"Luck is a facet of warfare," Ashiri shrugged. "Luck has lost and won as many battles as strategy. Sometimes it's better to be lucky than good." I shrugged. I didn't feel all that lucky. In fact I felt pretty darned unlucky. After all, I had people trying to kill me.

"Anyway, second place in one of the last drills? That's got to hurt, especially since Cadet Commander Argunpet of Dust Company was just ahead of him. That means he's a little further back."

"But what's the difference between ten and eleven?" I shrugged.

"Would *you* want to come in top ten or top twenty?" Ashiri replied.

"Top ten," I responded.

"Exactly," Ashiri nodded. "He's trying to make the cut-off. You have to keep looking the next ladder rung higher, all the time. Sometimes that's just enough to keep the person behind you from taking your spot."

"Seems pretty cutthroat," I said nervously. I could imagine that if someone really wanted to, they could sabotage an event to bring down someone's score. Especially since commanders seemed to have the highest risk.

"It *can* be, but at a certain point, we're all expected to behave appropriately," Ashiri shrugged. "I mean, there's the honor code, there's regulations... and it's not like Mackenzie or any of the others up at that level hate one another. They're just jostling for position, you know?"

I considered it. I tried to think about how I'd feel if Sashi Drien or Bolander were just ahead of me. I couldn't imagine doing that, especially not over something as simple as a class ranking. But what about Bolander? What about Sashi Drien? *Would I trust them not to sabotage me?*

I'd have to watch my back, I supposed. Then again, I had to do that anyway.

***

Chapter Fourteen: It's Good To Get Some Recognition

"Wake up, on your feet!" A voice bellowed, seemingly in my ear.

I rolled out of my bunk, dropping to the floor even as someone bashed two metal trash-can lids together out in the hallway. "Get up, get up, now! Get out here, get out on my line, now!"

I recognized Cadet Salter's voice and for a moment, I felt a trill of fear that I was back in Academy Prep School. I was out and on line, haphazardly dressed, braced at attention. Some of my gear was still damp from cleaning and the awkward weight of my rifle seemed to drag at me even more this morning. The lights were on and I blinked tiredly, trying to figure out if this was some kind of drill or something.

"Plebe Armstrong!" Salter stopped in front of me and leaned over me, "Do you know what day this is?"

By my best guess, it had to be sometime around two in the morning. I'd finished my homework and with the early end to the drill on Saturday, I'd gone to bed around sunset. "Ma'am," I replied, "Uh, Sunday, ma'am?"

"No, Plebe Armstrong!" Salter shouted. Her serious expression faltered, "It's Recognition Day!"

I stared at her, not really understanding for a long moment.

Then Cadet Third Class Trask slammed his metal trashcan lids together just down the hallway. "You heard her, plebes, this is Recognition Day! You survive the day and you'll never be plebes again!"

None of us knew how to respond to that. Before we could come up with anything, they chased us down the corridor and out onto the parade field. All across the space I saw former Cadet Instructors lining plebe sections up into formations. We barely had time to fall in before I saw the Regimental Training Officer stand up on his platform. "Class of Two-Ninety, congratulations! You have finally earned the right to prove yourselves to the rest of the regiment! If you survive today, you will no longer be plebes!"

All this talk of survival had me feeling nervous. I hadn't really heard anything about Recognition Day, not beyond the fact that we'd be Cadets Fourth Class afterward. I wondered just how arduous this was going to be. "Company Training Officers, take charge of your companies!"

Cadet Lieutenant Webster stepped in front of our formation. "Section, left, *face*." He snapped. "Forward, march!" Before I could even get my bearing, he brought us into a run. Our former Cadet Instructors fell in around us, yelling at us to run faster.

I felt disoriented and confused. We ran up the ramp and then out onto the surface. The night was dark, a haze over the stars and we stumbled over the uneven ground. Cadet Lieutenant Webster ran us past our section's fighting positions and then out into the desert. We were running at what amounted to a sprint and I gasped for air as we continued to run.

We came to a broad gully and Cadet Lieutenant Webster stopped us. "Cadet Petty Officer Salter, take charge."

"Yes, sir," She snapped off a salute. She was still smiling. So was Trask, I saw, and behind them I saw Cadet Commander Mackenzie with a broad grin on his face. Cadet Lieutenant Webster stalked away, his expression hard. Apparently he didn't approve of all this, I guess.

"Plebes," Salter snapped, "To get to this point, you have had to work together. Now you have to show us all that you can work together in the future." She gestured at the deep gully, "You have to cross this obstacle, with just the resources behind you. If anyone falls, you have to start over. Other sections are completing their own obstacles and you're on the clock. This is a timed event and it counts towards your rating... is that clear?"

"Ma'am, yes ma'am!" We all shouted.

"See you on the other side," Salter snapped, "Get to it."

***

The tools they gave us were a couple of two and a half meter long metal poles and a meter of thin rope. The rope didn't look strong enough to hold much weight, and the individual poles weren't long enough to reach across the four meter gap.

"Do we jump?" Dawson asked, looking across the gap.

"I can't jump that far," I pointed out.

"We could throw you," Alexander Karmazin grinned.

"Let's save that option, shall we?" I growled.

"Okay," Ashiri held up the poles. "These are thick enough to hold our weight, that's good, right?"

"Let me see that," Josephic said. He took the poles from her and then held them together, overlapping a bit, but extending out to either side. "Tie the rope around this, and it *might* work," he said.

"Better tie that really well," I muttered. I watched as he and Alexander Karmazin tied the poles together, then extended it across the gap. It reached, with a bit on either side of the gully.

"Someone should check it," Dawson said. "Someone light."

Everyone looked at me. "Sure," I said, "Why not?"

"Someone stand by to catch her if she falls," Ashiri snapped.

Yeah, that's going to go well, I thought to myself. Yet I felt a bit of relief as Dawson and Karmazin got on either side of the pole.

I started across, the pole surprisingly steady under my feet. Apparently they'd tied the rope better than I'd feared. I wobbled a bit near the middle, but then I found my balance again and covered the rest of the distance. "It works," I couldn't help but laugh in relief.

We worked the rest of the section across as quickly as we could. The gap was just short enough that we could reach out and help balance people across most of the distance, other than the very center gap. Karmazin was the last one across and we fell in to formation in front of a sour-faced Cadet Lieutenant Webster. "Left, *face*," he snapped, then he ran us on to the next obstacle.

The next event was a shooting event. We all had to take a shot at targets at different ranges. Between Mikuluk, Karmazin, and I, we picked people for each of the shots. We all had our full combat loads, but we all winced at the couple shots that missed. Somehow I had the feeling we'd need all the ammo we'd brought.

After that they ran us over to a large metal frame. Up close we could see a laser net running through the frame. "This," Cadet Third Class Trask said, adopting a smug smile, "is a laser net trap. Your goal is to get your entire group through the gaps. However, once you pass through a gap, the net will shift to close that gap. There are only twenty-one gaps. If anyone interrupts a laser, then you all fail this event."

I felt my stomach sink as I looked at it. There were some big gaps along the bottom, but there were also some smaller gaps near the top, including one well out of easy reach... and we had no tools to use. "Sir," I asked impulsively, "will a gap close if we pass our gear through it?"

Trask's eyes narrowed. "No, Plebe Armstrong, so long as no part of your body passes through, the gap won't consider the passage of equipment as counting towards a person."

"Drop gear," I snapped to the others. Without our body armor and weapons, we'd be able to fit through those gaps much easier. I pointed at a narrow gap near the bottom, "Ashiri, you go through that and we'll pass our gear through to you through one of the other gaps."

"Roger," she nodded. We moved as quickly as we could. For the medium height gaps, we braced one another and acted as ramps and stools. I tried to keep the biggest and lowest gaps for Dawson and Karmazin, as the two biggest guys in our section, but we were rapidly running out of gaps. In the end, there were only three left.

I stared at the gap at the top, then looked over at Karmazin and Dawson. I sighed, "You're going to have to throw me."

Dawson gave me a goofy grin, "You sure?"

"No," I said, "but it's probably our best bet." I nodded at the others on the other side, "Please ty to catch me, okay?"

I saw Josephic and Mikuluk move opposite us. Dawson and Karmazin caught me under my arms and at my knees. I closed my eyes as they swung me back and forth for a minute. "Ready, Biohazard?" Dawson asked.

"Just do it," I snapped.

I opened my eyes as they threw me upwards and forwards. For a moment, I thought they'd thrown me *too* hard, as the top bar of the frame came at me, but then I was diving through the gap, headfirst. I sucked in my stomach and tried to roll through... and the tips of my boots just barely passed over the top of the beam. I'd made it.

They caught me on the other side, though I managed to elbow Mikuluk in the face in the process.

We assembled on the far side and Lieutenant Webster looked positively disgusted with us. He ran us through the next three obstacles, seeming to grow more and more angry as we went on. I didn't know what we'd done to irritate him.

We did another shooting event, then a buddy carry where I ended up having to carry Dawson for fifty meters. Here and there we came to an obstacle where another section was still at work, and Cadet Lieutenant Webster would run us in circles while we waited for them to pass or fail. It went on, and on, one obstacle after another after another until they all blurred together.

The sun was just starting to come up when he led us to a halt in front of a tall sloped wall. The entire surface was covered in thick, slippery mud, and it was at a steep enough angle that I hated to even think of trying to climb it.

"Plebes," Webster snapped, "This is the final obstacle between you and Recognition! When you get to the top of that wall, you will have earned your place in the Regiment. You have shown the ability to learn, to be a part of the Cadet Reserve Regiment. All you have to do is reach the top."

He gave us a nasty smile, "Of course, anyone who doesn't reach the top is a washout. You give up, you go home." He waved behind us, "Here comes Ogre Section. You better get moving, you're still on the clock."

He stepped out of the way and we ran at the wall. Even before I reached it, I found myself slipping and stumbling. I slid into the wall and scrabbled at it, barely finding purchase. It wasn't working, if anything, my tired arms were working against me, and I found myself sliding backwards on the slight slope at the base of the wall.

"We have to work together," I shouted. I pushed and shoved at my squad and I saw Karmazin and Mikuluk doing the same. "Form up," I shouted. We leaned on each other and one by one, we started climbing over each other... but it still wasn't enough. I grunted in pain as someone's boot drove into my eye. I gasped in pain as Ashiri climbed over my back... but we were still too short. "First Squad," I gasped, "Climb us, Third Squad, brace us."

I felt a pair of hands brace me in place and then more hands and feet on my back. Someone stepped on my head and nearly drove me to my knees. Sweat and mud stung my eyes and it was everything I could do not to collapse... but then I heard a shout as someone reached the top.

"Third squad," I gasped, "Climb, first squad, pull."

I slipped and nearly fell as Third Squad climbed across my back. Yet our human pyramid had reached the top, and they were pulling us up as much as the people climbing us were pushing us down. It was painful and I felt like I'd been beaten with a stick, but soon enough, Third Squad was at the top.

It was our turn, now, and they leaned over, forming a human chain to help pull us up. I pushed Ashiri ahead of me and I was the last one, my feet finding no real purchase, my legs feeling like rubber and my arms aching, and my hands barely able to hold on.

They pulled me over the top and I lay there gasping, too tired to move, too tired to think.

"Congratulations," Cadet Lieutenant Webster said, "you're at the top. Head down to the finish line and you're done. You can go back, shower, and change."

Behind me, I heard Ogre grunting and shouting as they tried to climb the wall. I could picture Sashi pawing at the wall below me, stuck under the weight of Bolander or Thorpe. I could picture Bolander's face peeled back in anger, anger that we'd finished ahead of her, anger that Sand Dragon had done better than Ogre.

I saw a few of my section headed down the stairs. I didn't say anything, I just stood up and leaned over the wall. Just below me, I saw someone reaching upwards, face covered in mud and sweat, just a grimacing set of teeth and eyes. I reached out and caught the outstretched hand.

The weight nearly pulled me over the side, but I braced my feet. A moment later, Ashiri reached down next to me and caught the plebe's other hand. Someone started climbing up the woman's back. A moment later, all the other Sand Dragons were reaching over the side, pulling up Ogre's plebes.

I half expected to hear Cadet Lieutenant Webster shout at us, but as I had a moment to catch my breath, I saw him off to the side, watching us with a calm expression, arms crossed as he considered us. After what seemed like an eternity, the last of the Ogres had climbed up the human chain and Ashiri and I scrambled to pull the last over the top. The three of us collapsed in a pile on the far side, just as the sun rose over the horizon, shining on us.

I recognized Bolander, then. She stared at me, looking miserable under the caked mud, her hair wild. I didn't want to think about what I looked like. "Thanks," she growled.

"Yeah," I said back to her. I didn't know what else to say.

I heard shouts and grunts on the far side of the wall. Someone else had arrived, it seemed. Despite my exhaustion, despite my aching body, I found myself laughing. To my surprise, Bolander started laughing, too.

"Should we help them?" Bolander asked as she stumbled to her feet.

"Might as well," I said. She gave me a hand up and we went to work.

***

A couple of hours later, assembled as a mass formation, we stood on the parade ground, dripping mud, aching, sweaty, and utterly exhausted. We had started the recognition run as separate sections. We had finished it as a group. One, long, staggering chain of muddy, dirty figures.

I didn't know if our feeling of unity would remain. I didn't know if Bolander would try to pummel me the next time we ran across each other. I didn't know if Sashi would try to stab me in the back. I didn't really care. We had finished together and it gave me a feeling of exhilaration.

"Class of Two-Ninety!" The Regimental Training Officer snapped. "Congratulations!"

Behind his platform, the rest of the regiment had formed up. They watched us, their expressions stern. I wondered what they thought of the muddy, bedraggled group that stood in front of them.

"Raise your right hand, and repeat after me," Cadet Commander Trindale snapped. "I, state your name..."

"I," I said, "Jiden Armstrong, do solemnly swear that I will support and defend Century Colony against all enemies, foreign and domestic, that I will uphold the Colonial Charter, that I will bear true allegiance to the Colonial Charter and the Colony of Century." I repeated the words, feeling a weight settle on my shoulders as I said them.

"Class of Two-Ninety, you are hereby recognized as Cadets Fourth Class, with all the rights, duties, and obligations thereof... *WELCOME TO THE REGIMENT!*" The entire regiment shouted the last words with him, rocking us all back on our heels.

"Dismissed!" He called out.

We fell out of formation. Cadets came forward, shaking our hands in congratulations, offering towels, slapping us on the shoulders. Cadet Commander Mackenzie waved two of Sand

Dragon Company forward armed with hoses and they rinsed us down as we formed up outside the barracks. The cold water was a shock, but it was the only way to get the caked mud off our skin, clothes, and hair.

I looked back, over at where Ogre's newly minted Fourth Classmen were receiving the same treatment. I saw Bollander and Thorpe, at the center of their group, laughing and talking together. Bolander caught my eye and she gave me a slight nod. It wasn't much. It might not even mean anything... but then again, it might mean everything.

Off to the side, I saw Sashi Drien. Cold and miserable, looking like a drowned rat, her hair hanging down in her face. I couldn't find it in me to hate her, not with how miserable she looked. If anything, I pitied her. She'd betrayed me... and it didn't look like it had made her life any better as a result. *If she's willing to give up our feud, like Bolander seems to be, then so am I.*

***

I was cleaned up in time for chapel services and feeling a little lost. So much had changed in the past few hours and I didn't really know what to do with myself. The other cadets of Sand Dragon had been downright friendly to all of us. Cadet Lieutenant Webster was the only exception, of course. He still kept aloof and he looked as if he'd swallowed a lemon.

He'd ran us through a quick briefing after we had time to clean up. We still were the lowest ranking cadets at the Academy. We still had to clean the bathrooms and common areas. We still had inspections. We still had far more restrictions than the other cadets. But we had far more freedom than we'd ever had before. It felt strange to walk around the campus without having to run and to not always feel like I had to watch over my shoulder.

The chapel was mostly empty. It seemed as if most people were getting some rest. I'd come out of habit. There wasn't any training to avoid, it was simply a quiet place for me to think.

The Chaplain went through his service and I listened with half an ear as he talked about the importance of coming together, of putting aside differences. I wondered if he was talking about the plebe class in general, about us being recognized, or if it were something aimed a bit more personally at me. *Nah,* I thought, *he probably has no idea about my troubles.*

The unspoken truce between Sand Dragon and Ogre seemed to be holding. I had no idea whether it would last or not. While I didn't really hate them, I still didn't understand why they'd focused on me, which left me nervous that they might do so again. I'd have to keep up with my martial arts training, I figured.

I wondered if Sashi Drien would continue her grudge against me. Part of me hoped that she did. At least then I knew one person who was out to get me. The real threat, the person who'd tried to kill me, I didn't have a face, a name... I had nothing to go on besides the suspicion that it was someone who wore the same uniform as me.

That realization hit me hard. That was where my uncertainty came from. This felt like another betrayal. I had counted on Champion Enterprises and I'd been betrayed by Tony and Tony's father Isaac Champion. I'd decided to join the military and now someone from the military was trying to kill me, presumably over what had happened at Champion Enterprises.

As the services wrapped up, I found myself wondering about that. If I survived, if I did find out who'd been trying to kill me, could I leave it behind? Could I trust the military after someone betrayed that trust?

***

Chapter Fifteen: Family is the Worst

The next week seemed to fly by. Family day was on the following Saturday after Recognition. I had exams in all of my classes that week, we had a formal inspection of our dress uniforms and rooms that Friday, and I had to go through an interview board for being a Cadet Instructor.

I managed to do well in my exams and the inspection was almost routine at this point. The Cadet Instructor selection board left me shaking and trembling mess of nerves. I couldn't even say why. They asked me questions about myself, what I wanted to do, what I would do in complicated situations. It wasn't much different from some of the questions I'd gone through as a server for the Regimental Staff or that I'd dealt with from Cadet Instructors. Somehow it felt far worse and I left feeling sweaty and barely made it back to my room before I collapsed.

We did a formal parade, all of us marching in formation with the rest of our company. I felt proud, finally wearing the shoulder patch for the company on my uniform. I felt even prouder when they released us and my parents came up and gave me a hug. Of course, mom ruined that.

"You look almost like a real soldier," she said.

"Militia," I corrected automatically, "and I *am* in the Militia, I'm a Cadet Fourth Class, and--" I saw her face tense. I remembered how she'd lost her father when she was only a child. It wasn't worth the fight. "Nevermind."

"Well," Dad said, "you look good."

"Thanks dad," I replied. I looked over at Will, who looked like his head was on a swivel, trying to take everything in at once. He'd be fourteen next year, graduated with his classes... *He's going to apply.* Somehow, I knew it. He'd attend the Academy Prep School and then he'd go on to the Academy afterward.

I didn't know if my parents realized it yet or not.

Thinking about Will going through what I had gave me mixed feelings. If he did, then I'd do my best to get him ready for it. I didn't want him to go into it blind, like I had. I felt oddly protective of him... yet at the same time, I knew he'd be capable of doing it. *He'll probably do better than me,* I thought.

"So," I said, "want me to give you the full tour?"

"Sure," Dad said. Will nodded eagerly, while Mom just sort of looked around, her pinch-faced expression in full force. *She hates it here.*

"Where would you like to start?" I asked. "There's a grav-shell demonstration that we're doing for families later this afternoon, but we could try the firing range or the obstacle course..." Mom's expression grew more strained as I went on "... or how about my room or the chapel?"

"The chapel sounds good," Dad said with a smile.

I led them that way. Unfortunately, it seemed like everyone else had the same idea. The main corridors headed towards the chapel were jammed and unlike the cadets, most of the parents and family didn't move with any sense of urgency.

I paused, trying to get my bearings. There was a longer route using some of the side corridors, but I couldn't see over the crowd to judge whether we'd missed it or not.

"This way, right?" My mom nodded towards a gap in the crowd. I followed her and only after we started down the right corridor did I pause to wonder how she'd known. *Maybe it was luck,* I told myself.

We made good time, taking the side corridors and I pointed out some of the art that my section had done, our contribution to the murals on the walls. None from me, of course. I didn't have an artistic bone in my body, but I did point out one that Mikuluk and Phillips had done for our section. Most of the murals on this level were memorials to ships or units lost in combat.

My mom, though, paused in front of one I hadn't pointed out.

I recognized it instantly. It was the same one that had struck me during Academy Prep School. It was probably the best painted of the murals. The details were amazing, almost life-like. It depicted a ship, damaged beyond saving and falling into the atmosphere, but the crew remained at their posts, continuing to fire their weapons, the surface of Century far below them.

They were dying to save the planet that was going to kill them, and like every time I'd seen it, I felt a chill go over me. My maternal grandfather, the Admiral's husband, had been Captain of that ship, the *Comet*. His name was at the top of the crew roster painted below the mural. *Captain Brett Armstrong.*

My mom's father. I pulled my eyes away from the mural and saw her standing there, her eyes filled with tears. I didn't want to understand her. She was my mother. I much preferred thinking that she acted to spite me, rather than realizing that she didn't have things as together as I'd wish.

"That's your father's ship?" My dad asked, his voice low.

"Yes," My mom's voice startled me. It was controlled, hard. It sounded like the Admiral's voice. She straightened and gave us all a smile. I knew it had to be fake, but it shocked me that she donned the expression so easily.

I led the way onwards and we managed to beat the crowd to the Academy's chapel. I pointed out the heavy blast doors as we went through, "These are doors from the *Liberty,* she was destroyed in the Three Day War."

"Century's first cruiser, yes," My mom said quietly.

I shot her a glance, but she ignored me and so I just led the way on. I pointed out the stained glass windows, backlit by artificial light, then we managed to squeeze out the side door just as the crowd arrived. My dad puffed a bit as we closed the door behind us. When I gave him a look, he shook his head, "You kind of forget what the crowds are like, back at Black Mesa. It's a bit overwhelming."

I couldn't argue with that. Black Mesa had all of thirty adults in the coolest parts of the year, and during the summer that number dropped to about fifteen. It was the closest permanent settlement to the equator on the planet, so it wasn't anything resembling comforting. The closest that we ever came to a crowd down there was when everyone showed up to an event.

I led the way back through the corridors to the barracks area. My mom raised an eyebrow as we went up the stairs. "Sand Dragon?"

"Yeah..." I frowned, "How did you know?"

She didn't answer. I was starting to get a weird vibe about all of this, almost like my mom could have run the tour. But she'd never served a day in the militia. She barely talked about her mother, the Admiral, and never talked about her father.

I found Ashiri Takenata and her family just coming out of our room. It was a bit daunting, because first there was Ashiri, then her parents, and then what seemed like a constant stream of younger and older siblings. *How did they all fit in there*, I wondered. It wasn't like our room was that big...

"Jiden!" Ashiri gushed, "Mother, father, this is my roommate, Jiden Armstrong!"

"Ah," Ashiri's father gave me a slight bow, "We have heard much about you." He had a pronounced accent, which startled me a bit. It shouldn't have, I supposed. I sort of remembered Ashiri saying that other languages were more common back at Ten Sisters.

"Thank you," I nodded in reply. "Uh, this is my mom and dad, and my brother Will. Mom, Dad, this is my roommate, Ashiri Takenata."

My dad frowned, "I thought I remembered you roomed with some other girl, last year. What was her name? What happened to her?"

My smile grew a little strained. "Uh..." I really didn't want to go into it about what had happened between Sashi Drien and me.

"Drien," Mom said the word like a curse. Like a really bad one, the kind that one just didn't say in polite company. She smiled at Ashiri, then, "It's a pleasure meeting, you and your family, Ashiri."

"We were about to go get lunch, would you like to join us?" Ashiri's mother asked.

I had a flash back to my horrid experience the last time I'd gone out. Before I could decline, though, my parents both agreed. It put my back up, how they assumed that they would make the decisions, how, despite all I'd been through, I was back to being a child. I wanted to speak up and tell them I didn't want to go, but I couldn't in front of Ashiri's family. I didn't want to look bad.

Ashiri gave me a wink and muttered low enough that no one else seemed to hear, "Don't worry, Biohazard, we'll go someplace without spicy food."

That made me feel a bit better, right up until my mom brushed some speck of lint off my shoulder, once again setting the impression that I was a child. Family was the worst.

***

We made it to Bahta Town, taking the train and then emerging into the sunlight and chaos. Ashiri's parents led the way, their parade of children following behind and my parents, Will, and I in the back. My family seemed as overwhelmed as I'd felt on my first visit to Bahta Town.

We wound through the streets and I felt lost after a few minutes, but soon we stepped out of the noise and heat and into a restaurant. I sneezed a bit at the strong smells. This looked like more foreign food. I tried not to wrinkle my nose.

"Ah," Dad said, "*hokkai miso*." To my surprise, he spat out something in a different language at the hostess, who gave him a broad smile and nod in return.

"You speak *hakubu hitora*?" Ashiri's dad asked.

"I did my archeology internship on Ten Sisters," Dad said. "I picked up a bit. Their food is fantastic, I hadn't realized there was one of their restaurants on Century."

"This is the only one outside of New Albion," Ashiri's mother said. She smiled, "My husband used to cook at this one, but now we own our own restaurant at New Albion."

"That's great!" Dad said. "We'll have to come visit sometime! That's really fantastic!"

The three of them began discussing intimate details of the food that I didn't understand, even as they showed us to a long table. I ended up near Ashiri. I leaned in her direction, "What should I order?"

"Tell them number five," Ashiri said back to me. "It's rice with some dumplings. It should be fine to eat in uniform, way less messy than anything else and not spicy at all."

"Thanks," I muttered.

Now that everyone was seated, I was able to tell that Ashiri had five siblings, rather than what had seemed like ten or fifteen. I wasn't sure, but I thought that two of her brothers were older, while both her sisters and her youngest brother looked younger. "This is San and Tinan," Ashiri pointed at her two older brothers. "My sisters, Hiroe and Megu, and my little brother Eiji."

"We're so proud of Ashiri," her mom said, "she's wanted to attend the Academy since we immigrated, but we were so nervous for her, she's always been such a shy thing..."

"Thanks mom," Ashiri said with a tone of resignation.

"Oh, she's really come out of her shell," she replied quickly, "but she *used* to just sit in her room and study and play games all the time. Never any boys around!"

"Mom!" Ashiri protested.

"I'm only saying," her mom waved a hand. "I want grandchildren some day! You know I was already engaged to your father when I was your age, I had half the boys in our neighborhood courting me..."

Ashiri had buried her face in her hands, her ears turning bright red as her mother went on. I looked uncertainly at my parents. My dad had a slightly amused expression, while my mom didn't bother to hide her smile. *They think this is funny...*

Thankfully, food arrived before Ashiri's mother could go for too long. I dug into my food. It was bland, but after my last experience in eating out, I didn't want anything remotely exciting. Bland was good. And since I was wearing my dress uniform, I didn't want to get it dirty, either.

Everyone ate in relative silence, with Ashiri's younger siblings pausing to talk about this or that. They all seemed pretty excited to visit the Academy and it was pretty clear that they all wanted to attend as well. I finished eating quickly and I nodded at Ashiri's older brothers, San and Tinan who had been silent until now. "So," I asked politely, "what are you both up to?"

They looked at each other. "We help father with the restaurant," San said. Like his parents, his accent was noticeably stronger than I'd expected.

"Oh, that's neat," I wasn't really certain how to respond to that. Ashiri had seemed so eager to get out and do things, I was a bit surprised that her brothers weren't.

"In our culture," Ashiri's mother said, "it is typical for the men to stay at home or to work menial jobs, while the women pursue higher education. I've achieved multiple engineering degrees, my daughters will do the same, and my sons will follow in our family's traditions. That's what we are comfortable with."

"What if they want to do something else?" I blurted. Too late, I saw Ashiri shake her head in warning. Apparently this wasn't a good topic for dinner.

Ashiri's mother gave me a smile, "Jiden, they wouldn't want things differently. This is our family, our culture. We are perfectly content."

I glanced at San and Tinan, whose expressions were hard to read. Were they really happy waiting tables or cooking in their father's restaurant while their little sister went to the Century

Military Academy? I looked at Ashiri's youngest brother, Eiji. From the way he looked at the floor, I didn't think he was exactly excited to look forward to a career of working in the restaurant.

Ashiri gave me another warning look. She wanted me to leave it be. But it struck me as unfair. I didn't want to leave it be. "Well, what if Eiji wants something different?" I asked. "I mean, my brother will attend the Academy, what makes your son any less capable?"

Ashiri's mother's face went hard. Before she could open her mouth, though, my mom spoke up. "Jiden, don't say such things! Will just finished his work study with Nelson's University. You don't have any plans to go here, right?"

Will shot me an angry look and I realized that I probably should have kept my mouth shut. "Mom, I meant to talk to you about it..."

I saw Mom's eyes widen and she started to get that angry look on her face, the one that meant I'd really screwed up. I saw my dad put his hand on her shoulder and she pinched her lips together. She wasn't going to make a scene, not here, but...

I'd managed to ruin dinner. Ashiri's parents didn't talk for the rest of the meal. My dad made some small talk about the food. My mom looked like she wanted to scream. Will wanted to kill me for outing him. Ashiri looked like she wanted to crawl under the table.

Family is the worst.

***

We made our way back through Bahta Town and then down to the underground train station. It was nice to get out of the heat, but I felt like a child again as my mom played her silent game and my dad tried to smooth things over with Ashiri's parents. He managed to get them talking and laughing again. I wish I had a way with people like he did. I just seemed to mess things up.

Ashiri moved to stand next to me and I whispered at her, "Sorry, I shouldn't have opened my mouth."

She shrugged slightly, "It's not your fault. Family... what can you say, right?"

We stood in silence, waiting for the train. Just down the platform I saw another group of parents and cadets come down the stairs. The first thing I noticed was my mom's posture shift. She went from quietly angry to something entirely different. It was like her entire body shifted, to something predatory and watchful. She also moved over to stand between Will and I and the other group.

It was almost like she was a mother predator defending her young from another predator. The way she moved, the quiet, utter focus on her face made me drop into a defensive stance, without even realizing it.

I looked past her and felt a bit of a shock as I recognized Sashi Drien, in her cadet uniform. Then I realized who the other two cadets next to her must be. They were similarly short, and their features were so similar to Sashi's that they could only be her brothers. The man standing next to them wore an officer's uniform, and he could only be their father.

Next to him was another officer, slightly taller, with white hair and olive skin. Even from a distance I could see the stars on the shoulder boards of his dress uniform. A half dozen more men in uniform stood behind him, all of them talking and smiling, their features all so similar that they were clearly related. This was Sashi Drien's family.

Admiral Drien, I realized, *the man that didn't help the Admiral... the man she blames for her husband's death.* From the way my mom stood, clearly she placed some of the blame upon him as well... or else she just didn't trust him.

I saw Admiral Drien's expression harden as he looked past my mother and saw me. The group with him seemed to notice that change in expression and their laughter and chatter stilled, too. Admiral Drien stepped forward, standing between his family and my mother. The entire platform dropped into an awkward silence. Technically, I suppose I was supposed to greet him or something, but I kept quiet.

My eyes went from Admiral Drien to Sashi's two older brothers. The eldest wore second class rank and the younger wore third class rank. Both of them had Ogre patches on their shoulders. They both had confident smirks on their faces. They knew that they had nothing to fear. They had eight commissioned officers present to back them. Me, I had my mom and dad. I didn't even count Ashiri's family, they had no part in this.

I looked at Sashi Drien, expecting a similar smug expression... and then I realized that she stood off to the side, trying to draw as little attention as possible. She was the only woman in the group. I remembered, then, what she'd said about her family, how she was the only woman who'd ever tried to join. I noticed how she stood at the edge of the group. In fact, her grandfather stood between my mother and his grandsons... but not in front of Sashi.

She's only barely tolerated, I realized. In fact, her expression was one I recognized. She was miserable and trying to hide it. I thought about how badly my lunch had gone with my parents, how I'd managed to put my foot in my mouth, to annoy Ashiri Takenata's parents, and even to ruin dinner, but my mom still stood in front of me when she saw a threat.

Sashi's grandfather didn't do the same for her. I saw the same realization on her face, too. Worse, she wasn't surprised by it. She *expected* it. I saw her hunch her shoulders and she met my eyes, her expression miserable.

I had half an impulse to call to her, to tell her to keep her chin up, that her dad and grandfather were jerks. But before I could work up the courage, the train came, the roar of it making normal conversation impossible. As the doors to our car opened, I trailed behind the others, watching Sashi, wondering if maybe I'd misjudged her. Maybe I should have tried to understand her a bit more.

The last look I got as I stepped aboard the train was of her being the last one to board in the car, her older brothers gestured ahead of her. She met my eyes as we both boarded the train, her dark eyes suddenly angry as my mom put her hand on my shoulder.

But that anger wasn't about me... it was about her. *Family is the worst.*

***

As we made our way back to the upper levels of the Academy, the Admiral found us.

"Joy," she nodded at my mom, "Steven," she nodded at my father. "I try to make time to talk with many of the parents this weekend, especially of our younger students. Do you have time to meet with me in my office?"

I felt suddenly nervous. I tried to think of anything I might have done wrong. Anything outside of the disaster at lunch, anyway.

"Yes, we have some time, I think," Mom glanced at Dad, who gave a nod.

"Excellent," the Admiral said. She led the way through the corridors to her offices. I nodded politely at the yeoman outside who pretty much ignored me as I'd expected. Inside the Admiral's office, Mom and Dad took the two available seats. I stood. I felt uncomfortable and finally went to a sort of parade rest. Will walked over and looked at some of the awards on the walls.

"So, I wanted to tell you both that Jiden is doing well, very well at her classes and acceptable at everything else," the Admiral said. Mom's mother had a detached tone to her voice, as if she were reciting something she'd rehearsed. "She's received a good rating from her superiors and I think she's fitting in well, here."

"Really, that's all you can say?" Mom snapped. I suddenly wanted to melt into the wall. I knew mom was already riled up, the last thing I wanted was to be in the middle of a fight between her and the Admiral. No matter how it went, I knew it wouldn't end well for me. "You dragooned my daughter into the military and--"

"You came to me," the Admiral snapped back. "You are the one who asked for *my* help. And believe me, without the skills she learned here, you two would have had to bury her. Those skills saved her life--"

"She shouldn't have even *gone* to that stupid internship—"

"Ladies," Dad said, "Sorry, but perhaps we should all be adults?" He jerked his head in my direction and then over at where Will stood, holding some kind of trophy, staring at all of us.

Mom and the Admiral both pursed their lips. It was bizarre how similar their expressions were. "Yes," the Admiral nodded. She let out a tense breath, "We should. I'm sorry."

My mom looked far less willing to let things go, but she moderated her tone into something a few levels below full meltdown, at least, "I'm not happy about the situation. I know that coming here was Jiden's choice," she looked back at me, and for a moment, her expression slipped and I saw real concern, not just anger, but worry. "But I don't think she fully understands the situation."

"You can't protect her for the rest of her life, Joy," the Admiral's voice was almost gentle.

My mom glared at the Admiral, "I can be there for her when I can. And I don't think you've done a very good job of protecting her. *You* are the one who put her in a room with Toshi Drien's granddaughter."

The Admiral's expression slipped a bit, "I didn't arrange the rooms. The Cadet Instructors select those, you know that."

"You may not have set it up, but you didn't stop it," Mom snapped. "I came here, I know that every decision cadets make come under a molecular microscope, every detail of this place gets back to you..."

"Wait," I blurted, "You came here? You came to the Academy?"

My mom froze, her mouth dropping open and she stared at me. I saw my dad staring at her too, like he was waiting for her to go on. *He knew,* I realized, *but he never told me either.*

That didn't make any sense. My parents had graduated from Nelson's University with degrees in Archeology. They'd met in my dad's sophomore year, my mom had changed degrees from art to archeology after they'd fallen in love... I knew that. That was the story they'd told Will and I since we were born.

"Your mother attended Academy Prep School and completed her Fourth Class Year," the Admiral said, her voice detached. "When the time came to start her Third Class Year, and enter her contract with the service obligation, she resigned and transferred to Nelson's University."

"What?" I looked between her and Mom. "You *lied* to me?"

Mom's lips pinched together. "I didn't lie. Well, I didn't lie *much.* I transferred to Nelson's University to pursue a degree in art, a few weeks after I did so, I met your father and then I transferred degrees to archeology."

My knees felt weak and I swayed a bit. My parents had lied to me. They'd never lied to me. The one time I'd ever did the slightest deceitful act, they'd shipped me off to the Admiral over it.

"I did it to protect you... to protect *both* of you," Mom looked between Will and I. "Look, Jiden, this all may seem like fun and games to you, but this is deadly serious. I didn't want either of you coming here because I didn't want you hurt."

"What are you talking about?" Will asked.

The Admiral spoke, "While your mother was here, there was an... incident. Several cadets were injured. Your mother was nearly killed. A combat skimmer crashed. The official investigation ruled it was pilot error."

"Someone ordered the pilot to fly lower than the minimum safe altitude in a sandstorm, I heard it and I remember it, even if no one else had the guts to speak up. It was Toshi Drien and you know it."

"The investigation was inconclusive and no communications records survived the crash," the Admiral replied. "And while I believe you, that isn't enough for a court of law. Especially not to overturn an official crash investigation findings."

"Wait, Admiral Drien tried to kill my mom?" My hands clenched into fists. I'd known about the grudge over the Three Day War, but this was something else entirely...

"Don't go out and pick a fight just yet, girl," the Admiral cautioned. She shot my mom a look, "She's a hot-head, just like you, Joy."

"I wonder where they get that from," I heard Dad mutter.

All three of us glared at him and he just raised his hands, "What, did someone say something?" Behind him, I heard Will snort with laughter.

"The situation is complicated," the Admiral went on after a moment. "And circumstances have changed here since your attendance. I'm the superintendent here now, for one thing. Admiral Drien's family doesn't have the connections they once had here. I'm taking precautions and I am protecting your daughter, even if some of those protections aren't immediately visible."

"Someone shot her out of the sky earlier, then there was this grav-shell crash," my mom snapped. "Are you saying that you know the Driens aren't behind that?"

The Admiral looked uncomfortable. "Joy, you're asking about an ongoing military investigation. I'm not authorized to discuss details to a civilian."

"This is my daughter, your granddaughter," Mom hissed. "Tell me."

The Admiral glared around the room. "None of this leaves this room, am I understood?" We all nodded. Even Will looked somber. "The investigators believe this is tied to the smuggling ring that your daughter uncovered. They think that her attacker is a military officer who facilitated things from within the Militia. This attacker is either out for revenge or worried that she might be able to identify him somehow."

"Can you?" Mom asked of me.

"I would if I could," I said. "Three attempts on my life is more than enough for me, thanks."

"Three?" Mom asked.

"There was an... incident with a burst pipe," the Admiral shot me a look. "Any sign of sabotage is inconclusive."

I kept my mouth shut. I wasn't going to dig my hole any deeper. Besides, I was still trying to come to terms with the fact that Mom had attended the Academy. It made sense, what with how she'd known her way around and all, but still...

I tried to picture her in the khaki uniform and I just kept drawing a blank.

"I don't like this. I think it's best for her to resign," Mom said.

"I'm *not* quitting," I snapped.

"It's not worth your life!" My mom snapped in reply. "You don't understand, Jiden, the people that hate our family, they're willing to stab you in the back while they smile at you..."

The Admiral's expression shifted, ever so slightly, "Joy, Jiden is not you and Sashi Drien is not Jotaro Drien."

"What?" I asked.

"Your mother was... close to Jotaro Drien," The Admiral said.

"We are *not* talking about this right now!" Mom interrupted. I had no idea what *that* was about, but I definitely had no desire to ask. "Look, Jiden, I really think its best that you resign. Let all this blow over. I know you seem to enjoy all this, but there's other things you can be doing! It doesn't have to be archeology, it could be engineering, science, whatever you want!"

I swallowed. I hated to hear my mom plead like that. I hated how she was so worried about me. I wished I had a way to explain it to her, how I felt like I had to be here, that there wasn't any other place that I *could* be... this was a calling, not a choice. "Mom," I said, "I can't leave. This is what I need to be doing."

Mom looked over at Will, then back at me, "Think about your brother. He thinks this is cool, he doesn't understand the stakes..."

Low blow, Mom, I winced. I thought about the attempts on my life, about how I'd had to kill to protect myself, about the sick feeling I had when I thought about it and the flashbacks I had to the crash. I thought about Will going through that. I opened my mouth, not really sure what I was going to say.

"It's my choice, Mom," Will said. "And, sorry, but this is what I want to do, too."

I'd never felt so proud of my brother in my life. I couldn't help it, I walked over and gave him a hug. Before I knew it, my Dad was hugging me too.

Mom stared at the three of us and then she said, "Fine." She seemed to wilt a bit, then, and before I knew it, she came over and hugged the three of us too. "And I'm proud of you. Both of you. I just... *God* I wish there was some way to protect you from all this.... that's half of why I never told you any of it. I thought that if you didn't know..."

I thought about how ignorant I'd been back at Academy Prep School. I thought about how everyone else had seemed to know all the details about my family's feud with the Driens... and how powerless and confused I'd been. My mom had done that to me by not telling me the truth. She'd done it to protect me, but it had only hurt me.

I wished she'd told me the truth.

I looked up and saw the Admiral staring at the four of us. For just a moment, her expression was unguarded. There was sadness on her face. Sadness for what she had lost. *She's buried her husband and her son,* I thought, thinking of my uncle and aunt who'd died offworld in some kind of terrorist attack. *She's barely on speaking terms with her daughter.*

"Promise me that you'll take care of yourself, Jiden," My mom murmured, squeezing me tight.

"I promise, Mom," I responded, squeezing her back. Maybe family wasn't so bad.

***

Chapter Sixteen: Saying Goodbye Is Hard

After Parent's Weekend, it seemed like the rest of the semester flew past.

We had a few more big exercise events, one of which went the entire weekend. We had finals, and then everyone was rushing to get ready for the summer. With Academy Prep School going on during the summer, there weren't standard classes for the rest of us. Each class had separate duties. First Classmen, the seniors, went out on their five month tours with the Militia. Some of them went to ground forces, some to space, either to reserve or active Militia units. Since many of the Militia units conducted their big training exercises in the heat of the summer, there were lots of units for them to join.

A handful also went offworld, mostly on exchanges with the Star Guard or one of our allies. A handful elsewhere, and it was quite the event when the seniors got the news.

"Hanet!" Someone came down the hall shouting. "I got Hanet!"

I popped my head out in the hallway. I wasn't the only one, there were quite a few people gathered in the corridor. I saw Alexander Karmazin smile, "Congratulations, sir, what ship?"

"The *Victory*," Cadet Commander Mackenzie grinned. "I'm *so* excited. I've got to leave in six hours to make all my connections. I should be packing, but..."

Salter came running down the corridor, "I heard you got Hanet, that's awesome!"

"What do they mean?" I asked Ashiri.

"He's going to the mercenary company," she replied. "They're technically Militia ships, operating under charter, and their crews are all reservists."

"What?" I asked, "That's crazy..." I didn't know much about the Hanet Mercenary Guild, but I'd just sort of assumed they were all no-neck thug types. I certainly hadn't imagined that they were part of our Militia. "Why's that?"

Apparently I'd spoken louder than I'd realized. "Cadet Fourth Class Armstrong," Mackenzie grinned, "Don't worry, you aren't the only one who doesn't understand."

Salter grinned, "Our mercenary company is a sort of open

secret. Lots of Planetary Militias do it, it's a way to offset the cost of our forces and get additional combat experience for our people... without fighting a costly war at home."

"Oh," I said. It still seemed crazy. Fighting and dying for money, rather than to protect our nation, our people. Evidently my expression showed my opinion of that.

"Look, Armstrong," Cadet Commander Mackenzie said, "we've got a huge amount of ships and equipment, far bigger than most Planetary Militias do, right?"

I nodded. I'd picked that up when I'd been doing one of Commander Bonnadonna's research papers. Century stood out for that, most single planet star systems maintained far smaller forces.

"Well, keeping them maintained and especially keeping them stocked with antimatter is expensive. We produce it on our own, but it's *still* massively expensive. Most of the income from our mercenary company goes to offsetting that cost. All the rest goes to buying the Militia more ships. So it's not like we're doing it just for the money. We're doing it for the experience and to keep the lights on."

I nodded in response. It made some sense, but it still struck me as an odd way of doing business. Then again, it wasn't like it was up to me.

"You'd better get packing, sir," Alexander Karmazin said.

"Yeah, I know," Mackenzie adopted a goofy grin, "but *Hanet*. This is going to be great!"

He walked off down the hall and the crowd cleared out. "That's a good sign," Karmazin said in a low voice to Ashiri and I. "They only ever send ten cadets to Hanet, at the very most."

"That's good," I said. I had no doubt that Mackenzie was going to do well. I worried about him a bit, going that far away from Century, but he was so confident that I couldn't help but think he'd do great.

"Cadets," another voice snapped out as we stood there. We all turned and found Cadet Lieutenant Webster standing there. "Fall in."

All of us lined up. He wore a sour expression, like someone who'd just received terrible news. "I've got my orders, I'll be staying on as Sand Dragon's Cadet Training Officer through the summer. Which means that I'll be working with those of you who stay on as

Cadet Instructors. I'll be helping to select those who get such important responsibilities," he said. "Those who I help to select will end up working closely with myself and the Senior Cadet Instructor. We'll be setting the conditions for next year's Plebe Class, and I promise all of you, I won't be selecting any who don't meet my exacting standards, am I clear?"

"Yes, sir!" We snapped back. *Great,* I thought, *no way am I going to be a Cadet Instructor.* Webster was the most distant of all the senior cadets in Sand Dragon, he barely seemed to tolerate any of us, and with me...

He walked down the line and paused in front of me. "Some of you," he said, shooting me a look of distaste, "Aren't going to meet those standards. Don't worry, if you've applied to be a Cadet Instructor and you aren't selected, there are plenty of other assignments for the summer semester. You are dismissed, fall out and good luck on your summer assignments."

As our formation dissolved, I felt a mix of disappointment and relief at his words. On the one hand, I'd wanted to see if I *could* do a good job as a Cadet Instructor. On the other hand... at least I wouldn't have to deal with Webster. Five months more with him sounded about as miserable as could be. I couldn't help but wish Mackenzie was the one who'd been selected for Cadet Training Officer for Sand Dragon. I'd bet he would have selected me... and I wouldn't have minded spending five months working closely with him.

But Mackenzie is going to Hanet. He'd be going to our mercenary unit. He might be going into combat... and he might very well die. I could never see him again.

I felt a chill go over my body. I looked at my friends, "I'll be right back," I said.

I hurried down the hallway and found myself outside of Cadet Commander Mackenzie's quarters. As the company commander for Sand Dragon, he had a bit more space than the rest of us: he warranted his own room. He'd always had an open door policy and like usual, his door was open. His back was turned, though, as he was seated, cleaning and packing his gear on a folding table beside his bed. I hesitated, wanting nothing more than to run away, but instead I knocked on the door frame.

"Yes?" Mackenzie spun his chair around, his expression

distracted. "Oh, hey Armstrong, what's up?"

"May I come in, sir?" I asked, still hesitating at the door.

He gave me an amused smile, "Of course, what's up?"

I took a hesitant step inside. I hadn't been in his room before. I'd tried to avoid being called in here for any kind of disciplinary reasons and I hadn't felt I needed to talk to him in any kind of official setting before. We'd interacted on the grav-shell team so much that I guess I'd just felt that I could talk to him there.

"Headed out soon, sir?" I asked.

"Yeah, I need to start getting packed," he sounded the slightest bit impatient.

Seated, he was still tall enough that he was eye level on me. "Well, I just wanted to wish you good luck, sir," I said. Before he could respond, I crossed the two meters between us and kissed him on the lips. It was sudden, it was impulsive, and as he went still, I regretted it instantly.

I pulled back, my face flushing, feeling so embarrassed that I didn't know what to do or say. I backed away, and then, as he opened his mouth to speak, I turned and rushed out. I found myself running down the hallway and I took the stairs down to the lower level and just started running.

I'm such an idiot, I told myself. What I'd done was stupid. It was more than stupid, it could get me in trouble for fraternization and it could get me expelled. Worse than that, it could get *Mackenzie* in trouble for the same reason.

I didn't know what else to do, so I found a quiet section of corridor, far from everyone else and put my head against the wall. The cool surface of the bricks burned against the heat of my face. I wanted nothing so much as to melt into the wall, to forget I existed, to disappear.

How could I have been so stupid?"

***

I finally managed to get up the courage to return to my room later that night.

To my surprise, no one seemed to be looking for me. There wasn't any messages on my datapad, no instructions to report to the Admiral's offices, and Ashiri didn't even look up from her datapad as I came back inside. "Hey, Jiden."

"Hey," I forced myself to sound as natural as I could. "Did I miss anything?"

"Not really," she said, "lots of people shipping out to their summer assignments. Cadet Commander Mackenzie was only the first, the upperclassmen rooms are all pretty much empty. Word is that we'll get our assignments tonight..." She trailed off and I heard her datapad and mine both pinged at the same time.

She pulled up the message first and gave a whoop, "Yes! Cadet Instructor School selection, *with* Sand Dragon as the assigned company after completion!"

I scrolled through my message, feeling a goofy grin go across my face, "Me too!" I had no idea *why* I'd been selected. I had assumed that Webster hated me enough that I wouldn't make it, but it seemed I'd assumed incorrectly.

"Guys!" Alexander Karmazin stuck his head in the room, "I just got my assignment orders! Sand Dragon Cadet Instructor!"

"This is great!" I gushed. All my worries from before were forgotten.... but now I had a whole new set of worries. Would I do a good job? Would I succeed?

"Ash," Karmazin grinned, "this is going to be awesome. We should call my mom and give her the news."

"Yeah, I bet she'll be really excited..." Ashiri looked at me, "Uh, Jiden, if you want to stay..."

I found myself flushing. They wanted time alone together, I realized that quickly. "No, no, I'm good. Uh, you guys have fun..."

I found myself in the hallway, and I couldn't help but watch as the two of them moved close together, peering over their datapads as they talked. I envied them that... and no matter how much I told myself that it wasn't any of my business.

I moved down the corridor to the common area and pulled out my datapad. Maybe some kind of gaming or something would settle my nerves.

"Hey Armstrong," I heard a female voice behind me. I turned quickly, and recognized Cadet Second Class Salter. The big woman gave me a smile, "I heard you're one of the Cadet Instructors selected for Sand Dragon."

I nodded nervously, "Yes, ma'am."

"Well, *I'm* glad to hear they took my recommendation," she replied. "Especially since they selected *me* for Senior Cadet

Instructor for Sand Dragon."

I smiled in reply, "Congratulations, ma'am."

"From what I hear, I'll have you, Takenata, Dawson, and Karmazin, plus some others from outside the company," she replied.

I frowned at that, "Why outsiders, ma'am?"

She shrugged, "They like to keep us from getting too insular, I guess. Sometimes it helps identify plebes who need a different approach, sometimes it doesn't work out so well."

"Like Hilton?" I asked on impulse.

Her eyes went narrow and I saw anger flash across her face. "Yeah... though I wouldn't normally talk about that, since he was senior to you, you should know some of the details since you'll be a Cadet Instructor." She shook her head, "Definitely don't mention him or Rakewood, too much. The pair of them were pretty much nuked out of this school." She shook her head, "Bad enough that he got Peterson injured, but that he and Rakewood were dating before, during, and after..." She shook her head. "Huge abuse of power and then an honor code violation on top of that..."

"What happened to them?" I asked, flashing back to my encounter with Mackenzie. *It's not the same,* I told myself. *I kissed him,* I reminded myself, *I shouldn't have done that.*

"Well, Rakewood got offered an administrative recycle, she may actually come back in this prep school class... though I doubt she'll show," Salter said. "Hilton had a full administrative review and a discharge for conduct unbecoming. If Peterson had been hurt more seriously, then he could have faced jail time."

I felt a bit sick as I remembered the sound of Peterson's arms breaking as he fell from the obstacle. I didn't know how I felt about the punishments, but the last thing I wanted to do was encounter Rakewood again.

"Well, I'm going to go check in with the others, see you later, Armstrong," Salter said.

I was left staring at my datapad, feeling more than a little nervous. I was about to be in charge of training the next class of Sand Dragon. *I really hope I don't screw up...*

***

"Welcome, ladies and gentlemen, to your first day of Cadet Instructor School," Commander Bonnadonna's deep voice greeted us only a few days later. I hadn't realized that he would be one of the overall trainers. I felt a pit in my stomach as I stood in formation in front of him.

I was still certain that he was the one trying to kill me. It made me feel a bit better to see Commander Pannja and Commander Scarpitti standing behind him. At least there were other officers present.

I couldn't help a glance down the line at where the Ogre Cadet Instructors stood in the formation. Bolander, Thorpe, and Drien were there, along with a few more that I recognized but couldn't name. I just hoped I wouldn't have to deal with them.

"Now, some of you may look back at your time during Indoctrination with something less than enthusiasm," Commander Bonnadonna smiled. "Some of you may ask yourselves whether you should be nicer than your Cadet Instructors. Some of you may even tell yourselves that you should help your candidates in small ways, to make their experience easier. After all, this whole experience is a shock, there's no need to cross the boundary into cruelty for cruelty's sake."

Despite myself, I found myself nodding. I wasn't the only one, there were quite a few of us nodding at his words.

"Think about this, however... One day, these candidates, like all of you here, may find themselves in combat. They may face an enemy who will stop at nothing to kill them. An enemy where they may be the only obstacle in the path of slaughtering innocent civilians. Do you think they will thank you, then, for being less harsh than their enemies? Do you think they will look back at their indoctrination and be glad that it wasn't so harsh?" Commander Bonnadonna said the words in a thoughtful tone. "For that matter... how would you feel to learn that the men and women you trained failed in their charge? To learn that pirates, slavers, or a Culmor extermination force breached their defenses and civilians paid the price?"

My stomach sank. I thought about having to defend myself in the wreckage of the crashed skimmer. I thought about how easy it would have been to give up. Would I still be alive if I hadn't been put through the ringer as a candidate? I couldn't answer that question... but I could see Commander Bonnadonna's logic.

"Indoctrination and the rest of the Academy Prep School is

hard in order to challenge our cadet candidates. It is difficult so that they will handle combat better, when they are faced with it. The harshness, the stress, we do this to make them stronger, not to break them," Commander Bonnadonna waved at the two officers who stood behind him. "Commander Pannja and myself have both seen combat. Commander Scarpitti has worked search and rescue operations after a pirate attack. We know the value of intense training. The Senior Petty Officers and Sergeants First Class who stand behind you are here to act as your advisers. We want you to succeed, just as you want your candidates to succeed. Take heed, learn from us, do the best job that you can do... and never forget that everything we do is to produce the finest officers for the Century Planetary Militia."

He stepped back and Commander Pannja stepped forward, "Drill NCO's," he barked. "Show them how it's done!"

Before I knew what was happening, forty or more shouting men and women piled into the formation. They seemed to be everywhere, shouting at us, screaming in my ears, in my face. For one surreal moment, I thought that the past year had been some weird nightmare and I was back in Indoctrination on my first days as a candidate.

The feeling passed and I found myself reacting far more calmly than I could have on that first day. They formed us into smaller formations and bodily moved us where they wanted, but I simply rolled with it. I didn't feel the fear, the terror, that I'd once felt. I knew the purpose, I knew the intent.

Before it went on more than a few minutes, they put us at ease. A moment later, I recognized Senior Petty Officer Kennedy at the front of our formation. "Cadet Instructors," he growled, "What we just went through is a basic sorting technique. You've experienced it before, during your first day. We'll put you through it again and again... and then you all will take turns doing it to each other. The task is to move your people where they need to be in the most efficient manner possible while impressing upon them the importance of doing things properly."

He gave us all a cold smile, "Understood?"

"Yes, Senior Petty Officer!" We all barked in response.

"Excellent... *Now get on your faces and push!*" He screamed at us. We rushed to obey going through pushup as he and the other

Drill NCO's screamed at us. It was surreal, again, at how it both unnerved me and yet felt like the most natural thing in the world. *There's something wrong with me.*

"On your feet," Senior Petty Officer Kennedy snapped. As we quickly rose, he put us at ease again. "There's a method to the madness," he said calmly. "Your candidates need to come to fear you. Not because you enjoy it. In fact, if you *do* come to enjoy it too much, then you're doing it wrong. No, they need to fear you so that they pay attention to everything you do, everything you say. That attention to detail should cover every aspect of their lives. We are shaping them, molding them. We're taking young kids and we're turning them into killers."

I shivered at his words. I was a killer. I knew that far more clearly than I had any purpose knowing at my age. Kennedy went on, "...it's for the good of our world, for the good of the boys and girls you'll be training. But make no bones about it, it's an ugly business."

"We'll rehearse commands and the methods of instruction. Dawson, Regan, Connors, and Karmazin, out front and center."

The four of them rushed out. "You five will be the Instructors. Get them formed up over there," Kennedy waved at an empty patch of desert sand. "Execute."

The next few days were more than a little crazy. One minute I'd have someone screaming orders in my face and the next I'd be in front of a formation doing the same thing. I lost my voice after a couple of hours. We practiced giving orders, we practiced demonstrating drill moves and exercises. We did a lot of running. I'd been working out on my own, but that wasn't nearly enough preparation. We had to be able to run our candidates into the ground. We had to be stronger, faster, and better in every way.

It led to some of the most ridiculous interactions I'd ever had in my life. At one point, I found myself screeching at Karmazin's chest while he tried to keep a serious expression... the next I was standing on his back while he did pushups and I shouted at the formation, "Who else thinks this is funny, huh?"

I think we all went a little insane. And then, as the course wrapped up, we had to get everything ready for our candidate's arrival. We'd already moved out of our old rooms. It was eerie to move one level upwards. I knew it was only temporary, that we'd move back downstairs when Academy Prep School wrapped up. But it was still strange to be living in the upperclassmen's rooms.

They were surprisingly similar. In fact, they were laid out the same way: a set of bunks, two desks, a sink, a pair of wardrobes, all in the same layout. But I still felt strange to be there.

Sand Dragons' Cadet Instructors gathered in the common area to plan. There was a lot to setup. "We assign their bus seats?" I asked, thinking back to how I'd been partnered up with Sashi Drien from the very beginning.

"Yes, indeed," Salter grinned. "A little tip, putting the bigger and slower ones at the front of the bus is great for getting them bottlenecked at getting off the bus. It puts them in a panicked mindset from the first go."

"Huh," Ashiri muttered. "I didn't remember that."

I shot her a look. *I* certainly remembered the experience. I'd nearly been trampled. In fact, if not for Alexander Karmazin, I might have been injured. He'd helped me off the ground... of course, at the time I hadn't been very grateful. "Isn't it a bit dangerous?" I asked.

"We can monitor the flow, generally we put one person at the bus doors and two of us get at the back of the bus. If there's any issues, we stop them and fix it." She shot me a look and seemed to read my dubious expression. "*Hilton* was assigned to the doors for Sand Dragons' bus, last year."

"Hilton?" Regan asked. The red-haired cadet from Dust Company raised an eyebrow.

"Admin discharge for misconduct," Salter replied.

"Ah," Regan nodded. He and Connors glanced at each other, then he spoke, "Just so you all know, we're not Sand Dragon, but we're still going to do our best. You won't have any complaints about us. I sure wouldn't want to make Biohazard angry, after all."

I gave him a smile in reply. He'd been nice to me since the story had gotten out. It looked like we would have more time to get to know one another.

"Okay," Salter rolled her eyes, "Back to business. Most of these are easy enough to match up, the system makes recommendations based off their psych-evals. But some of them are going to be tricky... and then there's the late additions."

I didn't have to ask about that. I'd been a last-minute

addition. So had Karmazin. "When do those come through?" I asked.

"As late as one of them getting on the bus," Salter frowned. "But we should be able to match up most of them. Any last minute adds we can sort out at that point."

Sashi Drien had hinted that last minute additions were the rare exception. I wasn't exactly sure why… but I had the feeling that Sand Dragon received those kinds of candidates. *Flexible, that's what we're supposed to be…*

As I looked at my datapad, I wondered if we had anywhere near enough time to get everything ready. I'd celebrated my birthday only a few days before. I was fifteen years old… some part of me insisted that I should have had a party, some kind of celebration. Instead, Ashiri had woken me up early and given me a present, a hologram of me as coxswain in a grav-shell race that her older brother had done up a in a fancy frame. Alexander had clapped me on the shoulder and said happy birthday with one of his rare smiles. My parents had sent me a gift card and my grandmother had sent cookies, which I'd shared out among the other Cadet Instructors in my group. Some part of me felt a little cheated. *I'll do something special next year, maybe, when there's more time,* I told myself.

Salter went on, "Karmazin and Takenata, I want you two—"

"Senior Cadet Instructor Salter," Webster stepped into the room, interrupting her and ignoring the rest of us. "Have you got the room lists complete, yet?"

I didn't miss a flash of anger on Salter's face. "No, Cadet Lieutenant Webster, I haven't. I was going through the details with my Cadet Instructors, *sir.*"

He looked around at us, impatiently. "Well, get me your draft list, soon. I've got to vet it and make sure we don't have any mistakes, not like last year."

Salter's expression went hard, "Sir, normally final room arrangements are left at the Cadet Instructor level."

"Not this year," Cadet Lieutenant Webster waved a hand. "Now, I'll be in my office, bring it by in a couple hours." He turned and left the room. No one spoke for a long moment.

Salter let out a tense breath. "Alright, I guess we need to knock it out now." I was surprised she didn't say anything more about Webster's behavior. Then again, she was in charge of us, she shouldn't talk bad about *her* boss to her subordinates. It startled me a bit how quickly I realized that.

We worked out the room plan and Salter passed me the draft sheet. "Take that to the Company Training Officer, would you, Armstrong?"

"Aye, aye," I replied. I couldn't entirely hide my lack of enthusiasm, but she didn't call me on it. I headed down the hall and paused outside of what had been the company commander's office. The door was closed and I felt oddly disconcerted by that. The door had almost always been open when it was Mackenzie's room.

I rapped on it, "Sir, Cadet Instructor Armstrong, reporting with the room assignments."

A moment later, Webster pulled open the door. He glared at me and I passed over the papers. He scowled down at the hand-written names. "What?" he demanded. "This isn't even typed up."

I fought down a spike of anger. "Sir, you said you wanted it as soon as possible."

He scowled at me and stepped back from the doorway. Webster pointed at the chair in front of his desk, "Sit there. Type it up and give it to me in a useful format."

"Sir," I didn't trust myself to say more than that. I took a seat and I couldn't help a flashback to the last time I'd been in this room. Apparently it wasn't good luck for me to be here.

I'd rather be kissing Mackenzie than sharing a desk with Webster, a rebellious thought popped up in my head.

Webster went back to work on his datapad. I couldn't help but sneak glances at him, wondering what he was doing. I thought I caught glimpses of some kind of maze or structure of some kind, but it was hard to tell from my angle. It looked oddly familiar, but I wasn't sure how.

I typed up the rooms and names and forwarded them to him quickly enough. "All done, sir."

He looked up from his datapad, "Right, hold on." He toggled his desk display and the image of the maze appeared again for a moment. He scowled at me as I stared at it and then quickly swiped it over to the room list. He scrolled through it quickly, pausing to look at a couple names. "You put Beckman and Shade in the same room?"

"Yes, sir, is that an issue?" I asked. I'd actually made the decision. Beckman didn't come from a military family while Shade had an older brother who had graduated last year. I'd been thinking of how Sashi Drien had helped me.

"Just an interesting decision," he said after a long moment. When I didn't respond, he went on, "Candidate Kate Beckman is the niece of Charterer Theresa Beckman. Who isn't a big fan of the Planetary Militia. In fact, she was the deciding vote that prevented Candidate Alethea Shade's father from promotion to Rear-Admiral."

I put that together after a moment, "They won't get along."

"They might not. But maybe Beckman isn't her aunt and Shade isn't her father," Webster shrugged. "Also, neither of them are quite as... volatile a combination as an Armstrong and a Drien." There was a tone of bitterness in his voice. Something flashed across his face then and he shot me a look, like he realized he'd said too much.

"Fine," he said, "we'll try it. Tell Salter that I appreciate the good work."

"Yes, sir," I replied, standing quickly. As I stepped out, I saw him switch the display back over to the maze. He saw me staring at it and jerked his head at me in dismissal before closing the door.

What was that about? I wondered. Still, I didn't have any more time to think about it, there was plenty more to do before the candidates showed up.

***

Chapter Seventeen: Through The Looking Glass

"Get on your feet, get moving!" I screamed as loudly as I could. "Move, move, move!"

Candidates scurried ahead of me, rushing off the bus in a fashion that would have almost been funny... except for the fact that they were all terrified. I didn't have time to think as I shouted, screamed, and pushed at them. Ashiri was next to me in the narrow confines of the bus. I saw Regan at the base of the stairs, shoving candidates on, preventing any kinds of accidents like the one that had nearly trampled me.

Looking good so far... I squashed the thought and continued moving candidates off the bus.

Within a few minutes, we had them formed up, more or less, in what someone might generously call a formation. I found myself bellowing in the ear of a young woman as I caught her scratching her face, "Candidate, who told you to move? Did I tell you to move, did I? The only things you're allowed to do are breathe, blink, and respond, do you understand?!"

"Uh, yeah," she replied.

"The proper response is 'Ma'am, yes, ma'am,' and you will respond as such!" I screamed.

"Uh..."

I got the wayward cadet candidate doing pushups, then ended up putting them all to doing pushups. A minute later, Salter signaled me and I had them all on their feet. The sudden reprieve and the lack of screaming left them all still and paying attention. Despite my misgivings, I couldn't help but agree with what Commander Bonnadonna had told us. *He's right,* I realized, *we're making them pay attention and learn in the most efficient and direct manner possible.*

"Hello Candidates," Salter said, her voice relaxed, her expression calm. "I am Senior Cadet Instructor Sara Salter. I'm in charge of your section. Now that Cadet Instructors Armstrong, Karmazin, and Takenata have put you in some semblance of a formation, we'll have a quick chat." She gave what some of the candidates might mistakenly interpret as a friendly smile. I saw some of them respond. *You poor, dumb fools,* I thought to myself.

"You are now part of Sand Dragon Section. If anyone asks your unit, you will respond Sand Dragon Section. You are here for a variety of reasons. My job, and the jobs of the Cadet Instructors you see here plus some more that you'll meet soon enough, is to turn you into cadet candidates. Right now, you're just candidates. We have very little time to do it. Century's Planetary Militia does not need individuals incapable of following orders... right Candidate Michaels?"

"Uh, yeah," he replied.

"The correct response, is 'Yes, Senior Cadet Instructor Salter,' and if that's the correct answer, then *why are you not following orders!?*" Even I winced as Salter bellowed the last words into the hapless candidate's ear. "All of you, we're going to practice following orders. Get on your faces, we're going to do *pushups...*"

The first day of indoctrination had started. It was going to be a long day, for some more than others.

***

"They all look so young," I muttered to Ashiri as the candidates stood in line for their medical screenings. We had a bit of a break as they went through. I'd drank two liters of water so far as the day went on, but I'd already started to lose my voice. Apparently, my voice breaking as I screamed at them was still frightening enough, however.

"Yeah," she shook her head. "But a couple of them are older than us."

I shot her a look. I didn't believe it. I mean, I'd just turned fifteen, but still... I checked on my datapad. Sure enough, our oldest candidate was eighteen. I found myself shaking my head. I picked him out. Candidate Green was a big, dark-skinned young man. He was three years older than me, but he still had an earnest, nervous expression on his face. They all had that same expression, like they would do anything they were asked.

Had I looked like that, only a year ago?

We stepped away as the last of the candidates went into their medical screening rooms. "Regan and Dawson have them on the far end, right?" I asked.

"Yeah, we have four hours," she replied.

Since we'd both been up since the previous morning trying to get everything ready, I knew exactly how I intended to spend those four hours. Ashiri seemed to feel the same way. Back at the room, we both shut the door and climbed into our beds, pausing only to pull off our boots. I heard Ashiri start snoring and only a moment later, lulled to sleep by the distant sound of shouting, I fell asleep as well.

***

"Get up, get up, *now!*" I shouted. Beside me, Regan smashed two metal trash can lids together. It was just after four in the morning. We'd let the candidates get back to their rooms around midnight. Sleepy looking candidates stumbled out of their rooms, fumbling with their uniforms. I paused in front of one candidate who'd managed to pull on both his shorts and shirt on backwards. "What's your name, candidate?"

"Ma'am," he stuttered, "Candidate Hall, ma'am."

"No you aren't," I snapped. "Because you are backwards, candidate. Your name is Llah, do you understand?!" I shouted at him. Really, I shouted it at his chest, he stood at least twenty centimeters taller than me, but he still rocked back.

"Ma'am, yes, ma'am!" he shouted in reply.

"Get back in your room and fix yourself!" I shouted.

I heard someone give a nervous giggle and I spun. I found myself glaring at a pair of young women, both of them with trimmed-short hair. One blonde and the other dark-haired. "Candidate Beckman, do you find something funny?"

Her expression went worried, "Ma'am, no, ma'am."

"What about you, Candidate Shade?" I snapped.

"Ma'am, no, ma'am," Shade snapped back.

"We wouldn't want Candidate Llah to think we're laughing at him!" Regan bellowed from down the corridor. "Candidates, get in the front leaning rest. You will now do the pushup, to *my* cadence. Repeat after me," he started doing pushups, "We're waiting on you! We're waiting on you!"

The candidates shouted the cadence back as they did pushups. I honestly felt kind of sick. It felt mean, and petty, and cruel...

Hall stumbled out of his room, properly dressed and joined them at their pushups. I would be willing to bet he wouldn't make that mistake again. "Candidates, on your feet!" Regan shouted. "We will now commence room inspections!"

I started at one end and he started on the other. We worked our way down the corridor, flipping rooms. Here and there someone had done somewhat of a good job of putting things in the appropriate places. Green and his roommate were the closest to right... but we still destroyed it, spilling drawers and dumping their clothing in a pile. It wasn't fair, it wasn't nice. It was to impress on them the importance of attention to detail. Everything was going smoothly until we got to Beckman and Shade's room.

I paused as I saw the neat, perfectly done rack, the boots and uniforms aligned, the shirts folded properly. Everything was perfect... in exactly half of the room. The other half was haphazardly stacked, the bed not made. One of the candidates knew what to do, the other clearly didn't.

"Candidate Shade," I said in a calm voice. "Is that your gear properly stowed?"

"Ma'am, yes, ma'am!" She snapped.

"Candidate Beckman, your half of the room failed inspection," I said calmly. I could see her expression tighten. She knew what was coming. "Candidate Shade, because you didn't help your roommate, you *also* failed the inspection."

I turned around and started to destroy their room.

"Ma'am," Candidate Beckman blurted, "that's not fair!"

I froze. Before I could even begin to come up with a response to that, Regan was there. "Candidate Beckman, who asked your opinion?! Get on your face. *Everyone* get on your faces!"

I finished tearing the room apart and stepped out into the hallway. I felt sick to my stomach. I knew it wasn't fair. This wasn't about fair. This was about doing what had to be done.

That didn't make me feel any better as I did it.

***

"Armstrong, how you doing?" Salter asked me later that day.

I shrugged, "Okay, I guess." Oddly, we'd dropped most of the formalities at this point. The Cadet Instructors were a team. Just among ourselves, we didn't have time for ranks and titles, it was about getting the job done. That didn't mean I didn't respect her, it just meant we were both far too tired to go through all the formalities.

"Look, I know it takes it out of you," Salter said. "I've been through the same thing. I hated being a petty tyrant to your class, believe it or not."

I shot her a surprised look.

"Don't get me wrong, there were times it could be fun," Salter admitted, "but this first few days is going to be rough. They don't understand. They're tired, they're afraid, they're just kids..." Salter snorted, "*we're* just kids for that matter. But we've got to set them up for success...and that means we have to pretend to be monsters to prepare them for *real* monsters. You know that... you know that better than most."

I nodded. It came back to my experience. I'd had to fight for my life for real. How could I do less than my best effort, even if it did tear me up inside to do it?

"We're meeting to select squad leaders," Salter said. "Dawson put them on cleaning detail. Do a walk-through on your way down, okay?"

"Yeah, no problem," I replied.

I went downstairs and then walked slowly through the candidate barracks. All of them were so focused that they didn't seem to notice me as I walked slowly, quietly down the corridor. I listened to them talking and working, here and there I heard snippets of them talking, mostly helping one another out... some of them more friendly about it than others. "Flores, you idiot, I swear if you screw up our room inspection tomorrow, I'm going to murder you..."

The next room, the conversations were even more amusing. "I think Karmazin is the scariest one," Micheals said softy.

"No way," his roommate muttered, "It's Armstrong. She comes at you out of nowhere, I don't even see her coming and then she's screaming in my ear…" I filed that interaction away and kept walking.

"I can't believe how unfair they are," Beckman was muttering to Shade. "Especially Armstrong..."

I paused outside their door and listened. "It's just the way it is," Shade replied. "Look, they're doing all this for a reason. Go along with it, okay? If you start making trouble, it's going to make things worse."

"Worse?" Beckman hissed, "How could this get any worse?

This sucks. I wish I hadn't come here."

"This is nothing," Shade replied. "Wait until we get to the Grinder. Look, just follow my lead, okay? Keep your mouth shut. We'll get through this just fine."

I flashed back on my interactions with Sashi Drien and I couldn't help but empathize with Candidate Beckman. She was in an unfamiliar situation. She didn't know what was going on... and her roommate was the only support she had. In fact, her situation mirrored mine more than I cared to consider.

I walked on and arrived at Cadet Lieutenant Webster's room. He'd positioned a few chairs in front of his desk, but there was only so much room. I ended up standing near the doorway. I realized now how I'd been able to overhear the Cadet Instructors talking during my indoctrination. There wasn't room for eight people in the room, not without leaving the door open.

"Took you long enough, Armstrong," Webster scowled at me.

"Sorry, sir," I replied, "I took a walk through to check on the candidates."

"Oh, right, good idea," he waved a hand. "Any issues?"

"Green doesn't seem to like his roommate Flores," I said.

"Big shocker," Dawson shook his head. "I wouldn't bet on Flores lasting the week."

I didn't argue. It still shocked me how ill-prepared some candidates were. I had hardly been a stellar example, I knew. I'd had no idea what I was getting into, but most candidates really wanted to be here. They really wanted to join the Militia. *Maybe they just can't handle the stress...*

"Beckman was complaining again," I noted.

"She's going to be trouble," Salter nodded. "There's one in every class."

"Going to be worse with her political connections," Webster scowled. "I've already received a message from her aunt asking why she hasn't heard anything from her niece since her arrival."

"What?" I asked in surprise. The candidates weren't allowed communications outside until the end of the first week, and that was just a form letter where we basically dictated to them what they were allowed to send. Their families were notified by the Academy that communications would be limited. I didn't think it should even be possible for someone to find out who was in charge of their family member and then to message them directly.

Webster shot me a look, "This doesn't leave the room, understand?"

"Of course," I replied. The other Cadet Instructors nodded as well.

"Commander Scarpitti notified me that Charterer Beckman has been requesting additional civilian oversight over the Militia. She implied that the presence of her niece might be tied to that."

"*What?*" Salter demanded. "You think the Admiral would allow..."

"I don't know *what* to think," Webster snapped back. "We're just cadets. This is echelons so far above us that I don't even want to consider it. But Commander Scarpitti told me to keep an eye on Candidate Beckman and to make sure that she's not given treatment any different from the other candidates... and not given any grounds for a legitimate complaint."

The room went so quiet that you could have heard a grain of sand hit the floor.

"Now," Webster said, "Who do you recommend for squad leaders?"

"Green," Dawson said instantly, "He's a bit older than the others. His maturity is making him a bit of a leader already."

"Agreed," Salter nodded.

"Who else?" Webster asked, writing down Green's name.

"Hunt?" Andrews asked. Andrews was from Tiger Company, our other contribution from outside like Kyle Regan from Dust Company. "He's handling the stress well, he's pretty good at following orders."

I shifted uncomfortably. Webster noticed and looked at me. "Armstrong?"

"He's not a good fit for a squad leader in Sand Dragon, sir," I said. "He doesn't have much initiative." Hunt rather reminded me of Dawson, actually. He was capable and quick-learning, but he didn't think outside the box and he didn't seem to have the initiative to ride herd on his fellow candidates. Not that I disliked Dawson, but he hadn't been a squad leader in Sand Dragon either.

"Agreed," Webster nodded. "Who do you recommend?"

I felt sweat break out on my forehead as everyone stared at

me. I almost suggested Beckman, with how she reminded me of myself. I opened my mouth to say that. Instead I heard myself say, "Shade. She's smart, she's picking this all up quickly, and she's looking out for her roommate."

"Good point," Salter nodded.

Webster nodded. "Fine. We need a third squad leader."

"Wallace," Alexander Karmazin said. "He's a bit stand-offish, but I think if he's put in a position of responsibility then he'll step up."

"Sounds good," Webster said after a moment. I saw him adopt a distracted expression I'd come to recognize, he was receiving a call on his implant. Whatever it was, he scowled. "Okay, apparently Commander Scarpitti needs me to address something. Senior Cadet Instructor Salter, please get me a finalized list of squads. I have to deal with this... you're dismissed."

We left. Karmazin and Dawson headed straight for the candidates and I heard them start bellowing orders a second later. Kyle Regan paused and yawned, looking at me. "How you holding up?"

Neither of us had time before now to say more than a couple words to each other. "I'm doing well. How're you doing?"

"More tired than I've been since... well, since the Grinder," He winced, "I'm *really* not looking forward to that."

"Yeah," I said. Supposedly we'd have a lot more visibility out there. Regan, Dawson, and I would head out two days early to familiarize ourselves with the way things worked out there and set everything up. But we'd have to be monitoring three separate squads of candidates, plus the locations of individuals across the massive training area.

"You see that they already have rankings posted?"

"No, I hadn't," I said. That had been the furthest thing from my mind. "How are we doing?"

"Good," he grinned. "Dust is third, we're second, Ogre is out front."

"Ugh," I groaned.

"Yeah," he shook his head. "I think they've got an advantage in that their candidates are all the take-orders types. Dust is too, mind you, but I swear, if someone told an Ogre to jump off a cliff, they'd be halfway to the bottom before they even thought to ask for a parachute."

I snorted at that. "Assuming they didn't push someone else over the side first to break their fall..."

Kyle Regan laughed at that. He had a nice laugh, I noted. "You're not wrong there." He shook his head. "Honestly, I'd thought the Sand Dragons were all just a bunch of sneaky, devious types, until I got to know you."

"Oh?" I couldn't help but return his smile, "What do you think now?"

"You're a perfect example of a Sand Dragon, Biohazard," Kyle winked.

"Spare me my blushes," I grumbled.

He waved a hand, "Just messing with you, Armstrong. But I got to say, you guys spend a lot more time thinking about things. In Dust, we'd pick Hunt, Green, and Wallace in the first couple hours. If one of them didn't work out, we'd cycle someone in their place and keep going. You guys like to do things right the first time."

"Is that a bad thing?" I asked.

"Not at all, it just takes some getting used to. I'm more of the opinion that good enough in time is better than a perfect solution that's *late*, but it isn't like you guys are slow at making a decision, you just spend a few extra seconds thinking about the consequences."

"I didn't realize we were that different," I admitted. I hadn't really dealt with the other companies that much. Well, not besides having Ogre trying to beat up on me. "Maybe we should spend some more time together learning how we think."

I hadn't really thought about what I said until he winked at me, "I'd like that... Jiden."

I suddenly lost any ability to string words together. Thankfully, at that moment I heard the shouting down the corridor redouble and candidates started racing in our direction towards the parade ground. Our break was over. Time to get back to work.

Saved by the candidates, I thought to myself.
***

A couple days later, we'd just finished up our evening run and I was leading the jog down one of the ramps. I'd found I liked running at the front of the formation. I didn't have time to feel tired, if I stumbled, they'd run me over. It kept me moving, even when all I wanted to do was collapse and curl into a ball.

Dawson slowed them to a jog and then a walk. After he walked them for a bit to cool them down, he started leading them through stretching exercises. I saw Salter cock her head, a clear sign she was getting a call on her implant. Normally that would have made me uncomfortable. After the hectic past few days, I could only think of how convenient it would be not to have to have a datapad or comm unit on hand to send messages.

I saw Salter's expression change. Whatever it was, it wasn't good. She waved me over. "Escort Candidate Beckman to the Company Training Officer's quarters and then back here when she's done."

"What's going on?" I asked.

"She has a call she needs to answer," Salter's expression was hard.

Candidates didn't get calls. I knew that. It was Academy policy. They could send messages after they got back from the Grinder. Generally those were monitored. In part it was a security measure, after all, we were a military installation. But mostly it was because candidates were unhappy, we didn't want them sending the wrong impression to their parents, at least, not until they had a chance to adapt to their circumstances.

Beckman's aunt, I realized. I turned to the candidates. "Candidate Beckman, front and center!" I snapped. She bounded up and ran over to me. I saw wariness on her face. "Follow me," I snapped. I led her off at a jog. I could tell she wanted to ask what was going on. Either she'd learned to keep her mouth shut or else she was too short of breath to manage. Just in case, I sped up the pace.

"Sir," I knocked on Webster's door, "Cadet Instructor Armstrong and Candidate Beckman reporting as ordered."

Webster opened the door, behind him, I saw Commander Scarpitti standing next to his desk display, a woman's face on the display next to her. Webster gestured at Beckman to enter and he stood to the side. "Cadet Instructor Armstrong, please standby. We wouldn't want anyone getting the wrong impression." He said it in a cutting fashion, clearly aimed at Beckman, but I got his meaning. Academy policy was that upperclassmen weren't supposed to be alone with candidates in private.

I stepped in the room and left the door open.

"Candidate Beckman, you have a phone call. Against Academy policy, I have been instructed to allow you to take this call. Before you do so, I must instruct you that candidates are not normally authorized to make or receive calls during the Prep Course."

"I would like to speak to my niece in private," the woman on the display snapped.

"Our policy, ma'am," Cadet Lieutenant Webster said, "is that we do not leave a candidate unattended."

The woman's eyes narrowed and she glared at him. Despite the dislike that I'd had for him, I had to admit that he didn't back down. The Charterers were massively powerful. The twelve of them ran most of the planet's government. She had to own or represent at least one twelfth of the planet to have a charter seat. I didn't even want to be in the room... and Webster didn't as much as flinch.

"Fine," Charterer Beckman snapped. "Katherine, dear, how are you doing? Are they treating you well?" Candidate Beckman shot us a look. "Don't worry, you can speak up. If they're treating you unfairly..."

"It's not good, Aunt Theresa," she stumbled over the words. "It's all so hard. And they don't give us the chance to explain things. They're just so mean," she shot me another glance, "especially Cadet Instructor Armstrong..."

My stomach dropped as I listened to her. She rattled off a dozen complaints, everything from the food quality to her treatment. Charterer Beckman, meanwhile, adopted a broader smile as her niece went on. *She wanted this,* I realized. I didn't know why. I didn't see how one girl's complaints would be important, but I didn't need to understand it to know it wouldn't be good.

"Well, Katherine," Charterer Beckman said after a moment. "I'll be sure to place a complaint on your behalf. Believe me, there will be some changes taking place..."

"No," a calm voice interrupted from the doorway, "there will not."

All of us looked over and I did my best to melt into the wall behind me as I recognized the Admiral. She wore a calm expression, but her blue eyes glittered in a dangerous fashion. She stepped forward and stood over the display. I couldn't help but notice that Charterer Beckman seemed to hunch on herself. "Charterer, you're violating Militia and Academy policy by conducting this conversation."

"It's a health and welfare check," Charterer Beckman protested. "I hadn't heard anything from my niece. My sister's family hadn't even received a message--"

"I have a log of receipt, acknowledged by Patricia Beckman, two days ago, for a letter from your niece. Perhaps you should confirm that they hadn't received anything from her?"

Charterer Beckman's expression soured. "That doesn't change the fact that she has legitimate complaints..."

"About food quality and instructors being 'mean' and 'rude' to her, yes," the Admiral said dryly. "I'm sure that all of the other Charterers will be very concerned. They'll have to hold an inquiry about it... whereupon I'll have to show seven direct violations of Militia policy conducted by your office... including a direct call to an officer by a political figure in a fashion that could be construed as conspiracy."

I didn't understand what that meant, but I heard Charterer Beckman hiss in anger. "This isn't one of your games, Admiral. I'll not be threatened..."

"It's not a threat. If you involve yourself any further with *my* Academy, I will request a formal inquiry and I will make certain that all of this is made available to the rest of the Charter Council." The Admiral's face could have been carved from marble. The room seemed to shrink, or maybe she grew, I wasn't sure. It was like she filled the space.

"This isn't over," Charterer Beckman spat. "But I won't press for a formal investigation... at this time. But I will remember this." She cut the call.

"Add it to your list," the Admiral muttered, so low that I barely heard her, even though I was standing almost right next to her. Clearly the two of them had plenty of bad blood. *Good to know,* I thought. Apparently my family had another enemy.

"Candidate Beckman, I believe you need to get back to your section," the Admiral said. She looked at me, "Cadet Instructor Armstrong, please see to it... and Cadet Lieutenant Webster, accompany them and please make certain that Candidate Beckman's complaints are made known to her Cadet Instructors. I'm certain they'll want to address them."

I didn't miss how Beckman's shoulders hunched. Her litany of complaints had just backfired rather badly. I no longer felt any sympathy for her. Part of me hoped that she'd quit.

I started for the door. Behind me I heard the Admiral say, "Commander Scarpitti... a word, if you would. Please join me in my office."

I would have wanted to be a fly on the wall for that conversation. I didn't know how things had unfolded, or who had given the order for Webster to send for Beckman... but part of me wondered if Commander Scarpitti had done it. *Surely not,* I thought, *or if she did, maybe she did it so the Admiral could trap the Charterer...*

I didn't want to think about all that. Instead, I focused on my job. As we got back to the section, I saw Webster go over and speak with Salter while Beckman went back into formation.

A moment later, Salter stepped in front of the candidates. "Well," she said, "it seems that some of you are under the impression that we don't care about you." The entire group went still. I think they stopped breathing. "Well, that couldn't be further from the truth. We care *very* much about all of you. We want you to be stronger, better, and to prove that, we're going to take you all on a motivational run! Everyone, you have one minute to go get your full combat load from your rooms and return here. After that, we're going to go for a nice run through the evening! Doesn't that sound fun!"

The candidates didn't respond.

"I said, doesn't that sound fun!?" Salter bellowed.

"Ma'am, yes, ma'am!" they shouted back.

"Great!" Salter said. "Fall out! Sixty seconds, fifty-nine, fifty-eight..."

***

Chapter Eighteen: Grinding To A Halt

"Second squad is back at their bunker and Regan and Dawson have them for the next few hours," I reported as I came into the Cadet Instructor bunker. Senior Cadet Instructor Salter gave me a nod of acknowledgement and went back to her discussion with Cadet Lieutenant Webster.

I flopped to the ground next to Ashiri, "Thank God there's only a couple more days." The Grinder was every bit as bad as I'd remembered. I had thought that keeping track of my squad was bad as a candidate. I hadn't seen hard until I tried to track and watch them across four hundred square kilometers of training area. The rugged terrain was a mix of rocks, jagged hills, and clusters of ruined buildings, all of it designed to be as confusing as possible.

We'd initially split duty between the three squads, with two Cadet Instructors per squad. In theory, that meant we'd work in twelve hour shifts. But what happened was that as a each squad took casualties and those casualties were evacuated to the medical facility, someone had to cover down on them. Since that happened every few hours, I think I'd managed two or three hours of sleep per day over the past five weeks.

Ashiri didn't answer me. I looked over and saw that her head had rolled back. She was snoring faintly. *Figures.* I thought. I should sleep while I could, too... but I'd hit a point of exhaustion where I didn't think that I *could* sleep. I pulled out my datapad and checked over the notes on upcoming missions for the squads.

It had surprised me at just how much planning went into the Grinder. During my time as a candidate, it had purely been chaos. I hadn't had any idea that it all tied together. There were Militia units conducting their yearly training. There were basic training units doing their initial combat training. All of our missions had to be coordinated with them. Training rounds, food, water, all of that had to be positioned. It was a huge endeavor and I had a new-found respect for Salter and Webster for managing it all.

In our training we'd had a crash course on how to handle everything. Our datapads had a software update that let us pass messages on missions and supplies, to call for evacuation of candidates struck by the incapacitating training rounds, and in case of emergency, to request actual medical support. We also had an emergency override where we could shut down training in case of some real life emergency. They'd cautioned us against using that unless it was something really important, because it would shut down the entire Grinder. Needless to say, I had no intention of ever pushing that button.

I went through the upcoming missions and saw that Second Squad had an upcoming mission out to the north-west. They were supposed to raid one of the militia units out there and I winced in sympathy. That was the ruined town and generally our candidates didn't do well against the defenses that the regular Militia units would have. I'd been hit by one of the heavier training rounds they had for their larger weapon systems in a similar attack last year.

Out of curiosity, I switched over to the rating system. Sand Dragon was doing well, I saw. Our candidates as a whole were pretty close to Ogre, Dust, and Tiger. Ogre's overall section score was a bit better than ours, but that was because we had some special candidates. Most of the other candidates were several points behind, with Reaver being the closest after Tiger.

I frowned as I considered that. Beckman had refused to give up, I'd give her that, but she'd been the cause of a few issues. It was all the more maddening for the fact that I understood her viewpoint. She didn't like the rough treatment, she didn't like the unfairness of it all. What she didn't seem to realize was that was the point of all of this. *Life isn't fair*, I thought to myself.

The thing was, her rating was the lowest of any of our candidates. In fact, it was low enough that most of the other Cadet Instructors had begun to grumble. She didn't seem to understand that her actions had greater consequences... and she was having an impact, not just on herself and her squad, but also on her whole section and even the Cadet Instructors. *We* would be rated on the performance of our candidates... and Beckman was one of mine.

As if on that cue, I got a message on my comm unit, "Armstrong, this is Regan, we've got an issue with second squad. I need you down here."

"On my way," I replied and climbed to my feet. I saw Cadet Lieutenant Webster look over and note my departure. I wondered if he tracked all of us Cadet Instructors, like we tracked our candidates. The Cadet Instructor bunker was just over the ridge from our section.

The close proximity had led to a bit of humor when a couple of exhausted candidates had mistakenly walked inside. It also meant that I was able to get to Regan in less than a minute. The intense sun made me squint, even with the auto-adjusting visor on my helmet. "What's up?" I asked.

"Beckman is refusing to go on this next mission," Kyle Regan said in a low voice.

"She's *what*?" I stared at him in shock.

"She says that she's not moving until she gets some rest," Kyle Regan said. "I was so angry I nearly jerked her to her feet, but I ordered the rest of the squad outside and briefed their squad leader. They roll out in a couple of minutes." He let out a tense breath, "I'm at my wits end about what to do about her. Can you talk to her? You might have better luck than me."

She hates my guts, I thought to myself. But I nodded. Regan was in a hard position. If the candidates saw one of their number rebel, they were tired enough that others might. I'd never even considered it a possibility. It was an unspoken rule that everyone seemed to get.

We weren't supposed to get physical with candidates. There were a host of reasons for that. But if faced with complete passive resistance, I knew we didn't have many options. The main one was that Beckman would be cut from the course. She'd get her rest, alright, but she'd take it at home.

I walked into the bunker. It was cool after the intense heat of the sun. I found Candidate Beckman just inside, she glared up at me sullenly, "I'm not going. You can't make me."

My first impulse was to grab her by her shoulders and jerk her to her feet, but I restrained the anger and tried to see things her way. She was tired. She thought she was being treated unfairly. I squatted in front of her, "You're right, I can't make you."

She stared at me warily and didn't respond.

"If you sit here, you'll get your rest. And in a couple hours, someone will come to fly you out of here. You'll get time to get showered, get cleaned up, and turn in all your gear. Then they'll put you on a skimmer and you'll go home," I said it all in a calm voice. "You'll be done... and everything you went through so far will have been for nothing."

She scowled at me, "You can't threaten me. I've done

everything I've been told to do."

"No, you haven't," I replied. "You think we want to do this? Do you think I enjoy it?" I shook my head, "We're doing this to train you. This has nothing to do with you personally, we treat every candidate the same way. Every one of those candidates in your squad are just as tired, just as sore, as you."

"Yeah, right," she spat. "I've heard all about the high and mighty *Armstrongs* from my aunt. I'm supposed to think it's coincidence that you're my Cadet Instructor? I bet your grandmother gave you orders to make sure I quit."

I stood up, "If that was the case, I wouldn't have given you that warning, would I have?" I asked. "Now, you can keep thinking of yourself as a victim, or you can get out there and do your job. And before you refuse again, let me put it this way... if you stay here, it won't be anyone making you quit, it'll be you quitting, do you understand me?"

Beckman looked down at the ground and didn't answer me. I turned and walked out of the bunker. I wasn't even really sure why I'd tried so hard to talk her into doing the right thing. It would have been better for me if she'd just quit. Maybe I still saw some of myself in her. Maybe I just didn't like giving up on someone.

A moment later, I heard her come out of the tunnel. I watched as she jogged to catch up to her squad. *Good choice.*

"Thanks," Kyle said as he came up. "Though part of me wishes she'd quit."

"Yeah, well," I shrugged, "she's a pain, but she's our pain, right?" I looked over at him, "You get any rest?"

He snorted, "No, I had to help sheepdog some lost candidates back to where they were supposed to be."

"I'll take this patrol," I said.

"You sure?" He asked. "You just got back."

"Yeah," I nodded. "I got it, get some rest."

He headed off without another word. Clearly he wasn't going to argue. I jogged to catch up to the candidates and kept just to their side and rear as they moved. Now and then I'd pause to check my datapad and see where the other units in the area were. I frowned, though, as a message came up. Apparently there were changes afoot.

I flagged down Wallace, the squad leader. He halted them

and put them on security positions and then ran over to join me. "Change of mission," I said. "There's a blockage on the main route, go to your alternate route."

"Ma'am, aye-aye, ma'am," Wallace replied. I saw him hesitate. Last time they'd gone to an alternate route, it had been right into an ambush. I saw him think about it for a long moment. While we'd told them to treat this like a real event, I could see him considering whether that covered taking extra precautions.

He didn't ask, though. Wallace jogged back to his squad and started snapping off orders. I couldn't help but feel a bit proud of him as he ordered two of his squad ahead as scouts. Because, after all, it *was* an ambush. Ogre had a squad in that area who'd been told to ambush any foot patrols coming through.

And while I wasn't going to help Wallace and second squad, I wasn't going to be unhappy if they figured it out on their own. Especially if it meant they got the upper hand against Ogre. I turned the noise dampening down on my helmet headset, so I'd be able to hear the ambush as it began.

They moved into the ambush area a few minutes later and the scouts triggered the ambush early. It was unfortunate for them, but it meant that Wallace started maneuvering his squad against the ambushers. I saw several of Ogre's candidates go down to the counterattack. Everything was going well, right up until I heard the unmistakable crack of a real bullet going past.

"Candidates, down, now!" I shouted. Second Squad went to the ground and I searched for the shooter. A couple of Ogre's candidates were still up and my eyes tracked to one female candidate, only fifty meters away. I saw her sweep her weapon around, searching for targets... and the barrel came in line with me. She squeezed off a round.

The unmistakable crack of a real bullet almost sent me diving for the ground. Instead I remained still, "Candidate!" I barked, "Lower your weapon, now!"

She stared at me for a long moment, only now seeming to recognize that I had the white markings of a Cadet Instructor. Slowly, she lowered her weapon. I ran over and pulled it out of her hands and checked the magazine. Live rounds.

Ogre's Cadet Instructor ran over, "What are you doing!?" she demanded.

I recognized Sashi Drien. "Your candidate has live rounds," I snapped. "She nearly killed me."

"That's impossible..." Sashi looked at the magazine in shock.

"We have to shut this down," I heard myself saying.

"I'll check the rest of my candidates," Sashi said, her voice resigned. "I don't know how this happened..."

"No," I said, "We have to shut down the Grinder. There were *live* rounds in one weapon, there could be others."

"What?" Sashi shook her head, "You're insane. This was probably just a mistake somewhere, there's no sign that there is a problem anywhere else! If you shut down the Grinder, this whole exercise is over!"

"Someone nearly died," I said, pulling out my datapad. I brought up the emergency commands and stared at it for a long moment. Someone, somewhere might have a loaded weapon that could kill another candidate. I really didn't have a choice.

"Armstrong, don't you dare..." she trailed off as I pushed the button.

"You don't listen! Why don't you *ever* listen!?" Sashi snarled.

I looked up at her, "Disarm your candidates, I'll do the same with mine."

"This isn't the end of this, Armstrong," she hissed at me as she turned away.

"Uh, ma'am," the candidate next to me spoke up, "I think you're bleeding."

I looked down and saw a spreading red stain on my arm. "Well," I said, "that's unfortunate."

***

Luckily, I'd only been winged. I had Candidate Wallace slap a pressure bandage on it while I talked them through the field first aid. The way they were all staring at me, you'd have thought I was seriously injured or something.

The entire Grinder had gone eerily silent. The normal rattle of gunfire and distant sound of explosions had ceased. Even as I thought that, I heard the drone of engines and then a combat skimmer settled to the ground a few meters away. Commander Scarpitti jumped out. "Armstrong, what's going on?" Commander

Bonnadonna came down the ramp a moment later, followed by Commander Pannja.

"There's an issue with ammunition, ma'am," I reported, holding out the magazine and rifle for her inspection. Sashi Drien had asked for them back, but I'd refused. "One of the candidates from Ogre section somehow had live rounds mixed in with their training rounds.

Command Scarpitti stared at me. She took the rifle and magazine from me, her eyes lingering on the wound on my arm. "You okay, Armstrong?"

"I got winged, ma'am," I admitted. "I'm fine."

"Right," she said, her voice harsh. She checked the rifle and magazine and then nodded, "Yes, no mistaking it... but why shut everything down? It looks to be just the one weapon..."

"We couldn't confirm that other candidates didn't get issued live rounds, ma'am," I said.

"Good point, Cadet Armstrong," Commander Bonnadonna nodded. He donned gloves and took the magazine from Commander Scarpitti, "Which candidate? Who all has handled it?"

I felt my back go up as I met his gaze. I didn't trust him and I still suspected he'd tried to kill me, but I spoke as professionally as I could manage. "Candidate Heavey, sir. Myself and Cadet Drien have handled the weapon and magazine besides her. And yourselves, of course," I said.

"Sir," Sashi hurried up. "I have to protest this! Cadet Armstrong shut down the exercise before my candidates had time to react. I think this was a way for her to game the ranking system!"

Commander Bonnadonna stared at her. He didn't speak, but he put one of Heavey's magazines in the weapon and worked the action, ejecting one round after the other. Past the first one or two rounds that alternated live and training, the remainder of the magazine was live rounds. I swallowed nervously as I considered that. The training rounds were light, they had a bit of bright colored paint and delivered a tranquilizer on impact with skin or clothing. The live rounds, on the other hand, were composite rounds that would kill, and they traveled far faster and further. The two types of round made different noises when firing, but a candidate probably wouldn't have understood the difference. Most Cadet Instructors, if they didn't have their sound dampening turned down on their helmets, wouldn't know the difference unless they were really paying attention to their candidates.

The large number of live rounds at the bottom of the magazine meant that the longer an engagement went on, the more likely it was that she would have killed someone. I felt sick as I stared at all those possibilities of death. They'd been aimed at *my* candidates. I couldn't help but look up and glare at Sashi.

"She made the right decision given what she knew at the time," Commander Scarpitti was the first one to speak.

"Did we question the candidate?" Commander Pannja asked.

"Yes, sir," I replied. "She drew the magazine just before the mission. It was one of the lot issued to their squad. Cadet Drien told me that they expended most of their ammunition in an earlier engagement and they received a full restock just before they went on this mission."

He stared at the live rounds on the ground in front of Commander Bonnadonna. "We'll need to do a full investigation and inquiry. You were right to shut the exercise down. There could be other contaminated lots of ammunition. Good work, Cadet Armstrong."

***

"Biohazard shuts it all down!" Kyle Regan gave me a grin as I got back to the bunker. Behind him, I saw Cadet Lieutenant Webster and Salter, and most of the other Cadet Instructors for Sand Dragon. I just shook my head and then leaned against the wall. "Hey, Jiden, you okay?" He asked.

"Yeah," I said quietly. "Just tired of people taking shots at me."

"I didn't mean anything by it," Regan said. "And what happened, anyway? I got the stand-down message and then a few minutes later we were told to check every bit of ammo on our candidates. What happened out there?"

I showed him the bandage on my arm. "One of Ogre's candidates had live rounds."

"*What?*" Everyone in the bunker started talking at once.

"Quiet!" Webster barked. He hurried over, "You're saying one of Ogre's candidates *shot* you?"

"Yeah," I said. "But she was shooting at *my* candidates.

With live rounds. Which is why I shut everything down." I was tired and angry and I realized that I probably was coming off the adrenaline spike of being shot at.

"Right, we probably need to get you to the aid station and get you checked out," Webster turned away, "It'll probably be a few hours before the exercise goes back up..."

"No, sir," I said. "The word should be going out soon. As soon as everyone reports in clear on ammunition, they're pulling us all out of the Grinder. There's going to be a full investigation."

"They're shutting down the *Grinder?*" Webster turned around in surprise, "What, *all* of it?"

"From what I heard from Commander Pannja, yeah. He was on the net to the overall exercise commander. Until and unless they know none of the training ammunition is contaminated with live rounds, they're putting a halt to all of it."

"That's never happened," Salter shook her head. "Oh, man, Armstrong, when you do something, you don't do it in a half measure."

I wanted to say this wasn't my fault. I couldn't manage it though. Someone had taken shots at me. Sure, I could imagine there was an accident where live rounds got mixed in with training rounds. But that should have been more than the one weapon. As far as we'd been able to tell, the only one with live rounds had been candidate Heavey. And it would have been something else if she'd loaded the rounds herself. Maybe someone could have made a case for her pocketing some live rounds from target training before the Grinder and loading them here. It would have made her one of the stupidest candidates ever, but it would have been possible.

But the magazines had been issued to her. That meant someone, somewhere, had loaded those rounds in it. Then there was the change in mission, which had only happened after I'd taken over from Kyle Regan. *This feels like a set-up,* I thought. I'd taken the time, on the flight back, to look up Candidate Heavey. She had the lowest rating in Ogre section. She'd been penalized twice during the Grinder for shooting Cadet Instructors, both times she'd admitted to firing without identifying a target.

This didn't feel like an accident. It felt like someone had tried to kill me... again.

***

Chapter Nineteen: That's The Real Killer

"In all probability, we probably won't know how exactly those rounds got into Candidate Heavey's magazine," Webster finished briefing us.

"Sir, this is insane," Kyle Regan shook his head. "Armstrong was shot, several of our candidates could have *died*."

"I know," he nodded. "But the lot of ammunition that the rounds came from was no longer on inventory." He'd already explained that. For that matter, I'd read the report myself. The lot of ammunition had been reported destroyed as "out of date." What that told me was that it was probably made to disappear in the same way that Tony Champion and his father Isaac had been making military parts and equipment disappear.

This was tied to the smugglers, again. Only no one in the room knew that besides me.

Well, me and Ashiri and Karmazin, I reminded myself. Both of my friends had solemn expressions. I figured they'd put two and two together already. Regan didn't seem willing to let it go, though and he didn't know all the backstory. I put my hand on his shoulder, "Just let it go, Kyle, it's fine."

"It's *not* fine," he snapped in reply. He let out a tense breath, then, "Sorry, it's just... God, this is so frustrating."

"It's that way for all of us," Webster replied. "Believe me. This is the last thing I wanted happening on my watch. The training staff officers are the ones who put you all in these circumstances. I'm just happy that no one was seriously injured."

This time, I thought. But whoever had made the attempt was bound to do so again, I knew.

"Moving forward, we're past the big hurdle of the grinder," Webster went on. "The candidates are in their classes, so we have a bit more time. I want all of you using that time. We don't get a lot of it at the Academy, be sure you take the opportunities to get out and have fun."

I stared at him and I wasn't the only one. I would never have expected Cadet Lieutenant Webster to tell us to have fun.

He seemed to realize how odd that sounded and he coughed, "Admittedly, that may sound strange coming from me." He shot a look at Cadet Salter who gave him a nod. "What most of you probably don't realize is that this is my sixth year here at the Academy."

I frowned in confusion at that. The Academy was a five year program... My eyes widened as I realized what he meant.

"I'm a set-back. I... had some issues, last year, I wasn't allowed to graduate. It's not a path I recommend. But one of the things I realized was that I pushed myself too hard. I burned myself out, taking every assignment I could and additional classes as well," He looked over at his datapad and I wondered if the maze I'd seen on its surface was related to that somehow.

"We're going to have a lot more free time over the next few weeks, right up until we do their final exercise," Webster said. "So make the best of the time, go out, play some games, get a chance to relax." I didn't know how I'd relax, seeing as someone had tried to kill me again, but I appreciated the sentiment.

"Now, besides duties of moving the candidates around where they need to be, we will be doing the last preparations for the final exercise for the summer," Webster said. "I volunteered to help draft it up, and I hope that all of you are willing to help." He keyed up his desk display and then projected a map. It was the maze I'd seen him working on before. "Four of you in here were among the best scorers for last year's run. I'd like to see you give this a crack when we demonstrate it to our candidates, right before they go through."

"Sure thing, sir," Karmazin said.

"No problem, sir," Ashiri said.

I didn't answer, I was staring at the diagram. There was something oddly familiar about it, but I couldn't put my finger on exactly what it was.

"Armstrong?" Webster asked.

"What?" I looked up, "Yes, sorry, sir, I guess I'm more tired than I realized. Of course I'll help out."

"Good," Webster said. He shut off the display. "It'll be a maze run, as you saw. I'm favoring total darkness with entry points along the outer ring and, of course, completion by anyone who reaches the central chamber. There's the three outer sections that all feed into the inner section, so it'll be a good challenge, I think."

"Where'd you get the idea, sir?" I couldn't help but ask. I couldn't think of any mazes I'd been in, or diagrams that I'd seen with the ring-inside-rings pattern. The whole thing looking familiar enough to bug me, though.

"Oh," he grinned, "a game that I picked up when I did my assignment last summer at Duncan City. Commander Scarpitti actually introduced me to it. Hopefully none of our candidates have played, or that might give them something of an advantage. Luckily it doesn't seem to have been very widely available."

"Oh," I said. That might make sense, why it seemed so familiar. It might have been one of the games distributed on the military network. I'd played a bunch of games last year and a bunch more this year, including a few that Commander Scarpitti had distributed as part of her class.

"Yeah, I've been working on adjusting the overall design for twenty participants. Thankfully I didn't have to change much," Webster said, "most of the rest was filling in details and trying to figure out how to build it all..." He looked around at us, "Though, if you're doing the run, then I can't really give you any more details."

"Of course, sir, not a problem," Regan said.

"All right, then," Webster said, "thanks for your time."

We took that as a dismissal. Ashiri and Karmazin gave me a wave as they headed over to pick up our candidates. They had them the rest of the morning. I waved back and then I found myself standing out in the corridor, not really sure what to do. I didn't have candidate duty until the evening. I didn't have any classwork... I didn't have any classes, either. Some part of me itched to go check out the maze, to see which game it was that I remembered it from, but I figured it would be cheating, so I didn't want to do that...

"Armstrong... Jiden," Regan said from behind me. "Got any plans for the rest of the morning?" He gave me a friendly smile and I couldn't help but smile back. We'd spent a lot of time together over the past couple of months.

"Not really, you?" I asked.

"Well..." he shrugged, "they opened the Scuttlebutt to Cadet Instructors, to give us a place to relax out of sight of the candidates. Could I buy you lunch?"

I stared at him, taken off guard. "You want to buy me lunch?"

"Yeah, I mean, unless you don't want to..."

"No," I said in a hurry, "I'd like that. A lot, I mean."

"Great," he said. We found ourselves grinning at each other and I felt a little bit like an idiot... but at the same time I didn't care.

Someone cleared their throat and we both turned. Salter raised an eyebrow at us. "You two should probably vacate the area, the candidates will be back soon."

"Yes, ma'am," we both said at the same time.

For some reason, we both found that hilarious.

***

I'd never been inside the Scuttlebutt. I'd sort of known it existed. It was a restaurant of sorts that the Academy staff and faculty used. It was totally different from the chow hall, it actually felt like a nice place and as we came through the doors, I immediately felt out of place.

"Two?" the waitress asked. We nodded and she waved at the empty tables, "Pick a spot."

Most of the walls were hung with historic military memorabilia. There were brass plaques with weapons, bits of hull, and other strange items. There were pictures and holograms of men and women in uniform.

Kyle picked a table back from the door, next to a large section of hull plate. As I took my seat, I found myself reading the text on it. *Fragment of Culmor Dreadnought armor plate from the Battle of Rowan III.* After I placed my order, I rapped my knuckles on the armor and it was dense enough that it didn't even make noise.

"Impressive, huh?" Kyle said. "They opened the place up during Parent's Weekend, my dad and I sat here. I guess *his* granddad was at the Battle of Rowan III, he wanted to show me this."

"Wow," I said. Apparently he came from a military family. I was a bit flattered that he'd shared it with me. "You hear a lot of military stories from your family?"

He grinned, "Oh yeah. My dad and mom met in the military. She got out to raise us kids, but my dad has stayed in. My granddad retired ten years back, lots of health issues, he, uh, got some of the first generation of life extension treatments."

"Oh," I winced. There were stories about bad batches of those, when quality control had been an issue and a lot of the expensive drugs had been either diluted or falsely labeled. I'd heard rumors about first generation treatments, about some people suffering from organ failure or other issues, while outwardly they looked healthy. "Sorry."

"It's life, you know?" He looked away. "Anyway, my mom and dad both have the second generation treatment, and we'll be getting that too, here at the Academy in only a few more months. It's a lot more time than most people used to get... a lot more than some people get even now, you know?"

I nodded. On core worlds in Guard Space, the life extension treatments were commonplace. They weren't cheap, but there were plenty of options to get them. Out here at Century, the process was far more expensive and there was far less support. There were loans for it, but most of those had very long pay-offs... and lots of people didn't like the idea of living longer just to be in debt for the rest of their lives.

On the other hand, to live a few extra centuries? I'd planned on joining Champion Enterprises for that reason. It was a perk of joining the Century Planetary Militia. Yeah, both came with a set of costs, but I'd thought the ten year contract with Champion Enterprises would have been worth it.

And it's a five years of active service, twenty years of reserve service with the Militia, I reminded myself.

Our food came, the waitress gave us smiles but she didn't stick around. Kyle and I both ate quickly, habit, I suppose. Afterward we sat in silence for a while. I wanted to thank him for asking me to lunch. I wanted to say something nice, but I didn't really know what to say. Finally, I asked the question that had been bugging me since earlier.

"So," I said, "what do you think of what Webster said?"

He shrugged, "You mean about him being a set-back?" I nodded in reply. "Well, there's a lot more of them than you'd realize. Did they do the whole line-up and count-off thing for you as a plebe?"

"Yeah."

"Well, that's not as much of a scare tactic as you'd think... or at least, it's not *just* a scare tactic. I've already heard from a couple of my section-mates in Dust, they're not coming back to school in the fall."

"What?" I asked in surprise.

"Yeah, some of them got to their summer assignments and they just didn't want to come back. One of them, he said he had a panic attack just thinking about coming back. He sent in his resignation the next day." Kyle Regan sighed, "I can understand it, I mean, this is all way harder than I thought it would be, but the thought of quitting..."

"Yeah," I said. "It would be like throwing away all this effort. It would be for nothing."

Kyle nodded. "Anyway, from what I get, about twenty percent fail out or quit in the plebe year. Another ten percent or so fail or quit after that."

"I thought we were under our obligation after that, right?" I asked

"Yeah," he nodded, "from what I understand, those that fail out during that time go in front of a board. If they're viewed as having potential, they offer them enlisted assignments. I wouldn't want that, personally. I mean, could you imagine running into a former classmate and having to take orders from them?"

I shrugged. It didn't sound all that strange... right up until I considered it being Sashi Drien or Bolander from Ogre. *No way.* "That doesn't sound fun."

"Yeah," Kyle nodded. "Those that don't, they end up having to pay back the Militia for their training, their implants, and their life extension treatments. I guess there's a pretty good market for them, though, either as mercenaries or in industry. I haven't heard of anyone *not* being able to pay it all back within a decent amount of time."

"How would they accept a resignation after the first full year?" I asked. "I thought we were locked in."

"There's family emergencies and such," Kyle replied. "There was a cadet first class earlier this year in Dust who resigned. Her parents were killed in a ground-vehicle accident and she went home to take care of her siblings."

I blanched a bit at that. I couldn't imagine that happening to my parents. Especially not when I'd joined to protect them. "And set-backs?" I prompted.

"Generally when you get to your second or first class years," Kyle said. "At that point, the Academy has spent enough time and effort that they don't want to let you go, not unless you totally crack or there's something seriously wrong with you."

"Wrong?" I asked.

"Honor code or ethics violations are the only thing I've heard of," Kyle answered. "But my dad told me that he had a classmate who just stopped talking, stopped eating, just sort of broke down. Couldn't take the stress, I guess."

I shivered at that.

"But anyway, if you fail one of the higher level exams or you get a bad review, or you do something you shouldn't have, they generally send you home for the rest of the year with a bunch of assignments and a chance to come back the next year in the next graduating class."

"What do you think Webster did?" I asked.

He shrugged, "Who knows? Maybe he started drinking. Maybe he failed a class. He seems to be doing a good job, now. I mean, he's in a key leadership position and he's in charge of the candidate's summer exercise. That seems like he's on the fast track to graduate. Whatever he did, it doesn't matter to us, right?"

"I suppose you're right," I replied.

"Anyway," he said, "enough talking about me, I feel sort of like I haven't given you a chance to talk. How're you handling things? I mean, you nearly got killed out there!"

I snorted, "It's hardly the first time."

Kyle blinked at me, "Jiden, you were nearly shot. You're awfully calm about that."

I licked my lips as I wondered just how much it was safe to tell him. Probably best to keep it to what was generally known. "It's not the first time. There was the business at Champion Enterprises. There was the grav-shell crash. No one was seriously injured, that's enough for me."

He shook his head, "Wow, I hope I can be as mellow about it if and when that happens to me."

"I'm sure you'll do fine," I replied.

"Have you told your parents about it?" he asked.

"Are you kidding?" I snorted. "My mom would flip. My dad wouldn't understand, either. No, I just told them there was an accident and we came back early. I didn't go into details."

"Parents," he shook his head. "My mom always worries about me, too. And then she found out that my sister wants to come here next year..."

"My brother too," I nodded. "I thought my mom was going to lose it."

"Parents," we both shook our heads.

His datapad chimed. He looked at it and I saw his expression fall. "Dang, my duty time is coming up, I've got to go..."

"Sorry," I said, "I had a really good time."

"Lunch tomorrow?" he asked.

"Yeah," I replied, "it's a date." I flushed as I realized what I'd said. Kyle gave me a broad smile, though, as he stood up. "I'll see you later, lunch tomorrow, I'm holding you to it!"

After he left, I sat there, wondering about what I was doing here. I liked Kyle Regan. He was nice. He seemed to have a good sense of humor, he made me smile. I felt good for the first time in a long time. *You're putting him in danger,* a part of my mind whispered at me, *you should tell him what he's getting into...*

I shut that part of me up. It might be selfish of me, but I was going to enjoy what time I could. And if it looked like Kyle might get caught in the crossfire, I'd let him know. Besides, if *Webster* had to tell us to take some time, then I wasn't going to argue with him.

***

The candidates were playing games and I was off duty.

I grinned as I logged into one of their practice games as Biohazard. It was one of the simple strategy games that I'd played last year and it surprised me at how... basic it felt. Most of these games were focused on a small number of units. They were to teach tactics at a small level, to hone the basics. I realized that now.

All of us Cadet Instructors took our turns beating up on them in practice matches. It was good for them, it made them try to get better. Plus, it was fun to hear them howling about it, especially because they didn't know who we were.

We could see their actual names, next to their avatars. Those of them that didn't use their regular names for their logins, of course.

I grinned as I logged into a match with Beckman. The past few games I'd played against her, I'd gone a bit easy on her, letting her nearly beat me. I wondered if she realized that or if she was just overconfident as she started off the game in full-on attack mode.

She's not quite as clever as she thinks, I smiled to myself as I let her get all the way to my base... and then I closed off the trap behind her. I detonated the structures of my base in a cascading series of overlapping explosions that cut down her digital team. Down the corridor, I heard her start to yell.

Got you.

"Jiden, are you beating up on the candidates again?" Kyle asked from the doorway.

"Got to keep them on their toes," I replied. "Lunch?"

"Yeah, but I thought we might go for a run, first? Just a short one."

I still hated running, but I didn't want to say that. "Sure," I said, "let me get changed."

"Cool, I'll meet you at the stairs," he said.

We'd been meeting for lunch for the past couple of weeks, talking about all kinds of things. I closed the door and changed quickly, then did a quick walk-through the candidate barracks. Most of them were either studying or gaming. Beckman was angrily jabbing commands on her datapad's holographic screen. *She needs to learn to control that temper of hers.*

I met Kyle at the stairs and we jogged up. Normally, most of the runs I went on, I'd go out to the parade ground and then either take one of the underground tracks or go up a ramp to the surface. I didn't relish the idea of running in the heat of the day, so I was glad when Kyle led the way down one of the running tunnels. We didn't go far, though, until we were jogging up a spiral ramp. The slope was steep enough that I was really panting when we finally popped out at the top.

Kyle moved to the side and stopped and I followed him. I was startled, then, by the view. We were on some kind of covered track, near the top of one of the bigger Academy structures. We were high enough up that a cool breeze blew through and it felt surprisingly good. "Wow," I said, "where are we?"

"On top of Bunker Seven," Kyle grinned. I realized then why we were so high up. Bunker Seven housed the Academy's largest hangar, it was where the Academy's corvettes launched from. "It's one of the schools hidden secrets. Awesome view, right?"

I nodded in reply. I could see the entire Academy laid out below us. Concrete bunkers and roadways stretching off into the distance. "It's huge," I said. I'd seen maps, of course, but I hadn't really thought of how big it all was.

"Pretty view," he said off-handedly. I realized he wasn't looking at the Academy grounds, he was looking at me.

My breath caught as I realized that we were all alone and he stood very close to me. Kyle started to lean in and I met him halfway, our lips touching in my first *real* kiss. I couldn't help but compare it to my horrible attempt to kiss Mackenzie. This was far different. There were sensations and feelings that were almost overwhelming. My whole body seemed to tingle. It was too much for me to take in, too complicated for my brain to catalog... yet as Kyle stepped back, I was sad that it was over. I realized I was clutching at his shirt collar and I wasn't really sure if it was to hold him close or if I had started to do one of Commander Pannja's self-defense moves.

"I, uh, wanted to do that for a while," Kyle said.

"What took you so long?" I asked, smiling back. We both stood there, grinning goofily at each other.

"What do we do now?" He asked.

"I'm sort of new at this, how about we enjoy the view?" I suggested. He came over and stood next to me. I leaned against him. It felt good. Kyle felt solid. I liked him. I didn't want to lose him. So of course, I opened my stupid mouth and ruined everything

"Kyle," I said after a moment, "there's something you should know."

"What, do you have an older brother who's going to threaten to break my legs?" He joked.

I ignored his comment and spoke quickly, "The skimmer crash I was in, the grav-shell crash, too... and then the live rounds that candidate had, they weren't accidents," I regretted the words as I said them.

"What?" He pulled away and looked at me, his expression dubious. "Is this some kind of joke?"

"I'm not joking," I said. "Someone is trying to kill me. It ties back to the thing at Champion Enterprises, last year."

He stared at me for a long moment. "Are you sure? I mean, you've been through a lot..."

"Trust me," I snapped, "the Admiral confirmed it, there was also a bombing attempt and the grav-shell I crashed was sabotaged."

"You're not joking... jeez, Jiden, you're serious..." I expected him to do the smart thing. I expected him to say he needed some time to think about all this. Instead, he did what I never would have expected. He stepped forward and embraced me in a hug.

I stiffened in surprise. "What are you doing?" I asked, my voice muffled in his chest.

"I thought you were under a lot of pressure before, but you've been going through that and keeping it a secret. Don't worry, Jiden, I'm not going anywhere."

The words and the secure feeling of his arms around me made me fell all warm and tingly. I felt good. For the first time, I felt *safe*. It was irrational. I knew that Kyle wasn't any better able to protect me than I was. But just then, feeling his arms wrapped around me, knowing that he cared about me... that meant far more to me than anything else.

**

Chapter Twenty: History Repeats Itself

The rest of the summer seemed to fly by. Kyle and I spent as much time as we could together. He seemed to know all kinds of cool places on the Academy grounds. We spent hours together walking and talking. It was the first real relationship I'd ever been in and I took things slow. It was hard to open up to him, especially after how Tony Champion had lied to me. I ended up telling him the whole story with that, and to my surprise, he was pretty understanding.

Training the cadet candidates went on. We lost a few more to grades and it made me sad every time we had to give one of them the news. Some of them we saw it coming, they'd start falling behind in one of the prep classes and then, normally within a week, the instructors would make the call.

We had a lot of work to do prepping for their final exercise, too. Cadet Lieutenant Webster's course design used huge basalt blocks, and while those of us who were going to run it first weren't allowed inside, we still ended up helping to coordinate deliveries and move crates of training ammo, traps, and other supplies to the staging area. The sheer amount of supplies needed stunned me as I watched the piles get bigger and bigger. Around eight hundred candidates were going to tackle the course, each of them with a full combat load of three hundred rounds of ammunition. That was almost a quarter million rounds of ammunition just for them. Then the defenders had to have ammunition. Then there needed to be enough traps to reset the entire maze for all the iterations.

It was a massive expenditure. I overheard Cadet Lieutenant Webster and Cadet Commander An'Jirrad, the Regimental Training Officer, going over budgets, arguing details, and trying to get the most out of the money they'd been allotted. "These pillars weigh seventy tons, and you don't want to anchor them?" the RTO asked. The tone of his voice suggested he thought Webster was crazy. It was an interesting enough comment that I stopped in the hallway and listened, feeling a bit guilty.

"They're two meters across and made of solid basalt. Once we get them in place, they're not going to move," Webster said. "Not without a lot of leverage in the right place, anyway, and I don't see anyone climbing one of them to try to pull it down. The mass of these things will keep them in position. And the cost savings will let us save almost five thousand dollars per pillar. That's almost two hundred thousand dollars in savings."

That we were dealing with that level of money as cadets boggled my mind. I mentioned it to Salter, a few days before the final course. She snorted. "Yeah, it's a lot of money. You think it's crazy they have that kind of responsibility?"

I shrugged. I wasn't really sure.

"Think about it this way," she said. "A Mark V Firebolt costs over ten million dollars. The antimatter core on it costs almost four million to replace after it wears down. Assuming Cadet Lieutenant Webster graduates on time and gets a posting to a Firebolt squadron, he's going to command four of them and three pilots. That's forty million dollars of responsibility, not including other equipment."

"When you put it like that..."

"Besides, the final exercise is something of a tradition. The first class, every year, try to build it bigger and more complex than the previous year. The funds are a tiny portion of what we have for general operations, and *they* manage that budget, it's part of their rating. Each class saves as much money from the training budget as they can for it."

"Huh," I said. That actually seemed pretty clever.

"Yeah, the Admiral set it up that way over a decade back," Salter said. "So it gives the regimental staff more incentive to work hard and be tight on the funds they're given. Plus, we'll leave it up for the rest of the year. Cadets will use it for training and team building events. The one last year got used as a park... it was so cool we were all sad to see it go."

"Okay," I said, "well, I guess it all makes more sense."

"Don't hesitate to ask questions, Armstrong," Salter grinned. "And by the way, in case I hadn't said it yet... you're doing a good job."

"I am?" I asked in surprise. I mean, I'd known I'd done alright, but any kind of praise caught me off guard. "Thanks."

"I'll catch you later," she said.

I was kind of shocked how well things were going. The candidates were doing well, I was doing well, and I was in a relationship... and *that* was going well.

It kind of made me worry when things would get bad again.

***

"All right," Ashiri gave me a thumbs up as we gathered in the arena holding area. I couldn't help giving her a nervous grin.

"Listen up!" Cadet Lieutenant Webster shouted from near the door. We all turned to face him. He looked the most confident that I'd seen him, possibly ever. "The maze has three parts. Three rings, the central area will be the most heavily guarded. It's laid out to be confusing. Don't feel you have to beat the thing, you're just here to show the candidates what to do."

"Sure," Ashiri muttered from next to me, "that doesn't mean we don't want to beat it."

Webster gave us all nods, "Go to your start positions. Oh, and draw your ammo," he waved at the piles of loaded magazines, each one labeled with our names. "Good luck... but don't beat it too easily, this was about ten months of planning and work, okay?"

We laughed at that. In truth, I didn't plan on being able to get very far. I knew that, in theory, there were several different sets of lanes through the maze, but being unfamiliar, I probably wouldn't get very far. That wasn't what we were here to do, after all. We were here to give the first run of cadet candidates an idea of what *they* were supposed to be doing.

I went and drew my magazines, instinctively checking the top rounds in all of them. They were training rounds, but I had to fight the urge to unload and check the rest of the magazines. *Don't be paranoid.*

I went to my lane and waited. I couldn't see the viewing stands above me. I knew I'd be down below my candidates, I expected that they could see me and I thought I heard voices carry through the holographic field over us, but the field distorted the noise. Or maybe it was the maze, I wasn't certain.

Standing outside it, I didn't have that feeling of familiarity anymore. The crisp basalt blocks simply seemed ominous.

"Candidates!" I heard the Regimental Training Officer shout, "The course in front of you is the final exercise. It consists of three rings, each with increasing numbers of traps and enemies. You will compete against those enemies and each other to reach the central chamber! You will be graded on time to completion and how far along you get! Activating the lever at the center of the maze will end your time and award you full points!"

I knew what would come next. "Your Cadet Instructors will now demonstrate!"

A light blinked to tell me to move in. I entered the maze at a cautious pace, my eyes sweeping for threats. It was pitch dark black and I activated the light amplification on my helmet visor. Above me, I was sure the holographic projection would amplify light for the candidates so they'd be able to watch us move. On instinct, I turned down the noise canceling features on my helmet. If we were firing live rounds, that meant I'd damage my hearing, but we were using training rounds and I wanted to be able to hear if someone was sneaking up on me in the dark.

I found the first trap just a few meters inside, a trip wire that I cautiously stepped over, making certain there wasn't another trap beyond. As I went further down the corridor, I froze. Somehow I knew there would be another trap, something in the floor. I saw the edges of the basalt blocks in the floor looked a little too smooth and I poked at them with the barrel of my rifle. The blocks swung open, dropping into a deep shaft. *Of course.*

I bypassed a few more traps, spotting mines and trip wires, and somehow knowing where the deep pits would be. In fact, as I took turns, I started to feel as if I knew this place. It was hard to figure out where. The light-amplification made everything into shades of green and made it seem alien, but the turns and twists felt so familiar.

I left the first ring and moved into the second. There should be armed opposition at this point. I was proven right as I rounded a corner and, less than a few meters away, there was Thorpe from Ogre.

We brought our weapons up at the same time and I fired at his unprotected legs. His rounds struck my chest armor and I heard him swear as he fell. *Got you,* I thought to myself. I suppose I shouldn't be surprised that Ogre supplied the defenders for Sand Dragon's lanes. At least there wouldn't be any accusations of favoritism.

I continued on, slipping around the edges of an open pit, then crawling under a set of trip-wires set at various heights. In the dark,

I should have been disoriented, but I felt like I knew exactly where I was going. In fact, if I was right, there would be a large chamber ahead, the perfect spot for an ambush...

I eased around the corner in a crouch, and then rolled into cover behind a basalt pillar. Just as I did, I heard shots echo through the chamber and I smiled, my caution had paid off.

I popped my head around the pillar down low. Another shot rang out and this time I caught a muzzle flash. The flash illuminated my opponent's face. It was Sashi Drien. *Of course it is.* The training round smacked into the basalt floor near me.

Upper gallery, I realized. It was a good spot for an ambush, a platform that ran along the back wall of the chamber. I didn't have any cover to get across the open ground. I didn't have a lot of options. Three shots fired so far, and I was certain if I stayed here too long, then support defenders would shift in my direction. I rolled to the far side of the pillar and fired in the general direction of where I thought my opponent was.

I froze, though, as my rifle fired a real bullet. The unmistakable crack of the round shocked me into stillness... and a moment after that my opponent fired a live round right back at me. The round struck me square in the chest and the heavy impact jolted me back into motion. I dove to the side as more shots rang out.

I didn't know if she knew we were firing live rounds at one another. The only reason I'd noticed was because I'd had my noise canceling tuned down in my helmet. She hadn't noticed the live rounds during the Grinder. She might not notice them now. She could shoot me, kill me, and she'd just think she was playing the game. *Unless maybe she knows...* I banished that thought. Sashi had betrayed me, but I didn't think she'd try to kill me, not for real.

That didn't leave me with many options. I couldn't trust my magazines. I cycled the action on my rifle and ejected a round. It was a real one. I worked the action and emptied the magazine. All of them were real rounds. *All but the first three...*

I pulled out my spare magazine and checked it. The first three rounds were training, below them, I saw a real round. I threw the magazine to the side and loaded the three training rounds into my rifle. My best bet was to just wait here. Surely *someone* would have heard the real shots and they'd call it, right?

Except the holograms were distorting the sounds, I

remembered. They might muffle the gunfire enough that no one would know. I felt a chill as I realized that despite the fact that I was right in the middle of the entire school, none of them had any idea that my life was in danger. *No one is coming to help me, I need to do this myself.*

I felt like someone had replaced my blood with ice-water, but the strangest sense of relief washed over me. Here, it seemed, was the bad news at last. Things had been going so good over the past weeks that it felt good to know where the threat would come from.

I loaded the magazine with the three training rounds and took stock of the situation. Sashi Drien would have support coming soon. There were doors at either end of the chamber, which almost certainly led to other lanes. Her support would come from there. There was a chance that they only had training rounds, but I didn't want to count on that. My best bet was to get to the center. If I got there, it would end, and I could tell them what had happened.

But I had to get past Sashi, first.

* * *

I heard movement and the sound of footsteps and I knew I had to move.

I'd stopped wondering how I knew where things were. I rolled out of cover and then dashed across the chamber and into the shelter of another set of pillars. Gunfire cracked out at me and I heard the malignant whine of bullets ricocheting through the chamber. *Please,* I thought, *someone please notice...*

The pillar I hid behind was big, two meters across, carved of solid basalt. It was huge and comfortingly solid, especially seeing as Sashi was shooting live rounds at me.

I knew there'd be a set of stairs off in the darkest part of the room and I wasn't wrong. I ran up them and squeezed off a round at a dimly seen form in the shadows, the light amplification barely showing me the movement in time. *One.*

Bolander fell at my feet, a big welt on her throat from where I'd hit her. I spun and fired in the other direction and I heard Sashi swear and saw her duck back into cover. *Two.*

I had one round left. I cleared the stairs and took shelter behind a low stone block. On impulse, I shouted out to her, "Sashi, you've got live rounds!"

"Shut up, Jiden, I'm not listening to anything you have to say!"

"I'm not lying, someone set us up!" I snapped. In the hope that it would make her hesitate I bounded out of cover and rushed towards her. She leaned out and I was staring down the barrel of her rifle. I flinched as she squeezed the trigger.

The bullet caught me in the thigh and I gave a shout of pain as my leg went out from under me. I saw her freeze then. I didn't give her time to rethink and possibly kill me with the next shot, I fired at her... and my round struck her right on the side of her chest armor. That was my last round and I'd botched it.

"You faker!" Sashi snapped. She rushed forward, bringing her rifle up to fire at me from point blank. As the muzzle came in line with my face, the only thing I could think of was that maybe if I'd paid more attention in Commander Pannja's training, I wouldn't die.

I'm not going to die, I told myself. I swung my rifle into her stomach and as she doubled over, I swung the butt into the side of her helmet. Sashi crumpled to the ground. I levered myself up, leaning on the weapon. I had to get to the center chamber. I had to let people know that someone was trying to kill me.

But instead I fell down. The cool basalt of the floor felt good against my face. *I'll just rest here a moment*, I thought to myself.

Then the world went dark.

***

Chapter Twenty-One: Luck Is My Middle Name

"You're very lucky to be alive, young woman," the female doctor told me for what seemed like the hundredth time. She also seemed to think it was somehow my fault that someone else had shot me. *Then again, last time she saw me, it was because Sashi shot me in the face with a training round...*

Maybe it was my fault, in a way.

I just lay there, trying to make sense of things. Soon enough, the Admiral showed up. She stood at the end of my bed, staring at me. "What a mess this is," she said.

"Is anyone else hurt?" I asked. That had been my big worry, if someone else had live rounds, then one of the other runners could have been hurt or killed.

"No one else on the course was injured," the Admiral answered. I caught the distinction right away.

My eyes widened, "Not one of the candidates..."

The Admiral closed her eyes and looked down. For the first time ever, she looked weary and sad. "Jiden..." To my surprise, she took a seat. "God, this isn't easy. I had to break the news to his mother a few minutes ago."

"What happened, who..."

The Admiral looked up and met my gaze, "Cadet Lieutenant Webster was the architect of the maze. Not long after you were injured, someone noticed that he was missing. He was located in his room. He'd..." She looked away, "he took his own life."

"What?" I stared at her in shock. "Why?" It didn't make any sense. This had nothing to do with him.

"We found drugs in his room," the Admiral said softly. "We haven't finished testing his blood samples, but..." she shrugged, "Cadet Lieutenant Webster tested positive for Rex on his return from his summer assignment in Duncan City last year. I made the decision to set him back a year and give him the option to attend rehabilitation."

"Rex?" I asked in shock. It was a drug, a dangerous drug, I knew. "But..."

"He took the punishment, he came back clean, but it seems the stress was too much for him," the Admiral said. "And his assignment in Duncan City last summer was working in logistics for the military. He would have had access to alter logistic and maintenance records."

My eyes went wide, "You think he was the one behind the other attempts on my life."

"It seems possible," the Admiral said, her lips pinched together in distaste. "I interviewed him, Jiden. I didn't think he had it in him, but the Militia's investigators have gone with it and they put together a pretty convincing case. The rounds in yours and Sashi's weapons were from the same lot of ammunition listed as 'disposed.' As a Training Officer, he could have slipped real rounds in the lot sent to Ogre. The launcher and the explosives used... he could have had access to those things, he would have known how to use them."

"What was his assignment in Duncan City?" I asked, feeling hollow as I considered all that.

"He was assigned to the logistics department of Admiral Drien's staff," the Admiral replied.

I looked up in surprise at that and the Admiral gave a slight shake of her head, as if to tell me not to ask. But I couldn't help but feel there was some kind of connection. But accusing an Admiral of some kind of ties to this... that seemed a little outside my league.

"Is there going to be some kind of service for him?" I asked.

The Admiral gave me an odd look. "All the evidence suggests he tried to kill you multiple times."

I understood that, yet at the same time, all I could feel was pity for him if it was all true. All this time I'd thought I was facing some kind of evil mastermind... and it was just another cadet, one who was in over his head and didn't know what to do.

"He might have made some bad decisions," I said, "but that doesn't necessarily mean he was a bad person." It wasn't all of what I wanted to say, but it was the best I could manage.

The Admiral gave me a nod, "We'll have a service. He wasn't exactly popular and most of his friends graduated last year, but I'm sure there will be those who will wish to attend and pay their respects."

"Does everyone know?" I asked, feeling sick to my stomach as I considered that.

"Yes, Jiden," the Admiral said softly, "Most of the

candidates are in the dark, we cleaned everything up and let them run the course once we confirmed there weren't any other lethal surprises, but the rest of the school and all the Militia either already knows, or will know over the next few weeks. It's bound to get to the media, too. Bad business."

I nodded. I understood, now, why Webster had seemed to hate me so much. I thought about the school's memorial wall, "Will his name go up on the wall?"

The Admiral's face hardened, "No, it won't. That's a wall for heroes, and whatever his reasons, Webster tried to kill a fellow cadet before he took his own life. Webster will get a memorial service, but he won't be buried with military honors and his name will not go up on the wall." Her expression went bleak. "And it's my fault for not stopping him sooner."

"Ma'am, you couldn't have noticed..."

She looked at me and she shook her head, "Jiden, I have this entire facility wired. I see when you and your boyfriend sneak away to kiss, I see when a candidate sneaks food in his room against regulations... I *should* have seen when Webster started taking drugs again. I should have caught him when he put live rounds in those magazines and I should have stopped him. I shouldn't have let him come back here. But I did... and that's on me."

There wasn't anything I could say to that. The Admiral seemed to take Webster's actions personally, as if she could somehow have seen inside his head. I wanted to tell her that it wasn't her fault, but I didn't see a way to make her see it.

"Get better, Jiden. Fall semester starts in just another week," the Admiral said as she stood up. "Now, I'm going to go. Your boyfriend has been wearing a hole in the waiting room floor."

"He's not my..."

I didn't get the chance to finish as she left. For that matter, I wasn't really sure I wanted to finish that thought. I mean, I hadn't thought of Kyle as my boyfriend but...

The door opened and he hurried in. Before I knew what was going on he was bent over the bed, hugging me, "Oh, man, Jiden, you put a big scare in me!"

"Ow," I managed to say. I was on some pretty good painkillers, but he was almost lifting me out of the bed and I had a big hole in my leg.

"Oh, sorry," Kyle gently laid me back down. "Sorry, I just... when they pulled you out of there, you were so pale and there was blood... well, there was blood *everywhere*. I thought for sure you were dead."

"I could do without too much description, thanks," I replied.

"Yeah, well, I'm glad you are alive," he said.

"I'm glad to *be* alive," I replied with a smile. For a moment we just smiled at one another. It felt good. My smile broadened as I remembered the Admiral's parting words. "The Admiral called you my boyfriend."

His eyes went wide and he adopted a worried expression. "The Admiral... she knows, I mean, she what?"

"I kind of like the sound of that," I said.

"You do?" His voice broke a bit and we both chuckled. "Well, I kind of like the sound of that too," Kyle admitted. His eyes narrowed, "By the way, this is the second time you've been shot in two months. You're not allowed to make a habit of it."

"Fine," I grumbled, "take the fun out of life. I'll try to avoid it in the future."

We didn't talk much more after that. He stood there, just being there and it was rather nice.

***

Ashiri visited me a few hours later. "Ashiri!" I said, with a smile. Kyle had just left, promising he'd come back after he got something to eat. That he seemed willing to set by my bed while I just lay there was both endearing and sort of alarming. I wasn't sure I was ready for that level of commitment.

"Jiden," She took a seat. "You sure do spend a lot of time in the hospital. Maybe I should find another roommate."

"Nah," I smiled, "then you wouldn't have the room to yourself nearly as much."

"True," Ashiri snorted. Her expression went serious. "You had us all worried, there, Jiden. When the coroner van showed up, I thought it was for you, at first."

I remembered about Webster, then. "Yeah. I guess it was pretty close. You heard about Webster?"

"The whole school has heard about Webster." She shook her head, "There's a lot of shocked people. Commander Scarpitti and

Commander Pannja are the ones who found him. The inspection of his room wasn't even done before we'd heard a lot of the details."

I grimaced at that. It seemed unfair to Webster. *It wasn't like he was a bad person,* I thought to myself. Yet even as I thought that, I remembered the bombing attempt and the missile that had shot down the commercial skimmer I'd been on. Those didn't fit with what I'd seen of Webster. He'd been irritable. I felt like he hadn't liked me… but a mass murderer? I couldn't see that. But I didn't see a way to explain it.

"The investigators interviewed all of us, but it was like they already knew what they were going to decide before they even started asking questions," Ashiri shook her head. "As soon as they found the drugs in his room, it was over."

"Yeah," I couldn't help but shiver. "I heard he was a Rex addict."

Ashiri rubbed her arms, clearly unsettled by the idea. "Yeah. Rex is nasty stuff... my mom's brother, back at Ten Sisters, he got into Rex Tertious, it really messed him up."

"What's it do?" I asked, despite myself.

"From what I heard, it made him confident, smarter, more focused," Ashiri said. "But it also ate out his brain after a few years. By the end of it, it drove him nuts. He started screaming about alien parasites in people's heads and they locked him up so he wouldn't hurt anyone." She hugged herself, "Bad stuff. Really, really, bad stuff."

I didn't argue. I'd never seen the appeal of that sort of thing. Tony Champion had used alcohol and he'd convinced me, back when I was a bit more impressionable, to have some, but I'd never done much more than sip at it. I didn't even like the painkillers they had me on here in the hospital.

"Where's Alexander at?" I asked, eager to change the subject.

Ashiri blinked at me, "Karmazin? I dunno, probably in his room. I'm sure he'll come by sometime." The way she said it was odd but I wasn't able to quite put my finger on it.

"Aren't you guys hanging out in all the free time we've got?" I asked.

My friend's expression went blank. "Uh, we're not together anymore."

"What?" I asked in shock. "But, you guys were good

together."

She shrugged, "I dunno. I mean, I respect him and everything, but..." She sighed and flopped down in the chair, "You know when you spend so much time with someone that even when you like them, you just kind of want to kill them to get some space?"

"Uh, no," I replied.

"All of Indoc, then the whole Grinder, and then for the rest of the Prep Course we worked together the *whole* time. And it was like, I guess week three of the Grinder that I realized that I wanted some space. That I was tired of all the little things that I'd found cute. We had a talk after the Grinder, and we just sort of decided to take a step back, be friends, you know?" She shook her head, "And did you know that he snores? Ugh, it drove me nuts back at the bunker. Every time we'd get a break and I'd finally get time to sleep, I kept waking up because he snored. When I told him, he just stared at me like I was crazy."

I found that hilarious. I started laughing so hard that I had to double over in bed, gasping for air. "Jiden, what's wrong with you?" Ashiri demanded.

"He snores..." I shook my head, wiping tears out of my eyes. "Ashiri, *you* snore."

She stared at me, "I do not."

I started giggling, imagining Alexander's put upon expression when Ashiri must have told him he snored. "You sound like a freight train," I giggled.

"Oh," Ashiri said. "Okay, maybe I owe him an apology on that, I suppose..."

***

"Hey Jiden," Alexander Karmazin visited me the next day. He gave Kyle a respectful nod. "The Doctor told me that she's ready to keep a room open just for you."

"Hah," I said, "ha, ha."

"Might be a good idea," Kyle admitted.

"Don't you start," I waggled a finger at him. "I'll be out of here tomorrow. They're doing quick heal. I'll need to do a full physical therapy program, but I'll be able to hobble around on my own."

Kyle just gave me a wave as he stepped out in the hallway to answer a call on his datapad.

"Good," Alexander replied. "I got a message from Mackenzie, he wants us ready to start grav-shell practice as soon as he gets back. And Commander Pannja says he saw your clumsy take down of Sashi Drien, he told me to tell you that he expects you at *kerala* practice next Monday."

"Ugh," I said. I thought of the early morning practices. "Maybe I should stay in the hospital a few more days." That wouldn't be much of a reprieve. *Maybe I'll get lucky and injure myself again... where's a good assassination attempt when you need one?*

Before I could even voice that joke, I had another visitor.

"Cadet Armstrong," Commander Bonnadonna nodded at me. "I hear you're doing better."

"Yes, sir," I nodded. Some part of me wanted to apologize to him, to tell him that I'd thought *he* was the one out to get me. But then again, I'd be taking his classes so I probably shouldn't give him reason to dislike me.

"Excellent," he said. "I just came by to let you know that you can take a couple of extra days to finish your military history and your civics papers."

"My what?" I asked.

"The assignments for this coming semester," Commander Bonnadonna replied. "I'm sure you worked on them during your free time in the summer, but you might have lost a few days here in the hospital." He had the slightest smile as he said that. *He knows very well I hadn't realized there were research papers due for those classes.* "So take a couple extra days on them."

He turned and left before I could come up with an appropriate response. My stomach sank as I thought about it. I shot Alexander a look, "Did you..."

He nodded, "Yeah, I knocked them out a few weeks back... you didn't see the read-ahead assignments?"

I hadn't done any of the readings. I'd done the homework for the other classes, but I'd put the rest of the work out of my mind. I had a week before class started. *Plus two more days...*

Alexander gave me a sympathetic look, "I guess you've got a lot of work to do."

"Yeah," I said, "I guess I do..."

Commander Scarpitti stepped in the room, "Cadet Armstrong! I'm glad to hear you're doing better!"

I adopted as friendly a smile as I could as she came over and patted me on the leg. The big blonde woman used a bit more force than I think she realized and I winced as she hit my leg. "You're a very lucky young woman! First that terrible crash and now this... this horrible incident." Her harsh accent put added weight on it.

"Yeah," I said. I guess someone could call it luck. Certainly not *good* luck, not that it all happened to me. Not for the first time, I wondered if I was cursed or something. I remembered that she'd worked with Webster, so on impulse, I asked, "Are you going to the services for Cadet Webster?"

She cocked her head, clearly taken by surprise, "Why would I do that?"

"You worked with him, at Admiral Drien's staff in Duncan City, right?" I asked. I remembered that he'd said she'd given him a game, so that implied some kind of familiarity, right?

"I believe I encountered him a few times, not really enough to make more than an impression," She shook her head. "Maybe if I had more contact with him, I could have steered him away from the poor decisions that led to all this. As harsh as it sounds, I'm glad he took his life, so that he didn't do further damage to the Militia." The coldness of her words startled me. It was one thing to regret what Webster had done. It was quite something different to express gratitude that he'd taken his own life. Even I, who'd been endangered and injured by his actions, regretted that he'd come to the point where he'd taken those actions.

I didn't really know how to respond to that. The room fell into an awkward silence.

"I've already received your engineering homework," she said. "I really appreciate you doing that, especially with what happened. You always have such excellent attention to detail. You'll make a fine engineer, I'm certain. I just wanted to tell you that I'm pulling for you."

Her enthusiasm apparently got the better of her and she patted me on the leg again. "Thanks," I gritted out, trying to be as friendly as I could.

"Ah, Cadet Karmazin, I'm sorry I didn't see you there," she turned and gave him a broad smile. She looked between us, "Are you... together?"

I didn't like the weight she put on that. I was seeing Kyle, not Alexander Karmazin. "No!" I blurted quickly. The *last* thing I wanted was the too-friendly officer giving me some kind of dating advice, especially since Kyle could be back at any moment. "We're just friends."

"Well, I'm glad young Armstrong has such good friends," Commander Scarpitti smiled. "Another bit of luck for you, right Armstrong?" She gave my leg a squeeze and I let out an involuntary groan.

"Oh, sorry," she pulled her hand back. "Lots of weight training, sometimes I forget my own strength." She took a step back and gave me a nod, "Keep up the good work, Armstrong, and keep up that lucky streak!"

I actually breathed a sigh of relief as she left. Sometimes the people trying to help were the worst of the lot. *I've got plenty of luck,* I thought to myself, *all of it bad.*

***

Chapter Twenty-Two: Racing The Clock

Classes started and before I knew it, things went back to the hectic cycle from the spring semester. But there was a different dynamic to it. A lot of cadets gave me a wide berth. The official story hadn't broke yet, but all kinds of rumors were flying. I tried to ignore it, but it was kind of hard when I'd hobble into a room on crutches and everyone would go quiet.

It was something of a relief when the Admiral had the entire school assemble a week into the semester and briefed us. She didn't linger on what Webster had done, she read off the investigation results in a brisk tone. Thankfully, the investigators didn't comment much on my role. If anything, they made it sound like I was just an innocent bystander. I was grateful for that.

The whole dynamic changed overnight. Suddenly no one was talking about me. It was a huge relief. Kyle Regan and I could spend the little bit of free time we had. I could focus more on classes. Things were actually much better.

Of course, better was relative. Cadet Commander Mackenzie was back. He hadn't sought me out to talk about my kissing him. Karmazin had been right, he'd taken a position on the Regimental staff. I'd messaged him once about grav-shell racing, telling him that until my leg healed, I didn't feel up to attending practice. He didn't respond to that.

There was no getting out of Commander Pannja's defense classes though. He seemed to take my injury as some kind of personal challenge. He had me practice moves with my crutches. He had me fight while standing on one leg. He seemed to relish getting me right after I came back from physical therapy and working me until I was trembling with exhaustion.

Ashiri wasn't very sympathetic when I'd drag myself back into our room every night. "You should have just shot her," she said as I was complaining.

"What?" I asked.

"Drien," Ashiri shrugged, "You should have just shot her."

"I didn't want to *kill* her," I said, feeling aghast.

"Well, not somewhere lethal... but she *was* trying to kill you. You could have winged her or something," Ashiri said.

"Could *you* have been certain enough of your shooting not to kill her on accident?" I asked.

Ashiri shrugged, "No, but better her than me. Or her than you, I suppose."

That was all a bit more cold-blooded than I'd expected. "Do you really dislike her that much?" I asked.

"I don't dislike her at all," Ashiri said. "I just don't trust her... and that's the thing. Has she come by and apologized for nearly killing you?"

I shook my head. I hadn't really thought about it, actually. Technically, she'd been in the same set of rooms at the hospital for a few days. I'd hit her hard enough to give her a concussion, or so I'd heard. She hadn't come by once. Then again, I hadn't gone out of my way to see her either.

"Yeah," Ashiri shrugged. "If she'd been in the same circumstances, she would have shot you. In fact, she *did* shoot you, even after you warned her."

"I tried to warn her," I pointed out. "She didn't believe me. She thought I was lying."

Ashiri gave me a stern look, "Jiden, I love you like a sister... but I don't think you *could* lie well. You're painfully straightforward. Whenever you even think something isn't right, you get uncomfortable. There's no way that Sashi really thought you were lying." She frowned, "That's something *she* might try, but you? Not likely."

I wasn't really sure how to take that. I wanted to admit that I'd been sent to the Academy Prep School because I'd deceived my parents... but I almost felt like that was a different person. And in some regards, she was right. I did want to do the right thing. I hated to think I wasn't. That gave me pause though, especially as I considered the ethics classes I'd taken so far... and what Sashi had told me about them when we'd been roommates. *She said that her brothers called it time to sleep.*

Did Sashi feel that way? Did others? I couldn't say that I enjoyed those classes. I always came away from one of Commander Bonnadonna's lectures with a headache, thinking about the implications, thinking about how there were no easy answers. Had I bought into the idea of being a virtuous person, or was it just part of who I was?

***

"Welcome, ladies and gentlemen," Commander Bonnadonna said. "We've covered a lot of material in our civics classes, and today we're going to take a look at the idea of the citizen-soldiers."

I restrained a groan. I recognized the term, because we'd just finished a section about Rome and Sparta in his history class. I found some of it interesting, sure, but it was *ancient* history. I didn't like the names and dates. It seemed silly to me to try to point out where battles had been fought on Old Earth, when it was so impossibly distant that none of us would ever go there in our lifetimes.

"Mister Regan," Commander Bonnadonna pointed, "as members of the Militia, we swear our military oaths to the Colonial Charter and the Colony of Century, why not to the government of Century?"

"Sir, because the Colonial Charter is the foundation of our government," Kyle answered quickly. I couldn't help but feel proud of him. He always seemed to have an answer.

"A point... but not entirely correct," Commander Bonnadonna said, his deep voice clearly amused. "Is the Charter Council not the embodiment of our government? Do they not represent the people of our world? They pass our laws and they allocate our funding."

"But the President is the executive power," Duchan spoke up.

"Indeed, and she's also our Commander-in-Chief," Commander Bonnadonna nodded. "Why not give our oaths to President Patricia McIntosh and the Charter Council, then, as our reigning government?"

No one answered. As the silence grew long, I heard myself speak, "Because the Colonial Charter guarantees our rights."

"Ah... an interesting point, Miss Armstrong," Commander Bonnadonna's dark eyes glittered as he looked at me. "Someone has clearly done the read-ahead. Please explain further."

I flushed a bit, but I spoke up, "The Colonial Charter lays out what the government can and can't do, and it says what rights that citizens possess, it establishes how the government is supposed to do business." I swallowed nervously as I considered how to say the next part. "We swear an oath to it and to the people of Century, in case we need to act to defend them from the government."

The room had gone still. I'd basically said that we had a duty to take up arms against the Charter Council and the President... if the situation warranted it.

"That is correct, Miss Armstrong," Commander Bonnadonna nodded. "It's a point I want all of you to understand. Our loyalty is to our world and the people of this world. As officers, we must always examine the intent of our orders and judge that against our oath to the Colonial Charter." His deep voice went stern, "You will see it in our history classes again and again, it is often not the external foes that destroy nations, it is their internal foes, ambitious men and women who will twist and distort the law to suit themselves. As military officers, it falls to us to be the final guardian of our nation to defend it from itself, if necessary."

I found myself holding my breath and let it out in a gasp. I wasn't the only one. The very idea of some kind of civil war terrified me. Especially with what I'd read about how nasty those could be.

"Now, let's talk a bit about *why* we have some of the things in the Colonial Charter," Commander Bonnadonna went on. "First off, we'll get this out of the way right now, it is not a perfect document. It was drafted in a very different time. That said, there are processes to amend it. We'll get into those later. But first, let's talk about the circumstances of our Colonial Charter... Cadet Drien, perhaps you could speak to it."

I looked over at Sashi. Her dark skin flushed as she realized why she'd been selected. Most of the rest of the class realized it too, which meant we all paid a lot more attention to her words. "There were two initial waves of colonists to Century," Sashi said. She cleared her throat, "What we call Firsts and Seconds. The Firsts all came from North America and Europe on Old Earth. They'd purchased the rights to Century and they intended to set it up as a sort of religious enclave." I felt uncomfortable when she said it that way. The Firsts had been very homogenous, Elder Duncan Michaels, the main backer of the colony, had centered it on religious grounds, yes, but it wasn't like they were religious fanatics.

"The Seconds were deportees from parts of Asia and India," Sashi went on. "They were a mix of political prisoners, convicts, and other undesirables. A few months after the Firsts arrived at

Century, the Seconds showed up in a UN Colonization ship, with a military escort to ensure that the Firsts would take the additional colonists."

"Yes, it was quite the shock, I'd imagine," Commander Bonnadonna nodded. "Go on."

"There was a lot of conflict between Firsts and Seconds," Sashi said. "Firsts had claimed most of the arable land, most of the areas with fresh water. They had all the best equipment and they had supplies for themselves. The Seconds didn't have anywhere to go. There were some clashes, some violence..."

"Riots and murders," someone muttered.

"There was talk of war, until Lawrence Snow called a council. He met with Lorenzo Phan and Li-Ang Chen from the Seconds and they drafted the Colonial Charter together," Sashi said.

"Very good," Commander Bonnadonna nodded. "And it's a little-known bit of history that Brigham Drien was one of the Charter signatories, a First who married a Second. Miss Drien can trace her lineage right back to one of our major historical figures."

My eyes widened a bit at that. Sashi, though, just sort of hunched on herself as we looked at her. Apparently she didn't think that was a good thing.

"So what did the Colonial Charter do?" Commander Bonnadonna asked. "First off, it established limits on land ownership. Land was the main point of contention. Firsts had claimed the majority of the farmable and inhabitable land. The Colonial Charter established that you could only own land that you put to use. What that meant was that many Firsts had to either give up vast tracts of land or they had to allow Seconds to come and help them work that land, often with some kinds of incentives such as parcels of that land for themselves and their families."

I remembered that, now. Technically, my father was a Second. His grandfather had been one of those workers, though he'd turned around and sold the land to pay for an education and he'd eventually gone into archeology. He'd been one of the first xeno-archeology professors at Nelson's University.

"It also established the government structure that holds to this day. The Firsts were outnumbered by the Seconds, so they didn't want to lose control over their world. They established a representative government where land-ownership equated to votes...

and where the twelve men and women who owned the most land, or had the votes of the majority of land-owners, were the law-makers." He looked around the room. "Does anyone see any issues with this?"

"It kept the Seconds out of government for a long time," Kyle noted from next to me.

"They saw that as something of a benefit," Commander Bonnadonna noted. "More of a feature than a bug, you might say. Miss Martinez, what do you think?"

"It meant the wealthy families with the money and the land made the laws," Martinez said after a moment. When Commander Bonnadonna gave her a nod, she went on, "So, wouldn't they make laws that kept them in power?"

"Indeed," Commander Bonnadoona nodded, "Just that, Miss Martinez. That led to the Landowner Crisis. Which we will cover later on in this class. The intent was that the executive branch would counter that power. Our popularly elected president has veto power... but often that president has come from the same families as the Charter Council."

I hadn't really thought about it that way. I couldn't help but think of Charterer Beckman, and the way she'd seemed to think that rules didn't apply to her.

"There have been some changes in more recent times. Sometimes minor upsets, such as when Mister Champion of Champion Enterprises managed to temporarily gain a seat at the Charter Council. But these types of events tend to be rather rare. By and large, our government has been rather static. That's been a boon to stability, but we'll dive into some of the pros and cons in our later classes. Now, then, ladies and gentlemen, let's talk about this week's research paper..."

***

Commander Pannja stared around at the gathered class. We stood on a section of pavement. In front of us, there was a row of skimmers, ranging from a sleek, two-seater civilian racing skimmer to a pudgy-looking utility skimmer to the predatory form of a combat skimmer.

"Who here has flown a skimmer?" He asked. "I'm not talking about in a simulator. We've all done that plenty to this point,

I'm talking a real skimmer."

I hesitantly raised my hand, along with a few others.

"Armstrong, put your hand down, you got shot down; that doesn't count."

I sheepishly lowered my hand. A few of my classmates laughed at that. Kyle clapped me on the shoulder and grinned.

"Alright," Commander Pannja said. "Three of you. Martinez, I know you've got your civilian license, so that gives you some marginal ability to help out. We've done the simulator training for the past month. I've taught you all the theory. Today I'm going to take you up. You'll get some stick time. Hopefully you won't smash us into the ground and wreck one of my aircraft."

We chuckled at the joke. I was nervous. My one foray into flying had hardly been what anyone would term successful. At least I should have the opportunity to watch some of the others take their turns. I was halfway back in the group.

"Now, I'll take you up, one by one. When you're not in a skimmer with me, I want you in the seats running the simulation programs. Today is just a familiarization flight, so you can get the feel of real flying and see the differences from it and simulators."

He pulled up his datapad, "Armstrong, you're up first." *Of course,* I thought, *today we do things in alphabetical order...*

I hurried forward and followed him to the little red racing skimmer. He guided me through an exterior inspection and then he waited for me to climb up the ladder and then watched me as I strapped myself in. He quirked a smile as I double-checked the seat restraints. "I suppose I don't need to give you the lecture about safety devices, do I, Armstrong?"

I flushed, "No, sir."

He took the other seat and strapped himself in. "Go ahead and go through the preflight checks.

I did as I was told, cycling through the checks and then starting the skimmer up. The whine of the turbines sent a bit of a jolt through me. I'd been through two crashes... was I ready for this?

"Take her up, Biohazard, nice and easy," Commander Pannja said. I rolled my eyes at the nickname, but I did as I was told.

My nervousness vanished as I brought the turbines up and the light craft seemed to leap into the air. My hands went across the controls and I stabilized it, but it had so much power that I felt like the thing wanted to blast straight up into the sky... and part of me really wanted to let it.

"Nice and easy," Commander Pannja said again. "Slow loop around the landing area."

"Yes, sir," I said. It startled me how easy it felt after the simulators. The racer really wanted to surge ahead, but I kept the speed down and did a slow, steady loop around the landing strip.

"Good job, Armstrong," Commander Pannja said as we came back to where I'd lifted off from. "I've got the stick."

"Aye, aye, sir," I replied, just as my controls went dead. I had a moment of panic, but then I realized that he'd just shut my controls off as he took over.

He settled us towards the landing spot. "I think you could have landed it, but you're not certified yet, and I don't want to ruin a perfectly good day for flying if you manage to prove me wrong," Commander Pannja said. "I was a bit worried that you'd be skittish at the controls after what you've been through, but well done. Go ahead and do the post-flight and then tell Cadet Do to head over."

I did as I was told, and as I jogged away from the skimmer, I found my hands itching a bit. It was odd. Flying the little red racing skimmer shouldn't have felt different from the ones in the simulators. But there had been something *alive* about it. Something free and exciting and *pure*.

I hadn't expected to like flying. My one earlier experience in actual flight had started with me trying to escape from people trying to kill me and ended with me crashing after those same people had shot my skimmer up. *Plus I crashed into their skimmer in the process...*

But I had liked it. In fact, I really hoped I'd get a second chance to go up again today. And while before I'd viewed the idea of getting my skimmer license as just another hurdle, now I wondered if that meant I'd get to fly some of the Academy's skimmers more often. I thought I remembered something about a skimmer racing team...

I'd have to look into it.

***

Cadet Commander Mackenzie cornered me on the day I got my clearance from physical therapy to have the full use of my leg.

"Armstrong," He gave me a brisk nod, "you're going to be at grav-shell practice tomorrow."

He'd caught me by surprise and I started a bit. "Sir!" It took me a moment to form words. Before I could respond more than that, he was gone. I didn't know if he was angry with me for avoiding practice, or for the whole kissing him thing, or if he was angry at all. But I guess I was going to find out.

I showed up the next morning and before I really knew what was going on, I was back in the seat of a grav-shell and we were going through a practice race. I didn't have time to worry about what Mackenzie thought about me. I didn't have time to do much more than shout commands and steer. The familiar rush of the speed and the ground speeding past banished all my worries and fears and I just enjoyed the moment.

We coasted back to the shed just as the sun rose over the horizon. Mackenzie gave me a hand in climbing out while Stroud shelved the Daisy. I was suddenly aware of how close I stood to Mackenzie and I took an awkward step back. He looked over at me, his expression odd.

"I should head back, I suppose," I said. He held up a hand, then waved at Stroud as he headed off to get changed. Quite suddenly, we were alone in the grav-shell shed. I swallowed nervously.

"You've been avoiding me," Mackenzie said.

I wasn't really sure how to answer that.

"I'd like to know why," he said.

"I could have gotten us both in a lot of trouble last time I saw you," I said. The words came out in a rush. "It was stupid of me and..."

He waved a hand, "Ah, *that.*" He shook his head, "Look, Armstrong, you're a nice enough girl... but you're a little young for me. It's flattering, but..."

I flushed as I realized he was trying to let me down easy. "It's *fine,*" I interrupted him. "I'm seeing someone, Kyle Regan from Dust Company."

"Oh, good," he said. "I'm glad that worked itself out then." His expression went serious. "I thought you were avoiding me because of this business with Webster. I thought you didn't trust me. I thought you suspected I was working with him or something."

"No!" I protested. "That's ridiculous. I mean, all the evidence the investigators found suggested he worked alone. Besides, you've helped me out... it's not like you tried to kill me."

"If I wanted to, I'm sure I could have done it," Mackenzie snorted. His expression went solemn, "I still find it hard to believe, honestly. Webster was one of my Cadet Instructors when I was a candidate. He was a friend of mine... last year when I heard he got set-back it was a shock. Then this..." His blue eyes were clouded as he looked out at the sunrise. "I wish there was something I could have done for him. I wish I could have helped him, you know?"

I nodded. People threw out lines about tragedy, but this was what that felt like. Everyone said that Webster had been a promising young man... where had he gone wrong? His death left everyone with more questions and for all that he'd nearly killed me several times, I couldn't find it in me to be glad that he was dead.

"Well, anyway, I hope you'll stick with the grav-shell team," Mackenzie said. "We've got a lot of races coming up soon and this is my last season."

"Of course, sir," I replied. "I'm in."

"Good," he said, "because you've got a lot of catching up to do. We need to shave a good thirty seconds off our start times if we're going to place in these next few races." He closed his eyes. "I just forwarded you race footage from some of our competition, I want you to study it, get to know their tactics..."

He started laying out strategy and I realized that maybe this was going to be a bit more involved than I'd hoped.

***

"The important thing to remember while you calculate the strength of the warp field generated, is power versus cost," Commander Scarpitti said. "Most people generally correlate the strength with the size of the ship, which is true to a point. The main limitations are power and cost. Building a powerful warp drive smaller requires a massive expenditure of molecular circuitry and a great deal of engineering to attain decent efficiency, and a sufficiently powerful antimatter plant to operate it. That's why larger ships, which have more space for bigger drives and larger powerplants, typically have stronger warp fields."

The first few weeks of Fall Semester had flown past and now

classes were going full swing. All of the classes had grown much harder and I almost felt like I was trying to dig sand with a dinner fork. There was just so much to learn... and I wasn't the only one wondering why we were tackling some extremely hard subjects in our first full year on campus.

"Ma'am," Duchan asked, "why are we *designing* a warp field? I mean, most of this stuff is off the shelf, we don't exactly have shipyards, after all."

"We don't have *military* shipyards," Commander Scarpitti nodded. "We do, however, have several civilian shipyards in the system. True, they aren't exactly able to build ships to military standards, but we do have military engineers on liaison with them. During war-time, they could be converted to production of smaller warships."

That didn't seem like a great idea to me. The two shipyards she spoke of, Secundis Station and Century Station, were tiny things. Secundis built mining ships, which didn't even have an FTL warp drive, just in-system drives. Century Station was bigger, it was owned by Champion Enterprises, but it built small freighters and transports. The size of vessel they could produce probably wouldn't be much use in a real war.

"There's also an element of knowledge here that you need to learn in order to repair these systems," Commander Scarpitti went on with a friendly smile. To me, she seemed condescending, like she was talking down to us. "If you know how to design a warp field, you'll know how to repair it."

"Before we go into the deeper math, let's refresh on the importance of a deeper warp drive, shall we?" She looked around the class expectantly. Her harsh accent made her otherwise innocuous words somehow seem almost threatening.

"Ma'am, the deeper or stronger the warp drive, the higher overall relative velocity that a ship can produce," I said, not really understanding why we were discussing something so basic so far along in the class. So far, we'd already gone through designing the antimatter containment fields on reactors, radiation shielding, and a variety of other complicated things, comparatively, this was child's play.

"And?" she asked.

I considered it for a moment, wondering what else she

wanted me to say. *We are talking about military ships, and stronger drives mean they take more damage...* "The deeper the drive, the more damage it can take."

"Ah, there's a key point... and it's totally wrong," Commander Scarpitti turned to her display and started sketching a simplified diagram of a warp drive, the curvature of space looking like a wave. "That's a common misconception and that's why we're bringing it back to the basics. You can have a deeper drive that isn't resistant to damage." She turned and smiled at me, as if to suggest there was no insult meant. Still, it irritated me that she'd set me up that way. I'd known the answer wasn't exactly right, but she'd prompted me to say it anyway.

"It's normal for most people to correlate a deeper drive with a stronger drive. Most engineering programs teach it that way. But that's *wrong*. In fact, there's a geometry of the warp field that comes into play. Until relatively recently, most warp drives were built to project a gradual curve, like this," she said, gesturing at the display. The long, smooth curve looked like a normal warp field to me.

"Merchant vessels typically use a compressed curve because you can get one with lower power requirements." She brought up a second warp field curve, this one just as deep, but with less length. "What observation showed, however, is that a compressed curve drive can produce equal relative velocities, but with far less capability to take damage."

Next to both images, she created an explosion. That represented antimatter and matter combining, releasing a massive burst of radiation and particles. On both diagrams, the waves were squeezed by the detonation, the curve bowing. On the military drive, it resumed its previous shape, on the civilian one, the two edges bowed together until they touched and the warp field collapsed.

"This is fairly common knowledge among professional engineers," Commander Scarpitti said. "And all ship commanders know that merchant ships and military ships have different capabilities to sustain damage. This is the key reason... and until the past decade, it was generally assumed that a deeper and *broader* drive field was necessary to sustain a military grade warp field."

She brought up a third warp field, this one very different from the other two. It was sharp, almost angular. "This, is what we've begun calling a Zubaran Field, a variation of the standard

Alcubierre Field. It looks radically different because it was designed to be radically different, by a military engineer on Drakkus Prime."

I frowned as I looked at it. The curve was asymmetric, the inward side went down steeply while on the outward side it arced up more gently. Commander Scarpitti detonated the simulated bomb again. The other two diagrams bowed, the new field barely quivered. "This is a modeling projection based off of observed data. We haven't been able to learn exactly *how* Drakkus does it, but this drive is far more robust than a normal military drive. It seems they're keeping their secrets to themselves on how to make it, but we also suspect, from the size of the vessels mounting them, that it's also more efficient. This is a military grade drive with a depth equal to a cruiser... and it's mounted in a destroyer."

The class went silent. It wasn't just that that was impressive. It was that Drakkus was sort of infamous for being aggressive. They'd recently conquered the Oberon system. They'd conquered other star systems. And in reality, they weren't very far away from Century.

"Warp theory is old. We've managed increases in efficiencies by using newer solid state technology, but this, ladies and gentlemen, is something that changes the entire paradigm. This is why we study warp theory, because something like this could be incredibly valuable... and someone in this room might learn how to do it."

***

Chapter Twenty-Three: Something Rings A Bell

The semester continued to fly by and I started to have less and less time to do anything other than sleep, go to class, train, and occasionally go to grav-shell races.

Now that we'd learned our roles for drills, they put us through rotations where we learned every other job. Some of them seemed easy at first, until they threw in more complicated scenarios. We learned how to load up the warp-fighters, running the antimatter warheads from the deep bunkers to the hangars. We learned how to operate the aerial defenses. We learned how to load and arm the combat skimmers. We ran through scenarios where we were the attacking force or where they'd do an aerial transport and put us on the defense in a different location. Sometimes it was to the Grinder where we'd operate against a unit training there. Sometimes it was other places on the planet where we'd act as defenders or attackers. Half the time we got a briefing on the fly and it was clear that our team and section leaders had no more preparation or information than they gave us.

Every weekend it was something different. Every exercise, our training officers watched us, evaluating our every move. I quickly saw that while my plebe class struggled to learn and become proficient with all the new skills, the next year's upper classmen were preparing to take over. In just a few months, the first classmen would graduate and then the second classmen would take over... and they were trying to get ready for that.

Everything continued at a furious pace. I got more time in skimmers. Not just in the simulator, but actually flying. It was like grav-shell racing, only with far more power. I actually felt guilty when I thought that... and when I realized that I liked flying a skimmer more than driving a grav-shell.

Through it all, there was class and there was my friends and Kyle Regan. It startled me, one day as we were running, just how much of a part of my life he'd become. We studied together, we hung out together, and that started to feel natural. It felt far better than my crush on Karmazin or the weird feelings I'd had for Mackenzie. With Kyle, I really felt like we worked together, I felt like we complemented one another.

The breakneck pace didn't slow, either, as we came up on our final exams for classes. The scariest part of it all was listening to upper classmen and even the first classmen. I figured they'd have a handle on things, that this would become easier.

They were struggling just as much as the rest of us. Cadet Third Class Trask failed too many of his engineering exams, he was getting set back and he'd return next year. He'd be in our class, which was really strange to think about. Gault failed out, he just couldn't keep up with the work and one day he was packing up his stuff. The first classmen were putting in their requests for their assignments for after graduation, but some of them weren't even sure they *were* graduating.

Could I handle three more years of this... or worse, four? What would I do if I hit another class like Commander Scarpitti's, only this time I failed it? The constant pressure, the constant stress, it was unlike anything else. Yet part of me loved it. I didn't have any distractions. No one was trying to kill me. All I had to do was focus on classes and duties.

I stopped gaming. Grav-shell season ended and I stopped going to practice. I wasn't the only one. Dawson came by and told me that the whole shed was empty, no one had time. I stopped going to Commander Pannja's *kerala* classes, mostly because I had too much to study for, and I put up with his stern looks during our flight training and told him that I'd be back as soon as I finished finals.

I was nearing the end of the first year... but I realized this wasn't a sprint, it was a marathon. I had another three years... and this was only the beginning. All of this was to prepare us to be officers in the Century Planetary Militia. Was I really going to be ready for that?

Struggling with questions like that made me feel like I was writing another of Commander Bonnadonna's papers.

***

"Is finals over with yet?" Ashiri asked plaintively.

"Not yet," I said. We'd spent most of the past week studying hard. I'd knocked out the final edits on my civics paper for Commander Bonnadonna. Despite myself, despite my previous distrust for him, I'd actually come to like the class. The history class, too. I didn't *want* to like the subjects. They were way outside of my interests, but the constant engagement, the struggle to find answers to complicated problems... I'd started to find myself caught up in it.

It was like a game, or a puzzle, one where there wasn't a predetermined answer. In this puzzle, trying to find the right answer, or even just the questions we asked ourselves, was the point as much as any answers we came up with.

I'd already signed up for one of his classes for next year.

"There's only so much we can be expected to do," Ashiri groaned. "I can't believe this test review from Commander Scarpitti... it covers *everything.*"

"Yeah," I nodded. She'd seemed to find it amusing to lay out the entire semester in her review. I was more than a little aghast. Normally, at any other school, each of the subjects we'd covered in her field theory class would have been separate senior-level classes. In fact, if I understood things right, we'd cover each of them in separate classes over the next few years.

But her review had gone into exhausting detail and she'd told us that we'd have to run through the calculations for a ship design to a set of parameters she'd send us, covering the antimatter plant, the radiation shielding, and the warp field design. It made my head hurt thinking about it. I'd spent hours studying with Kyle and I still felt like I barely had a grasp for what I needed to cover.

Most of my other classes weren't nearly as involved. "Ready for the flight test?" I asked.

"Yeah," Ashiri nodded. "I saw you and Kyle down at the simulators earlier today, you having issues with meeting the checkpoints for Commander Pannja?"

"Uh, no," I flushed. Kyle and I had been playing games together, going through a racing sim that his father had sent him. "We were just spending time together, you know?"

"Oh," Ashiri said. There wasn't anything I could put my finger on, but she almost sounded disappointed. I thought about how her relationship with Alexander Karmazin had sort of fizzled.

Probably best to change the subject. "How's your family doing?"

"Good," Ashiri smiled, "they can't afford to fly out for the end of the year, but they're doing well. My little sister is trying to knock out all the prerequisites for the Academy."

"Oh, she's got two years, right?" I asked, trying to remember. When Ashiri nodded, I couldn't help but smile, "Maybe my brother will be one of her Cadet Instructors."

"Oh, your brother is attending for sure, then?" Ashiri asked.

I nodded. "He sent in his packet for the Prep Course as an early submission and he got his acceptance letter yesterday. My mom's not all that happy about it, but she's supporting his decision."

"That's good!" Ashiri nodded. "That's really good." She went quiet for a moment. "My brother, he's interested in coming, but I don't know... my parents are very against it."

I remembered. "What do you think?" I asked.

Ashiri shrugged, "I want him to do what he wants to do, but I worry about what my parents will say about it. It shouldn't be an issue, but my mom is very traditional..." She sighed, "In Ten Sisters, it wouldn't even be an option. In many ways, my parents love Century, but in some others they cling to the way things *were...* you know?"

I didn't, really. But I thought about Sashi Drien, how she'd attended the Academy against her father's and grandfather's wishes. Her situation was different, yet it wasn't, really. I saw that Ashiri expected some sort of response. "Everyone has disagreements with their family, I guess."

"That is for certain," Ashiri nodded. She bit her lip, "Have you seen that we're in the first group scheduled for implants next year?"

I nodded. Doctor Aisling's classes this semester had focused on how to gain the best use of the neural computer and how to integrate its functions and avoid typical issues. I still felt uncertain about the whole idea. Part of that was the stigma, the fear. Part of it was that it was something so *permanent.* Once we had the neural computer, we'd have it for life. There wasn't a safe way to remove it. Doctor Aisling said there was a way to shut it down, to make it inert, but it would still be there.

"I guess it's bound to happen sooner or later, right?" I asked.

"Did you... do you think the special testing we went through will be involved, somehow?" Ashiri asked. She sounded a bit breathless as she asked it... and I felt my own heart race a bit as I remembered the feeling, the power, of being tied into her machines.

"Maybe," I shrugged, feeling uncomfortable. "I try not to

think about it too much," I admitted. I didn't like Doctor Aisling. She scared me, more than a little. The thought that she might have done something to my mind, to *all* our minds, terrified me.

"Me either," Ashiri said. "All the same, I hope we get connected like that again. It was just so... *amazing.*" She looked down, as if suddenly ashamed.

I didn't really know how to respond. Some part of me felt the same way.

***

"Final test results are up!" Karmazin shouted from down the hall, "We've got our final point ratings for the year... go Sand Dragon!"

I pulled the results up on my datapad. The first thing I checked was my score from Commander Scarpitti's final. I'd passed... and for that I breathed a sigh of relief. I hadn't done *great*, but the list of scores, each one with an alphanumeric identifier label instead of a name, showed that passing was an achievement in and of itself. She'd failed nine or ten people just from my class.

I already knew I'd passed my flight test and I wasn't worried about my other exams, so I pulled up the class scores and found my name. *Jiden Armstrong, ranking number two.* "Karmazin beat me out for first place this year," I commented.

"I'm third... *again*," Sashi gave a sigh. "Oh, look at this, your *boyfriend* is number six, that's a big jump..."

I looked down the list recognizing more of the names. Dawson had made the top ten as well. I wasn't surprised to see Bolander and Thorpe in the top twenty. I didn't think either of them were as good at the technical classes, but both of them had gone the pure tactical track, which meant they didn't have the hurdle of Commander Scarpitti's engineering class.

I kept scrolling down spotting names I recognized. My eyes widened, though, as I found Sashi Drien midway down the list. Her point breakdown showed a zero for a class and when I checked, I saw it was Commander Scarpitti's class. She couldn't have done well in her other classes, either, not with a serious drop like that.

She failed a class. I should have felt some bit of satisfaction. She'd shot me, she seemed to hate my guts. She probably would have done a cheer if our situations had been reversed. But I just felt empty. I didn't *want* her to do badly, I realized.

"Look at this!" Ashiri hurried over to my desk and switched over the display to the First Class rankings. "Mackenzie got top tier! He graduated first in his class!" Right next to his name was a big star... that meant he was clear to graduate and his final rating was confirmed.

"Wow," my eyes widened as I realized what that meant. A moment later, I heard some shouts and then a dozen first-classmen were running down the hallway, they were pushing Mackenzie ahead of them. They all looked so happy, so exuberant. I couldn't help but envy them. *It will be my turn, in three years.*

They rushed down the corridor and the rest of us followed. Out on the parade field, I saw the entire school had gathered, the First Classmen running for the decorative area at the front of the parade ground. There was a bunch of decorative statues and military monuments there, so at first I didn't understand what they were doing.

Mackenzie ran up to a platform, atop of which was a big bell. He gave a shout and rang the bell, yanking hard on the lanyard and filling the entire parade ground with discordant notes. The entire school cheered. I saw him throw his hands up in victory and I couldn't help but cheer with everyone else. Five years of hard work had paid off for him. He hopped down and another first classman hopped up behind him to ring the bell, then another. The cheering went on, but after a few minutes, the crowd started to thin.

As the seventh or eighth person rang the bell, I looked at Ashiri, "Is this going to go on for a while?"

She nodded, "*Everyone* rings the bell."

There were three hundred cadets up there to ring the bell. It looked like it would take a while. Hours maybe. The bell rang again and I suddenly had a headache at the discordant noise. "I'm going to walk around for a minute."

"What?!" Ashiri shouted.

"See you later!" I shouted back.

The press of the crowd, the shouts and the cheering were too much for me. I backed out of the crowd and then headed off as fast as I could go. The ringing of the bells and cheering making it hard to think. *The arena,* I thought to myself, *it should be empty right now.*

I leaned over the balcony of the arena, looking down into the maze that Webster had built. After the noise and disruption up at the parade ground, it felt good to be in the calm and quiet. From this perspective the familiar feeling gnawed at me again. I didn't know where I'd seen it before or why it felt so familiar.

I leaned against one of the big pillars that held up the arena ceiling, looking down at the maze. The idea was there, just outside of realization and it drove me. I didn't know *why* it bugged me so much. Webster was dead. It wasn't as if knowing why the maze looked familiar would really matter to anything. In a couple weeks, they'd tear the whole thing down anyway.

I looked down at the chamber where I'd nearly died. The massive basalt pillars jutting from the floor and terminating in open space, held in place by their own massive weight. *They'd be connected to the ceiling, though... or carved from the same rock as the ceiling and floor and walls...*

The idea started to coalesce.

"I'm not going to quit!" A raised voice interrupted my train of thought.

I went still, recognizing Sashi Drien's voice.

"You failed a class, you barely passed several others, and you switched your degree back to the tactical track despite father's advice," I peeked around the pillar and I saw Sashi and one of her older brothers a quarter of the way around the arena stands. "If you continue, then you will only bring further embarrassment to our family. Think of our grandfather, think of how it will look to have one of his grandchildren fail out."

"I thought *you* agreed with father, that it didn't matter how well a woman did," Sashi snapped. "Or was that only when I did well?"

"You still came in third to that *kutaya*," her brother sneered. I wanted to punch him, not just for insulting me, but for treating Sashi that way. "And that was *last* year. This year you are barely midway up the ranking. If you'd failed another class, you would be removed from the Academy and I wouldn't even have to ask you."

"I won't fail, and I won't quit!" Sashi snapped

I felt suddenly embarrassed, I didn't mean to be

eavesdropping, but this certainly wasn't a conversation they meant for others to hear.

"You *will* resign," her brother responded, his voice confident. "Father had me draft your resignation letter. All you have to do is sign and submit it. If you do not, then the family will not support you. You will be disowned, father will not recognize your name and *grandfather* will make certain that you have no career, even if you *do* somehow manage to graduate."

Sashi didn't respond. "I'll give you a few hours to consider your options. You will resign before the graduation ceremony. Do the right thing, Sashi." He turned and walked away towards the nearest set of doors.

Sashi turned and walked in my direction. I bit my lip and crouched back against the pillar. *Please don't see me...*

I thought she wouldn't. She walked right past me...and then my tablet vibrated to signal I had a message.

Sashi turned and saw me. "You..." Her eyes narrowed. "You heard that, did you? You must be gloating. You've ruined my life!"

"I didn't do anything, Sashi," I answered. "You did this yourself."

I probably should have been more diplomatic.

"I'll kill you!" Sashi hissed. She came at me, flailing limbs and anger and it was everything I could do not to let her shove me right over the railing. We struggled for a second. I caught an elbow to the sternum and I kneed her in the stomach. We both stumbled back.

"Cadets," a voice barked. "Stop right there."

We both looked up. Commander Bonnadonna stood there, his expression hard. For a second, I felt a spurt of real fear at the anger I saw there. "What's going on here?"

Sashi opened her mouth, I wasn't sure what she was going to say, but I knew it wouldn't be good for her and probably not for me.

"Just a misunderstanding, sir," I said. I didn't know how much he'd seen, whether he knew she'd attacked me or not, but I didn't want her to get in further trouble.

"A misunderstanding?" Commander Bonnadonna looked between us. "Well, *Cadets*, perhaps you should be more careful about what you say... and do. Cadet Armstrong, get out of here."

"Yes sir," I responded. I put my head down as I hurried away, feeling a bit ashamed that I hadn't told the whole truth. I hadn't lied, not really, but...

I shot a glance behind me as I left and saw him standing there, his face stern. *He knows,* I realized, *and he's not happy about it.*

***

Chapter Twenty-Four: The Pieces All Fell Into Place

I didn't really know what to do. I could still hear the bell ringing and the cheers. I needed to distract myself from the noise and from what had happened with Sashi and I. My mind went to the maze and I fixated on that and the random thought I'd had about the ceiling. When I got back to my room, I pulled it up on my datapad. The barracks was pretty much empty. Almost everyone was at the parade ground. I was glad for the quiet and lack of interruptions. I pulled up the map that Webster had uploaded and zoomed in on this area or that, but I wasn't getting it. It wasn't familiar from a game, it was somewhere I'd been... and it was driving me insane.

I stared at the map of the maze for a long time. On impulse, I printed it out and set the sheet of paper on my desk. I turned it sideways and it seemed more familiar. I took a pen and started drawing a long entrance shaft, where it would connect to the surface. I started drawing other details, crossing out sections that didn't seem right, areas where I could tell that Webster had altered the overall design for the exercise.

It wasn't until I started drawing the buildings of Black Mesa Outpost just outside the entrance until I realized what it was that I was staring at. It wasn't a maze, it was the ruins under Black Mesa. It was the access tunnels that my parents had excavated. That was why it was so familiar. I'd grown up there, following them from tunnel to tunnel. That was why the maze had seemed so familiar and alien at the same time. It wasn't weathered and old and it wasn't lit by portable lights. I'd seen it in the green shades of my visor's night vision.

In fact, the diagram pretty much exactly matched the sensor survey that my parents had taken a couple years earlier, back when Tony Champion and his father had been there. I remembered then. Tony had asked me to see a copy, and I'd sent him a digital copy that I'd taken off my mom's datapad. It had been a simple thing. I hadn't thought of it since...

How had Webster seen a copy of that map? The only answer I could come up with was that Tony must have given it to him, but I had no idea why.

No, I thought, *that's not right...* Webster had mentioned the maze, he'd said he got the idea from a game that Commander Scarpitti had given him. Commander Scarpitti had worked in Duncan City. She'd somehow had the image of the alien ruins at Basalt Outpost that I'd given Tony Champion. Webster had trusted her. He probably wouldn't have thought anything if she'd called him aside during the final exercise...

She would have had access to ammunition to swap real rounds for the training rounds during the Grinder and at the final exercise. She'd have had the experience to use the launcher and the explosives. She was an engineer, so she probably knew what parts would have been the most valuable for the smugglers to take.

I reached for my datapad and then I heard the door open.

I spun, half expecting Ashiri, "You're not going to believe..."

I trailed off. It wasn't Ashiri. Commander Scarpitti stood in the doorway. "Cadet Armstrong," she said with a pleasant smile, "What is it, exactly, that I won't believe?"

I didn't know how she'd got the door open. I didn't know how she knew I knew. I opened my mouth to shout.

She kicked me in the stomach. I doubled over, gasping for air. I felt like I wanted to vomit, but I couldn't control my diaphragm. I lay there, like a beached fish, gasping, unable to speak, unable to move.

Commander Scarpitti squatted next to my head, cocking her head, her smile still pleasant, as if we were discussing something casual. "I could have killed you just now, Armstrong. I pulled that kick, just enough. You won't suffocate with a ruptured diaphragm. You should be grateful. Don't feel like you need to thank me, though."

I saw her stand up and pick up my datapad. She typed in a message. "Now, I think it's time for you and Cadet Drien to have a conversation. Something appropriately dire, I think. How about, 'let's settle things, see you at the maze.' Hmm?"

I tried to force out words. I felt tears work their way down my face as I rocked back and forth, trying to get my body to move.

She pulled out an injector and touched it to my throat. "Now, time for you to go to sleep."

The world faded out.

***

I woke up in the dark. My hands were tied behind me, tied off to my feet. I shifted around, my stomach a ball of agony from where Scarpitti had kicked me. I managed to roll over and my fingers found warm flesh.

"Who's there?" I asked.

"Jiden?" I recognized Sashi Drien's voice. "What's going on, why am I tied up. What have you done?"

"It wasn't her, girl," Scarpitti's voice spoke from the darkness. "Well, not directly. If she'd just died the first few times, we wouldn't be here. I'd be enjoying a good drink and you'd be getting ready to go home and bask in the disapproval of your woman-hating family."

"You won't get away with this," I growled.

"But I *have,* Armstrong. I got away with this for *years...* right under Admiral Drien's nose. I made millions, Armstrong. And that was just the beginning. The Enforcers thought this was just about money... but that was just a nice perk. There's changes coming out here on the Periphery, and I signed on with the winners. The rest of Century... well, you're just going to be the losers. You just don't know it yet."

"You're nuts," Sashi said from beside me.

"I just have more information than either of you," she said. "And I was going to just let you two go on being oblivious until Armstrong here started getting nosy again. She set off a monitoring program I'd installed on her datapad, which is why we are gathered here today. I thought the information about my involvement was gone, safely dead with Webster when I murdered him, but I guess I was wrong."

"You killed him?" I asked in shock. I'd taken the investigators word that it was suicide.

"Poor Webster," I heard Scarpitti walk in a circle around us in the dark. "He wanted *so* hard to do well here. It was so easy to get him onto Rex when he did his summer assignment. Then I put him to solving the puzzle labyrinth there at Black Mesa. Then the whole Champion Enterprise news broke and having the data that they got from you was a liability... and so was Webster. He never saw it coming. An injector to the neck and he had enough drugs in his system to kill an elephant."

"You set him up," I growled.

"I needed someone to take the fall," Scarpitti continued to pace in a circle around us, the sound of her boots surprisingly soft on the hard floor. "What with you surviving all those attempts to kill you and all. Webster made the perfect stooge. A waste, but he was a liability anyway, what with him keeping the copy of the labyrinth program I'd given him."

"I'll kill you," I said, my voice calm.

"Doubtful, dear child. You see, the rest of this writes itself up as a report quite easily. You sent a message to Cadet Drien, telling her you wanted to meet and settle your little ongoing feud. You've been taking Commander Pannja's defensive classes. It only follows that you got a bit cocky. The pair of you met here in the maze. Drien took care of disabling the security monitors, or at least, they'll find her datapad plugged in for that purpose. Your fight here escalated, I think there will be a tragic fall... very sad."

"After the incident with Webster, I think your grandmother's career will be done for. Three cadets killed in just a year? One of them the granddaughter of her rival? That's going to look bad on her. It'll look bad on Admiral Drien, too, but I'm sure he'll make it work in his favor, he's good at snaking out of things." Scarpitti stopped her pacing. She came forward and I felt her press something on the restraints that held my hands and feet. A moment later, I could move.

I rolled away from her and kicked out blindly, but I might as well have just flailed in the dark. She chuckled. "Oh, please. This is your chance, Armstrong. Don't waste it fighting me."

I heard her release Sashi's restraints. "Now. I'm going to let the pair of you try to escape. It shouldn't be too hard. We're not far from where Drien nearly managed to kill you. Oh, here," she turned on a flashlight and threw it at my feet. "Run along, now, children... I'll be following you soon enough."

I snatched the flashlight and brought it up just in time to see her disappear around a corner. The way she moved, she had to be wearing some kind of low-light vision gear.

"She's crazy," Sashi muttered.

"Yeah, but she's going to kill us if we don't get out of here," I replied.

"We should split up," Sashi said. "She can't get us both if we go in opposite directions. Whichever one of us gets out, we get help..."

I waved the one flashlight around, "Go ahead. Think you can find your way out in the dark?" That wasn't very fair, I knew. It was a good plan, but clearly Scarpitti had headed that off.

I could hear her fuming. "I hate you."

I didn't respond. I led the way down the corridor, quickly realizing where we were. It was the inner ring. We were very close to where Sashi had nearly killed me. I hurried along, trying to sweep the flashlight in all directions while Sashi ran next to me.

I turned a corner and caught a punch to the face. The blow slammed me into the wall and I felt my cheek tear open. I dropped the flashlight and stumbled back, my vision blurred and my head aching. In the flickering shadows, I saw Scarpitti hit Sashi and then slam her into the wall. "The pair of you really beat each other down, the investigators are going to see that one of you ambushed the other here... but the fight continued onwards..."

Scarpitti vanished back into the shadows. She was toying with us, I realized. I felt sick to my stomach. The woman was clearly insane. All of the attempts on my life made far more sense, now. This wasn't revenge or the actions of someone in a panic... this was a game to her.

I stumbled to my feet, still seeing double. I stooped over to pick up the flashlight and barely caught myself from falling on my face. Sashi got to her feet. "This way," I said.

"It's no use," Sashi leaned against the wall. "She's just going to kill us."

"She'll kill us faster if we stay here," I replied. But that wasn't all. I had the inklings of a plan forming in my head. It was something that Webster had said and his words came back to me as I led the way. *Leverage,* I thought, *it's all about the leverage.*

***

"I'm sorry," Sashi said as we limped through the dark.

"This isn't your fault," I replied, still putting together the plan in my head. I couldn't tell Sashi. Scarpitti would overhear. I just had to hope that she'd understand and do as I told her.

"No... I'm sorry about, well I'm sorry about everything, okay?" Sashi sounded miserable as she said it.

I turned the flashlight on her in surprise and she winced away from the light. "Sorry," I said, turning it back down the corridor. "I... well, I'm sorry too, for what it's worth."

"You should be," Sashi muttered. "You ruined my life."

"*I* ruined *your* life?" I demanded. "You're the one who betrayed me."

"I had no choice!" Sashi snapped. "My father and grandfather were watching. You have no idea what kind of pressure that brings. They saw you save me, during the final exercise. When I nearly got shot from behind. If I hadn't shot you, they would have..." She trailed off, "Things would have been much worse. As it was, they said I brought dishonor on the family for coming in behind an Armstrong. Then I had to transfer to Ogre because no one in Sand Dragon trusted me anymore..."

"You did okay there, it seemed," I said.

"I'm miserable. Bolander and Thorpe are the only ones who talked to me at all, and then after Recognition, even they ignore me. I have no friends. I have to study on my own. My older brothers think it's hilarious. They keep telling me to quit. They say that I'm weak. That a proper woman would not come here."

I hadn't known any of that. I'd known that she looked miserable around her family, but the rest... "God, I'm sorry Sashi."

"You're *sorry*," She spat. "That doesn't help. Even if we somehow survive this, I'm going to end up failing out. Your future is set. You're at the top of our class, your grandmother is paving the way for your career..."

"I don't get any help," I said. "I barely speak to her, and when I do, it's generally about people trying to kill me."

"I wish I had one third of the luck you have, Jiden," Sashi said.

We reached the big chamber where Sashi and I had fought it out. I heard mocking laughter from Scarpitti as we moved towards the row of pillars nearby. "A nice set of symmetry, here, don't you think? Perfect for the two of you to end up."

We had come out near the same pillar I'd hidden behind when Sashi had fired on me. I aimed the flashlight upwards and as I'd remembered, the two-meter wide basalt stone pillar ended at the same height as the walls around us. There wasn't a ceiling and that gave us an opening.

I pushed Sashi into the gap between the pillar and the wall. "Climb!" I shouted at her and I started up, bracing my feet against the wall and my back against the pillar. "Go!" I shouted at Sashi.

I craned my head around, shining the flashlight around the chamber. As expected, I found Scarpitti quickly enough, she walked up, amusement clear on her face. She wore a set of night vision glasses, which darkened slightly as I shone the flashlight on her. *A little closer,* I thought. I kept climbing. It was slow moving. There was no way we'd reach the top, not before she could catch us.

She paused, cocking her head at us, "Clever," she said. "Get on top, then run along the walls. It won't save you, but it was clever. I'll almost regret killing you, Armstrong. You've stubbornly refused to die, I've got to say."

We were almost two thirds of the way up the wall. I kept climbing, inching my way up while I tried to keep my light on her and keep her in sight.

She took another few steps forwards and I could see her gauging the best way to climb up and catch us. *Just about....there.*

"Push!" I shouted to Sashi. I stopped trying to climb and instead I shoved against the wall with my legs and at the pillar with my back. Sashi seemed to realize my intent and she did the same. The huge stone pillar shifted ever so slightly. It had to weigh seventy tons or more... but we were high up, and it wasn't anchored. Webster had counted on its weight to keep it in place. It seemed oddly fitting to use one of his design points to defeat the woman who'd murdered him.

I turned over, pushing with everything I had, wondering if it would be enough. *I can't do it,* I thought, *I'm not strong enough... I'm going to die in the dark.* The pillar tilted then and I clung to it as it fell. It seemed to happen in slow motion, seventy tons of stone falling like a blow from a giant. I caught a glimpse of Scarpitti, her jaw dropping, her face going blank in shock. Then the pillar blotted her out and it slammed into the ground with a world-ending crash.

It was louder and more powerful than the skimmer crash. It felt like the entire world had shattered. The impact sent me flying and I slammed into the ground and rolled away. I lay there on the floor, feeling like a broken doll for a long time. After a moment, I managed to climb to my feet. I could hear the sounds of sirens and shouts in the distance. Apparently they'd heard the noise, so even if the attack hadn't worked...

I searched around and found the flickering flashlight, the whole thing bent from impact. I shone it over where I'd last seen Scarpitti. I flinched away from what I saw there, among the tumbled pieces of rock from where the pillar had shattered. "Cadet Lieutenant Webster sends his regards," I said. It didn't change the fact that he'd died, but at least I'd helped him gain some measure of justice. I stood up, keeping my eyes averted and feeling nauseous. "Sashi, you okay?" I asked.

"Yeah," she croaked. "That was your plan?"

"Yeah," I replied. "That was my plan."

"Terrible plan," Sashi Drien said. "Stupid plan. Thank God it worked."

"I love it when a plan falls into place," I said. I sat back down on the floor, feeling utterly spent.

"I hate you," Sashi replied, but there was no weight to her words when she said it. She came over and took a seat next to me on the floor. We sat there, listening to the shouts coming closer. "I'm sorry, Jiden," she said after a moment

"Me too," I said. I reached out and patted her on the leg. "You should come back to Sand Dragon. After this, we shouldn't be enemies." I wasn't sure I could be her friend, but there was no reason for us to keep fighting each other.

"My father would never forgive me," she said.

"Then don't go home," I replied. "Come stay with me during break, if you need. You're sixteen, now, you don't have to do anything your parents say, you're legally an adult."

She didn't answer for a long minute. "I'll have to think about it," she said. She sounded like she was actually considering it. I hoped she would. Well, not the staying at my place, part. I really sort of dreaded how my parent's might react. But her coming back to Sand Dragon would be good.

Before I could tell her that, the lights came on. We were rescued.

***

Chapter Twenty-Five: A Little Bit Of Closure

I got to see the same grumpy female doctor. She made a big point of telling me that my usual bed was open. I wasn't sure if she was being humorous or if she'd actually kept it open for me.

"We need to stop meeting like this," the Admiral said as she showed up a few hours later.

"I'm fine," I protested.

"You have two cracked ribs and a partially dislocated shoulder, along with a concussion. You're staying in bed until Doctor Force gives you a clean bill of health."

"Okay," I said, "maybe I'm not fine." I sighed, "I'm sorry I got into this mess..."

"You did well," the Admiral said. I could not have been more surprised to than to hear those words from her. Until, of course, she went on, "I'm proud of you."

"You're proud of *me*?" I stared at her. "I nearly got myself killed. This was all my fault..."

She waved a hand and cut me off. "I read the report. I know how this ties back to you giving a map to Tony Champion. That doesn't matter. You couldn't have had any idea how that would connect to all of this. Scarpitti, by any definition, was crazy. We found high concentrations of Rex in her blood samples. We also found cartridges of it in her personal possessions."

I shivered at that. "You think..."

"I'm certain she was the one who got young Cadet Webster addicted. I'm not sure *why* she did it, but I don't know that I *want* to understand her thoughts, from what I've seen of her actions." The Admiral shook her head, "She set Webster up for the attempts on your life and then she killed him, to cover her trail. You uncovered what a team of investigators *should* have found on their own. But they were too focused on the drugs she planted and they didn't look deeper like they should have."

Her expression went hard. "I've had some very select words for those investigators."

"Ma'am," I said, thinking back, "Why was she looking at a map of my parent's dig site, anyway?" That was the part I didn't understand. What did the alien ruins back at Black Mesa Outpost have to do with any of this?

The Admiral frowned, "We aren't sure, yet. There were some files that Isaac Champion had, that talked about underground trade in alien artifacts. There's also been some... interesting discoveries at your parent's dig site. There's some Militia involvement over some of the implications. It might be related to that, but..." She shrugged. "It doesn't seem to have gone anywhere, at least. I've had some words with some of my contacts in the Enforcers. They're going to open a station at Black Mesa Outpost, just in case."

I felt a wave of relief at that. Even a couple of Enforcers should be enough of a deterrent to keep any criminals away. I'd joined the Academy because I wanted to protect my family. Knowing that they'd be taken care of was a huge weight off my chest.

I just hoped that this really was the end of it.

***

"Hey Jiden," Sashi said as I stepped out into the hospital waiting room. I was still sore and bruised, but the grumpy doctor didn't have any reason to keep me. Though she had threatened to have me restrained to my quarters if she had to see me any time during the rest of my time at the Academy.

Personally, I wasn't sure I disagreed with her. I hoped I never saw the inside of another hospital. Kyle walked with me, more there for moral support than anything, but I was glad to have him.

"Hey Sashi, how's it going?" We hadn't had a chance to talk after they rescued us. I noticed she wasn't in uniform and I saw her bags next to her. My stomach sank a bit. "Did you..." I couldn't finish the question.

She looked down at the bags, then back at me. Realization dawned on her face. "Oh, no." She swallowed and gave me a weak smile, "I messaged my dad and told him to stuff it. He... didn't take it well. I was wondering if that invitation for a place to stay was still on the table."

"Yeah, of course!" I gave her a welcoming smile... then I thought about how my mom would react. Especially since she'd heard who shot me for real. *I'm sure it will be fine.*

"Great!" Sashi gave me a relieved look. "I was worried I wouldn't have anywhere to go."

"We'll take care of you," I said. I clapped her on the shoulder, "You're Sand Dragon."

"Well, they haven't approved my transfer back, yet," she shrugged, "But hopefully."

I would put a word in with Salter about it. Since she was the new Company Commander, I was sure it would work out. "You're already packed?" I asked.

"Uh, yeah," Sashi shrugged. "My older brother Nahka is Ogre's new Company Commander. He... sort of gave my room away."

I scowled at that. "Let's go talk with Salter. I'm sure she can fix that problem." Sashi's brother Nahka sounded more and more like a jerk.

I put my arm around her shoulders. Somehow, our situations had reversed. It was odd, feeling like the confident one while she seemed so uncertain. We'd had our differences, but when it came down to it, I wasn't going to let her sink without helping her.

She'd nearly killed me once. She'd betrayed me once. I realized that was as much my fault as hers... I hadn't understood the pressures she was under. From here on out, it was a new beginning.

***

Webster's parents got to hear that their son wasn't a crazy attempted murderer. I didn't know if it made them feel much better, but they came by and visited me and thanked me. I got interviewed by a bunch of Militia investigators and even a few Enforcers as well. They all seemed rather irritated with me for some reason.

Things settled down. None of it made the news. I was glad for that. The last thing I wanted was to make the news. I didn't want to be famous and I really didn't want my parents any more worried than they already were.

The Admiral sent me a few notes on updates to the new investigation. Some of it was random things. Scarpitti had been an immigrant from Drakkus, which she'd told all of us. What they found out was that she apparently was a bit older than she'd said. Records pegged her as having come here to Century to finish her secondary schooling. But if the investigation was right, then she'd already been twenty. That meant she'd been twenty-two when she started at the Academy, rather than the normal fourteen or fifteen. No one really had an explanation for why she'd pretended to be a kid... or just how she'd pulled it off.

There were other discrepancies. She had way more money in a variety of accounts, some under fake names. The really bizarre parts were where that money came from. I wasn't an accountant, but even I could see that money had gone from her to Isaac Champion and not the other way around.

I didn't know what that all meant, but on the last day before I went home, the Admiral called me to her office. There was a tall, thin man in uniform, his collar had a symbol for Militia Intelligence.

"Cadet Armstrong, this is Captain Douglas Spader, he's here to give you an apology."

"Me?" I asked incredulously.

"Yes," he replied. "Cadet Armstrong, my branch has done you a great disservice and I wish to give you my full apology. The previous investigators into the events at Champion Enterprises missed crucial details. They thought that this was just a smuggling event, and it looks more and more as if it was much more than that."

"Sir, I..."

He held up a hand, "Cadet, if not for your actions, a woman we suspect of being an enemy agent would have remained an officer in our Militia. She had high level access to all of our engineering projects. She had access to political and civilian leaders. We still don't know the extent of the damage she did or what her end goals were, but at least we have a starting point to dig deeper. Thank you."

He gave me a nod, then saluted the Admiral and left.

I stood there, dumbfounded.

"Good job, Jiden," the Admiral said. "You've managed to take Militia Intelligence down a notch."

I stared at her, not really sure what to say to that. "They tend to be a bit full of themselves," the Admiral smiled. "To be shown up by a fourth-class cadet... that stung them a bit. Captain Spader is the best of the lot and he at least admits it. The others are still sulking a bit."

"Ma'am," I asked, "how is it that they *did* miss this?"

"They shouldn't have," she said. "But that said, Commander

Scarpitti hid her actions very well. She had multiple layers of cut-outs... of which we think Isaac Champion was one, just as Cadet Webster was another." Her expression went bleak as she said that. "Each time something went wrong, there was someone who she could shift the blame over towards. I'm told that the Intelligence branch is going over every personnel file in far more thorough detail, especially for anyone hailing from Drakkus space."

I nodded in response to that. I didn't like how this came back to Drakkus, but I didn't really see what I could do about it. *At least the people in charge know there's a problem.*

"You're headed home?" The Admiral asked.

"Yes, ma'am," I replied.

"Your boyfriend is going?"

"Yes, and Sashi Drien too," I said. I watched her expression carefully, but she didn't show any sign of surprise at that.

"Did you break the news to your mother?" The Admiral's expression *looked* professional, but I heard what sounded like a smile in her voice. Of course she found the whole situation amusing.

"No," I replied, "I hadn't." I swallowed, "I don't suppose that you..."

The Admiral gave me a very real smile, "No, Jiden, I think that's one fight I'm not going to take on. But I'm sure it'll work out."

"Thanks," I said dryly. I wasn't sure what else to say.

The Admiral came around her desk and stopped in front of me. "I am proud of you," she said. "I know your mother is proud of you, too. You've done well and I think you'll continue to do well."

"Thanks," I said. On impulse, I stepped forward and hugged her. For a moment, the Admiral went still. Then, after what seemed like a long time, she hugged me in reply. I stepped back, feeling my eyes well up a bit. I could have been mistaken, but I thought the Admiral's eyes were a bit misty too. *Nah, I'm just imagining things.*

"Take care, Jiden," the Admiral said, "I'll see you in a couple of weeks."

***

I stood in front of the Wall. A freshly forged brass plaque had joined the wall. I touched the plaque, feeling at once happy and sad.

"Hey Armstrong," Mackenzie greeted me from behind.

"Sir," I turned around and snapped off a sharp salute. He wore the boards of an Ensign. "Sorry I couldn't be there at graduation."

"You were in the hospital, it's fine," he grinned. "Though you sort of put the whole event in the background." His expression went solemn, "I wanted to thank you. Webster was one of my Cadet Instructors. After that, well, we were friends... and when I heard what they'd accused him of, I knew it wasn't right, but I didn't know how to prove it wasn't him. You cleared his name."

My gaze went to the plaque. "I wish I could have saved him, sir."

"I wish I could have been there for him too," Mackenzie sighed. "But we don't always get what we want. Webster was a good guy, I think he was just coming back from that mistake he'd made. I think he would have been proud of you, Armstrong."

"Thanks, sir," I replied.

"I'm proud of you, for that matter. You'll make a fine officer," Mackenzie said.

"Thank you, sir," I choked up a bit.

"Well, I'm headed out on the next shuttle. Good luck and take care, Armstrong."

I watched him walk away. I wondered if that was the last time I'd ever see him.

"Hey, pretty lady, how are you doing?"

I turned and found Kyle standing there. "Waiting on my boyfriend. He's supposed to meet my parents and look somewhat presentable. I don't suppose you've seen him anywhere?"

Kyle grinned, "Nope, but I did find some nice flowers, but since you're snooty, maybe I should give them to someone else? Or would you care to hold them for me?"

I shut up and took the flowers.

We walked away from the brass plaque. Some part of me hoped that it would be the last name on the wall. I knew, it wouldn't be. And while that saddened me, it also left me feeling good. I had thought that this would be like a job, like working at Champion Enterprises. I realized now that I'd been wrong. This wasn't a job, it wasn't a career... this was a calling. There would always be men and women who answered that call.

###

The End
The Story will continue with Valor's Duty

About the Author

Kal Spriggs is a science fiction and fantasy author. He currently has five series in print: The Renegades space opera and space exploration series, the Shadow Space Chronicles military science fiction and space opera series, the Valor's Child young adult military series, and the Eoriel Saga epic fantasy series.

Kal is a US Army veteran who has been deployed to Iraq and Afghanistan. He lives in Colorado, and is married to his wonderful wife (who deserves mention for her patience with his writing) and also shares his home with his newborn son, three feline overlords, and a rather put-upon dog. He likes hiking, skiing, and enjoying the outdoors, when he's not hunched over a keyboard writing his next novel.